THE LAST OF THE WICKED

WHITE MOTH PRESS

THE LAST OF THE WICKED

A Novel By

ISRAEL BARBUZANO

This is a work of fiction. It's all made up. Your children are safe from wicked witches, as far as I know.

THE LAST OF THE WICKED

A heartfelt thank you to all beta readers for their invaluable feedback. Special thanks to Bliss Winters, who went above and beyond any reasonable expectations and did an editor's worth of work on the novel. He wrecked bad ideas with an oversize plow and smacked me upside the head with keen insight. This kid will go far.

And an enormous thanks to you, glorious backer of the 2019 IndieGoGo launch campaign (or recipient of the leftovers!) You're a real peach. It's my most fervent hope you won't be disappointed. Praise Shaglaroth!

First Edition: October 2019
IndieGoGo Edition
Published by WHITE MOTH PRESS, LLC
Printed in the United States of America
Paperback ISBN: 978-0-990-80828-2
eBook ISBN: 978-0-990-80827-5

Fiends in seeds to sow

Fain for spark to grow

Naught but lies to tell

Bethralled in wonders past

And ploys built not to last

So tolls their dying knell

Miscast from tarnished mould

In soot and shade I dwell

Through lines of rust and gold

Behold these hands foretell

The day the wicked fell

INDEX

PART I

CHAPTER ONE

THE BAIT

A PORTAL HAD OPENED on the wrong side of Earth. The little boy stared into it, his eyes as big and beady as boiled eggs.

"Sally!" the boy yelled into the open pantry, where only pots and pans should have been. "Sally, come here! I knew it, I told you!"

His big sister poked her head through the kitchen doorway. "Quit yelling!"

"Look!" the boy said, pointing under the counter.

The girl hesitated only a moment before stomping toward her brother. She looked in, and the swirling blend of light and color cast a rainbow of shadows upon her face.

Her eyes took on an egg-like quality as well.

"What's that?" she asked him, breathless. "Whatcha do?"

"Nothing! I heard Ma singing like she used to, and I opened up, and there it was!"

"But what is it?"

"It's a whatchamacallit!" said the boy. "A . . . a tele-portal, like in the stories! I *told you* it could happen!"

The big sister smacked the boy upside the head. "That's stupid, that stuff's not real. You're such a turd-brain."

"Ma said to stop calling me that!"

"That don't make you no less a turd-brain."

"It's a tele-portal, they're real, I'll prove it to you!" Without one bit of hesitation, the boy leaned in and dove head-first into the color vortex.

"Ceejay, don't you dare!"

The girl reached out for him, and grabbed his shirt, and got yanked in like she was caught in the undertow of a whirlpool. The back of the pantry didn't stop them from falling through.

Boy and girl tumbled together onto cobblestones. A female voice greeted them before they were done rolling on the floor.

"Yes! Wait. Two?"

"Ow," said the boy.

"Get off'a me," protested the girl from under a mess of limbs. With some effort the kids disentangled themselves from one another. The boy was the first to stand and look around.

"Whoa. . . ."

Tall pillars lined a courtyard that opened to a lush garden. Flowers of a dozen different colors bloomed between the pillars, and about them fluttered butterflies the size of pancakes, as did floaty translucent jellyfish, and ethereal will-o'-wisps that chattered in and out of the brush. Golden seedlings drifted above, sun-kissed twinkles sparkling in contrast to the deep green of trees wrapped all around.

The woman before the children, clad in black from floppy wide hat to robe two sizes too big, lowered her arms to a far less enthusiastic pose.

"This . . . doesn't look right. I think there was a mistake."

Her voice trembled slightly. The children looked at one another, then behind themselves. The tele-portal was contained in a doorframe contraption, swirling round and round like it was flushing a rainbow down the toilet.

"Told you," the boy said to his sister. She scowled and grabbed him by the ear.

"You jumped in!"

"Ow!"

"Now look what you did! I'm gonna whoop your rear 'til it falls off your backside!"

The woman sighed dramatically. "There *certainly* was a mistake. Neither of you look like the youth I was trying to lure."

The children focused their attention on her.

"She talks funny," the boy noted.

"She a foreigner," responded the girl, eyes narrow and nose turned up as though nothing could possibly impress her. "Sounds like one of them Brits. You a Brit, lady?"

"Wh . . . what?"

"Reckon you a Brit, alright. This one time this guy was talking real funny on the tee-vee, so I asked my Da and he told me them Brits are spineless patterguts 'cause we had to save you from Hitler, and y'all mad about tea getting thrown into the sea or somesuch so we had to kick you out of our land."

"Uh, I don't—"

"And I know it's true 'cause my Da don't tell me no lies, so don't you try say otherwise, lady."

The boy tugged at his sister's shirt. "Sally," he said in a wary hush, pointing at the woman. "Look what she got."

In one hand she held a gnarled rod, blue light sputtering on its tip. In the other, a glass orb with silver swirling in dark depths. A lectern stood to her side, propping up a large tome that had seen better centuries.

"She's a witch!"

His sister snorted. "Na-a-aw. . . ."

The alleged witch stared at them, blinking profusely. Her arms came down all the way. "What is that appalling drawl?"

The girl stepped up to the woman, arms folded, head tilted and brow furrowed. "You a witch, lady?"

"Don't be bothering her!" the boy said.

The woman's shoulders hunched in defeat. "I can hardly understand a word you're saying."

"She ain't no witch," the girl said crossly. "Just a crazy dum-lookin Brit hag who talks funny."

"She gonna get mad!" worried the boy.

The crazy dum-lookin Brit hag was quietly whining to herself. "How did the alignments get scrambled again?"

The young girl took another step toward the robed figure, pointing an accusing finger. "I dunno whatcher trying, but better send us back before my folks find out we gone."

The boy clung to his sister's sleeve. "She gonna get mad!"

"*Ma's* gonna get mad. Who you scared of most?"

He kept quiet. The woman cheered up. "Oh! Maybe you are immigrants, yes? You live in London, yeah?"

The kids looked at each other again.

"Did you just call us *immigrants*?" the girl asked, none too pleased.

"You . . . you're not from London? Rhoda and Swanfield?"

"We ain't from no stinkin London, you butt-ugly Brit hag! We're from Linden, Alabama, and damn proud of it!"

The butt-ugly Brit hag looked between them, back and forth. "What?"

"You deaf on top of dum-lookin, lady?" the girl said. "Dumb creepy Brit lady hag, you some kind of foreign pervert?"

"I'm, uh . . . no, I—"

"Brits are dingheads!" the boy joined in, emboldened by his sister's attitude.

"Yeah! Brits are dingheads! Go back home, dinghead!"

The foreign pervert shook her head, gaze turning inwards. "This is terrible. I'll miss the quota again. Frau is going to kill me."

"Go back home! Go back home!"

The human youths kept chanting until it progressed into clenched-fist screaming, but Meredith had made her decision.

"Can't believe it," she muttered, "not a lick of spark in them. Worthless." She left rod and orb by the tome on the lectern and rummaged in her big side-pocket for a bit. Her brow furrowed in frustration.

"Ah," she said at last. The munitions magazine was the size of a large box of matches, easy to misplace. She pulled back her robe at the hip, unholstered her semiautomatic hand-crossbow and loaded the cartridge into the weapon.

"Be still now," she told the accidents. "This is all a dream."

"What's—" the disappointing dud started, but never got to finish her question.

Meredith aimed and pulled the trigger once—*thwap-whirr-kachunk*—then once more—*thwap-whirr-kachunk!*

The darts plucked under their respective collarbones. A burst of words filled the air around them, the short lag between each string rendering both streams of sound unintelligible. The spell happened quickly after the stored incantations were done triggering.

A human girl, posed in recoil, shock dawning on her features. A human boy, fists still balled with intent, face twisted in toothy mockery. Both abruptly stuck in stasis.

The crestfallen witch unloaded the weapon, returned it to its holster and stowed the remainder of the *Paralysis* cartridge in its proper pocket. Reluctantly she neared the accidents, and with each step her spirits sank a bit closer to the soles of her slippers.

Their bare heels scraped like metal on stone as Meredith dragged the bodies to the frame full of swirling colors. "Ghh," the female youth somehow said, hardly a whisper above the breeze. The budget *Paralysis* cartridge certainly wasn't entrapment orb quality. At least it would wear off sooner rather than later.

Unpluck the darts. Push, grunt, shove.

Meredith watched as the accidents sank into the funnel. Another failure. She sighed, bent over the side of the device and flipped a switch. The blasted thing winked out with a muted whine.

She stared through the now-empty frame. It was a test of will not to kick it flat.

With a long-suffering grimace she took off her once-upon-a-time pointy hat, flapped it a bit, placed it back on her head. Made a few adjustments until it sat *just right*.

After one last look of disappointment, Meredith began her walk of shame into the cellar.

CHAPTER TWO

❂

THE SWITCH

AS SHE MADE HER WAY to the storage cabinet, Meredith Brena-Galvan-Neumann wondered why the Universe conspired against her.

A yearly quota about to be missed again, and not even a dud to turn in. She could already see it: another trip to the Tower to beg Frau for a waiver, another debt added to the tally. It would be the fifth year in a row. She'd never gone so long without a single spark retrieval.

Under the harsh light of a bare lightcoil she unbuckled her holster and hung it on its proper place. One by one she emptied her pockets of sensitive items, each one acquired in a number of questionable ways, each one returning to its designated home. Dart cartridges, middle shelf, alphabetical order. Smoke pellets, tiny drawer, right side. Firetape, above the ammunition, second peg. Odor neutralizer, why was she even carrying it? She set it on the bottom shelf, cradled into the old lightbend girdle. Those two had spent a good while together, they got on well.

She emptied all her pockets, but the oversize robe stayed on. It didn't go in the cellar, it didn't fit in. The robe belonged in her room's closet.

Meredith shook the imaginary dust off her hands and headed for the ramp back outside, past the freestanding shelves, the cauldron and the modest woodworking station. On the way there she continued to curse under her breath, cursed her disease and her incompetence and every indignity she suffered because of them—and most of all, she cursed the absurd relief she felt at not having snared a proper target. The litany of curses had become a bit of a ritual after every failure.

She turned off the light, swung the heavy doors closed, listened for the click, scrambled the code, slid the padlock in place and locked it. She took a few steps down the path around the house, then rolled her eyes, went back, took the key out of the padlock and dropped it into its designated pocket. Immediately she fished it out, put it back into the padlock, unlocked it, locked it again. Unlocked one more time, locked again. Better do it a third time, to make sure. And a fourth, just in case.

Finally she pulled out the key and put it away. She patted the pocket four times and resumed her downtrodden way back into the house.

Someone knocked at the door.

Meredith froze in place. She wasn't expecting anyone. The Council sessions were under way, surely Frau couldn't—

"Meri?" the Someone called. It was Frau's voice.

Wide-eyed, Meredith rushed to grab the lectern and toss it behind the nearest bush, critters dashing out of the way, pages rustling in their flight. She strode to the portal device and shoved it behind a pillar, squeaky wheels complaining all the way to a full stop. She dashed to the kitchen door, snatched her hat off her head, hung it on its hook and re-did her ponytail to its proper primness as she kept walking. Frau knocked again.

Meredith shrugged out of her robe and tossed it over the back of a chair. The protest was immediate and could not be ignored: she clicked her tongue off her teeth, went back to the chair, grabbed the robe and all but ran to the closet in her bedroom.

Frau's voice climbed over the open window and into the house. "I brought soup!"

Meredith's belly surged with excitement and sank with dread at the same time, leaving it uneasily squashed in place. She poked her head out of the closet. "What kind of soup?"

"Open the door and find out!" came the sing-song reply.

"I'm almost there!"

"What are you doing?"

"Reorganising the closet!"

There was a brief pause. "I should think you'd have a better reason to make me wait with hot soup in tow."

Meredith finished properly hanging her robe and strode toward the door, eyes scanning through the living room for potentially incriminating evidence. Everything seemed to be in order.

"As if you'd ever carry the pot with your bare hands?"

"Regardless! Open up already!"

She pursed her lips at her all-black long-sleeve-and-leotards outfit. No time to change. She reached for the key ring on its peg, rattled it some, selected the proper key and unlocked the door. Then she undid the deadbolt. Then she unclasped the security latch. Then she detached the chain.

The door swung open and a sealed pot of soup flew toward her face. It stopped to hover a fingerbreadth short.

"Truly, Meri," the voice behind the pot said, "why lock the door ten times over when you leave the window open?"

Meredith simply shrugged at the often-heard question. "Why is Tin-can so eager today?"

"I already set it to obey you. And I've told you not to give them names." Frau nudged the soup-carrying butler aside so she could give Meredith the once-over. "Did you just get out of bed?"

"No, I . . . well, yes, the sofa." She smiled self-consciously. "Nap."

"Nap," Mifraulde repeated. "You napped today, at dusk."

"Yes. I just had to, I couldn't—"

"And then you woke up and immediately decided to sort out your closet."

"Yes."

"Hm. At least you weren't wasting your time in that silly garden of yours. Will you stand there all evening, then?"

"No, sorry, come in, please." Meredith stepped aside and let her brood-sister through. Mifraulde was in Head of the Coven regalia still: tiara, medallion, ring and lush burgundy shawl, all imposing reminders of her vested authority. She laid soft fingers on Meredith's shoulder for a greeting and walked into the living room. Her intense latent power permeated the space around her in a heady aura.

Meredith tapped one of the butler's dangling arms and started toward the kitchen. The hovering golem faithfully hummed behind her, wordpaths glowing to the appropriate configurations all along its arms and torso. "I thought you'd be in session until late," she said as she walked, casual and conversational and not disappointed at all.

"I thought so as well." Frau tossed her shawl on the couch. She smoothed her velvet cowl along her buttocks before sitting at the edge of the cushion, back very straight, knees glued together. Her skin, pale as fog, practically glowed under the white light of the ceiling lamps.

Meredith shouldered her way through the kitchen's swinging door and engaged the latch so it would stay open. "But?"

"The swamp dwellers made such a ruckus over the new spark distribution that the session had to be adjourned before it came to actual blows."

"That bad?"

"Selma went as far as standing up and balling a fist at me. Imagine the nerve! We'll be incurring another deficit this year. No-one wants to give up *their* youth allotment, and yet all those traditionalist crones won't even consider rule changes, let alone an overhaul to the system. It's frustrating."

The topic was veering entirely too close to what Meredith had been attempting just a moment ago. "You should throw Selma in a cell."

"Would that I could, but her Tarkan cult of idiots would revolt. Foul bog lurkers, the lot of them."

Meredith tapped the golem again and pointed at the counter. "Drop the pot over there, Tin-can."

"Stop giving them names! It's as bad as naming the serfs."

She rolled her eyes and watched the butler settle the load. "No it's not," she quietly answered—very quietly—as the latches became undone. Heat roiled above the lid once Tin-can floated out of the way.

Meredith put on a pair of mitts, grabbed the pot by the handles and moved it over to the stove, soup sloshing noisily inside. She carefully pried the clasps on the lid and set it inside the sink.

Nose hovering over the pot, Meredith caught a delectable whiff of pure guilt.

"You brought piggy soup? Is, uh– is this an occasion?"

She didn't hear Frau's sigh, but she knew it was there. "Only for your deprived palate, Meri."

Meredith opened the cupboard and inspected the small collection of bowls. She had to reach to the back for the one that wasn't chipped or cracked in one way or another. "Yeah, well," she muttered, "some of us live on a budget."

"Did you say something?"

"I said I didn't make the fudge yet! I was planning to put together some fudge for dessert as soon as I was done with the closet."

"That's for the better, then. Your fudge is terrible, I don't know why you persist."

"Desmond likes it," she said as she poured spoonfuls off the ladle. Her brow was pinched as she watched it plop down. This soup was so hearty with piggies. Outright decadent. It was impossible to avoid them.

"You must stop talking to yourself, dear."

"I said Desmond likes it!"

"That little monster likes *everything*."

Meredith replaced the lid and fastened the latches twice, just in case. Thrice. Four times. She took her only ivory spoon from its case and put it in Mifraulde's bowl, then opened a drawer and fetched a steel spoon for herself. "Let's go, Tin-can," she needlessly prompted. She heard the sigh this time around.

Back in the living room, Meredith placed each bowl on either side of the snack table and moved the cloth napkins to optimal distance between bowl, table edges and diners. Mifraulde unfolded her napkin over her lap, brushed her immaculate waves of dark hair over to one side of her neck and took the daintiest of sips.

Meredith cupped her bowl to her chest and heaped her first carefully-selected mouthful. The carrots were sweet and didn't even need to be chewed. The peas were firm enough to pop satisfyingly. There was egg and onion and a delicate blend of spices she couldn't begin to decipher. A stew made to order from Greta's Mess, no doubt; Frau had a direct comms channel to their kitchen.

As she ate, Meredith's spoon would pick and prod into the stew like a raven's beak through a carcass. When she looked up, gelid blue eyes met her self-conscious smile.

"Why are you only eating the broth?" Frau asked.

"Huh?"

"The piggies are quality stock, not a single dudlet. You don't like them?"

"Oh, I do. They're delicious. Perfect."

"I don't see them in your spoon or in your bowl."

"No, there're piggies in there. See? Look."

Frau looked. She said nothing.

"Just saving them for last, is all."

The Head of the Coven chewed in deliberate silence for entirely too long. "Eat all your food, Meredith."

Even while Frau's gaze was focused on her own meal, her attention bore down on Meredith like a graduation tribunal waiting on her examination answers. Without outward hints of hesitation, she filled her spoon and closed lips around the whole lot.

"Mmm," she made sure to say, perhaps a bit prematurely.

The piggies were de-boned, de-nailed and cooked to soggy perfection, so tender they came undone on her tongue. The flavor went beyond mere spices and meat, it reached into some primal center in her brainstem that sighed in relief and contentment and said, *yes, this is good.* A tiny boost to her latent power tingled down her throat as she swallowed.

It was delightful and perfect and it sated the flesh-woven craving that would scratch at the bones of every witch. And yet, none of these things stopped the nausea that bothered the pit of her stomach.

Keep it down, she goaded herself. *You're going to keep it down this time.*

"So, then. Have you not set up yet?"

The words smacked Meredith upside the head. It was a challenge not to choke.

"Set up?"

"The retrieval."

"Oh, yes, of course, I . . . I slept past dusk, I didn't mean to. Forgot to set an alarm." She kept her attention fastened on her spoon, determined not to make shifty eyes.

"Yes, I see." Frau maintained a neutral expression. "Even though you knew your window would expire at dusk. And after I reminded you, only three days ago."

Meredith nodded, ever so contrite and disappointed in herself. No need to pretend, there.

The Head of the Coven took another sip, softly swallowed, tongued her palate. "It's curious you would take a nap at all, after going to the pains of reserving the space-fold for a two-day period. You can't sit still come retrieval time. Suddenly it didn't make you nervous anymore?"

Meredith licked her lips. "That's why, really. I didn't sleep well at all, so then I was too tired in the evening."

"Ah."

Mifraulde continued bringing spoon to mouth, letting her terse acknowledgement linger for a while. The knot in Meredith's gut kept tightening.

"That is unfortunate," Frau finally said.

"Well, I figured I could rest today and get it done at dawn."

"You, out of bed before light?"

"I can do it, I've done it before."

"Hm." Another calm sip. She patted her mouth with the corner of her napkin, then smoothed it back in place. "Do you think I'm gullible, Meredith? Do you think I'm stupid?"

"What? No, why would you say that?"

"If you are going to lie to me, at least think of better lies."

"Lies? I don't lie to you, I would never lie—"

"Are you certain you want to finish that sentence?"

Meredith went quiet. Her mouth made a few false starts. "I haven't had time yet, is it so hard to believe?"

"So you're saying if I went to Travel and Transportation and demanded to see the nexus registry logs for today, I wouldn't find your entry there?"

The pause was only for outrage, not incriminating in the slightest. "No. No, of course you wouldn't."

"You truly are committing to it. What did you do this time? What went wrong?"

"Nothing! You always doubt me, it's no wonder I can't—"

"What did you do this time, Meredith?"

"I don't know why—"

"*Meredith.*"

"Alright! I made a mistake, I . . . I set the alignments wrong, or something, and all I got was a flush of sewage pouring through! I just finished cleaning up the whole mess, not even a dud to show for it. Is that what you wanted to hear me say?"

"No. What I want to hear you say, for once, is that you retrieved a youth fit for harvest without making another mistake." The Councilor's composure didn't fray one bit, every word delivered in an off-hand manner. Nonchalant sheets of sandpaper fluttering across the room to scrub Meredith's ears. "That would be too much to ask for, wouldn't it? It truly would be too difficult, for you to get something done right first-try, for once. Though at least I didn't have to rescue you this time, so there *is* something to celebrate, correct?"

A ball of shame and anxiety ballooned in Meredith's belly and made good pals with the nausea. She set her bowl down on the snack table. Whatever was left of her appetite was gone.

Mifraulde continued enjoying her soup with studied care. Miserable thoughts piled up with every spoonful.

"You're right," Meredith said in a quiet voice. "I don't know what's wrong with me, Frau."

"I won't listen to your self-pity again. Your talent shortcomings can't justify this. More and more I suspect it's a matter of will."

Panic surged among the misery and threatened to push up Meredith's throat. "What do you mean? Nothing would please me more than to get all my spells right."

"Then why do you get them wrong? You can speak well enough, and anyone with even a trickle of talent can get a space-fold going. You can't tell me something's malfunctioning every single time, it's ridiculous. What's left, if not self-sabotage? Do you enjoy the attention, is that it? Maybe that's the only way you can feel accomplished, making me look like a soft-hearted clod at every chance you get, because otherwise you'd be another nobody. A personal disgrace of mine I could at least keep secret without fuss. What am I to think?"

Her tone was reasonable, as if she was trying to have an honest discussion. As if the words wouldn't climb into her brood-sister's ribcage and clog her chest in a suffocating choke. Meredith shrunk in her seat, all of a sudden keenly aware of the fabric in contact with her skin, of the scarcity and shoddiness of her appearance next to the Head of the Coven.

Her eyes were cast down and adrift in the middle distance, because she'd long given up on holding Mifraulde's high-browed stare. "I wish nothing more than to get all my spells right," she repeated. Her freckled cheeks burned in humiliation.

Mifraulde shifted in her seat and regarded her in silence. After a few moments she blew out a breath and her features softened, though they remained more severe than compassionate.

"Alright," she said, "I went too far, that was unwarranted. Forgive me. It's been a taxing day, and learning about another of your failed attempts does nothing to improve it."

Meredith glanced across the couch at the Councilor, embarrassment and hurt mixing in a bitter cocktail inside her head. Despite the shift in tone, Frau hadn't exactly retracted her spiteful remarks.

She considered her next words carefully. After all, Mifraulde Brena-Galvan-Neumann was the only reason why she still drew breath.

"You only say the truth as you see it," she said. "There's nothing to forgive."

Neither one spoke for a while. Meredith took up her bowl again and made an effort to empty it. For the remainder of supper the silence was broken only by the occasional clatter of spoons, the Council signet clacking against Frau's bowl, the call of the duskaws, the cluck of ravens, the faint tik-tok of the clock on the wall. The tension eased slowly as they finished their dishes, yet still it stubbornly clung to the air between them.

Mifraulde set her empty bowl on the snack table and carefully wiped her mouth with the napkin. She folded it up and laid it upon the table at the end of a long sigh. "Dusk and dawn. Greenwich, yes? Or is it the Americas?"

"London. Haggerston."

"I see. Even easier. You have two more nexūs before your window is over. I shall help you tomorrow at dawn."

"Help? But, the law—"

"I know the blighted law. I will simply supervise you and correct mistakes on a mock attempt, without infusion. *Then* you will retrieve the youth we need, all on your own merit. Are we in agreement?"

The inclination of the Councilor's head and the arch of her eyebrows allowed for no other answer than "Yes. Thank you, Frau."

"Good." The High Seat medallion swayed on its delicate chain and bounced off Frau's bust as she stood. She gathered the Councilor shawl and draped it around her well-toned frame. The Head of the Coven tiara, intricately woven into her hair, glinted under the white lamplight. "Keep the rest of the soup. Cool it properly for storage, I don't want you to be sick."

Meredith's chin dipped. Her pressed lips quivered with the words she wanted to say: I don't want your soup, I can feed myself, I can at least manage that.

She nodded instead. "Don't worry."

"I wish I didn't have to. Rest well and early. I'll see myself out."

"You too."

Frau's slippers rustled through rug and wood. Meredith tracked them—it was as high as her eyes would venture at the moment. Her brood-sister stepped closer, within arm's reach. Maybe to offer a gesture of encouragement? She'd pat Meredith on the shoulder, reassure her everything was fine and even apologize for—

"Follow," Mifraulde ordered her golem, one hand cradled in its subtle indentations so it would switch back to her. She walked away and paused at the door. "I will return a span before dawn."

Meredith nodded again. The door opened, then swung closed, softly.

She swallowed.

One breath, half an exhale, and she bolted for the bathroom. She barely held it down long enough before reaching the toilet.

There was nothing witchlike about what followed.

Desmond trotted in at some point between wretched heaves, as if he'd been avoiding Mifraulde on purpose. He probably had. He waited until she was done, then rubbed his upturned nose against her calf and made a few consoling noises while she fought to catch her breath. Meredith's hand absently scratched at the thick of his ears, below the fluff and above the bristles.

"I'm alright," she whimpered despite all evidence to the contrary. She reached for some tissue and tried her best to dry her face. "Don't worry, I'm alright."

The barrel-bellied thog licked her knee with self-assured eloquence. Meredith gave a big sigh and wiped off the slobber he'd left. "Do you ever feel like you don't belong where you are, Desmond?"

He snorted and nudged her leg.

"No?"

More nudging.

"I know, you belong wherever you are."

He dragged his whole flank along her thigh and flopped on the tiles. He snorted.

"I'm moping again, aren't I."

Nudge, snort.

"Fine, alright, I'm getting up."

Fighting light-headedness, Meredith rinsed her mouth at the sink until her tongue stopped trying to escape; she was very conscious to avoid her reflection through the process. She stumbled to the front door and locked it four different ways, then gathered the napkins and bowls and spoons and brought them to the sink. Desmond trailed behind her, feet clacking on the hardwood at a relaxed trot. His damp snout nudged relentlessly while she washed the utensils, but Meredith had tuned it out for so many years that she hardly even noticed anymore.

Rinse, soap, scrub, rinse, repeat.

She left them to dry and turned to that galling pot of soup. It could feed her for a whole moon cycle, if she could manage to keep it in her stomach. It would feed her for several, if she fished out and pawned the piggies in there, even as soggy and diluted as they were. The way things were going, she could hardly believe a dish this wasteful was still legal. Perhaps it wasn't.

Nudge nudge nudge.

"I know you're hungry, you don't have to be such a bother."

Snort.

"Hm. How would you like a special treat?"

Snort.

Meredith hauled the heavy pot of soup outside and dumped it in Desmond's trough.

CHAPTER THREE

SISTERLY LOVE

 NLY HALF-AWAKE, MEREDITH couldn't fathom how the witches of yore had managed for centuries to create and maintain the portals manually. Some of her more conservative contemporaries scoffed at the use of space-folds and still relied on the old methods, the thought of which was enough to make her shudder.

She carefully rotated knobs until the doorway to a walk-in closet was centered between the swirly edges of the image. How had the meridian alignment shifted so radically the last time? Not one of the radial coordinates was even remotely similar between England and Central America—or was it North America? Earth's borders were so confusing. The mistake had surely been in her infused diction, and indeed the attempt they'd rehearsed a moment ago had revealed some minor flaws in her pronunciation, but they shouldn't have caused such a wild deviation.

Regardless, this looked the way it should. The youth was a modest mound under the covers, this time. The day previous she'd been weeping on that bed, hugging herself, constantly wiping at her eyes while staring into the middle distance. It would have been *such* an easy lure.

The room had been an utter mess then, but now it was tidy and proper, with its shelves full of colorful books, toys and figurines. The human was on the older side of the curve, but no doubt still viable. Everything should go smoothly, as far as Meredith could tell. She shot another bleary-eyed look at Mifraulde.

"Stop darting glances at me," Frau said from behind her shoulder. "Do as if I were not here."

"But you *are* here, watching me. I keep thinking you disapprove of every little thing."

"I do disapprove, but there's nothing I can do short of replacing you with someone else. So continue doing as you will."

Meredith clamped her jaw shut so her first choice of words wouldn't make it out.

"Well," she said instead, "it's not helping much. It makes me nervous."

"Perhaps it will also make you work faster? Dawn will be upon us soon. Stop doubting yourself. You *will* succeed this time, Meredith."

It was more demand than encouragement.

"Sorry. I mean, yes. I mean, I will, thank you."

"You will."

"Yes."

The image was slightly off-center. Meredith opened the polar angle a hairbreadth while decreasing radial distance the teensiest amount. She tilted the image up just enough to compensate.

"The alignment is correct," Frau said. "I cannot interfere from this point forwards. Do *not* make a mistake, now." She stepped away and continued observing by the kitchen door.

"How could I, with such reassurance?" Meredith muttered. The guilt was already throwing a fit, as nagging and unwelcome as usual. Under Mifraulde's judgmental eye there would be no way to spare the youth its fate, if it turned out to be a dud despite all the promising signs.

She closed down the metal flap to lock the controls and took her position at the center of the courtyard. The lectern stood to her left, holding her disheveled copy of *Folding Space and Other Non-Standard Transportation*. She leafed through *Chapter Four: A Comprehensive List of Proven Transportation Spells* until she found the appropriate section: *Establishment of a Portal to Earth – Models #27A and Newer*.

She could sense Frau's displeasure with the turn of every page, but Meredith would rather safely read it than risk reciting from memory. As she quietly reviewed the spell she warmed up her core and throat muscles, taking them through the Proctor Pre-Infusion Cycle for Safe Incantation. Infusion came as natural as breathing to her brood-sister, but Meredith needed every bit of her concentration to pull it off reliably.

Somewhat reliably.

After a good while of contractions, spasms and mostly suppressed burps, she felt as ready as she could ever be. She unsheathed the command rod from its belt loop and drew the entrapment orb from its pouch. Her eyes darted to the skyveil, then to the small clock on the outside wall. Dawn would break in a quarter-span.

Meredith pointed the rod at the center of the image. She reached for what little talent she harbored, consciously rousing every bit from toes to fingertips. Halfway through the exhale of a deep breath, she engaged her diaphragm at just the right tautness and coaxed her vocal cords into doing cartwheels.

"Şæ—"

Frau coughed, not even looking in her direction.

Meredith interrupted herself, blinked, looked around. Everything was well and ready, what bug had crawled—

Oh.

Heat rose to her cheeks as she shuffled over to the space-fold, reached under and flipped a switch. Hundreds of tiny sigils slowly brightened all over the frame, lines upon lines of miniaturized symbols packed into the paths dictated by automation protocols. Meredith kept her eyes on the cobblestones as she walked back into position.

She faced the device. She squared her shoulders, pointed the rod forward and took another deep breath. On the exhale, Meredith hooked a tether to the foundations of the Universe.

"Şæ ŕīd'ün vēr'vă'yun vă'in ŏńēş'ŷăn úm."

She read it slowly, clearly, voice reverberating with the shallow depths of her infusion. The effort wheedled forth her attunement to open the link between her and the rod, which would in turn link the rod and the portal device. Although it hadn't been flawless, it proved good enough to be functional: the pointy tip of the rod glowed blue; most of the sigils on the frame faded while the appropriate paths flared to a golden hue; the view of the walk-in closet became a swirling vortex of lights.

Meredith suppressed a sigh of relief. The link choked and died, leaving the portal to idle on its own energy well. Had Frau groaned?

Nah, she hadn't, everything was fine.

She held up the fist-sized orb and depressed the indentations where thumb and little finger were cradled. A tinny hum emerged from the orb, a mixture of frequencies with a dash of infusion that would worm into the psyche of human youths and irresistibly lure them. Most of the time. Her index finger caressed the knob on the front of the sphere, ready to trigger the entrapment as soon as she got a positive ID on the target.

With practiced care she smothered the voice moaning in the back of her head, that bothersome whine that would always implore her not to try. In that moment, she was glad for Mifraulde's presence. There would be no inner struggle this time, no queasy reluctance unbecoming of proper witches. A youth would come through, and Meredith would take care of it.

She continued to stare at the spinning vortex, dreading what might come out of it, looking forward to settling this ghastly chore for another year. The moving image was hypnotic, a rainbow caught in a whirlpool, eddies of color and wispy swirls fluttering whimsically about the edges. Meredith had to blink and shake her head a few times to stay alert.

Frau's voice poured onto the humming silence. "This waiting is why proper witches get an Earth travel license and get it done in hardly a cent. Will you stop fidgeting already?"

Meredith glanced her way and made an effort to stop shifting her weight from one foot to the other. "You forbade me from ever applying again."

"And why did I do that, Meri? Do you want to go into detail as to why? Don't let me stop you, now."

Meredith pressed her lips together and kept silent. She didn't need to see it to know Mifraulde had just rolled her eyes. "Give it time, some resist longer than others."

"I thought you weren't supposed to talk to me?"

"I'm not supposed to aid your retrieval or interfere with the spell. I have done neither."

"Right."

"Concentrate."

Meredith fidgeted some more before stopping herself. "Right."

Dawn would break soon. Dawn happened, the Sun taking a centispan to fade into being above their heads. Dawn came and went.

The humming silence dragged on. The brood-sisters exchanged a look.

"The nexus is closing soon," Frau said.

"I did everything right this time, I swear."

"Did you?"

"I did! I swear I did."

Frau pointed at the pillar behind Meredith, the one with the rough dent and web of cracks. "You claimed the same after *that* happened."

"And I still do! That hydrant flew out of nowhere, I still don't know how—"

Meredith was rudely interrupted by voices yelling. The yelling voices came from people bursting through the portal and stumbling directly in front of her.

Two males, one female, all grown. She had time to take a step back.

One of the two burly mustached man-things regained his footing ahead of the others. His eyes cast about the area wildly. He clutched to his chest a long tube with a handle and a trigger, while the other big male brandished a smaller powder-gun with revolving ammunition chambers.

"What's this place!" the face-haired human yelled at her. "What'd you do to my kids? You some kind of terrorist?"

"You hurt my babies!" the large female screamed. She held a humongous knife in her outstretched hand, pointed directly at Meredith.

She took another step back while her stomach made a backflip. In a panic she aimed the orb toward the nearest male and pressed the switch to trigger the entrapment. Immediately the trinket lit up in myriad threads of silver, and with a burst of sound like a hundred words crammed in an instant, the oblong sphere flew to the man's chest. It hit with an audible thump.

"*Hurk,*" the man said. There was a crack and a jet of rank steam, and the chromeflow burst from within the orb to wrap in full around the target. The other two deranged creatures stared aghast as the face-haired man-beast became one perfectly rigid lump of gray. It teetered on the balance. It collapsed on the cobblestones with a solid thunk and a short scrape.

"Rick!" the other male cried.

"Sweet Jesus in Heaven," breathed the female. The remaining man-person quickly stepped up and pointed the revolving-chamber powder-gun at Meredith's nose.

"Swear to God almighty, you gonna pay!"

After one look at the circle of darkness within the barrel, Meredith whimpered and shut her eyes.

Mifraulde's voice descended upon the scene, a gale of infused syllables that reverberated through Meredith's skull. She didn't understand all of it, but she recognized enough clauses to know she better duck and shield her face.

She heard the horrid crackle of flowers and bushes and fluttering critters withering into lifeless husks as a result of the spell's sourcing. The hair along her neck stood on end, the air became heavy with friction. Even through her closed and shielded eyes she saw the flash of lightning that struck the intruders.

The thundering whip-crack and electrified sizzle seemed to carry on forever. Two distinct thumps hit the floor, followed by the clatter of metal parts against the cobbles. The stench of charred flesh immediately inundated her nostrils.

Meredith squinted at her feet. As the world came back into focus, she caught sight of the grisly remains touching her slippers. White skull bone peeked through a melted eye socket. Her breath quivered and hitched in her throat—she stepped back, turned around and retched for a second time in as many days.

Mifraulde was next to her some time later. Meredith knelt on the floor, cowl pulled back, one hand on her breastbone. Her chest heaved with every anxious breath she took, the gulps of air hurt her ragged throat on every inhale. She lifted her eyes from the remains of her meager breakfast, and the sight of her black-clad brood-sister brought genuine dread to her gut.

"A witch does not whimper," the Councilor said in a terrible rasp.

"A witch does not cower."

"I'm sorry. . . ."

"Don't be sorry. Be *better*."

"I try, I'm sorry. . . ."

"How in Tarkai's name did you manage to get *that* through the portal? What were they going on about?"

"I don't know, Frau! The Universe hates me!"

Mifraulde's eyes narrowed. "The Universe doesn't hate you any more than it could hate a star or a mote of dust. Stop making excuses for your mistakes."

"But I did every—"

"Your infusion was poor and your diction imprecise. How else could you have attracted grown humans? Let me see that orb."

Mifraulde cracked the now-opaque spheroid off the human's chest and examined the set of dials behind its tiny concealed panel. After a suspicious frown, her features drew into outright scorn.

"This is the wrong frequency," she spat. "If you are going to bend the rules with trinkets, the least you can do is use them properly. How could you be this obtuse?"

Meredith's eyes found a cobblestone to cling to and stayed fixed on it. "I don't know. . . ."

"Of course you don't know." Mifraulde looked at the scene around her. "I would tell you to clean this up as punishment, but you are too weak to even do that, aren't you? You can't look at these human wretches without shaking. What little you did to defend yourself happened by accident. Don't you even try deny it."

Meredith wanted to stand, tell her sister to go burn in a pyre, maybe throw a punch at her jaw. Yet the smell, the hissing sounds, the exposed flesh, and how very close she'd come to *getting killed*— it all kept her clenched on the floor, helpless.

She feebly nodded agreement.

"I'm tired of taking care of you," Mifraulde continued. "I keep telling myself that you need me, that I'm doing right by you, but am I really? Maybe I coddle you. Maybe I enable you to be this way. I wonder if I've been mistaken all along, and you cannot be helped."

Meredith's chest seized at the words. She spoke tremulously, bile still burning on her tongue.

"I *can* be helped, I— I'm not hopeless, please. . . ." With a shaking hand she grasped the hem of Mifraulde's robes. "Please, Frau. I owe you everything, without you they'll tie me to a pyre, they'll wipe and banish me or worse." She swallowed, and she could very much feel a bitter mouthful of pride going down her throat. "Please forgive me."

The Head of the Coven stared for long moments, and in frightful glances Meredith followed the calculations running behind those gelid blue eyes. In horror she understood Frau was actually considering it, to withdraw her protection, to let the Coven do with her sister as they did with every broodling that turned out to be a dud.

At last Mifraulde exhaled a sharp sniff, pulling away so Meredith would let go of her clothes. "Pick yourself up and go get clean. I'll take care of this."

Meredith felt an immense rush of relief and hated herself for it. She gathered her robes and clambered to her feet, eyes well away from all the gruesome disfigurement.

Carefully holding her tears in check, Meredith fled into the house.

FRAU WAS GONE. She had left without saying goodbye. Meredith had forced herself to pay attention as someone else cleaned up after her. From the kitchen table she listened to Mifraulde engage the space-fold to somewhere else, and the spell to levitate the corpses and toss them through. Frau's power had permeated the courtyard and seeped into the house. Her diction was impeccable, her infusion flawless, she'd honed her technique to perfection and had a voice naturally pitched to shape reality. Huddled in her chair, Meredith had sweltered in a familiar blend of envy and admiration.

Frau had come inside and walked past without a glance, the otherworldly aura of unleashed magic trailing behind her like a transcendental perfume. She hadn't been gentle with the door locks, but at least she hadn't simply blown the door off its hinges.

Only after she was gone did Meredith let frustration take over. Even then she cried in silence, not making a scene, not making a mess. She was used to this feeling. It was simply stronger than usual this time.

Had she truly made so many mistakes? Even if the orb's frequency was wrong, the portal had also malfunctioned somehow. Everyone saw her as a bumbling fool where magic was concerned, and sure, she'd failed enough to earn it—but sometimes she couldn't understand what had gone wrong. It felt like Frau had laid the blame on her mostly out of habit. How was she supposed to be better, if she didn't know what to improve?

Maybe it would be for the best if they got rid of her. They'd burn her, or throw her into a pit, or slice her tongue and use her for brute labor along the duds and the stunts. At that moment it all felt like a small price to pay, if it meant freedom from the clutches of frustration.

Mired in self-pity, she left her chair to wrap up the cleaning outside. She opened the back door to find Desmond snuffing at the regurgitated breakfast.

"Don't eat that!" She hurried toward the thog. "Shoo, Desmond! Shoo!"

Desmond raised his snout from his prospective meal, snorted and trotted away through the newly withered bushes. Meredith eyed the remains of her lovingly nurtured flowers with resentment. Shriveled butterfly wings and flitglow husks littered the floor around them. It had taken forever to get them to nest in there.

"She didn't have to kill you guys," she told the dead plants. Mifraulde had made the spell needlessly complicated by using the plants as a part of the source. They couldn't even fuel it all on their own. She'd done this on purpose.

Meredith looked at the floor and wished she hadn't. There were clumpy patches of red on the cobbles, very obviously raspberry jam and not any kind of melted body part whatsoever. She went over to the corner and picked up bucket and mop. The water was still soapy from yesterday's pass.

She set out to clean all the spattered jam and scrambled eggs, and runny eggs, and spicy minced taters. On her knees she scrubbed at the pieces of . . . of ground beef, yes, charred ground beef stuck to the cobblestones *for some reason.* She was intently not looking at it when she spotted a silvery gleam under the space-fold.

With a mix of curiosity and dread she crawled the half-step to the device and pushed it out of the way. Squeaky wheels rattled on the uneven ground to reveal the muzzle of a revolver.

"Eep!"

She quickly pulled on the frame to cover it back up and scrambled away to a good safe distance. She spent a moment sitting and staring, legs bent to her chest, before feeling properly ridiculous in her reaction.

"Stop being an idiot," Meredith chided herself. Again she pushed the device aside and squatted by the artifact. Fretting at her lip, she inspected the weapon as if it was the carcass of an unknown pest.

She didn't want it. Lethal Earth artifacts were strictly controlled. She'd have to make a trip to Brena's repository, fill out all the forms . . . and then would come the questions, of course. Humiliating to answer, at best. At worst, they'd lead to a search.

Under no circumstances should a Judicar search through her spare room or cellar. Her collection had stretched plausible deniability several shelves too far.

Best to take the powder-gun to Mifraulde. She'd scowl and harrumph, but Frau would deal with it quietly.

And give a lecture while at it. And berate her, and make her feel like a worthless clump of dirt again. "Rather chew on a mouthful of worms than go to her," she muttered bitterly.

She eyed the space-fold frame. She could risk opening a portal to somewhere on Earth and throw the thing through—

Eugh, the idea alone made her recoil. The damn thing would open into a volcano and the magma would char half of Brena, she just knew it. The portal wouldn't go unnoticed by the Department of Travel and Transportation, anyway.

Blasted vermin in a teacup, just put it in a pocket. No-one would notice, no-one would know. Maybe one day it would come in handy. Maybe, one day, it could even save her life.

She was *saving her own life* by taking the weapon. Yes. Hard to argue against her very survival.

Meredith caved, as she often would, and went to stow the revolver in her belt pouch, only to realize her hands had already done it and were pulling the strings closed.

"Huh."

It wasn't the first time they seemed to have a will of their own.

"Just to keep it out of sight for now," Meredith said out loud. She wiped her palms on her robe and glanced at the clock. It would bother her all day if she went to work without tidying up everything.

The weight of the gun was a constant presence at her waist as she bustled up and down the courtyard.

CHAPTER FOUR

CRIME AND PUNISHMENT

 ITTING AT ONE OF SEVERAL workbenches in Assembly Chamber Three, Meredith peered into her current work assignment through the augment lenses. Her right hand adjusted the brace for the casing, tightening the grip. Her left hand picked the next cog from the container and lined it up by the unfinished device.

"I got mine back on Wane," Val continued yammering from the next station over, craggly voice raised above the din of laboring machinery. "First attempt, barely enough spark to qualify, but I'm not one to keep hunting. They'll take anything at this point. I truly don't envy you, winter's starting in Britain now, most grown ones are indoors with their youths. Harder to lure them out."

Meredith said nothing while lowering the tiny cog onto a tiny plate inside the tiny cube. She delicately eased the pressure on the pliers so the cog would fall in place at the right time. She pressed down on it, gently. It made contact with a soft click.

Satisfying.

As usual, Val's lips flapped relentlessly while she did her own tinkering. It was a constant in Meredith's workdays, as consistent as the drone of the machines in the distribution halls. At least today the other stations were quiet: Anna, Gretchen and Brienne were at the infusion labs for the rest of the week.

They never failed to rub it in. Meredith was not allowed anywhere near a soundstill.

"They should switch you with someone else so you could do it in the warm season," Val carried on. "All the grown ones are away while the youths do whatever they want. Much easier to get a good target hassle-free."

Meredith's eyebrow perked up. "Switch? Since when is it possible to switch dates?"

"Well, you're not *supposed* to, not officially, but trading's been going on since forever and the Harvest Department looks the other way. I've done it myself a few times, it's easy chud, but I never told you that."

"Oh. That's, um . . . I would rather not do anything illegal. It's not worth the trouble."

Val chuffled out a breath. "Ever the milksop, you are. There wouldn't be any trouble, but suit yourself. How's this for an idea? Ask that brood-sister of yours to rig the lottery in your favour. Let *her* cheat for you, and that way she won't have to yell at you later. What do you think?"

Meredith looked up from the half-assembled scent mask and give Val a rotten look. Her coworker's knobby pepper of a nose wrinkled with amusement. "I'm not trying to mock you, I'm only saying you have connections. Might as well use them, since you can't afford a harvest bribe."

"I already use them too much for comfort. And there's no such thing as harvest bribes, everyone follows the law and pulls their weight. Mifraulde said so."

"Oh, yes, of course, indeed. I'll have to check my sources, if *Mifraulde* said so. Why would she ever lie about something like that? It must be true, certainly."

"Alright, I caught your meaning, stop."

Devalka let out a low cackle. "You truly are precious, if you think those well-to-do Council crones are in the habit of turning in. That's pedestrian work and shortage be damned, mark me."

"Well, Frau does. Always."

"Yes, our dear Mifraulde does, I don't doubt that." She put down her fine-point iron to wag a finger in Meredith's direction. "You simply don't know how to take advantage, that's your problem. I'd be enjoying luxury in the Head of the Coven's shadow if I were you. Leaning upon the backs of my dozen stunts, chewing on flap jerky and sipping on eyeball cocktails." She chuckled at her own mental image. "But no, you toil away for a handful of clips at the manufactory, working on low-level assignments as if your brood-sister isn't the most powerful witch in existence."

Only after the next cog was in place did Meredith respond. "You've a strange concept of how Mifraulde spends her time on a given day."

"Ah, and how does dearest Mifraulde spend her time on a given day?"

Meredith had the good sense to ignore the bait for gossip. "You don't know her. She'd never let me get away with all that. And maybe I don't want to, maybe I want to stand on my own two feet."

"Pah, that's another problem, you stand on your feet while the rest of us fly far above your head."

Meredith pressed her lips together and carefully selected the next cog in the sequence. The gloriously rotund witch huffed out a breath while brushing her stringy mop of gray hair away from her forehead. "That was obnoxious, I shouldn't remind you. Have you tried appealing the suspension yet? It's been quite some time."

Meredith kept silent as the cog clicked in place. She reached for the conduit box and pulled out a coil of finespun filament. After cutting the appropriate length, she used pliers and thumb to wrap it in the prescribed pattern around the gears.

"I'm grounded in perpetuity," she quietly said. "You know that."

"But surely it's been long enough? You should talk to her about it, she won't hold a grudge forever. It wasn't *that* bad."

"I don't miss flying, I never liked it anyway. I'd rather walk and stand on my feet at all times, thank you."

Devalka eyed her colleague for a while, but said nothing. It wasn't long until words found a way out of her mouth again.

"They finally caught the forger, did you know?"

She prattled on unprompted about all kinds of sordid details Meredith didn't care about. If asked, she could've only remembered a few words here and there: tribal gorgon, big counterfeit stash, stunt accomplice, heinous deviant, gabber gabber gabber. Meredith kept to her work, now and then interjecting suitable acknowledging noises.

"Why do these fools even try?" Val wondered at the end of her story. "Every now and then fake coin turns up, and they never get away with it. Vanuuren's system is infallible."

Meredith carefully threaded the conduit into the switch, then connected the other end. She flipped the switch a few times, ensuring it made contact. She reached into the box for case bolts and found it empty.

"Maybe they do," she said after buzzing the button directly in front of the slot for the box, "but you only hear about the ones that get caught."

Val let out a blaring guffaw, much louder than the comment warranted. "Yes, good point. I hadn't thought of that."

From the hallway came the shuffle of chains, and a moment later a stunt walked in carrying a box full of screws. Chain links clinked with his every movement as he walked behind the desk and grunted the box onto it. The move wafted his unpleasantly intriguing scent into Meredith's nostrils, a pungent mix of sweat and iron. Had he jacked his odor neutralizer again? Perhaps it had simply malfunctioned.

He grabbed the empty container, slid it out from its slot, set it aside and snapped the new one in place, well-defined muscles shifting under his soot-covered skin.

"Thank you," Meredith said.

The stunt nodded and began walking away. Perspiration ran in streaks down the dirt on his bare back, making the scars clearly stand out.

Meredith made a conscious effort to stop looking and peered into the new container. "Oh, um, excuse me," she called after him. The stunt turned around.

"I'm sorry, these are A-4's. I need A-2's."

He frowned. He walked back to the desk, yanked the full box out of the slot and started toward the door.

"Stop right there."

Val's deep-set eyes stared darkly at the worker. She'd stood up, clutching in her knuckle-haired fingers the talisman around her neck. Her enormous artificer robe flopped around her body like a wet blanket on a mammoth's back.

"That is no way to behave before your superiors."

He remained in place, still facing the door.

"You have made a mistake. What do you say?"

The hand not carrying the box clenched into a fist. He turned around stiffly. After glaring at the fearsome hag, he bowed his head in Meredith's direction.

"Muh," he said.

"It's alright," Meredith responded, slightly wide-eyed. "Scathe undone. Please go now."

"I didn't understand you," said Val as if Meredith hadn't spoken. "You'll have to repeat that."

The stunt went from stiff to taut, like a predator about to pounce. His shoulders trembled with his breath. He bowed again, deep enough for Meredith to see the number seared on the back of his bare head. 413.

"Muh apogees."

"It's alright, really. Honestly. Please."

Val wasn't satisfied. A sneer twisted her features, tiny teeth and large gums in full display.

"What is your defect, boy? You are simple-minded, is that it? You must be, a simple-minded bell-bottom. No need for the mumjob, here, you are too dense to articulate words. I could bet my brood and estate it took decades to teach you even the simplest of tasks. Can you even understand the words I say, or should I limit myself to gesticulation?"

He took a step toward her. She smiled with dark hunger, the kind cf smile a hag of her caliber might reserve for a particularly succulent meal. The stunt halted, glaring so intensely Meredith half-expected Val to drop dead on the spot.

"Is that a threat, boy? Are you threatening me?"

He brought up his manacled hand.

"Sove!"

Though still no word could be understood, his upward-thrusting thumb left no room for interpretation. Not waiting for a response, he turned around to leave.

Devalka Tremmel-Stohlz-Vanuuren needed a moment to find her tongue. Her knuckles went white on the hand clutching her amulet. "Do that again. I dare you."

The human stopped. He turned back to her, chains clinking. He raised his hand again. He extended his thumb and made an up-thrust motion.

"Sov. Ig."

He let the gesture linger for a while, shook it a bit for emphasis. His scowl was deep, his chest was heaving. Devalka's eyes widened.

"I really need those A-2's!" Meredith hurried toward the stunt. "Better go get them now, before I get angry!" She shoved him through the door while darting glances at her coworker.

He finally left for the appropriate parts, his indignant shuffle fading under machine noises. Meredith frowned at Val. "You have to stop doing that."

Val burst out laughing. "Serves him right, I keep losing on wagers because of him."

"You *still* go to the fight pits?"

"There's nothing better to do on Naughtday, you're the mug for not coming. The odds keep going up, he'll choke on sand eventually, give it time." Devalka was chuckling, shaking her head. "I'm so tickled he still has a backbone. One day I'll get him to lunge at me."

Meredith rolled her eyes. "I don't understand why you won't leave be. They're already in chains, what more do you want?"

"After what they did? They deserve it all."

"*He* does? He couldn't have fought in the rebellions, it's been nearly a hundred years. *You* didn't fight in the rebellions, either."

Devalka's mirth faded slowly. Her tone became guarded. "I was still in the academy at the time. I remember enough."

"Regardless—"

"It's not the first time you defend them. You are no sympathizer, are you?"

Meredith tensed as if Val had pulled a knife on her. "N— no, I just don't want a corpse on my lap, I'd rather let them be!"

Val's expression didn't change. "You do look at him strangely sometimes. Don't think I haven't noticed. Should I be worried you might be a deviant?"

"What? No, he—" Meredith realized she'd raised her voice and switched to loud whispers. "He terrifies me! All of them do! You don't know what it's like for me, I can't defend myself the way you can. Not to mention Gertrude will be *livid* if she needs to report a death because of you, and she'll find a way to blame it on me, somehow!"

The clinking shuffle returned, making Meredith jump away from the door and line up next to Devalka. They watched in silence as the stunt installed the box on Meredith's desk—until Val's sneer twisted to a disgusted wince. "What is that foul stench?" She sniffed with squinted eyes and frowning lips. "Is it you, boy? Why is it that you *reek* this way again?"

Her face scrunched up in the most ridiculous way, and she sneezed. Meredith didn't believe her eyes when they told her a smirk had flashed on the serf's lips.

"Yeugh! You did it on purpose, didn't you?" Devalka sneezed again. "Get out, you! Begone!"

He calmly walked out with the empty box under his arm. Val called after him: "I hope the discipline report was worth it! Irreverence is expensive for a servant, let's see if you can afford it."

No acknowledgement came. Meredith and Devalka looked at one another. Val very pointedly leaned away from her.

Meredith scoffed. "I'm *not* a sympathiser," she said, "and I'm not a deviant, Malkin strike me. I want nothing to do with them, good or bad, and that's all. Can we please get back to work?"

"Hm."

Val returned to her station. The reserved, thoughtful looks kept happening. Meredith exhaled a nervous sigh through her nose. "Sanity's sake, I'm not a deviant! I was pining after Yurena for a whole year, remember? You wouldn't stop bothering me to say something to her, don't you remember that?" She went back to her seat and fiddled with her equipment, indignant in her every motion. A few moments passed.

"And yet you didn't ever approach her," Val finally replied.

"I *did*. I asked her for a job, and I got laughed at. So that's the end of that story."

"Hm. That's not the same as approaching her."

Hands held back from anxiously wringing her apron, Meredith hid the fear behind a scowl and faced Val head-on. "I can't believe you're accusing me like this. When you blabbed about your affair with human music, I didn't think of it twice. In fact, I never mentioned again, like you asked. And this is what loyalty gets me?"

Their eyes met, and Val's impassiveness broke into a tiny-toothed smile. "Oh, don't be cross, I don't truly suspect you!" She reached over to slap Meredith's knee. "I wanted to see how you'd react, is all. Now and then I like to test newer broods like yourself, and that deviant forger story gave me some strange ideas."

Meredith shrunk back, lips drawn to a line. Her voice trembled with emotion. "It's very upsetting to be accused like that. What if anyone heard you? The last thing I need is such a horrendous rumour spreading, on top of everything else."

"Come now, no-one would take it seriously. . . ."

"You don't know that. But you *do* know not everyone supports Frau around here. A rumour like that would be another way to smear her name."

"Fine, yes, you're right." Devalka let out a husky breath. "I wasn't serious, Meredith. I apologise. By my words and power, I swear I didn't mean any of it."

Meredith blinked a few times. She'd expected to be shushed and dismissed.

"That's, um." She cleared her throat. "That's alright." She turned to her work and needlessly readjusted the brace holding the trinket in place. "I'm glad we talked about it. Thank you."

"Mm-hmm." Devalka picked up her iron and flipped the switch to power it up, ready to continue etching wordpaths upon her current project. She spent some time paging through her manual.

"You know," she mused without looking up, "now I'm thinking I needn't go that far. Maybe I shouldn't file for discipline. What do you think?"

The question was posed casually, conversationally. It might have been sincere. It truly could have been.

"No," Meredith responded. "You did the right thing. He should be punished for his insolence. We don't tolerate that behaviour under any circumstances."

She spoke without tension, as though alluding to a rebellious pet that refused to do as taught.

Which was exactly the case.

"Of course, yes. You're right."

Meredith strove to set the matter aside and dive back into her work. Reaching for those accursed A-2 bolts, she noticed the sleeves of her blouse were now dark with soot and dirt. It would bother her all day.

It should've been an artificer robe getting dirty, but Meredith was never issued one. They never hesitated to remind her she was no artificer.

She dug into the box and found hundreds of bolts. It barely registered when a handful flew into her pocket, all of their own volition. More inconsequential gossip was soon flying out of Val's mouth, and Meredith feigned interest with practiced timeliness, though perhaps her efforts were more listless than usual. If her colleague noticed, she didn't care to comment on it.

Meredith's thoughts were somewhere else entirely.

CELL 12-D, BLOCK FOUR. The log said he was booked a span after midday, immediately following the incident.

The expansive cell blocks were a holdover of times past, when the building had another purpose entirely and the oversupply of retrievals would need to be held in captivity before harvest. Though she knew the blueprints well by then, it had taken a while to reach the holding cell without alerting the one team on patrol.

"Um," Meredith said. She nervously pulled her cowl tighter around the full face-mask. "Hey, you."

Calling them by their number seemed so rude.

He sat motionless on a cot, brooding. He was barefoot and dressed in threadbare rags. His chains hung from a peg outside the barred door.

"Human." She rapped a knuckle on one of the bars, her desire to be quiet conflicting with the sense of urgency. He finally looked at her.

"Um, hi. I know what happened today. I'm here to– to make amends."

He remained still, glaring. She was almost positive he could still understand her through the mask's voice distortion.

"I have something. For you. Just . . . a gesture. To say . . . to say we're not all alike. No-one should be treated like this."

The intruder produced a white handkerchief from one of her pockets. She unwrapped it to reveal a few dry leaves and a small vial containing a pasty white-greenish substance. They easily fit between the cell's bars.

"Hide this under the cot for later. The herbs are for pain. Two leaves per dose. Fold the leaf and place it under your tongue–" She darted a glance at his mouth. "Um. Just– just fold it until it cracks and suckle on it, don't swallow it. The salve is for burns. Just in case. Apply it generously, it'll sting at first but it's worth the trouble, you'll heal much faster."

She left them on the floor by the cell's entry. The stunt kept still. Then he stood, and Meredith hurried beyond arm's reach. He picked up the herbs and looked at them.

"It's gramrout. I grow it. It's not a trick, I promise."

He considered them for a little while longer, eyes narrow. He then held up the herbs so she could clearly see him crush them and toss them through the gap between bars. He grabbed a handful of hay from the cot, covered the salve container and proceeded to smash it with his foot, the sound of breaking glass muffled by the hay. Once he was done, he very thoughtfully slid the mess out of the cell.

"Go away," he managed to say.

She regarded the ruined items with a grimace.

"You didn't have to do that," she told him. The human kept staring.

"But I thought you might." She produced another handkerchief with identical contents. "Please take this. Please. Leave what remains under the cot, no-one will know. You're not my first."

Meredith went to slide the bundle across the floor, but she caught herself half-squat. Instead, she took a hesitant step forward. Her hand trembled as she extended it through the bars. Her insides were doing jumping jacks.

"We can trust each other," she said.

He stood motionless, tense—his hand lunged forth and clamped on her wrist. Meredith let out a strangled yelp, but didn't let go of the bundle. The words to a fatal temperature rise inside the human's skull tingled on her tongue, ready to be unleashed . . . and then vanished, dispersed by the overpowering scent of sweat and soot wafting through.

His fingers, grimy and dreadfully strong, dug into her skin. He glared at her for long moments. He could probably break her bones with a sharp flick of his hand.

"If you hurt me," Meredith stammered, "you will die."

They stared at one another. Meredith's breath was fast and shallow. He couldn't recognize her, could he? The mask's mesh obscured her eyes, though it didn't fully blot them out. She wanted to squirm and struggle, maybe gibber a little at how *dirty* everything was, but she forced herself to hold her ground.

His fingers stopped threatening to crush her wrist, and the stunt laughed, a low and bitter laugh that was almost a cough. His eyes seemed to shift, tempered steel crumbling to brittle rust. *I will die?* Meredith all but heard. *What is my life worth?*

The mewlings of the sentries resonated through the hallway.

"Take it. Please. Just take it."

He released her arm and stepped deeper into the cell. "Go," he said. He didn't take the bundle.

"I'm leaving it here." Meredith ignored the groan and tucked the items to the side of the door, pressing them against the wall between cells. She glanced down the hallway. A four-legged silhouette was projected on the stone bricks, around the corner. She hastily scooped the ruined items and dumped them in another pocket. "Stop being stubborn," she said as parting words before gathering her robes and scampering away from the approaching shadows.

It wasn't too difficult to keep a good lead: the patrolling juditors were bored out of their minds, complacent by rote and quietude. Her path turned several lefts and several rights, doubling back to the surreptitious staff access she'd used to sneak into the laborers' wing of the manufactory.

Back in daylight, she heaved a sigh of relief, unclasped the mask and deactivated the scent suppressor. Meredith leaned against a nearby wall, letting all the adrenaline and nervous jitters work their way out of her system. There was no-one around to see her panting.

"I can't believe I did this, today of all days."

She readjusted her robe and resumed walking at a brisk pace, eyes darting around for witnesses. It wasn't just guards she had to worry about. The Circle would chew off her fingers if they caught wind of her unsanctioned escapades.

Meredith noted the position of the sun. "Thank the Stones, there's still time."

The market wouldn't close for at least another span. Long enough to get her deeply embarrassing shopping done.

There was only one more chance to capture a youth for harvest, and she was willing to try anything by this point.

CHAPTER FIVE

JANETTE

VERYTHING WAS READY.
Her command rod functioned properly. The new
entrapment orb, bought at an outrageous premium on
such short notice, was meticulously configured. She'd
scrambled the space-fold coordinates and aligned them from
scratch, thrice. Every switch was in the correct setting, none of it was
stuck or half-cocked. Her chalk marks were still fresh on the cobbles
from measuring the exact distance and angle at which to stand, she'd
recited the words well over a hundred times and practiced her
infusion for a whole half-span.

She'd also burned five candles at the points of a pentagram,
sprinkled salt and iron filings in front of the portal, tediously
braided and feathered her hair. She'd dabbed paint on her face
(Enchanted Indigo), poured raven blood (bought by the vial) on goat
bones (minor contraband) and drawn sigils on each pillar with a
lump of coal (they didn't say anything magical, as far as she knew.)
Her stomach grumbled from the day's fast—having thrown up in the
morning counted as fasting, in her book—and her skin was roused
with goosebumps from wearing only bead strings and leather straps.

All proven obsolete or worthless, but Mifraulde's anger begat
desperation. It had felt different, this time. Like genuine contempt.

Like an ultimatum.

"Let's get it done," she muttered without much conviction.
Inspecting the wordpaths on the space-fold frame had revealed a

fleck of gunk stuck to some of the output grooves, definitely interfering with the alignment on the back end. She would be filing a strongly worded complaint about that.

She powered the device and got in position. An uneasy squirm continued to bother her stomach, half reluctance, half trepidation. The walk-in closet door from the attempt at dawn was in display, slightly cracked open, and through the sliver of light she peeked at the youth. She lied belly-down on her bed, features somber as she wrote on a notebook while listening to something on one ear-wire. Unwitting, defenseless, isolated. A perfect opportunity.

The quarter-span to dusk struck, and she opened the gateway without fuss. The image morphed into the standard funnel of flushing colors, a frustrating quirk of light as it warped through the active threshold to Earth. Meredith raised the entrapment orb and let it begin humming.

A proper witch would've been thrilled with such a clear-cut retrieval, yet Meredith felt nothing but dread. In fact, a proper, *licensed* witch would have gone into the portal, scouted ahead, made sure it was worth the trouble, and then she'd have quickly snatched the youth.

The thought further tightened the knot in her gut. No, never again. She still had bad dreams about the license field test and how wrong it had gone. The screams, the chaos, the savage beating—and that atrocious human jail cell, where she'd been too bruised to cast even the smallest cantrip. If Mifraulde hadn't rescued her. . . .

Ancient stones, she'd been livid at the mess. No wonder she was fed up. She'd been burdened with her brood-sister's failures ten times too many. The bond of their youth seemed so far away, now: the tag-teaming on chores, the hushed instructor mockery, the bunk bed battles, the sharing rations and punishments and toilet prank buggery in the dorms. It had all changed after Frau was plucked from Brena's academy and sent off to the posh Valeni conservatories, and again after her years at the Tarkan practicum. But even when she'd come back groomed and empowered beyond her already considerable talent, they'd always shared—

The colors buckled, and a young human girl stepped into view.

She climbed down from portal to courtyard as if it was the last step in a set of stairs. Her chin-length hair hung about her face in flaxen waves, bobbing from side to side as she turned her head this way and that. Her eyes, big and blue, drifted in wonder before anchoring onto Meredith. Or rather, only one of them did.

"Finally," the youth said, voice hushed with reverence. Her white nightgown fluttered in the twilight breeze. "It finally happened."

Meredith stared, barely hearing the words. Her finger, gingerly resting on the entrapment switch, should have already pressed down on the trigger—and yet she stared, thoughts seized in gridlock, breath caught between lungs and teeth.

The youth was oozing with spark, yes, at last. It was easy for a mature witch to detect the spark in a human child, easy even for a witch of her lackluster attunement. It was an unmistakable buzz, an alluring bend to the senses charged with untapped potential. The human had enough of it to fashion its own gravity well, but this was not what held Meredith as if spellbound.

Latent magical power was a much subtler sensation. A perceptive witch could get a whiff of it when close enough to another, touch it with her mind and take measure of it, if she concentrated. It was a tenuous aura, a scent that wasn't smelled, a sound that was felt more than heard. In all of Meredith's life, only when close to Mifraulde had she ever felt it in a significant way.

It definitely wasn't a presence that jumped at somebody, and grabbed her by the ears, and yelled *"look at me!"* right in her face. It didn't visibly radiate from a thaumaturge like heat off of molten glass.

It wasn't supposed to, at least.

"I've dreamt of this for so long," the youth said, eyes round with awe, bright with zeal. "Is this Avalon? Are you . . . are you the . . . the Arcanist?"

Meredith's belated response came through the fog in her mind.

"Witch. I'm a witch. You are in our realm. Galavan."

"Oh, a *witch!* I didn't want to say it, they always say witches are bad, but I knew it wasn't true, I knew it!"

There had been no mistake this time. She looked the same as on the viewport. This youth, this human girl Meredith had scouted only last night . . . she was a spark't witch, an Earthborn witch. Attuned to magic while brimming with spark. The most precious find.

Spark't witches used to be the norm, before the Civil War, before the Desolation. Back then, the witches of Galavan would seek out the Earthborn and rescue them from the rabble. These days they were sought for a much different purpose. How could one so plentiful slip past the Department of Harvest for so long?

"I've never read of Galavan," the youth continued, "but it makes *so* much sense. The real thing is what you never hear about." Her little smile was one part sheepish, two parts impish. "The real thing is the secret. Right?"

Meredith blinked. "It's named after the Galvan brood. She was the first of the furies."

The girl gave a few giddy little jumps, dainty fists shaking with delight. In her hand she still carried her screen-gadget-thing, with its ear-wires neatly rolled around it.

"Oh, I knew it, I knew it! This is marvelous!"

In current times, the spark was the exception instead of the rule, and magical talent alongside it nearly extinct. For hundreds of years the lineages had diluted, the sites of power and leylines within Earth dwindled to trickles, no longer able to infuse vast swathes of the population. Many regions could no longer produce harvestable youths at all. The systematic retrieval and exploitation hadn't helped matters, either.

"I've dreamt of this my whole life," the girl repeated. "I've wished so hard for you to be real, and you've finally come for me!"

And yet here was this youth, this . . . girl. Enough spark to drown the power grid for a year all by itself. More attuned than anyone Meredith knew, certainly more attuned than the current Head of the Coven. Her latent power was a brick-stuffed cushion in the middle of a pillow fight.

"You . . . what?"

The girl nodded excitedly. "I'd go into the closet and wish for it. Wish with all my heart. Magic had to be real, it *had* to." She stepped forward, hands clasped to her chest. "I promise to do my best for you, I'll learn everything, I won't ever want to go back."

Meredith blinked. She had a wandering right eye, this girl. Half-lidded, glazed, unfocused. A well-documented witchmark, mostly found in the Tremmel brood.

In the ensuing silence the girl shrunk in place, as if a terrible possibility had just occurred to her. "You . . . you are taking me in, right? To be your apprentice? Oh, please say yes, please."

"Abbabbah," Meredith uttered mindlessly.

This was not a good thing. This was the *furthest* from a good thing. It would cover her quota this year, sure—but it would also lead to interviews and close scrutiny of her retrieval process. They'd want to analyze every square meter of her courtyard, maybe even give credence to some of the superstitious tripe she'd employed.

And they would search the house, of course. They'd poke their noses in every corner of her privacy, looking for a cause beyond the most random of coincidences.

"I'm Janette. You can call me Jane if . . . if you like. Not Nettie, though. I hate that."

The protocol was clear. She ought to have engaged the entrapment by now. The girl would never learn to use all that power, they would plug her into a pod and eventually take her to the breeding grounds. It was procedure.

"Your garden is beautiful. What happened to all those dead flowers over there?"

"My brood-sister killed them."

"Oh."

A shame. No, a tragedy. The girl had *so much talent*. Meredith felt a twinge of envy as her senses explored the youth's aura. Just one high-end trinket infused through that kind of attunement, backed with such an obscene spark-load, could afford an entire year's worth of food. *Good* food, none of the moldy cheese and wilted cabbage from Reva's ramshackle market stall.

"It's such a pretty house, really. Very cozy. Just lovely."

"It was a decrepit ruin when I moved in."

"Oh."

What wouldn't she give to have such power at her disposal? To break free from mediocrity and humiliation, to have Mifraulde's respect, to forget the meaning of the word "budget" and never again deprive herself just to add a couple piggy coins to her pitiful stash. And the tools she could buy! A full set for the garden, her own manufacturing bench, a functional sewing machine, Ferris steel knives and shiny new pots and pans for the kitchen. . . .

"Your accent is so old-fashioned. I wish I spoke like that."

Meredith couldn't get past the wave of resentment coming over, resentment at the youth for her power, resentment at the Universe for its crass sense of humor. Here she was, found wanting every day of her life, while this girl's potential as a witch would never come to fruition. The spark throbbing in her flesh guaranteed her own undoing.

What a *waste*.

"Is . . . is this a test?" The girl fidgeted in place. "Am I being tested? Should I keep quiet?"

Unless. . . .

Meredith's eyes widened at the idea that sprung in her thoughts.

It was crazy. Deranged. Beyond illegal.

"I'm worthy, Muh– Madam, I swear. Let me prove myself, I won't disappoint you. Please."

To pull it off, she'd need equipment she didn't have. A soundstill. A workbench. A dead room. She could make it work with some inventive thrift. And none of it had to be permanent: if the youth became troublesome, if she was too dense or too much of a handful, she'd just abort the plan and . . . dispose of her. Still a better fate for her than being turned in.

"Oh, I get it! The crystal ball . . . you're predicting my future, right? Divining my soul, to see if I'm worthy, right? I'll be the best apprentice you ever had, just . . . please, let me in. Let me stay. I'll do anything to learn from you, whatever you ask."

Meredith looked back and forth from the entrapment orb to the wide-eyed youth. The sixteenth span chimed from the living room clock, marking the start of the sun's fade from the skyveil.

"I used this to draw you here," Meredith said. "It serves no other purpose whatsoever." She quickly tucked it in one of her pockets—except her current outfit was nothing but beads and leather straps. The trinket bounced on the cobbles with a metallic clatter.

The girl tracked it as it rolled to a stop between seams. Her right eye dragged behind, as if interested in something else altogether. "Oh."

"Yes."

"Yes?"

"Yes, you may be my apprentice. Yes. That's why I lured you here.

I'm in need of a new apprentice."

The youth clasped her hands together, face lit up with the brightest, most joyful smile Meredith had ever seen. "Oh– oh, my god, truly?"

"Y– yes. Yes, you may start–"

With a giddy jump and squeal the girl ran forth and threw her arms around her new mentor, pressing one side of her face onto Meredith's chest. "Thank you thank you thank you thank you!"

"Um, that's alright, ah. . . ." She kept her hands out to the sides, breath catching in her throat. Didn't humans often carry contagious diseases?

"I'll be the *best* apprentice you've ever had, I'll work so hard, I'll do all the chores, I'll study for hours and do everything you say!"

Meredith awkwardly patted her head. The girl's hair was a bit coarse, like freshly spun flax.

"I'm sure you'll surpass all the . . . um, the *many* other apprentices I've had. Settle down, now. This . . . this isn't proper."

"Oh, sorry! I'm so sorry!" The youth quickly let go and stepped back. She squirmed a bit before resolutely squaring her shoulders. "I mean . . . I apologise, Mah– Madam. Mistress. Is that how I should address you? Mistress?"

"Yes. Yes, that will do." The witch cleared her throat. "Mistress Meredith."

"It's an honour to meet you, Mistress Meredith. I'm ready. I've wanted this for so long. Everyone made fun of me, but I knew it would happen eventually, I knew it."

Meredith walked over to the space-fold, wooden beads chattering, thoughts racing. She was doing this. Yes, she was doing this.

She laid a finger on the off-switch. "My . . . previous apprentices would tell you that you must be committed. There will be many rules, and you must follow all of them. You understand? You must . . . you must prove yourself worthy. Yes, indeed." She glanced at the portal. "Once I close this gate, you won't be able to go back. Are you *worthy* of staying on this side?"

"Yes! Yes, Mistress." The girl's nostrils were flared like she couldn't fit enough air in her chest. Fervor glinted in her eye. "It's my fate, it's finally happening. There's nothing for me back there. I don't want to see them ever again."

"Um, alright. I mean, yes, that pleases me." Meredith flipped the switch and the swirling colors blinked out of existence. The low-pitch hum revved down and died a slow death. "And so your fate is sealed," The Mistress said in a very official capacity.

The girl smiled a hungry, near manic grin. She looked her new guardian up and down. "Should I take off my nighty and don the beads now? How should I paint my face?"

"No, no. No beads, no paint. This is all" *superstitious bunk* "ritual garb." Meredith's eyes ambled through the courtyard. "Apprentices wear . . . grey cowls." She paused briefly. "Your first official task is to sew your own. An ancient tradition."

"Oh." The youth looked crestfallen. "I don't know how to sew."

"I'll, um, I'll teach you in the traditional way, as is common and proper. We have a lot of tradition. You will see."

"Oh, okay. That sounds like fun, Mistress Meredith."

"Good."

Meredith's stomach grumbled loud enough for the girl to dip her chin at it. The hunger and the cold helped brush aside the mind-numbing prospect of getting caught doing this. For the moment, at least. There was a lot of cleanup to do before bedtime, and just getting the space-fold ready for tomorrow's pickup would take a third-span.

She looked at the youth. Janette. *I'll do all the chores,* she had said.

"We'll begin immediately, then. You will help me tidy up every-thing. The cold will keep our pace brisk."

Janette nodded, very solemn, very eager. *This is a terrible idea,* a voice kept repeating in Meredith's head. She studiously ignored it, focusing instead on the intense aura emanating from the girl and the intense hunger rumbling in her belly.

"There's much work ahead of us, apprentice."

Janette beamed at the word. "I'm ready, Mistress." She offered up her gadget. "Should I throw the phone away? I'm ready to embrace magic, one hundred percent."

Phone. Right. Devalka had said something about half of Earth's humans being permanently attached to one of those, nowadays.

Meredith gravely took the device in her hands. "That is com-mendable," she said, and carried it to the small table full of containers she'd set up for the evening. "But know that magic and technology don't exclude one another."

"Oh. Well, it's hardly more than a music player, anyway. It's all locked up so I don't. . . ." She rolled her eyes. "You know."

Mistress Meredith didn't know at all, so she simply set the thing down and moved on. Focus on one problem at a time, that's all she had to do. "Bring the mop, broom, dustpan and bucket from the corner. The scrubbing brush and soap are on those shelves." She pointed. "I'll instruct you on what to do while I work on the space-fold device."

The girl took off running toward the cleaning tools, bare feet slapping on the cobbles. Meredith walked up to the machine and began unlatching clasps around the frame. *This is the stupidest idea you've ever had,* the voice said.

I'm tired of listening to you, she replied. *This is my chance to do better. It's worth the risk. It'll work out.*

Janette returned with sloshing bucket and stringy mop, left them on the floor and went back for more. Meredith continued her inner dialogue as she worked her way through the latches.

You can still change your mind. Entrap the youth, turn her in, answer the questions and enjoy a year of peace. They won't even glance at your precious shelves.

And then nothing changes, and I'll have to meet the quota again next year. You heard Val. I could bribe my way out of the yearly turn-in. You know it happens.

You are missing the quota now. You won't make this work in a year's time, it's impossible. Mifraulde will be furious, you will be executed or worse. Turn in the youth.

Meredith clenched her jaw.

No.

Janette dropped brush, bar of soap and broom next to mop and bucket. She eyed Mistress Meredith expectantly.

"Start by picking up all the debris," Meredith said. "We'll salvage the candles, but throw everything else. There's an empty sack on the table."

The girl set to work, broom and dustpan in hand. Meredith continued relaying instructions as she finished unlatching clasps and disengaging safety pins. She separated the functional device from the base and spent the next fifteen centispan wrapping it in canvas for safe transport. After that, she worked the spring mechanisms on the bulky support structure until it was folded into a tight bundle, then wheeled it over to the wall and leaned the wrapped device over it. She flipped a switch nearby and the lamps overhead came on, illuminating the scene with white-green light. The girl lifted her head to look at them, but didn't comment.

Meredith took up mop and bucket and joined the cleanup, working in silence whenever no new instructions were necessary. It was simple, one task at a time. The sun finished fading and a full moon appeared in its place, at the mid-point between zenith and horizon.

Janette asked no questions and voiced no complaints, fully focused on the work even as her skin roused with gooseflesh, her feet turned so pale they were almost blue, her knees got skinned against the cobbles and her hands became raw from handling brush and cold water. She did often look longingly toward the kitchen door by the time she was done scrubbing coal marks off the pillars.

"This is good enough," Meredith finally declared. "Let's stash away all this and go inside."

The girl wasted no time gathering all the tools and taking them back to their corner. Meredith loaded a tray with the evening's materials and carried it in one arm, hauling the sack of refuse with the other. Janette met her halfway to the door and wordlessly took hold of the sack, looking up adoringly at her new mentor.

Meredith let go with a pleased smile. "We'll leave it by the fire. Between Desmond, the chimney and the compost pile, nothing ever goes to waste in this house."

"Desmond?"

"He's in his pen. You'll meet him tomorrow." Meredith tilted her head toward the door. "Let's go warm up."

Janette nodded emphatically. Mistress and apprentice all but ran into the kitchen.

THE GIRL SAT AT THE TABLE, huddled in a blanket. Her nose and cheeks were ruddy and she sniffled occasionally. The abused remains of a cloth napkin lay crumpled in front of her. Meredith leaned against the counter in her thick red robe, braids undone, face paint washed off and beads put away. She was looking at her charge with carefully concealed dread. The extent of her unpreparedness was an ever-growing chasm gaping between her feet, made apparent from the moment the girl had asked for a "Kleenex" to blow her nose.

The newly-invested Mistress couldn't guess at how to properly care for a human youth. She had no spare bed, no wardrobe that would fit the girl, no sanctioned gruel to feed her. They didn't eat regular witch food, did they? What she'd been fed *that one time* on Earth had not resembled anything she'd ever choose to eat.

This is the absolute worst idea—

Shut up shut up shut up shut up.

"Mistress Meredith?"

She gave a little start. "Yes?"

"I don't mean disrespect, but . . . is supper going to be any time soon? I left right before dinnertime."

"Oh, yes, of course. Dinner." Meredith walked over to the frost-box with purposeful strides, as if she knew exactly what to fetch. She unlatched the hook and lifted the lid. "Hmm."

Her heart sank at the sight of the meager contents. She'd blown her budget on today's shopping, and no payday until Sixday. She might have to do the unthinkable and borrow from her sad little stash before then.

"I've been so busy, I forgot to stock up on a few things. I might have to feed you something you're not accustomed to."

"Oh, I– I don't mind. I'm . . . I'll become a witch, true? I should eat like one."

"True, yes." Meredith leaned into the frost-box and rummaged for a bit, as if spoiled for choice. "Well then. We'll have . . . bread, fried eggs and sausage?"

Janette breathed out with relief. "Yes, thank god, that would be great. I was so afraid you'd say basilisk eyes and lizard tails."

Meredith fished out four eggs from the no-frost section, held them precariously in one hand and closed the lid. "Humans eat those? What's a basilisk?"

"No, um, they're . . . scaly, and bigger than an alligator, and turn you to stone with their breath. You don't have basilisks?"

"No, and rather glad we don't, by the sound of it."

"How about dragons? Surely you have dragons."

"Dragons." She left the eggs on the counter. "Big, leathery wings? Fire-breathing?"

"Yes!"

"No, no dragons." Meredith opened the pantry, unhooked her last bit of cured sausage and grabbed her second-to-last loaf of very definitely not stale bread. "That's a mythological creature, I thought. Do you have dragons on Earth now?"

"No, no." Janette looked disheartened. "Wizards, at least? Or . . . warlocks."

"No, wizards are an old myth, too."

"Oh. I guess druids, as well?"

"Druids? Isn't that like a wizard, but dirty?"

"I suppose, yeah."

"No druids that I know of."

"So no wizards at all?"

"I don't think they even existed in the first place, to be honest."

"Okay—trolls, then? Orcs and goblins? Ratmen? Elves? Vampires, maybe?"

Meredith kept shaking her head with a nonplussed pout. She set a cast iron pan on the stove-top, got a spoonful of lard from its jar and splatted it on the pan. She rotated the dial to *high.*

"Umm . . . fairies? Dryads? Necromancers?"

"Pfft. Necromancy, what a hoax, don't get me started. Fell for it once. Lil' Sumo just twitched and shambled for a while, it was horrific. So foolish, but he was such a good pet, and I felt bad about the accident. . . ."

"Oh. Um. I'm sorry."

"Why would you be sorry?"

"I'm sorry it happened."

"Ah. Right."

Lips pursed, Janette watched for a while as her new mentor cut the sausage in slices.

"Do you have *any* monsters?" she finally asked.

Meredith couldn't suppress the smile. "Well, I have a brood-sister."

"Oh! Is that some kind of– of monstrous overseer, watching over what you do? And you have to live up to the brood standards, or the brood-sister will come and punish you? Is that how it works?"

Yes to all of that, Meredith thought as the lard hissed and sizzled.

"No. We shared a womb, that's all. I was making a joke."

"Aw. So you have a twin sister? Does she look just like you?"

"No. Mifraulde and I could not be any more different."

"Oh. I asked because Brad and Bridget from my class kept saying they're twins, but they look *nothing* alike, so I looked it up and it turns out there are different types of twins. So I guess it's the same for you."

Meredith didn't quite know how to respond, so she didn't. Eggs were soon out of their shells and gaining color in a very satisfying way.

"May I ask more questions, Mistress Meredith?"

"Um, yes. Yes, of course."

"How many apprentices have you had so far?"

She gave the lie a short while to fully form as she sprinkled a pinch of salt and pepper over the rosy yolks.

"More than I care to count. Over twenty, certainly."

"Oh, wow. Do you . . . am I the only one, right now? Is there, like, a class?"

"No, one at a time. Always one at a time. It's a long and time-consuming process."

How long would it take to teach this girl magic, anyway? How long until she could infuse—

"Long?" the girl asked. "How long is the apprenticeship, Mistress?"

Such a great question. At the Brena academy, witches were introduced to the basics at eight years old and were not expected to cast even the simplest thing for years. Frau had been a precocious brat, sneaking forbidden tomes into the dorms to infuse her very first cantrip at nine. Meredith hadn't managed anything until she was thirteen.

For the plan to work, she'd need this girl to infuse trinkets worth selling within the span of a single year.

"It depends on you," was the belated response, "and how much you apply yourself. How old are you?"

"I'm . . . I'll be thirteen in May."

"So you're twelve."

"Y— yeah, but I'll work the hardest of them all, Mistress. I promise. I want to be the best."

"Yes. I expect as much from you."

The girl watched with great interest as Meredith transferred the eggs to the plates she'd prepared, distributed sausage and bread in equal amounts and brought dishes and forks to the table. She pulled a pair of tall glasses from a cupboard, took them to a fat clay jug on the counter and carefully poured brook-crisp water into them. Finally, she pinched Janette's napkin between thumb and forefinger, tossed it into the sink and brought two more napkins over.

"Thank you, Mistress Meredith."

"It's not much, I know. Witches eat frugally."

"It's plenty. Just the right amount."

Janette reached for the fork. Meredith's chest tightened at the sight of the girl's hands. "This might sound strange to you, but it is customary for us to always wash our hands before eating."

"Oh!" Janette looked down at her palms. "Oh, gross!" She hastily stood, her chair almost tipping over as it clattered backwards. "I completely forgot to wash, this is all so new, it didn't cross my mind! You must think I'm a savage now."

Meredith was slightly alarmed at the girl's aghast demeanor. "It's, uh, it's alright. Scathe undone. There's the sink, now, use as much soap as you need."

Janette shed her blanket, hurried to the counter, opened the tap, grabbed the bar of soap and began scrubbing.

"Bosh. I feel silly for saying it, but I didn't think there would be running water here."

"I'm at the edge of the wood farms, but this is still part of Brena. Running water is a basic commodity. Isn't it so for humans?"

"Well, yeah. Kind of, it depends where you live in the world. What I mean is . . . I thought this would be medieval times? Hauling buckets of water from the well, lighting candles and so on, but you have electricity!" Janette giggled bashfully. "I'm so relieved."

Meredith spoke while concentrating on cutting the egg whites in orderly squares. "Well, it used to be raw spark flowing through the power grid, but as supply dwindled we adapted a lot of Earth technology into our systems. It's far more efficient to generate electricity first."

"Raw spark?"

Meredith stopped her sausage placements mid-motion and realized what she'd so casually mentioned. "Oh, never mind that," she said, and waved a dismissive fork. "It's, um. Obsolete technology. We've come a long way, as has your own civilization."

"I can't wait to hear all about the history of Galavan, Mistress Meredith." The girl dried her hands with a rag and went back to the table. She pulled in the chair before sitting down, adoring smile on her lips. "I still can't believe this is happening. I'm so excited."

"Hm. I'm glad to hear it, but I hope you understand it's not all going to be frolic and harvest, here. You'll be working very hard for your magic."

Saying the word *magic* switched on a light behind the girl's eyes, every single time.

"Y– yes, I understand, I do. Thank you so much for choosing me, Mistress."

"Right, yes, well. You are smart and talented, or you wouldn't be here. I'm sure you'll prove yourself worth the trouble."

"Oh, I hope so. This is all so new. I'm worried I'll make too many mistakes."

"I am fully aware you will need time to learn and adapt, apprentice. You're not my first, remember?"

Janette fell silent for a moment. "I'm sorry," she finally said, "but is that the way I should eat this meal, Mistress Meredith?"

Meredith looked down at her arrangement of bread-egg-sausage towers.

"Um." She adjusted one of the towers slightly so it wouldn't tip over. "Yes, absolutely. It's tradition."

"There's so much I don't know. I'll work hard to get everything right, I promise."

Janette proceeded to emulate her, cutting and placing the food in neat little piles of bread at the bottom, slice of cured sausage in the middle and egg white on top. The yolks were at the center of a circle of food towers.

Meredith drew an entirely disproportionate amount of satisfaction from watching the girl copy her irrational compulsion.

"Yes, well done. We may now eat." Meredith grabbed her fork. "Observe carefully."

She pierced the yolks just enough for dipping and drove the fork through egg, sausage and bread. She dabbed the bread on the yolk before stuffing the whole thing in her mouth.

"Mmm."

Janette followed the same steps, precisely mimicking the motions. She imitated Meredith's *"mmm"* in exact pitch and duration, but she couldn't restrain a giggle as she chewed.

Meredith found herself smiling back. This wasn't so hard. Then again, why should it be? Humans did it constantly. They bred and brought them up a dozen at a time, and this one was already at a self-sufficient stage of growth, mostly.

She could get used to having an apprentice, Meredith told herself.

Then she remembered the girl wasn't an apprentice at all. The powerful youth was her ticket to financial stability and consistent quota palm-greasing. She'd have to dispose of her—of *it*—when *it* outgrew its usefulness, so best not to get attached.

Meredith watched the slim little human as they ate, hopefully not letting any of her thoughts show. Yes, she'd have to stay vigilant at all times around this girl.

That eager smile of hers seemed downright virulent.

MEREDITH PULLED an armful of bedding from her closet and brought it to the living room. Janette sat in front of a freshly stoked fire.

"This is so nice. I've never sat in front of a hearth before. I could fall asleep right here."

"That's just what you will do." Meredith dropped the sheets and blanket on the couch. "This is the Apprentice's Sofa. The spare room will be yours only after you've earned the right to your own bedroom."

"I understand, Mistress Meredith. Though maybe I could bed down on the floor right here? Just for tonight. I love this fire, and your rug feels very comfortable."

"Yes, that is acceptable. You can get started now. I must go speak to the Head of the Coven immediately, to report your retrieval and arrange the, um. The official record of your apprenticeship. There are some other errands I must run, so don't wait up for me. Stay in this room at all times and don't touch anything, understand?"

"Actually, Mistress Meredith . . . I really need to make a trip to the loo, if you don't mind."

"Yes, bathroom, yes. That's acceptable. The narrow door by the jade in the corner. You may also get water from the kitchen, but don't leave anything out of place."

"Thank you." Janette took off at a thigh-squeezing skip, brushed past the leafy potted plant and closed the door behind her.

Fidgeting silence. High-pressure tinkle. Flush. Running water. The door opened a moment later.

"There's even a sewer system! I'm *so happy* you didn't point me to a latrine outside."

"It's a magical septic hollow, actually. The bottom is connected via space-fold to the main drain into Earth, you simply give the coordinates to the database and they activate the line from off-site every year. It's a popular setup for suburb cottages."

"Oh, my god, I could ask twenty questions about all that, but . . . I'm sure you're in a hurry."

"Yes, I must depart now, apprentice. What are the rules?"

"Don't leave the room, don't touch anything, go to bed."

"Good. Rest as long as you can. There is much work for us tomorrow."

"I don't know if I'll be able to sleep, honestly. I'm so excited."

Meredith walked over to the shelves and pulled out a tome as thick as her palm was wide. *Complacency of the Learned,* the title read. *A Novel.* Mifraulde Galvan was the author.

She handed it to Janette. "This will put you to sleep in no time."

The girl accepted it with both hands and almost toppled over from the weight.

"Oof."

"It's pure fiction, everything in there, nothing to do with how things actually work in Galavan. For future reference, this shelf is allowed." She pointed at her meager collection of sanctioned Earth fiction and miscellanea, then pointed lower. "*That* shelf is off-limits, you may not touch it. We'll get to some of it together, when you're ready."

"Yes, Mistress Meredith."

"I'll be on my way. Lock the door behind me, but don't throw the latch or put on the chain, you'll lock me out."

"As you say, Mistress Meredith. Thank you again, Mistress. You won't regret choosing me, I promise."

Meredith patted the girl's shoulder. It registered as the most awkward thing she'd done this decade. "I, ah, have every confidence you won't disappoint me." She walked past Janette, put up her hood, undid all the locks and swung the door open.

"Wary's worth."

"I'm sorry?"

"Goodbye, I mean. Good night."

"Oh! Good—um . . . where is Worf, Mistress." Janette waved, smiling. Meredith smiled back.

She shut the door behind her and didn't have to wait long to hear lock and deadbolt engage. Leaving the girl alone in the house struck Meredith as foolhardy at best, but she had little choice.

She traveled down the fractured tile path flanked by gnarled bushes and properly eerie tree trunks, pushed the fence open and walked into the night.

CHAPTER SIX

LAST CHANCES

HE HEAD OF THE COVEN'S waiting room was a stone enclosure where opulence could be found in the details. The walls were mostly bare, but had been polished to a reflective sheen, as had the marble floors. The chandelier was simple and functional, but closer inspection would reveal high-artificer make and burnished Ferris metalwork. The window drapes were a plain midnight blue, but their weave was thick with the finest Valeni silk patterns.

Meredith sat on a stone bench she knew to be uncomfortable on purpose. Straight ahead was the secretary's nightwood desk, a window to its right, a doorway to its left. Mifraulde glared from her oversize portrait on the back wall, dreadfully constipated in her sober burgundy dress and Head of the Coven regalia. The only sounds in the room were the incessant scratches of pen on paper and Meredith's nearly-inaudible mutters.

"Another chance," she whispered, and pursed her lips. "A *last* chance, more urgent. It's the last mistake . . . no, no, don't remind her. Please, Frau, I won't let you down—I won't *disappoint* you, yes. Use bigger words, she likes big words."

"Are you ill?"

Meredith gave a little start and looked up. Coren had stopped writing and now stared from behind her desk, disdain clear in her dark features.

"Wh– what?"

"Is there a reason why you are talking to yourself?"

Her fingers wrung the hem of her robe. "No, I . . . I'm just nervous, sorry."

"Then be nervous *quietly*."

"Yes. Right. Sorry."

Coren returned to whatever she was doing. Meredith's thoughts continued begging and groveling and rehearsing, molding desperation into heartfelt promises. It seemed like several days passed as she waited.

The secretary abruptly lifted her head from her writing, and one moment later a robed figure stormed out of Mifraulde's office. The stranger's booming voice cut in mid-sentence as soon as she crossed the threshold.

"—every word you just said! *You* are misguided! *You* will lead us to ruin, not I. Humans are nothing but babes and pests, and as soon as I get you out of the way, the world will know the rightful order of things. It's time we come out of the shadows and claim what's ours."

She strode to the vertical transporter, traditional gorgon chimes rattling and jingling with every step. Once there, her sallow-skinned claw tightened to a fist.

"*Open it,*" she demanded without looking back. Coren glanced into Mifraulde's office. After a tiny pause there was a buzz at the secretary's desk, and the doors slid apart.

The witch marched inside the box and turned around to stare straight forward. Before the doors closed she had time to notice Meredith, pinch her lips and let out a contemptuous sniff. The waiting room fell into an uneasy silence as the transporter hummed on its way to the bottom.

Visitor and secretary exchanged a look. Meredith forced a smile. "Foul bog lurker, yeah?"

Coren did not find it amusing. She let out an irked breath and returned to her scribbling.

Another eternity passed before Mifraulde's voice finally emerged from her office.

"Send her in."

Meredith stood up and stepped forth as Frau's secretary made a needless beckoning gesture.

"The Head of the Coven will see you now," she said.

"I don't think I've ever seen your desk empty, Coren. Is there any time you don't work?"

"Do you ask so that you might avoid me in the future?"

"No, I—"

"I work any time the Head of the Coven works. I suggest you don't make her wait."

"Right." Meredith stepped away from the desk. "Thank you."

Coren rolled her eyes and filled out a line in the schedule. Meredith stole a peek. Below *09.50: Audits (all day)* and *18.41:*

Meeting with Selma Tarkai-Holtz-Grubber (unscheduled), the secretary wrote *18.72: Inconvenient meeting with dead weight (unscheduled)*.

She considered giving the snooty secretary Four-Thirteen's rude gesture from the day previous. The mental image eased some of the tension in her chest. Meredith turned away, parted the vaporous violet curtains and crossed the tall arcade into her brood-sister's office.

Her slippers rustled on the lush Valeni rugs as she stepped to the middle of the room. Her brood-sister looked exhausted, more so than usual this time of the year. She was surrounded by open ledgers, rolled-out parchments, black-and-red-ink treatises, all propped both on her enormous nightwood desk and several lecterns besides. The gaps in the usually crammed shelves reminded Meredith of Mistress Vera's grin whenever she punished a student.

It would've felt like a prison if it weren't for the panoramic window behind the Head of the Coven. Under the brilliant moon of early Wither, Brena cascaded downhill—orderly within the jagged old walls, cluttered in the suburbs beyond. Figures milled about Galvan Boulevard and its nocturnal market, the Crooked Garden trees cut a skeletal outline by the library, Blackened Square was a blotch in front of the Felling House and its clock tower. Several streets were still awash in eerie green lights from the Hallow's End decorations that lingered.

Mifraulde flipped a small switch on her desk and the thick window drapes whirred closer until they were fully drawn. At the same time, the subtle thrum of aural privacy enveloped them. She continued comparing lists on separate ledgers and noting down figures for quite a while.

"Meredith," she finally said. Her pen didn't stop moving.

"Hi, Frau."

The scratching silence crept on, the sound like tiny claws eroding Meredith's sanity.

"I saw Selma," she began, but Mifraulde interrupted her.

"Meredith, I'd like to apologise for this morning. I was on edge from all the meetings and I unfairly took it out on you. You're not useless. You've helped me with the Riven Circle and I can always count on you to listen when I need it. I'm still upset about your failure, but I was needlessly cruel. Please forgive me."

Meredith needed a moment to parse the words. Was Mifraulde having a stroke?

She seemed fine. Fatigued. Her wavy hair was uncharacteristically frothy.

"Meredith?"

"Oh, it's, ah . . . it's alright, really."

A small pause. It was a conscious effort to set aside all the pathetic groveling she'd planned.

"Is it? I know I hurt you."

"No, it's . . . I don't blame you, we were both upset. You couldn't have said anything I haven't already told myself. I'm glad you feel this way. I'm surprised you've put up with me this long, ha ha, ah."

Meredith winced and forced herself to shut her mouth. Mifraulde nodded and continued working with unsettling gravity.

Time passed.

"You look tired, Frau."

"That's because I am tired."

"You look terrible, is what I meant."

Weary eyes met Meredith's gaze. The brood-sisters shared a brief smile.

"You're one to talk," she teased. Mifraulde let out a sigh. "I'm frustrated, Meri. I can see the system falling apart within a decade, and no-one wants to change it. No-one wants to change *anything*. Look at me, surrounded by paper records, doing everything by hand simply because that's the way it's always been. Does it look superior to you? Does it in any way look magical? Adopting human computers realm-wide won't turn anyone into a dud."

"I know," Meredith said. The same two words she'd always say to Frau's private rants.

"I wish *they* knew. You saw Selma stomping off, yes?"

Meredith nodded. "Yes. She's crazy."

"She fancies herself the next modern fury, it's pathetic. And the worst part is that she's not alone in her delusions. Half the Coven acts as if it's two hundred years ago and humans are still afraid of their photographs. They have so much technology we haven't used yet, they're on their way to their own singularity, and yet here we are, chiding one another for naming a pet golem. But, no, of course, doing away with the span system and all the needless tradition is too high a price to pay. As if we'd be sullied, somehow. It's all a resource, just like any other."

Meredith nodded, sympathetic and thoughtful—her go-to when the rants became too erratic to follow. All throughout, Mifraulde's pen stabbed and slashed at the page.

"*They* voted for me, well over three-fourths of them, so the least they could do now is follow my lead. It's such an arbitrary line to draw—everyone uses human appliances, we adapted our powerlines to their voltages, and we certainly didn't *invent* proper sanitation, did we? No, we've always fed off them one way or another, adding our touch. And the Coven resists, every time. All the talk of young blood and new ideas back then, it was just that, empty talk. Sometimes I feel they gave me the shawl and patted my head like I was a pet they'd groomed to do their bidding."

"You're no-one's pet, Frau."

"I know that, but *they* don't. You'd think at least all the Brenan crones would support me, but Hedre and Yawleth and Branwen are as bad as the rest. Well, I'm going to push reform some way or another, and those that don't like it can jump into a pit. Coren and I are fed up with all this cumbersome nonsense."

Meredith let her sister work through her grievances. She wasn't prone to these outbursts, but they were common enough around the Council sessions.

The Head of the Coven continued intensely scribbling in silence for some time. Finally she put down her pen and despondently pushed the ledger away.

"So." She crossed her hands together. "Any progress at dusk?"

Meredith simply shook her head, ashamed and contrite. The less lies she spun about it, the better.

Mifraulde sighed again and reached into a drawer. She produced an official-looking sheet of paper and extended it to Meredith. It had the Council Seal already stamped at the bottom.

Bashful, she drew near and closed hesitant fingers on it. Frau didn't let go. Meredith looked in her brood-sister's eyes and saw both severity and regret in their wintry depths.

"This is the last time I'm waiving your responsibilities, Meri. Next year, you will fulfill your lawfully required quota of one youth viable for harvesting, or you will face the consequences. Whatever those may be."

Meredith's brow arched in understanding, knit with worry. "It's Selma, isn't it?"

Mifraulde let out an exasperated breath. "That Tarkan harpy has pecked at my heckles since we met, but all her misguided Return-to-Earth idiocy has become a credible threat, now. Undo the masquerade and go to war, can you imagine? All the delusional rhetoric lately about Earth domination is enough to churn vomit. Eugh." She shuddered in actual disgust. "So you see, I can't afford liabilities anymore. They look at the way I care for you, and they see weakness. This is the most I can do."

Meredith nodded. "I understand."

Fine eyebrows lifted in mild surprise. "You do?"

Meredith nodded again. "Thank you for all you've done for me. No-one else would have cared."

Mifraulde blinked a few times. Her grave mask cracked around the eyes, at the corner of the mouth, revealing a smile that couldn't decide whether to be affectionate or bitter. She let go of the paper, and the smile was gone.

"Well, good, then." Her attention returned to the pages full of dreary lists and numbers. "I'll be busy for the foreseeable future, trying to keep our world from falling apart. I'd appreciate not being disturbed."

"Not even. . . ." Meredith needlessly lowered her voice. "About the Circle meetings?"

"No. You're done with them. Disengage from those mercy-ridden fools as soon as you're able without rousing suspicion. I won't use you anymore, and they're no menace to the realm, anyway. You know where I stand on the issue."

"Um, alright. I'll . . . I'll play up Selma for you before I leave them, I'll make sure they know she's the one to keep from power."

"Feel free, but it's not necessary. I'm dealing with her already. You need to take care of yourself from now on. Don't come calling until you're in good standing with the Coven."

Mifraulde didn't look up. Meredith lingered. "Thank you for your time, Frau."

"You're welcome. Help yourself to a snack on the way out. You look malnourished."

"Yes, alright." Meredith stepped toward the exit, head down. "Farewell."

The Head of the Coven's response was to switch off the privacy shield and continue with her work. Meredith walked out of the room, ignored Coren's glare at the paper she carried, and pocketed from the snack table a fistful of dried flaps she had no intention to eat. She passed the double doors by the bench and hurried toward the spiral staircase. She would've jumped into a pyre before asking that stuck-up wart of a secretary to unlock the vertical transporters.

The tiny service door clicked shut behind her. Meredith leaned against it while letting out a lungful of nerves.

What had just happened in there?

The ultimatum was clear. Frau was cutting her off and had no intention to associate with her again until she stopped being a failure. As Meredith carefully read the waiver in her hands, she couldn't decide how to feel about that.

"All the better," she muttered to herself, and realized she was panting. "I don't think she'd approve of the new guest."

Meredith started on her way down once her heart rate regained its normal rhythm. She had to squint a little to make out every step in the twisting stairwell.

Four hundred-odd steps and a few grandiose halls later, she left the Tower grounds, turned Tarkisward onto Galvan Boulevard and made her way downhill across the eerie glow and sparse crowds of the nocturnal market. Already the Kestrel Memorial Library peeked above storefronts and stalls, tucked around the Five Furies monument and past the Centennial Crooked Gardens.

Books had taught her most of what she knew about botany, and optimal etherfish habitats, and cottage construction and maintenance. From books she'd learned advanced mechanical tinkering, salve and toxin brewing, how to keep a pet thog happy and healthy and how to stay alive in general.

How to care for a human youth should be no different.

YURENA VALEN-FROST-MERGAT lounged behind the front counter, nose buried in a book. A usual sight. There was placid surprise in her smile when she looked up.

"Meredith?" Her sandaled feet came off the counter as she let the reclining chair smoothly lean forward. "I didn't know you came here so late."

Meredith's chest tightened, just a bit. Nothing like it used to be.

"Hi, Yurena. I didn't expect to see you here, either. I thought you kept to a diurnal schedule?"

"Council sessions," she said, as if it explained everything. "How about you?"

"Oh, I . . . I can't sleep, so I figured I might as well read. It's not a habit."

Yurena propped her bony elbows on the counter, ivory-gray eyes looking at Meredith over the rim of her glasses. A slim forefinger was sandwiched between the pages of the book in her hand. *Gallia's Burning Desire,* the cover read, along with a zero-subtlety rendition of Gallia and the buxom object of her desire.

Meredith had read it already. It was pretty good.

"And what troubles your sleep, Meredith?"

She gave a tired smile while eyeing the dim, book-lined halls. "Too many things to count. There is truly no-one else here?"

"Not one wicked soul. The nocturnals get too tired at this time of the year, so I always switch with Martha. It's nice to have the place to myself—and now you, of course. What can I get for you? You've more burning questions about your garden, I'm sure."

"No, well, actually, I didn't have anything specific in mind right now. I was wondering if I might browse for a little while?"

"Mm, I don't know, all by yourself? Can I trust you not to bump into my precious shelves and topple the whole lot?"

"Um, no, I mean, I wouldn't—"

"I'm joking, Meredith. I've seen the way you treat my books. If there's someone I'd trust around them, that's you."

"Oh. Oh, well, I'm glad you feel that way. I think I'll go to the second floor. Mind turning the lights on?"

"And ruin the magic of a night-shroud library? No, just take one of these." Yurena slid a bookmark between the pages of her novel and bent under the counter. She pulled up a portable lamp and held it out to Meredith.

The lamp was an opaque glass orb encased in an ornate wire frame, with a stable metallic base and an overarching handle. Meredith hesitated. "Aren't they expensive? You never hand them out."

The librarian waved the question aside. "Hardly, they're not even magical. I simply don't trust most to bring them back." She pressed the handle onto Meredith's palm, then reached down to catch her other hand. Yurena's cold fingers guided Meredith's to a small knob under the frame.

"The switch is underneath," Yurena said affably. She pressed Meredith's fingertip against it, and with a click the orb lit up with white light—bright enough for comfortable reading, soft enough not to be a nuisance to fellow readers.

"Um. Thank you. I'd have wasted a span trying to find it, I'm sure."

Yurena smiled broadly, showing her slightly crooked, pointier-than-usual teeth. Her fingertips lingered on Meredith's hand. "You'd have figured it out."

Meredith's chest got a bit tighter. Before she could come up with an answer, the librarian let go and sat back down. "You're all set." She crossed one leg over the other and propped the novel on her knee. "I'll be here if you have a question, then. Or . . . if you'd like to talk."

"Alright, thank you. I'll just. . . ." Meredith gestured vaguely toward the shelves.

"Enjoy."

Flustered, a bit wobbly, she headed toward the lavish set of stairs a bit faster than necessary. The brief conversation left her ill-at-ease, it had been so pleasant. Yurena had gradually shifted from dismissive to friendly in the past year, and Meredith had no idea how to handle it.

She went up the steps, very definitely not looking for any section in particular. The Kestrel Memorial Library was five stories tall. Climbing one flight of stairs to start browsing was hardly suspicious, she'd decided. Though by all appearances Yurena's attention was once more devoted to her reading, Meredith didn't breathe easy until she went out of sight behind the shelves. She meandered a little, her steps a quiet shuffle on the tile floors as her eyes wandered through the dimly-lit aisles.

Mostly packed shelves were arranged in a grid pattern that at regular intervals circled around cozy reading areas. The wooden shelves were ancient but well kept, the smell was necessarily musty but pine-scented, and the books ranged from flesh-bound relics to modern paperbacks. The late Victorian architecture and décor lent the whole building an air of sophistication and exclusivity that belied the horrid, outrageous, sordid and banal contents of many of the texts it housed.

Meredith raised the lamp as she strayed farther from the chande-lier above the stairwell, long shadows parting just enough for her to see one shelf ahead. Her tenth-span of meandering had very casually led close to the back, well within the third of the floor devoted to non-fiction on humanity. *Human Youths,* read the cursive rubric between the aisles in front of her.

She went in, passing several sub-sections, her eyes scanning spines as she went:

Six Efficient Methods to Harvest the Spark.

The Viable Youth Decline: Our Dwindling Supply and How to Solve It.

Missing Children Statistics and Acceptable Thresholds.

One Hundred and Five Succulent Recipes: The Ultimate, No-Waste, No-Nonsense Way to Cook Children!

Sugar-Candy: Wunderfull Drug – Rightly Lure a Fat Tiddler to Thine Cottage.

She reached the Proper Upkeep subsection. Though every shelf in the library was routinely cleared of dust, the air here was heavy and stale. These books were old and largely obsolete, written or compiled before the time of stasis pods, entrapment orbs and streamlined harvesting; before even the exodus to Galavan. Several were in languages other than English, or in an English so archaic it might as well have been Shaglaroth's forbidden tongue. Meredith ran a finger through the spines, muttering out loud the titles she could read.

"*Indoctrination and Obedience* . . . no, that won't work. *Effective Torture blah blah* . . . hardly useful here. *Anatomy of* whatever . . . hmm. *The Young Human: A Comprehensive Guide To a Healthy Youngster*—oh, by Caterina Galvan? Must be an English reedition."

She pulled the tome out of the shelf, along with a fairly modern *Earthborn Witches: Truths and Myths*—possibly a Doctrine text, it sported the Hexe Wardja seal—and a small *What To Feed Your Pet Human* booklet wedged between ominous Slavic spines. She brought them all to the reading area by the back wall and almost dropped everything when she noticed the harsh pair of eyes boring straight into her skull.

After some moderate panicking, she realized it was but a life-sized portrait. Helena Tremmel, the Marrow Banshee, Prime Surgeon, Haunt of Brattenburg and Caterina Galvan's contemporary Fury. Her foreboding glower was particularly sinister in the half-light of the portable lamp.

Such a fitting area to hang her likeness, Meredith thought. Tremmel's thorough research on youth anatomy had been a building block for converting the spark into storable energy.

Meredith shrugged the ancient witch out of her mind and neatly piled the books on the table by the portrait. After some consideration, she went back and fetched the large cookbook she'd passed, leaving it at arm's reach from her seat. She placed the lamp on a comfortable spot, sat down and grabbed the book at the top of the pile: *Earthborn Witches*. Etched in relief under the silver lettering was a figure with a line splitting it down the middle: one half was a stylized staff-wielding witch, the other a malevolent toad-mouthed slob. She wasn't sure what to make of it.

Meredith stifled a yawn, cracked the book open and began reading.

* * *

MYTH: Earthborn Witches Could Control their Hunger through Discipline!

TRUTH: The Hunger of Earthborn Witches is Uncontrollable until Sated.

Apostates would have you believe the Hunger could be managed in reasonable ways before the Desolation, and the thousand cautionary tales are embellishments and exaggeration. These are False arguments pushed by Dire Criminals to rewrite history and undermine Puritan Doctrine. Any such arguments should be Immediately reported to a Judicar near you.

It is Truth that every Earthborn Witch (and, indeed, every Spark't Witch Galavan-born) was afflicted by Sparkwane upon reaching maturity, and so the Well within them dwindled until only Hunger remained. It is Truth that every Waned Witch found the need to sate their Hunger overpowering. It is Truth that even the Furies struggled with Hunger, and in fact it was Helena Tremmel herself who first formulated the theoretical principles that would become the Desolation. Our society is their vision, free at last from the Tyranny of the Flesh. Beware the deceit of the Merciful.

MYTH: An Earthborn Witch can be fully assimilated into Galavan!

TRUTH: All Earthborn Witches will eventually yearn for their homeland and turn against Us.

Apostates sponsor recruitment of Earthborn Witches as the desired path, spinning a fantasy of cognitive integration and learned loyalty to Our Realm. They will claim Earthborn Witches as sisters-in-waiting, and blatantly ignore Our History in order to attribute greed and malfeasance to the Puritan Doctrine.

It is Truth that Earth taints its spawn from Birth. It is Truth that this Infection will sully any and all efforts to assimilate an Earthborn Witch into Galavan, poisoning their every thought with considerations for their birthplace. Whatever relations were present before recruitment shall sicken their minds with Doubt and Conflict and Mercy.

Our History proves this Truth, from myriad individual incidents, to the American Crisis, to the Conveyance and beyond. In their Wisdom, the Furies shunned life on Earth, and so we embrace and perpetuate their Legacy. Beware the folly of the Merciful.

MYTH: Earthborn Witches are just like Us!
TRUTH: Earthborn Witches reek of humanity and the Stink never washes off.
The Apostate will argue upon Kinship. She will invoke Mercy and inclusion as though an Earthborn Witch is an estranged brood-sister, and not tainted by Human Filth. . . .

* * *

"Meredith?"

She gave a start and flapped shut the *What to Feed* booklet. Meredith quickly lined it up next to the other two, reached for the large cookbook and opened it on a random page, covering the incriminating texts as surreptitiously as she could.

"In here," she called. "I'm here."

She'd lost track of time. How long had it been, a span? Two span? She hadn't planned to take so long, but there was an awful lot to learn.

The shadows brightened around the shelf straight ahead, and Yurena's figure emerged shortly after. She walked toward Meredith with easy steps, her frame a gauntly thin Grim Reaper between the shelves, near-white irises glinting eerily in the parting darkness. She held two long glasses full of dark purple, with the portable lamp hanging from her forearm.

She neared Meredith with a smile and offered one of the glasses. "I got myself a drink and thought maybe you were thirsty."

"Oh. Um. Yes, sure." Meredith took it. "Thank you."

Yurena left her lamp on the table. Her ochre librarian's cowl was unclasped, revealing the white blouse and knee-length skirt underneath. She casually leaned against the nearest chair and sipped from her drink. "I wasn't aware you cooked such fancy recipes."

Meredith glanced down. *Tongue and Glut with White Pheasant over Wylde Herbs.*

"Ah, hah, I'm not so fond of it, but Mifraulde keeps saying I can't cook and I'm determined to prove her wrong."

Yurena chuckled and took another sip. Meredith did the same.

Spiced hansel and grape juice, warm. Quite delicious.

"I hope she'll provide the ingredients," Yurena said. "That recipe costs a small fortune."

"Oh, yes, of course. *She* can afford it without problems. She brought this piggy soup just yesterday. . . ." Meredith rolled her eyes. "I felt like spilling even one drop would be like wasting a year's worth of salt."

"It must be nice to be her." Yurena looked at her surroundings with contentment. "I'd never want to trade places, though."

Meredith took another sip that turned into gulps.

"I can't blame you. I'd feel the same way."

"You would, wouldn't you? I've been meaning to talk to you about it. You asked to work here years ago, are you still interested?"

Meredith blinked. "Are you . . . is that an offer?"

"It is. I have an opening coming up. Full time, the whole ten span shift. Sleeping quarters provided, you could have your pick in the labyrinth down there. Not that you would. I know you'd never abandon your garden."

Lips pursed and eyebrow raised, Meredith eyed the near-depleted glass in Yurena's hand. "You didn't spike these with ludebark, did you?"

The librarian laughed good-naturedly. "I've simply changed my mind, is it so hard to believe? Or, what, did *you* change your mind?"

No, she had not. Spend her days surrounded by books, moving them from shelf to shelf, arranging and cataloguing and lining up the spines *just right?* She would've done it for free. The half-day shifts would have been a welcome respite from her otherwise pitiful life.

Or they would've been, before she'd taken into her home an Earthborn witch and acquired a literal deadline to make things work.

Meredith played with the bookmark tassel dangling from the cookbook, rolling it round and round her finger. "You said it would make you look bad to have me here."

"Yes, I . . . I apologise for that. I thought so at the time, but not anymore. I've seen the way you treat books. You carry them out of here as if they're made of glass. You'll return them without a scratch on the cover or a bend in the pages, always in a timely manner. You'll touch the shelves like they might whisper in your ear, and don't think I haven't noticed you dusting off a few. Even right now, look at where you placed your cup on the table, so far from everything so you don't risk a spill. I notice these things. I think you might be an excellent caretaker."

Meredith couldn't help the flustered smile. "I don't know, you might be horrified at my copy of *Non-standard Transportation.* I tossed it into the bushes recently."

She laughed again, softly. "I think we've all done that at some point." She finished her drink and wiped the corner of her mouth with the back of one finger. Meredith's eyes lingered on the gesture.

"So," Yurena prompted, "what do you say?"

"Oh, well. . . ." She bit her lip and looked to the side. "I'm really flattered, and I wish I could, but, um, I'm tangled in a few projects right now, and the manufactory, they . . . they kind of need me? And I've been expanding my garden—and by the way, your order is ready, but I forgot to bring it." Her glance touched clear gray eyes for an instant before fleeing back to the bottom shelves. "I'm afraid I'm just too busy right now to give the library the time it deserves."

"Oh." Yurena set her empty glass on the table. "I see."

"I'm really sorry. I'm honestly surprised you changed your mind. No-one's opinion of me seems to ever change for the better."

She spoke the truth in jest, but the librarian studied Meredith's defeated-amused expression without mirth. "It must be hard for you to be Mifraulde's brood-sister. I don't think you could ever live up to the Head of the Coven's expectations, no matter who you are or how much you try."

Meredith's mouth quirked at the corner. Thoughts of Mifraulde's anger clouded her vision. "Her standards aren't as high as you might think."

Yurena gently pushed herself off the chair and drew a tiny step closer. "What I think is that you sell yourself short."

"That's . . . very nice of you to say."

"Clearly you're dexterous with your hands or they wouldn't have kept you at the manufactory."

"I wouldn't say . . . *dexterous*. More like *adequate*. And even if I were, what good is it, when I can't distill a sound worth half a clip?"

"Well, you fixed up war-torn ruins into a cottage worthy of any witch I know, largely by yourself."

"Yes, and you know why? Because I couldn't afford anything else when Frau left for the Tarkan practicum, and I couldn't even qualify for designated quarters. Nearly two decades of cobbling materials together, that's what I'm good for."

"You're good for more than that. You grow the best natural leaves, roots and petals I've ever used."

Meredith snorted. "Natural, exactly. Inferior in every way to infused botany. You *don't* want to see my attempts at chanted growth."

"Does infusion even matter that much? I've cast exactly four spells in as many years, and it's always to engage the space-fold for retrieval. It's not like the old times."

"It's different for you. This is your profession, you don't need to prove yourself to anyone."

"This is my profession *now,* and I'm fortunate. But you want to talk about stigma? I specialised in golemancy back in Devalen. The classes might as well have been held in secret, it was so frowned upon. Even now I'm wary of asking for a few golem permits to help at the library."

"You have a specialisation? Of course you do, you're smart. I have a barely passing grade. I spent every day on the verge of failure."

"Meredith."

She looked up and noticed the librarian standing much closer than she remembered. Yurena bent forward, left hand resting on the open book.

"I've been watching you for years," she said. "I know better, now. Your reputation is not deserved, and I was wrong about you."

She was close enough for her thigh to graze Meredith's knee. "Uh. . . ."

"I enjoy talking to you, about botany, and books, and . . . what I mean is, I look forward to seeing you, I have for quite some time. Hasn't it been obvious? I truly thought it was. Although you're not very perceptive of these things, are you?"

"Uh—"

"I can't ever seem to catch you in private. It makes me wish you'd have trouble sleeping more often. Is that selfish of me?"

"N— no, I don't think—"

"I better confess while I have this chance. I won't ever do it, otherwise."

"Confess?"

"Yes. Confess." Yurena shifted her weight and sighed. "You see, the way you handle these tomes?" She caressed the aged texture of the pages, drawing out the whisper of skin on paper. Her hand drifted closer until it rested on Meredith's fingers. "I find it . . . very attractive. Intoxicating, even."

Meredith's gaze shifted from their touching hands to Yurena's face. The librarian met her with a timid smile, as if actually afraid of how she might react.

"Yurena. . . ."

"Yes?"

"Is this . . . are you—I mean, is this really. . . ."

She sniffed with amusement. "You look so shocked. Is it truly that horrifying?"

"What? No, it's just, I'm not. . . ." Meredith swallowed, her throat dreadfully dry. "Me, of all people?"

"Why? What is wrong with you, exactly?"

Meredith had to look closely to make sure she wasn't being mocked. The question seemed good-natured. "You know I'm a disaster," she responded.

"No, you shouldn't believe that." Yurena placed her free hand on Meredith's shoulder. "I don't think you are."

"Well, you might be the only one this side of the Froth. Mifraulde is fed up with me, she almost threw me off to the flipside today, and another failure next year will be my last. I'm a burden, don't you see? You don't want anything to do with me."

Silence stretched for a few breaths. Yurena's hands didn't move.

"I think you should let *me* decide what company I want to keep."

"Yurena, I . . . I don't know, I don't think I should be in a relationship right now."

The long-legged witch got down on one knee, bright eyes piercing straight through. Her right hand moved from shoulder to neck.

"It doesn't have to be a relationship." She caressed Meredith's jawline with the back of her fingers. "It could be just . . . whatever you want it to be."

For one brief, wild moment, Meredith was convinced she was trapped in a fantasy. For years she had thought about this, almost exactly *this*. Maybe she never left the bedroom that morning. Maybe she was about to gasp awake in her bed.

Incidentally, Yurena was at just the right height to see the spines of the other books.

Nervous jitters surged into a jolt of panic. Meredith cupped the librarian's hand and subtly moved their arms to the surface of the table, blocking line of sight.

"Could I, maybe, ah, think about it? I, ah, I'm so dumbstruck right now, I can't even process—I mean, it's so sudden, and you're so— you're so *you*, and I'm not even. . . ."

A trace of hurt flickered in Yurena's eyes. "You don't find me alluring?"

"Well, yes, of course. That's part of it, you're *so* alluring, I'd have never thought—"

"Then what is there to think about?" She leaned a bit closer, her breath lightly brushing Meredith's cheeks. "Call me a spook, but I'm enthralled by your freckles."

"Ah hah, hah, that's just silly."

Another bit closer. "Is it?"

The close proximity stirred a hot, vibrant tangle in Meredith's core that had nothing to do with the fear of getting caught. She fought against it, pressing herself harder against the backrest. Getting close to anyone was the very last thing she should do in her situation.

Her answer came out as a tremulous squeak. "I don't know, I suppose not so much?"

Yurena's inviting smile faltered. She took a moment to look Meredith up and down. Her features crumpled in disappointment.

"You really don't want this, do you."

The jittering tangle spread in a flush all through Meredith's limbs, a vigorous protest against restraint. She *had* wanted it, even after dismissing it as an unattainable fancy. Couldn't this have happened two days ago?

Meredith cringed through the words: "It's not like that, I'm simply . . . it's been such a hard day, and I can't even think straight at this point. It's not about you, I'm just—"

"Of course, yes." She drew back slightly, looking away. Her right hand left Meredith's jaw, hovered self-consciously in the space between them, came to rest on Yurena's own knee. "I . . . I should have known. I shouldn't have done this, I didn't mean to pressure you. I'm not the kind."

Meredith worried at her lip. "I don't know what to say."

"It's fine. This is my fault, I read too much into you coming here, tonight of all nights, wearing nothing but your robe. I let my thoughts get carried away, it's not like we. . . ." Her fine eyebrows drew into a confused frown. "Are those more cookbooks?"

"What? Oh, those, yes, I skimmed through them, they're not very good, couldn't hold my interest. You were saying?"

"They don't look like any cookbook I remember."

The librarian's tone was merely curious, as was the hand that rose to the large tome on top.

Meredith's heart jumped to her throat. She shouldn't have tried to hide them. She could've passed off her interest as curiosity, or research for retrievals, or *whatever,* but now it was too late, too suspect. Visions of Yurena's mistrust flashed through her mind, events unfolding in rapid succession: narrow-eyed questions, a quiet report to the Judicars, a demand to search her house, the human girl being found, iron cuffs, a gag, being dragged through the mud and humiliated and then just screams, horrible screams in the dark depths of the holding pens.

In that moment of terror, she could think of only one way to stop it all from happening, short of murder.

Meredith leaned in and pressed her lips to Yurena's mouth.

The librarian drew in a sharp breath. Meredith's hand sought curious fingers and firmly entangled with them, while her other arm snuck between robe and blouse and wrapped around a narrow waist.

The half-lifted book cover returned to its previous position.

It didn't take long for Yurena to respond with startling intensity, lips locking and caressing with avid hunger. Her hand cradled Meredith's nape, pointy fingernails tingling on her scalp, and she felt Yurena's tongue briefly grazing her lips, as if dying to go further but wary of being unwelcome. Sweet grape and the scent of fresh-bound pages permeated Meredith's nostrils.

Their mouths parted with some reluctance. Yurena appeared stunned, eyes half-lidded, breath torrid. Her smile was eager and slightly crooked. "I thought you didn't want—"

"I couldn't resist anymore."

"Thank the Crones. I shouldn't say this, but I was about to be heartbroken."

"I'm sorry."

"Don't be." She leaned in once more. This time her kiss was slow and delicate, as if she actually cared. Almost as if. . . .

As if Meredith was someone worth kissing.

Yurena tugged on their clasped hands, mouths still sharing a breath. "I want more," she whispered. "My bed is only two floors away."

She succeeded in pulling Meredith to her feet. The first few steps were even eager, thoughts addled by the hint of sugar that lingered on her lips. She only remembered herself at seeing the one gap on the shelf.

"Wait, the books. I need to put them away, they'll gather dust and could be damaged out here."

Yurena stiffened, only to exhale a body-wide shudder. In such close proximity, Meredith could watch the pupils dilate. "What are you doing to me? You said that on purpose, didn't you?"

"What?"

She brought Meredith's hand to her lips, kissed the fingers, lightly nipped at the knuckles. "Hurry downstairs. It's the first door off the stairwell. I'll get everything ready."

She grabbed her lamp and empty glass and with quick steps she glided past, heading for the stairs. She turned in her stride for one last look full of anticipation, then broke into a skip and disappeared around the shelves. Meredith watched her go, her heart beating like it wanted to break loose from her ribcage.

She needed this new complication as much as she needed a raven pecking at her buttocks.

Meredith hastily put every tome back in their place, lining up the spines *just so*. The double doors at the front creaked shut as she returned the chair to its original position. She didn't hesitate at all to grab lamp and cup and start walking. In fact, she found herself smiling as she rushed down the steps, toward the basement, toward Yurena's quarters.

If her life was going to be complicated, she might as well enjoy it.

Yurena,

I need to get up early and I didn't want to wake you.

As I said, I'm very busy at the moment, so I don't know when I'll be able to see you again. I'm likely to be unavailable if you come calling, but rest assured you will be in my thoughts. Especially late at night.

I wish you'd approached me earlier. ~~You made me feel I am glad I'd never felt~~

I can't think of the words I want to say, so I'll just say "thank you".

I'll be in touch,

— Meredith

(It truly was great)

CHAPTER SEVEN

THE ALLEGED PAST

ROWSY, BLEARY-EYED, paste-mouthed, crazy-haired, Meredith opened her bedroom door and stepped into the living room. She shambled right up to the clock and stared, for the longest time unable to understand what it said.

Just a little past the seventh span mark. Two days in a row with hardly any sleep felt like too much for her brain to endure. Thank the Stones for having the day off. She was tempted to flop back into bed, but the soft snoring coming from the couch dissuaded her. There was too much to do, and none of it could wait.

Meredith went into the bathroom and quietly shut the door. After taking care of basic needs she started the shower, slipped out of her nightgown, clenched her teeth and shoved her head under the dreadfully cold stream. Only through sheer willpower did she hold in the multitude of ululating shrieks that fought to escape her lips.

She resisted the temptation to turn on the water heater and focused instead on wetting and lathering, wiping and scrubbing. The cold did its job, and soon she felt somewhat sapient, almost rational. Definitely clear-headed enough for the worry to make a comeback.

"What am I doing," she whispered through the frigid water running down her face. Her mind ran through the crazy events of the previous day, from the gun in her face to her sister's ultimatum, from a bound human awaiting discipline to the stupefying draw of Yurena's scent. And on top of all that, the spark't witch not-quite-snoring on her sofa.

"I should've just turned her in. Why didn't I turn her in?"

Meredith pressed the ball of her palms to her eyes, rubbing until it hurt. It was too late, now. She'd already lied to Mifraulde and pocketed the waiver, and a change of mind would be outright incriminating. There was no turning back in that respect.

Not that she actually . . . *wanted* to.

"You know why. You're sick of living like this. The human youth is your way out."

She wasn't stuck with the girl, in any case. Getting rid of her would always be an option. It'd be a terrible weight on her disease-ridden conscience, but still preferable to a single turn on a Judicar wheel.

She finished rinsing, turned off the shower and wrapped herself in her enormous towel. Still shivering, she brushed all the tangles out of her hair and pulled it into a wet ponytail, water mist sprinkling all over with every stroke.

The freckled witch in the mirror was a pitiful sight to behold. Her ears colored at the bite marks on her shoulder.

"You can do this," she told her reflection. "Just be smart about it."

Her reflection stared back blankly, bags under her eyes, cat-paw-print towel hugging her unremarkable frame. Among the rustic décor and earthy colors, she didn't precisely look like the sharpest knife in the block.

Meredith sighed, cracked the door open and peeked through. Janette's undignified pose and the volume of her breathing evidenced she was still asleep. Meredith gathered her dirty laundry and snuck back into the bedroom, water droplets tickling on their way down her calves.

The message blinking on the trans' froze her in place. Had it been there all night? Had it just happened? It couldn't be coincidence, this message—they were on to her, it was already over. Oh, she could already hear it, a voice in the most chilling tone imaginable: this is the Department of Mercy, we know what you've done, report to the Tower at once.

Her heart thumped in her temples as a shaky hand neared the Reproduce button.

"Tidings, denizen. The Department of Mercy informs you of the imminent pyre to be held at Brena's Blackened Square tomorrow, Seventh day of Wither. One Bellina Tarkai-Holtz-Drogo shall answer for her Most Dire Crimes of forgery, stunt-minding and terminal deviance."

Meredith exhaled her held breath. Shaking her head, she got started on her dressing routine as the rest of the announcement played out.

"Every denizen is encouraged to attend and engage in tradition-al jeering as befits these Most Dire Crimes. Ceremonies will begin

one span before dusk. Complimentary rots will be provided, though you are welcome to bring your own. It is all of our duties to conduct a successful and orderly burning. That is all.

"*Always beware deceit. Wick't Wardja.*"

Yugh. Even if she weren't engaged in a deranged plan to get ahead, Meredith would have found some likely excuse not to attend a public pyre. They never failed to make her terribly queasy.

A tenth-span later, she came out of the bedroom wearing an all-black ensemble: long sleeve shirt, leotards and slippers under the official Coven-sanctioned black cowl. She found Janette sitting on the sofa, face scrunched up as she rubbed her eyes raw.

It was time for Meredith to put to work all that she'd learned.

"Good morn, apprentice."

Janette smiled drowsily. "Good morning, Mistress Meredith. The sofa is very comfortable. Much better than the floor."

Meredith blinked in mild surprise. "Slept without problems, then?"

"Better than I have in years."

It wasn't what Meredith had read she should expect, but it would be silly to complain about not having a "*fussy youngster*" scared of every shadow.

"I didn't know what time I should be up," Janette continued. "Your clock only has twenty hours."

"Span."

"I'm sorry?"

"Twenty span to a day. Ten days to a week, and thirty to a moon cycle. Twelve cycles in a year plus a hundred and five span of night for Hallow's End."

"Oh, Hallow's End? Halloween?"

"Close enough, yes. Never mind that, there's much for us to do." She waved a hand in the bathroom's general direction. "Perform your morning routines, and we'll get started over breakfast. Use the smaller hairbrush and towel. They're yours now. There are hair implements in the left drawer, pick your favourite." A small pause. "Not the raven hair tie."

"Yes, Mistress Meredith."

Janette got up and shuffled into the bathroom. While the girl got ready, Meredith headed into the kitchen and brought fruit and sugar to the table. Running awful low on sugar. She left some milk to heat on the stove, went outside, walked around the house to the small attachment by the cellar doors and let Desmond loose. Soft squeals and happy grunts followed her around as she dumped a day's worth of oats into the thog's trough. Still good on feed.

Meredith left him to his eating and went back inside to cook breakfast. The girl walked in some time after, bright-smiled and fresh-faced. She wore black barrettes at her temples, very sober, very professional. The word *adorable* sprung to Meredith's thoughts;

ever vigilant, she wrapped the word in a bundle of cloth, set it on fire and tossed it down a dark pit.

The Mistress took a seat and gestured for her apprentice to do the same.

"I know you have many questions," she said while pouring scalding-hot porridge into Janette's bowl, "and you won't be able to concentrate until you have some answers."

"I would love to know more, Mistress Meredith. Thank you."

"Sugar?"

"Yes, please. Thank you. That's good, thank you."

"I will tell you the history of Galavan. It's important you know where we come from and why we do things a certain way. I need you to listen to this story and hold it to mind. After that, I'll lay out the rules of your apprenticeship. You must never, ever break these rules. There will be *dire consequences* if you don't follow them to the letter. Do you understand?"

"Yes, Mistress Meredith. I'll do my very best."

"Stir and eat at your leisure." She gestured at the pieces of fruit in front of her. "Have a hansel or two."

Janette reached out and grabbed the golden-green fruit. "Thank you," she said, inspecting the ovoid shape with curiosity, rubbing her thumb on its soft, fuzzy skin. It fit comfortably in her hand.

"Are these not common where you come from?" Meredith asked.

"I haven't seen one before."

"Bite in. You'll like it. They're my favourite."

Janette did as told after a tiny hint of hesitation.

"Guh!" Pinkish juices from the hansel ran down her chin before she could slurp them. She cupped a hand under her mouth. "Igh sho shweet!"

"They're in season now. I picked them only two days ago."

Janette swallowed and wiped at her lips. "You grow these?"

"Just a small patch." Meredith stretched over the table and placed a cloth napkin where the girl could reach it. "The soil here is very good, I can grow most everything. I'll teach you the basics of how to tend to my garden, I won't have as much time for it now that you're here."

Janette cringed. "I'm not great with plants."

"Well, that will change, won't it?"

"Oh, um, yes, Mistress Meredith. Of course." She took another, more timid bite.

Satisfied, Meredith fixed her own dish with not nearly as much sugar as she'd have liked. She spoke over the soft scrapes of spoon on bowl.

"I know from my extensive experience that in the next few days you will begin missing your parents and the comforts of your old home. It is a difficult time but—"

"I won't, Mistress."

"Oh, you may say that now, but—"

"Forgive me, Mistress Meredith. But I won't miss them, and I want nothing from that house. I'd burn this nighty if I had anything else to wear."

Meredith blinked a few times. The girl's expression was eerily intent. Even her wandering eye seemed full of conviction.

"You truly won't miss *anything*?"

She looked aside, seriously considered the question. Her brow twitched, but soon enough she was looking back up, shaking her head with lips pressed together. Her frown was bold and determined.

Meredith ended up shrugging. "Well, good, then. Soon you'll perform your first task as an apprentice and sew your robe. It sounds daunting, but don't worry, it's a very simple project. I will help you, of course."

Janette's excitement returned. "Will we weave enchantments into the fabric, Mistress?"

She couldn't help but chuckle. "No, it's only a robe for you to wear. Infusing objects will come later, as soon as you prove yourself capable. I haven't even prepared a soundstill yet."

"A soundstill?"

"We'll get to it. I've a story to tell—"

Desmond trotted in through the wall-flap next to the kitchen door. Janette startled. Her eyes widened in delight. "What is *that*?"

Meredith rolled her eyes. "Desmond, this is Janette, my apprentice. Say hello to Janette, you rude little mongrel."

The small thog bumped Janette's leg, grunting softly. Her grin was wide enough to take up half her face. "Can I pet him?"

"I don't see why not, but wash your hands afterwards. Who knows where he's been."

The hairy little barrel snorted with good enough timing to seem indignant. Janette patted him on the head and scratched behind his ears. "Never seen one of you before," she cooed gleefully, using both hands to properly pet him. "You're so ugly, yes you are, you're so, *so* ugly, look at you—oh, um. . . ." She looked up. "He can't understand me, right?"

"I'm convinced he only pretends like he doesn't."

She giggled and returned to her cosseting. "Well, I meant cute-ugly, not *ugly*-ugly, right, little guy? My goodness, you slobber a lot, yes you do. . . ."

"Don't get too attached, he'll be food one day."

Janette froze mid-pet. The girl's horrified expression made Meredith snicker. "I'm joking! He's my refuse disposal, I couldn't do without him." She nudged the thog away with her foot. "Off with you, now. Go sleep."

Desmond ignored her, nudging at the girl's hand for more attention. Meredith stomped her foot. "Off!"

The thog wabbled into the living room among grunts and little squeals. Meredith gestured toward the sink. "Just rinse. He's very clean."

She waited until Janette was done and back in her seat.

"As I was saying, I have a story to tell you. Are you ready?"

She nodded her usual eager nods while taking another bite of the hansel. Meredith let out a deep breath and prepared to tell the collection of carefully selected truths she'd gathered.

And a whole lot of lies as well.

THERE HAVE BEEN WITCHES and covens for most of human history, but we didn't become a global organisation until the advent of Caterina Galvan. She had a curious upbringing, but that's not important. She came into her powers, quickly rose through the ranks, defeated rivals, worked in the shadows, all very dramatic. What matters is that Caterina had a vision, and the special talent to make it happen. She sought kindred spirits all around Earth, witches of all creeds and ages, and over more than a hundred years she built a secret society linked through their power, with Galavan as their sanctuary. What was that?

Oh, yes, over a hundred years. Witches live longer than humans, it's a fact. The most powerful among us can surpass three hundred, it depends on . . . well, a number of things, let's leave it at that.

Me? Forty-seven. Um, a *hundred* and forty-seven, of course. Forty-seven years would hardly be long enough to rear even half the apprentices I've seen through, ah hah, hah.

Oh, believe me, I look my age. I'm about average, in fact. How long you wither depends on the brood, or, I mean, your genes. Like, say, the Tremmel hags? They'll keep showing age till their seventies, most of them. Brenan crones like myself stop between our thirties and sixties, it depends on other things. You're Earthborn, so . . . it could be anything for you. Anyway, it doesn't matter right now. Where was I?

Right. The Coven grew in influence, but that also meant becoming more visible. In truth, we became overconfident, arrogant and careless. Far too many witnesses told tales of our magic, secrets spread and, of course, fear followed. This is probably where most of our bad reputation comes from.

These days humans ridicule the witch hunt hysteria of the time, yes? Well, it's true a majority were innocent and harmless, but over time hundreds of real witches were found out and slaughtered. When the great witch hunt came knocking on Galavan's doors,

Caterina herself became under threat.

Yes, I should have mentioned that. This was during your sixteenth century. But you see, Caterina had prepared for it, as she always would. She'd rather have carved out her own eyes than see Galavan burn, it had been her mission for decades. The Tower was already centuries old by the time she made it her home, down at the foot of the Pyrenees. It went from remote laboratory to ever-growing academy, a sanctuary for all thaumaturges. Do you know what that word means?

Yes, that's correct. By the time tales of Galavan spread, it had already become a fortified city with sprawl all around. The nations sent their warriors. The church sent their knights. And so Caterina's inner circle, the furies, the founding witches of yore, they faced a choice they always knew would come: they could fight the populace in the open . . . or they could escape a world that didn't want them.

Some wanted to fight, but Caterina knew better. She'd been *counting* on eventually leaving, she was prepared. They weren't even a thousand witches, then. There would be no winning a war of attrition. Do you know that word, too?

Alright. How about you just ask whenever you don't understand? Good.

And so they left, taking *everything* with them. They named it "The Conveyance," the largest portal ever created. It wrapped Galavan in a dome, transporting the grounds to a place simple humans could never reach: a fold of space, a mirrored set of three dimensions we call "The Hollow." So once the transfer was—

Oh, don't worry about that, it would take days to explain the details. In very broad terms, it's like . . . a cellar, a cellar under a rug, and the conveyance took everything through the trap door, yes? Now we are thrice anchored to Earth as it hurtles through space, intangible to the Earthbound. Maybe someday human technology will be able to detect our little pocket of reality, but I doubt it'll happen.

So, the escape left a crater in place of a small nation, and a colossal landmass floating in the Hollow. Well, it doesn't quite *float,* but . . . it's not important. The times that followed were the most challenging of all. They built then what today we take for granted: reliable gravity all the way to the edge of the realm; a stable atmosphere with fine-tuned climate; rotations of stars, moon and sun on the skyveil; watercourses, wells and networks of pipes; the crops and the planning for today's industry and manufacture, and so much more. The Conveyance transported hectares of land, all the room we could possibly need to develop and grow.

Um, sure, I've a map in the shelves, somewhere. Let's move to the living room. How about you clean this up while I look for it?

Good.

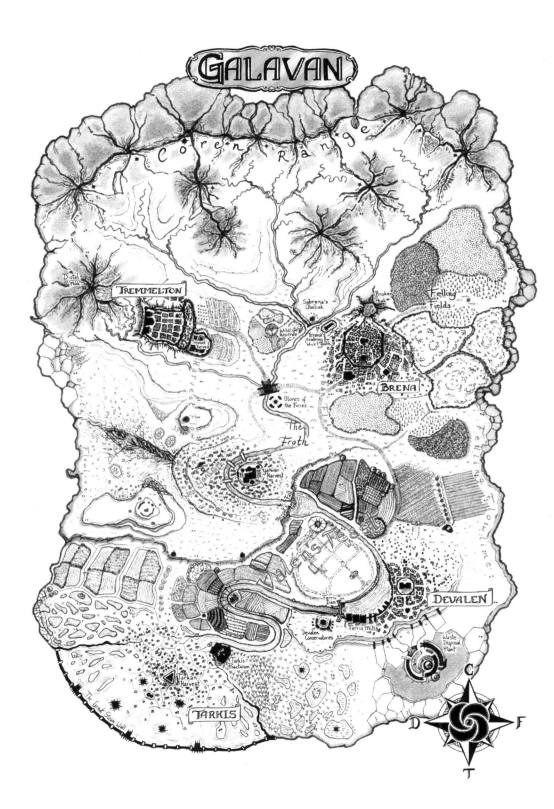

Hm, this is a bit old, but it'll do. We're right here at the edge of Brena, next to the pinewood. The big circle in the middle is Galvan Tower, the centre of our government. There's the Coren range at the top, and the Tarkis swamplands at the bottom. See all the crops along the Froth, and the nightwood farms, and the Ferris Craftworks next to Devalen? That's what I was talking about. Centuries of development.

Oh, we make a mite of everything, whatever makes sense to produce through magical means. These days there are countless mundane items that are far more cost-effective to procure from Earth. It's so much easier now, with all the automation and mass production on the human side. That's where my stove comes from. The Scouting and Supply Department takes care of it all.

Sure looks like a lot of work to build all this, yes? They must've been so busy, there's no way they had time to squabble and fight among themselves. Right?

No, no, it's rhetorical. They fought all the time. Remember what I said, all creeds and ages?

Our power bound us together, but that didn't mean we could live peacefully under the same roof, not without humanity as a common oppressor. Without them to worry about, it wasn't so easy to look past the differences. It became a serious problem as time passed: old friendships embittered, witches went separate ways and built their own communities and so on. Segregation became a matter of necessity in barely a few decades.

Just . . . different philosophies. It wasn't like now, with hundreds of years of communication and mingling. Back then, witches were plucked right out of Europe, and Asia, and Africa and the Americas, so the founding crones spent all their time herding cats decades after the exodus. There wasn't even an official common tongue, not until the Stonehenge accords.

In-between all the progress there was the War of Succession, Sabrena's Rift and the Purge of Old Yanwar, the American Crisis, the Golem Revolt, and, well, a lot of conflict. We could carry on all day. If you're interested you can study it in your own time, *after* the apprenticeship is over. There's only one thing that's important to us right here: our Civil War, over two hundred years ago. It's *very* important that you understand this part of our history.

You see, over time, for many reasons, two big philosophies came about. On one side, you have the Humanists. They understood humans were central to our long-term survival and should be treated accordingly. New apprentices, goods and commodities, manual labour, and . . . procreation, of course, it was all a symbiotic relationship, and mutual respect was necessary. We should still mingle with them, and bring the worthy into Galavan. Many of these witches had husbands, friends and families. It seems reasonable, doesn't it?

Right. On the other side, you have the Tyrants. These witches were bitter and rotten, corrupted by power. To them, humans were livestock to be processed and discarded as they saw fit: as slaves, as fodder for experiments, even as food. Child-devouring witches, just like in your stories. They saw mercy as a blight to be purged, and anyone who would show compassion was unworthy of the Coven. Witches were the favoured daughters of the Universe, nothing but complete domination over the lesser beings would do. They even plotted an eventual return as conquerors of Earth, as silly as that sounds.

As time went on, everyone became more polarized, horrified with the other group. Tremmelton and Brena mostly for one side, Devalen and Tarkis mostly for the other, and New Yanwar right there, split down the middle. It housed the Council at the time, you see, it was the capital for a short while. It didn't survive the war. In fact, that big circle by the bridges, Yanwar Harvest? It's a monument. A memorial monument, so we don't ever forget.

Tensions brewed for decades. The situation in New Yanwar became untenable, and the escalation led to the horrendous crime that sparked the war. This crime is the main reason I'm telling you all this, because I need you to understand why our rules exist.

The Head of the Coven at the time—by the way, her given name was Yanetta, believe it or not. In fact, this entire incident is known as "Yanetta's Folly." It's true! It'll help you remember.

Yanetta was a very powerful witch, but power isn't everything, and her position was precarious. Even though she was a Humanist at heart, she constantly worked to balance the needs and demands of both groups, but it became impossible as tensions grew. Yanetta would favour the Humanists often, which progressively put her at odds with the Puritans. The– the Tyrants, I mean. There were fights in the Council, open hatred. It was a very difficult time to lead the Coven, as you might imagine.

Now, Yanetta, she had many Earthborn apprentices, her very own academy on Council grounds. She was elderly even by our standards, and in all her time she'd become nurturing of those under her care. Motherly. She was attached, *too* attached.

The Tyrants saw this as a dire weakness to exploit. They wanted to destroy her, and expose Humanist values for the sickness they were. In their hatred, they underestimated the consequences of their actions. What do you think they did?

Oh. That's, uh . . . that's close! But it was far, far worse, they didn't *just* kill them, they . . . they arranged to kidnap her apprentices, every last one, because they were such easy targets—and they did *gruesome* things to them, terrible things to force Yanetta to do their bidding. She would've been broken with simple murders, but that wasn't good enough for the Tyrant leadership, oh no. Yanetta was irrational and desperate, she complied with everything they wanted.

She became a puppet, manipulated through her weakness. The Tyrants got away with anything they wanted, for a while.

Others became suspicious, and the entire plot came tumbling down, but not before Yanetta and her apprentices had suffered through *unspeakable* things. The Greycoats were outraged, the Judicars got involved, and it all ended in more violence that spiralled out of control. Oh, yes, each group had their own branch of law enforcement. The Greycoats were Humanists, the Judicars belonged with the Purita-a-ah I mean, the Tyrants. That was another cyst ready to burst open, because New Yanwar was policed by either one depending on which side of the Froth you landed. It was a right mess from tip to boot.

So here's why I want you to know these things: after all the dust settled, lessons were learned, and those lessons became tradition that's observed to this day, even if it's not necessary anymore. Ever since Yanetta's Folly, apprentices must always be kept in secret. No-one but their Mistress may see them, sense them or even know about them. You will be sheltered at all times until your apprentice-ship is complete. Do you understand?

Another lesson: Yanetta's attachment to her apprentices cost her everything. We cannot allow such a thing to ever happen again. I mean, obviously, no-one is out there targeting apprentices these days, but our relationship will remain strictly professional, it's simply the way it must be. I'm friends with many of my former pupils, but that comes after, alright? You're here to learn magic and artificing, we won't be wasting any time with silly—

Good, yes. As long as you understand. You will always do as I say, no questions, no arguments. No complaining. No throwing fits. I will be *very upset* if you misbehave. Very upset. Nod your head and say, "I understand, Mistress Meredith."

Yes, perfect.

So. The Civil War broke out, and it was terrible. Thousands of witches died, and many more humans besides. So much destruction, such wasteful use of magic, it wasn't our proudest moment. Two years of hatred and carnage in our streets.

Mm-hmm, two years indeed. When it's neighbour against neighbour, you can't lob a fireball the size of a building at the enemy, and nobody wanted to destroy Galavan itself . . . though the ruins of New Yanwar tell a different tale. It was all-out warfare, there.

It took a very long time to recover from all that. You could say—

Oh, yes, of course! Can you imagine, if the Tyrants had won? You and I would not be talking right now. I can picture it so well, a society full of barren witches and dreary serfs, where your worth is measured in merit alone and any form of kindness to humans is suspect. It could never work long-term, I don't think. It's easy to imagine oppression getting so bad, they'd have to deal with a rebellion at some point. I'd never want to live in such a place.

Fortunately, we live in *this* reality. Not much of note has happened since then, we've simply been recovering from that terrible time. We lost almost half our numbers, damage was substantial pretty much everywhere, and our magical trinkets—

You're full of questions, aren't you?

No, it's alright. You're contributing to the number, after all. Right now we're eight thousand, five hundred and some. Far below the stable population cap, we have no shortages of anything whatsoever.

Except, well . . . so many of our invaluable trinkets and devices were destroyed or used up during the war. You see, raw incantations are complicated, and most spells require a fair deal of preparation. We understood centuries ago that artefact technology was the way to the future. They are the tools that allow Galavan to thrive, so you might say crafting these tools is about as important a job as there could be.

And that's *my* job. I am an artificer. The great majority of your apprenticeship will entail the construction and infusion of magical items. It's difficult and time-consuming work, but highly respected. And well compensated, of course. I live frugally entirely by choice, I assure you.

So there you have it, our history so far, or the abridged version of it. You can feel free to look up the details after your apprenticeship is done, but I don't want you to waste time with it now. I forbid it. If there's anything you truly must know, I can answer much more quickly than a dusty old tome, so don't hesitate to ask.

Any more questions?

JANETTE WAS LOOKING UP from her cross-legged position as though tripping on a double dose of ludebark. Her hand, which up until that point had been absently playing with Desmond's ear floof, was clenched against her chest in a heartened gesture.

"I am *so* happy you chose me. . . ."

"So you keep saying."

Meredith sat on one edge of the couch. Janette had plopped down on the rug by the dead fireplace. Desmond lay on his side, back pressed against the girl's leg. He'd zonked out fairly quickly.

"Why did the witches escape Earth at all, Mistress Meredith? They could've fought! They could've ruled the world!"

Meredith raised her eyebrows and thought of a suitably rose-tinted answer.

"Because, um . . . there are a number of reasons. The founding witches never aimed to rule over humanity, for one. It's complicated and impractical. And Caterina was a scholar, she only cared about knowledge, so ruling would've gotten in the way. And our numbers are too small, and public distrust and superstition were simply insurmountable. It would've been such a headache."

"But they had magic! Couldn't they just cast a spell and force people to obey?"

"Oh, no, magic doesn't work that way. Incantation is all about altering the physical world. No such thing as mass mind control."

"Aw. Really? But . . . but you *can* throw fireballs, or make it rain lightning, right? You mentioned fireballs earlier." She might as well have been wringing her hands together, she was so anxious about it.

"Lightning and fireballs are a definite option, yes."

"So that's it, then. Make people obey, or they go up in flames. If armies come, they won't attack for long if half of them get swallowed by the ground under their feet, or choke on clouds of poison, or—or! The battlefield becomes so hot, their brains got baked inside their skulls. Why didn't they do those things?"

Meredith looked on, a small frown on her brow. "You are more imaginative than my previous apprentices."

Janette fidgeted. "Well, it's just . . . it makes me so mad I grew up without magic because some angry blockheads drove the witches away a long time ago. It isn't fair."

"Yes, well. No sense wondering what could have been. Pay attention, now." She straightened her back and looked at her pupil over her nose the way she'd seen Mifraulde do a thousand times. "It's time I establish the rules of your apprenticeship. Tell me, what have you already learned from our history?"

Janette's pouty expression was immediately replaced by serious thoughtfulness.

"Mmm . . . no-one can know about me until my apprenticeship is done."

"Yes, that's *very* important. It's not only you that would get in trouble, I'd be severely punished for not teaching you properly. You don't want *me* to be punished, do you?"

Janette quickly shook her head as if her Mistress had just offered a switching across the knuckles.

"Good. Because if you wander off from the house, anyone that sees you will immediately know what's happening, and then we'll both have to answer to the Judicars. They're not known for their lenience, especially since the war. You'll be deemed unworthy, banished back to Earth or *worse*, and I won't be able to teach again for a very long time. I want this to be very clear to you. Don't give me a reason to put you on a leash, I absolutely will."

The girl appeared properly fearful, though soon confusion took over. "I thought the Judicars were with the Tyrants? I might have misheard."

Meredith blinked. "Oh, yes, of course, you're right. All this history got me turned around. The *Greycloaks* will make both our lives miserable if you break this rule. That's what I meant."

Janette nodded in solemn understanding. "I will never, ever leave without your say so, Mistress Meredith."

"Right. That pleases me. Now, if I ever get visitors, you must hide at all times. My, ah, my spare room used to be insulated properly, but it needs some work at the moment, so . . . for now, if there's a visitor, you will hide in Desmond's pen."

The girl tried not to look aghast, she truly tried. Meredith raised a placating hand. "Desmond is very clean. He might take exception at *you* getting your scent all over his home."

Janette's lips quirked in a slight purse as she looked down. "Yes, Mistress."

"It's only temporary, and I don't get many visitors, but that's irrelevant, isn't it? You'll do as you're told, no complaining, no pouting. Or are you having second thoughts?"

With some alarm Janette sat upright and erased any hint of displeasure from her features. "Not at all, Mistress. You don't need to worry."

"Good. I've been taking care of your needs so far, since this is all so new for you, but that will change soon. I'll expect you to fix our meals and do the chores while I'm not here. Teaching you will be time-consuming, so you'll be making up for it. It's only fair."

"Yes, Mistress Meredith."

"You will keep this house clean and Desmond fed. All your assignments will be kept up to date. I'll teach you to tend the garden, sew and mend, and cook if you don't know how. I'll also show you several traditions that must be respected at all times. They may appear senseless to you, but there are solid reasons behind them and you must respect it all."

"Yes, Mistress Meredith. May I ask a question?"

"Go ahead."

"Well, I expected . . . and I'm only curious, I swear, I'll do everything as you say—but I expected enchanted brooms sweeping the floors, and dishes that wash themselves, or maybe a golem that does all the chores for you. Don't you have those things? I mean, they exist, don't they?"

Meredith scrambled to find an answer that wouldn't include the words *ludicrously expensive.*

"There *are* some primitive automatons I could use," she began, "but witches have a bit of a history with golems. I glossed over this earlier, but it wasn't that long ago that we had a golem revolt in our hands."

"Ooh, really? What happened?"

"Well, you see, after the Civil War there was a big push for technological advancement, and no other field progressed faster than golemancy. It wasn't enough to have tireless labour that only needed a charge now and then for sustenance. No, the witches kept pushing at the boundaries of– of wordpath trees and miniaturization, making the golems smarter and smarter, able to understand and execute complex commands and even engage in conversation. They'd give them names, and personalities, and make them capable of basically anything a regular human—"

"Oh god, and they became too smart and rebelled against you!" Janette's good eye had widened steadily until she could no longer hold back the interruption.

"Y– yes, sort of. It was more complicated than that, Malkin and Vanuuren had this rivalry going and . . . well, anyway. There were a lot of golems. It was messy."

"So there was another war?"

"Not so much *war,* just chaos and more deaths and lots of destruction. Ever since, we keep very strict limits on the kind of automatons we use. It's only recently that they've become more widespread, but still with severe restrictions, and none connected to the nodework. We learn from our mistakes, we don't want to repeat history. Just like with the Civil War and all the rules you must follow, see?"

Janette nodded. "I understand, Mistress. No animated brooms."

Though the girl's expression didn't show it, Meredith could easily sense the disappointment. She cracked a smile. "Of course, if you were to learn enough to create your very own assistant in your spare time, I could hardly find a reason to argue against its use. Golemancy overlaps quite a bit with artificing."

Her face lit up. "I could learn to do that?"

"Well, it depends on how hard you work, doesn't it?"

"I'll do my best, Mistress."

"I don't expect—"

Someone knocked at the front door.

Only a twitch of her brow betrayed Meredith's panic. Janette looked at the door for less than a moment before she bolted out of the room and disappeared into the kitchen. The shuffle of borrowed slippers and the familiar *kah-clack* of the back door's latch shortly followed.

At least the girl was a fast learner.

She weighed her options. The windows were closed, the drapes drawn, the door bolted shut. Their voices had been quiet, surely not loud enough for the visitor to hear. Whoever stood outside would go away soon enough.

But who would come calling in the morning? No-one but Val and Taskmaster Gertrude should know she wasn't at work. She always fulfilled what few orders she had in the evening, and for the most part she'd deliver the goods herself instead of having people come to her home.

Meredith tip-toed toward the kitchen. They could leave a message in the drop-box, whoever it was.

They knocked again, bangs hard enough to rattle the vase on the fireplace shelf.

Yes, they'd go away soon. But what if they'd actually heard the conversation, and insisted on banging on the door, and without an answer they'd go around the house and peek over the fence, and what if then maybe they fly over the fence and go snooping—

Meredith clenched her teeth and silenced her neurotic thoughts by calling out in sing-song: "I'm coming!"

The knocking stopped abruptly, as if the visitor was embarrassed to have made so much noise. Meredith undid everything but the chain and cracked the door open.

"Hi, Meredith."

Yurena stood in a sleeveless white dress, long and fluttery in the light breeze. Her glasses were gone, possibly stowed in the small clutch purse she held in one hand. With her near-white irises, pale complexion, sharp teeth and wispy dark hair she was a spirit of the night caught in broad daylight.

"Yurena?" A flush of heat rushed to Meredith's face as she unlatched the chain and swung the door wide enough to step under the doorjamb.

"I'm sorry for knocking like that, I thought maybe you were in the garden and couldn't hear."

"I . . . yeah."

They looked at one another, then Meredith's eyes dropped to the Valeni sigil pendant resting on Yurena's breastbone, a tear-shaped opal surrounded by star-like studs. Yurena swayed subtly from one foot to the other. "I tried to find you at the manufactory and maybe save you a trip with the herb bundle—if, if you'd happened to take it with you, that is—but they said you were home today. So I figured I'd come here and save you that trip anyway."

"Oh, yes, the bundle, of course, it's right here."

Meredith side-stepped to the little table by the door and grabbed a cloth-and-string packet marked with a large *Y*. "You shouldn't have. Going to the library is never any trouble."

"Thank you so much. These are great." Yurena opened her purse. Shallow metallic clinks ensued as she rummaged.

Meredith pressed her lips together. She coaxed a smile. "You . . . you don't have to pay me anymore."

"What? Oh, no no no, that's nonsense, I wouldn't take advantage of . . . you know." Yurena's lanky fingers separated a handful of coins. "9P and 12? Unless it's changed since the last time."

"No, still the same." The money exchanged hands. Meredith dropped it in a pocket without counting it. "Thank you."

"You should charge more. You have the best I've ever tried, infusion or not. I mean it."

"That's . . . very kind of you to say."

"It's the truth."

Their eyes met. Meredith looked at the skyveil, at the neighbor's cottage down the road, at the brick trail to the outer fence. Yurena glanced at the doorknob, the side of the house, the thorned shrubs. They stood through the silence with stoic aplomb.

"I've always admired your frontage," Yurena said. "Very eerie, it strikes just the right note. Those withered vines go so well with the wood rot. Is that authentic?"

Meredith looked at the carefully arranged plant husks and rot mockups. It had been terribly time-consuming to give it that "barely held together" air of neglect.

"No, it's painted. Actual rot makes me . . . uncomfortable."

"Oh. That's fine."

A bout of wind rustled through the evergreens. A frantic split-feather called for its mate, a raven clucked back in open mockery. Yurena inhaled as if to say something, reconsidered, gave Meredith a sheepish look.

"I liked your note."

"Note? Oh! Um. Yes. It was all true. I just forgot I'd be delivering to you today, though I guess not anymore, hah hah, ah."

"You could stop by anyway, though. I mean, you should feel free. You don't have to. I'm not asking. . . ." Yurena trailed off into a cringe. Finally she gave a stormy sigh. "I'm so pathetic."

"What? No, why would you say that?"

"You're right, I should have waited, you'd be showing up in the evening anyway. This just reeks of desperation."

"What does?"

She gestured at herself. "This! Making an excuse to go find you. Dressing up. Harassing you at your home."

"Oh."

"See? I'm making you uncomfortable again."

"No, no, it's . . . it's very flattering."

"Please, Meredith. You're only humouring me, I can tell."

"I'm being honest. You look gorgeous. As intimidating as Valen herself."

Yurena colored at the compliment. She pinched at the skirt of her dress. "I don't even know what I'm doing here. I said I wouldn't pressure you."

"I don't mind, I'm happy you're here," Meredith said, and with some surprise she realized that it was the truth. "You're not pressing. Pressuring. Whichever."

Yurena took a step closer. "I don't mean to, I simply can't stop thinking—I . . . I just wanted to see you again. I never got the chance to say how much I enjoyed last night. I've never been with someone so . . . gentle." Her hand found Meredith's. A soft thumb lightly traveled the mounds and valleys of garden-worn knuckles. "I can't imagine how you left without my noticing, I wake easily."

Meredith's lips toyed with a smile. "I don't know, you seemed fairly spent."

Yurena laughed. Her pointed teeth brought her grin from impish to wicked. "I was, yeah. But I'd hoped to make you breakfast."

"I'm sorry, I just had so much to get done. I still do."

"No, no need to apologise, I know you're busy. You explained. That's why I'm not parsing earnest how you're not inviting me in."

Meredith blushed even more. "I'm sorry, I really am. I– I've been working hard on becoming a real artificer. I've made a lot of progress, I think I can find a way to get around my infusion problems, but it needs dedicated work. I'd like to spend time with you, but . . . I truly must get back to it."

"I understand, Meredith. Honestly. This isn't supposed to be a relationship, anyway. Remember?"

What if I wanted it to be?

Meredith held back the words before they escaped her mouth. Their mere existence was problematic enough to leave her in stunned silence. It was too fast, too sudden, too reckless.

"It was great seeing you," Yurena continued. "Thank you for the goods, I'll be back for more. Good fortune with your work." She leaned in and placed a light kiss on Meredith's stupefied lips. "I still owe you breakfast," she murmured with a wink.

Yurena followed the path to the fence and closed the swaying door behind her, then climbed onto the dais she'd left on the cobbled road. She pulled the controller out of her purse, waved goodbye with her fingers and took off toward inner Brena at a leisurely drift. Meredith raised a belated hand in response.

She went inside, absentmindedly locked the door, stepped around a snoring Desmond on her way to the kitchen. With pensive gait she walked all the way around the courtyard wall to the thog's den, opened and closed the door, leaned against it. The musky scent of hay barely registered.

"Mistress Meredith? Is everything alright?"

Janette sat on a small seat made of piled bricks, with armrests and everything. Her corner of the den had been cleared of clutter and then populated with more bricks and neat mounds of hay. She seemed to have been in the process of building some kind of brick-and-hay fort.

Meredith noted the scene in a bit of daze. The words overtaking her thoughts came out in a loud mumble, as if she was unable to believe what she was saying.

"I think I might've fallen in love."

A thrilled gasp filled the tiny room. Janette was sitting forward, hands balled into fists. "You *did?* That's *so cool!* Was that him knocking? Have you known each other long? I didn't even think witches would—but, of course, why wouldn't you? It's why the Tyrants lost, right? So we could fall in love. What's his name? Is he nice?"

"She's, uh . . . Yurena is. . . ."

The Mistress blinked for some time. All at once she realized the twenty different reasons why this was a terrible topic of conversation. In the meantime Janette's fingers rose to parted lips, her one attentive eye wide enough to make up for the slacker. "Oh! Oh, I'm sorry, she's . . . another witch, then? Or, um, are normal women allowed into Galavan? Bosh, I probably should know this by now, I feel so stupid. . . ."

"Y– yes, she's a witch." Meredith rubbed at her brow. "But never you mind about any of that. I was distraught. You and I cannot discuss such personal things. You remember the lesson, yes? Yanetta's Folly."

The girl deflated on the spot, yet did her best to keep her expression neutral. "Yes. Of course, Mistress Meredith. I apologise."

"Don't. It was my mistake." She made a big show out of her deep sigh. "You see, this is also an adjustment for me. I haven't reared an apprentice for a very long time. You could even say it feels new all over again." She opened the door and affably gestured for the girl to go first. "So we'll be adjusting together, I suppose."

Janette's smile returned, though far more bashful. "Okay," she said while getting up from her brick throne. The oversized slippers shuffled with her every step as they followed the tile path along the wall. "Back inside the house?"

"Indeed. It's time we honoured tradition and made you proper clothes. You're about to learn all about sewing."

"That's . . . nice." She stopped, fidgeted a bit. "Are we, um . . . are we also making undies? Is that tradition, too?"

Meredith stopped as well. She looked down at Janette, at the fluttery white nightgown she still wore, at the faint shade of silky blue around the hips. There were plenty of undergarments in her drawers, though certainly none that would fit. Perhaps with a few adjustments. . . .

"No. That's silly." She gently prodded to keep walking. "I'll go out and get you plenty of underwear while you practice."

"Oh. That's nice. Thank you."

She could've made it work, yes. Yet for some reason, it struck her as deeply unsavory to give the poor girl some hand-me-down, ill-fitting undergarments to wear.

She'd just go shopping again. There would be *a lot* of shopping the next day, and no-one would care about the size of her skivvies.

CHAPTER EIGHT
✸
INVESTMENTS

RAPPED IN HER THICK RED robe, Meredith pried boards loose from the wall next to Desmond's pen. She removed them in predetermined order, one by one, neatly piling them up on the path. Even while sluggish, her movements carried the casual precision of extensive practice.

She could barely see what she was doing, both because it was still dark and because her eyes wouldn't open past a squint. Thoughts of burying her face in the pillow and sleeping until she ached became harder to ignore as she progressed.

Meredith stuck her whole arm into the opening, hand reaching down as it searched for the familiar leathery feel. Her fingers closed around the worn material and hauled it out of hiding.

The bottom of the bag flattened on the tiles with a jingling thud. She undid the knot tied around it, tossed the flap open, and spent a short while staring at all the money she had in the world.

Frau would laugh at her "fortune," Meredith knew. Her brood-sister belonged to the Coven high market and didn't care about the bottomfeeder economy. She could spend in one evening what had taken Meredith over a decade to save.

"Well, I'll be doing just that today," she slurred.

She set the bag aside and took the time to replace the boards as they had been. The sacks full of sawdust followed, directly in front of the stash. She almost lost her footing in her drowsy state, and decided to sit on the sacks until her head cleared a bit.

"I hope this works out," she told the fat purse on the ground. "You were just a year away from becoming a space-fold of my own."

The purse didn't respond. Meredith rubbed at her eyes, pressed them shut, forced them open. The stash should be enough to buy what she needed, but no-one would sell her such sensitive equipment without a proper license. She did not qualify for a proper license.

She couldn't let such trifling details stand in the way of advancement. She bent down and hauled the bag up to her chest, cradling it under her armpit.

"Don't worry about a thing," she reassured the purse. "Everything will work out and I'll fill you up again. Soon you'll be too stuffed to carry."

She headed back inside, shambled past the girl splayed on the couch and collapsed onto the bed, bag still in hand.

PORTABLE STASIS TRAPS required larger parts and much less concentration than odor neutralizers. Meredith was thankful for it, because concentrating was a bit of a challenge today—both for lack of sleep and because she'd left an Earthborn witch alone and unsupervised inside her home. Somehow, she doubted the girl could sit through an entire day of sewing without going stir-crazy.

To fray her nerves further, it was a slow day for Val, who painstakingly brushed the glossy finish on her nearly-complete Wand of Pestilence. Words kept pouring off her lips like so much sewage off the Earth-ward pipe.

"The Duels last night were an absolute wash. I lost nearly eight peep notes thanks to that cross-eyed gorgon sweeping the whole roster—good thing I didn't get greedy, with the odds they were hawking. Everyone knows she won't last, she's got the raw attunement but lacks discipline. Not that a loss means much, now. Back in my dueling days, the drain from a loss could put you out for a few cycles. That's what made it thrilling. Now they have all these regulations and penalties, you never see anyone drop dead. I might stop going altogether."

"Mm."

"At least tonight's pyre should be good. Did you see her in the 'trans? She'll be a big screamer, I can tell. I'll be seeing you there, yes?"

"Oh, um. I would go, but . . . I have a previous arrangement I can't postpone."

"Ah!" Val's tone become conspiratorial. "Might you mean a *date*?"

"A date? No, whatever gives you that idea?"

"Well, someone visited us yesterday. She appeared *terribly* disappointed not to find you here."

Meredith kept her attention firmly fastened on adjusting the trinket's underside. "Oh, yes, right. She did mention she stopped by. I had an order ready for her."

Val snorted a quickly restrained laugh. "Those 'natural herbs' and salves of yours?"

Heat rose to Meredith's face. "She just so happens to think they're the best in town, Devalka."

"Alright, no need to take that tone." Val rang the buzzer by her workstation. She was frowning at the bristles of her brush, thumbing them critically. "So it's all strictly business, then?"

Yes, Meredith almost said, but she pressed her lips together. "I won't add fuel to your gossip machine. Not that it ever needs it."

Val barked out a laugh. "Truer words were never spoken. You needn't tell me anything, I can smell the attraction from two mountains removed. And the way she was dressed! She's an odd one, just like you—and I mean that in a favourable way. I'd ask you to keep me updated, but I near glean you'd sooner pull out your own teeth."

A stunt stood at the entryway. He was short, dark-skinned and dark-browed. Though slight of frame, the muscles in his arms stood out like ropes tight around steel rods.

He bowed deep at both witches and awaited instructions, at all times careful to keep his eyes low.

"This brush is worn out," Devalka declared, and threw the brush at the human. He didn't flinch when it papped against his dirty pectoral. Wood clattered on tile floor.

"None of these please me. Bring me a set so I can choose another."

The stunt bowed again—picking up the brush while he was at it— and left the room. The clink of chains faded into the halls.

Meredith forced herself not to show any interest. Her worry crept below the surface, an intruder as persistent as it was unwelcome. Whatever might have happened to Four-Thirteen? Had the discipline been so harsh that he needed two days to recover?

Val spoke soon after the chains could no longer be heard. "Remember our friend from Thirday?"

"Hmm? What friend?"

"The stunt that usually sets up our parts. The one that botched your retrieval."

"Oh, hah. 'Friend,' with quotes. I'd forgotten about that already. What about it?"

"Listen to this: they found salves and pain medicine in his holding cell."

Meredith went still, but quickly resumed bolting the pressure plate to the appropriate contacts. "Truly? How could he possibly come by those?"

"They're still trying to draw a line to that one. He won't speak a word about it, apparently."

The image of what the Judicars might be doing to make him confess flashed through Meredith's mind in vivid detail. She did her damnedest to keep her voice casual. "That is so bizarre. You think they have some kind of supply network?"

"I don't see how that could be possible. He must've had help from a witch, no doubt in my mind."

"Huh. Could anyone be so foolish?"

Devalka snorted. "You ask as if the rebellions didn't happen."

"I ask *because* they happened. And besides, wouldn't she get denounced in the first round of questioning? I don't see how one of these savages could have any loyalty for one of us these days."

"Don't be so certain. They're like starved mongrels. Throw them the smallest bone and they'll be yours forever, no matter how much you beat them."

Meredith drummed her fingers on the trinket case as if she was deeply intrigued by this mystery. "But who, though? No-one goes into the holding pens. It's restricted and patrolled."

"That's right. Which is why my wager is on a sympathising juditor."

In a small panic Meredith glanced all around to see if anyone might've overheard. She gripped her desk with both hands and hunched low, as if it would help conceal the words. "There is no such thing, you shouldn't say that aloud."

"Why? They try to pretend it's impossible now, but it isn't, it's never been. Wane through Yearning they're still witches like you and I, and if *we* are scrutinised for disease and affliction, then so should they. Nobody is going to forget that Faedre the Minder was one of *them,* no matter how much they pretend."

Meredith squirmed in place, still darting glances around. The last thing she needed at this time was Judicar scrutiny. "Can we please stop talking about the human rebellions now?"

"Soot and ash, it's idle conversation, what are you so afraid of? No-one is listening, nor would they care if. . . ."

Val trailed off and switched focus as chains shuffled closer. The stunt was back, small bundle in hand. After another bow, he approached Devalka's workstation and rolled the bundle open on the one clutter-free corner of the table. The worn leather skin revealed a diverse collection of brushes arranged by size, each one neatly sleeved in its own individual pouch.

Devalka grabbed the skin, upended it and shook it until every brush was clattering on the desk. She pawed through the pile until she found one to her linking.

"Ah, yes, good. This will do. Now clean this mess and get out of my sight."

As the human wordlessly gathered everything, Meredith didn't grit her teeth. She didn't roll her eyes, or raise an eyebrow, or sigh with disapproval. She was very conscious to simply tighten bolts, one after another after another.

Val resumed her work and hummed with satisfaction as she broke in the new brush. Words inevitably spilled forth shortly after.

"I often forget how young you are," she said. "You weren't even hatched during the rebellions, were you? You've no grudge. You didn't watch Faedre's disciples burn everything."

Meredith glanced over, very briefly. "I was taught well enough, Val. They spare no details at the academy."

"And yet look at you, worried about a Judicar overhearing, instead of watching for a possible traitor among them. You fear punishment more than corruption. That's the problem with the newer broods, too much doctrine and not enough zeal, and so the cycle continues. *'Mercy is the weeds of progress.'*"

Meredith kept quiet. Relief and guilt and worry tumbled on a loop in her thoughts, steadily driving her insane. Thank the furies, she wasn't a suspect. Did Four-Thirteen know it was her behind the mask? Could they draw a line to her regardless, if he talked? How long could Four-Thirteen hold out? How much would he suffer because of the stupid thing she'd done?

The evidence alone might do it. There were precious few artificers at the manufactory that grew all-natural gramrout. Exactly *one,* if she had to guess. Had Four-Thirteen simply left it all in plain sight, untouched? Had they only discovered the remnants? How long until they barged in with chains in their hands?

She tightened the last bolt until the contact cracked.

"Ogh, shrub-gobbling horsepork. . . ."

Val turned her head to look at Meredith's station. "What happened?"

"I ruined it."

"Did you?"

"I tightened the plate too much and it cracked, it's ruined."

"It's not so bad as that, I'm sure."

"That's because you're not looking at it."

"Fine, let me see."

Devalka abandoned her stool and waddled to her coworker's side. She leaned over the desk, unfastened the brace and lifted the trinket casing to eye level, turning it in her hands.

For a convenient stretch of time, her robe's side-pocket was wide and spacious and perfectly open to wandering fingers.

"It might still be serviceable," she declared after a while. "It will have a shortened range, I believe."

"Gertrude won't care, it's still a defective casing and it'll come off my pay." Meredith sighed. "At least these are cheap."

"Well, as far as I'm concerned, Gertrude doesn't need to know."

"What? No, I couldn't do that. You start hiding things and it always comes back to nip your tail. I'd rather just tell her."

Val chuckled and set the casing down. "You're sickeningly honest, Merth. You won't ever get anywhere with that kind of attitude."

"I'm right where I want to be, thank you." Eyebrows raised indignantly, Meredith gathered the unfinished trinket and made for the door. She stopped at the frame.

"Say, Val. . . ."

"Yes?"

"This pain medicine they found, might it be uninfused gramrout?"

"I didn't get so many details. Gertrude should know. Why?"

"Some days I come home to a mess in my garden, plants trampled and herbs missing. I thought it was some animal breaking in, but now I'm worried . . . maybe it's a thief. Uninfused gramrout is untraceable, perfect for a sympathiser. It all makes sense."

"A thief? It sounds more like there's a gap in your fence."

"There's no gap, I've looked. Some *thief* has been using *my* gramrout to help these savages, and she wants me to take the blame for it. What if they suspect me now? What if they accuse me of going back there and giving out—"

Meredith's speech was interrupted by Devalka's laughter. It went on for entirely too long.

"*You?*" Val finally asked. "*You* sneaking into the holding pens? Past the juditors? Past the *cats?*" She let out an especially loud guffaw, perhaps imagining the ridiculous image her words painted.

Meredith waited for the worst of it to subside, lips drawn in a line. "Well, *they* might not find it so funny! Or they'll think I'm the supplier, or a mole, or *something*. I can just see it already, the questions, the suspicion, the surveillance, and I did nothing wrong! What's more, what if that dirty stunt points his finger at us out of spite? He got disciplined because of us, after all. Oh, I can just see—"

"Alright, calm down!" Devalka had her hands out in a placating gesture. "Never saw you this worked up, it's so droll. Nothing will happen to you. They already took my statement yesterday, and between that and your reputation, you're as safe as can be. You can let Gertrude know about your garden thief, if it makes you feel better, but you said it yourself: uninfused goods are untraceable, so of course they'd use that. And a false confession? Who in their right mind would believe an unwashed serf over the Head of the Coven's own sister?"

Meredith looked on. Her arms were crossed over the unfinished trinket, plates flat against her chest.

"You vouched for me?"

"Of course I did. Is it so hard to believe?"

"Only two days ago you near gleaned I might be a deviant."

"And I apologised for it, didn't I? You're as harmless as a baked turnip, Merth. Everyone knows that."

A smidgen of pride surged in Meredith's chest, intent on listing all the deranged antics she'd been up to in the last fifty span, intent on grabbing the extraneous lump in her pocket and throwing it at Devalka's face.

The impulse was swiftly stomped flat. She gave Val a downtrodden smile.

"I suppose I should be glad I'm the town's bottomjosh. Thank you for speaking on my behalf. Though I'm still going to report both the theft and this disaster."

Val shrugged. "I'd hardly call that tiny crack a disaster, but it's your decision, I suppose. I'll be right here. Best fortune."

Meredith nodded and stepped out of the room. Holding in her sigh of relief, she turned into the appropriate hallway and began the stair climb that would take her to Gertrude's office.

G ERTRUDE WASN'T AT HER office. Meredith found her on a catwalk above the machine floor, yelling commands at the workers below, hands like talons on the rail as she leaned over it.

"One-twelve, be more careful with those, yeah? You're handling merchandise worth your skin a hundred times over! Wake up, Three-thirty-seven! Are you *trying* to get yourself disciplined? Walk faster or I'll make sure you won't walk again! Five-oh-nine, if I see you lean hands on that conveyor belt one more time I swear I'll come down there and toss you into the feeder!"

The laborers milled about below, minding their business, not changing their behavior in any way Meredith could notice. She cleared her throat and patiently waited to be acknowledged.

"Neumann." Gertrude eyed Meredith up and down. Her eyes lingered on the trinket casing. "To what do I owe the pleasure?"

She had the kind of imperious voice that was permanently set to Loud. It carried none of her skin's wrinkles.

"I made a mistake, boss." Meredith offered the incomplete stasis trap. "I was hoping you'd assess the damage before I fill out the paperwork. It could still be profitable."

Gertrude pulled up the teal sleeves of her taskmaster robes and gave Meredith a displeased look before snatching the item out of her hands. "What did you do?"

"I tightened screw T-3 too much. The plate cracked a hairline."

Another displeased look. Further studying.

"The range instructions got split," Gertrude finally declared. "This won't be more than an ankle biter. You *are* aware your assignment wasn't to produce an ankle biter, yeah?"

"Yes, boss."

She tossed the casing back at Meredith. "This will come out of your pay, of course." Her lips split in a wry smile full of highly respectable rot. "Congratulations on your purchase. Fill out the forms and drop them at my desk."

"I understand, boss. I apologise. I was distraught by worrisome news. This is the other reason I come talk to you."

"Is it, now. What could it possibly be? Let's hear it."

"Well, I learned about the stunt assigned to my station. He was found with pain relievers after he turned in for discipline, I heard."

"Yes. What of it?"

"Well, I was only wondering, might the pain medicine be gramrout? Uninfused gramrout?"

Gertrude seemed amused by the line of inquiry. "If that were the case, why should it concern you?"

"Boss, I . . . I dabble in botany and keep an uninfused garden. I grow gramrout there. I've become concerned, well . . . I'm not a suspect, am I?"

"You'd be in an interrogation room, if that were the case. Why are you bothering me with this? Are you looking to *become* a suspect?"

"No, no, of course not, I just thought . . . so it wasn't gramrout?"

"Yes, it was. It's also a common weed in Liddell Park, Neumann. You don't need a garden to procure it. Now, you have ten words to explain why you're wasting my time with this."

"Uh, I thought maybe I could help? With the investigation."

The taskmaster looked at Meredith as if she'd just spoken a different language.

"You see, boss, someone's been breaking into my garden—or well, they must have, because I found a mess of broken stems and a handful of strains missing, and they took my gramrout. I was thinking, if I could take a look at those herbs they found, I'd know if they were mine. And if they happened to be mine, then, maybe, the Judicars could keep surveillance on my cottage, and catch the thief next time she—"

Gertrude's laughter resonated through the machine floor, loud enough to eclipse the humming and clanging. Unlike Devalka's, there was nothing good-natured about it.

"Surveillance? Take a look at the evidence? You must've been made a Councilor and I didn't hear. Is that it?"

"Um—"

"That must be it. Otherwise you wouldn't presume to be entitled to such things, yeah? Maybe your brood-sister has decided to cede her position to you? Where is the signet, then? Where's the tiara?"

"I don't, uh. She didn't—"

"No, I didn't think so. That's unfortunate, because it would've been interesting to have the Judicars watch your home, only to find this 'thief' is nothing but the ravens pecking at your worthless plants. It would have given me a bigger laugh, then."

Meredith knit her brow in distress. The heat on her face went all the way up to the roots of her hair. "But . . . what if it *is* a thief? What if she steals from me again, and she tries to help those unwashed humans again? What if I'm already an unwitting accomplice? I can't stand the thought of being part—"

Gertrude cut her off with a brusque air-chop. "I've heard enough. Your concerns are foolish and not worth my time, or anyone's, for that matter. Return to your station immediately and concentrate only on the job in front of you. Understood?"

Meredith swallowed and nodded. "Yes, boss."

"Marvelous." The taskmaster shook her hands in a shooing gesture. "Now scram!"

Meredith complied without delay, metal walkways shaking and rattling with her every step. Soon Gertrude's yelling was once again directed at the stunts below.

As Meredith rushed on her way down the catwalks, her lips curved in a tiny smile that quickly vanished.

S HE'D BEEN EAGER to rush home after work, but all the shopping had to come first. Between restocking the neglected pantry, making some very casual underwear-related purchases and spending her life savings, it was hardly a span till dusk by the time Meredith made it back.

She stood at the front door, juggling a hundred bags to disengage multiple locks. By this point her arms were sackfuls of sand dangling from her shoulders, but she'd never paid the fee for doorstep delivery and she wasn't about to start today. Anyone looking on would have been understanding of her permanent grimace, even if the load wasn't the actual reason for it. Her thoughts were full of dread at what she might find on the other side. The girl seemed tame enough, sure, but everything she'd read said youths had terrible attention spans and would destroy everything in sight when unrestrained and unsupervised.

She pushed the door open, gathered the rest of her bags and stepped in.

"Huh."

Nothing out of place. Not at first sight, at least. Even the bedding she'd brought out for the couch was neatly folded by the armrest.

After thoroughly locking up, she headed for the kitchen with tentative steps. "Apprentice?"

A voice murmured beyond the swinging door, but Meredith couldn't make out the words. She pushed her way in.

Cloth and threaded needle in hand, Janette sat at a kitchen table that was a mess of cut discards, seamstress tools and practice scraps. Ear-wires ran up to her head, which gently bobbed from side to side as she sang to herself. Desmond snoozed at her feet without a care.

"I'll be waiting, all there's left to do is run
"You'll be the prince and I'll be the princess
"It's a love story, baby, just say—"

"Apprentice?"

The girl gasped and looked up. "Oh!"

She readily plucked out the ear-wires and stood at attention, subtly stretching limbs and back. She was already clad in the robe they'd only started the day before. Puffy eyes hinted at the fatigue behind her smile.

"Welcome home, Mistress. May I help you with those?"

Meredith stood blinking, cloth totes of groceries weighing down her shoulders. "You've truly been sewing all day?"

The girl seemed taken aback. "Y– you said I should, wasn't I supposed to?"

"No, I mean, yes, of course. It's good."

Janette reached for the bags and took half off her mentor, leaving Meredith lopsided and herself nearly tipping over.

"Oof. Heavier than they look. Where should I take them?"

"Um. There." She made a vague gesture toward the floor by the sink. "Over there is fine."

The Mistress watched as the girl tried to hide her struggle with the load. Meredith took note of the painstakingly joined seams and the well-balanced cut of a robe that used to be her warm season spare blanket, thin and soft and of the dullest shade of gray. The unfinished collar was rough all around, as it was designed as a cowled robe. Janette had been working on the hood's center seam when Meredith arrived.

Granted, a robe was a beginner's project, but every one of those stitches had been done by hand. Her rickety treadle sewing machine had given out years ago and she'd never bothered to scavenge a replacement.

Meredith headed for the counter. "I'll be honest," she said while getting on her tip-toes and rolling her loaded-down shoulder so the bags would make it over the edge, "I didn't expect you to stay focused like this. I am very pleased with you."

It was like a furnace came alive in the girl's cheeks. Meredith didn't know so much delight could be packed into a flustered little smile.

"I . . . I messed up a few times, but I think I fixed it. It's turning out okay, right?" She spread her arms, turned and twisted to showcase.

The garment was perfectly fine, but it was drab enough to pass for a discount bathrobe. There was no reason for the girl's clothes to be terrible, on top of everything else.

"It's a good job so far," Meredith said. "We'll add . . . a black satin trim, and an embroidered pattern along the hem." She smiled with sudden inspiration. "But that's for later, as you advance in your training. A symbol of your progress."

"Ooh, like going up in ranks?"

"Yes, just like that. Now, I'd usually let you put all this away, but—"

There was a knock at the front door.

Janette reacted with appropriate alarm, but her Mistress laid a reassuring hand on her shoulder. "I'm expecting visitors," she said. "Do you know what to do?"

"I will wait in Desmond's pen, Mistress."

If the prospect fazed her in any way, she didn't show it this time around.

"It won't be long."

Janette gathered cloth, sewing kit and screen-device and headed outside. As if summoned, Desmond perked up from under the table and followed the girl through the door flap.

The knocks repeated, seven thuds spaced at perfectly measured intervals. Meredith answered without further delay, eyes scanning everywhere for incriminatory evidence more out of habit than for real concern. After the usual rattle of locks and key, the front door swung open.

"That was fast," she told the visitors.

The pair of delivery crawlers answered with a gust of pressurized air as they settled on their multiple legs. Meredith eyed them with both interest and disappointment. Though she'd never before spent the kind of money that would warrant this kind of service to her door, these units were egregiously outdated, possibly going back to pre-rebellions times. Anti-gravity motivators were the standard in golem design, nowadays.

Using what must've been cutting edge sanctioned technology back then, they'd crammed over twenty legs per side on these models. Lines of pale blue glowed all over their limbs and broad torsos, constantly shifting and humming in accordance to their automation protocols. The cargo was low to the ground, strapped to the flatbeds on their backs, protected by a green-tinted repulsion dome that arched over it in a translucent shell. Both creatures had the well-worn, frayed feel of endless maintenance cycles.

The front crawler extended its three-fingered hand and offered a clipboard for Meredith to read.

~~~~~~~

TREMMELTON

TREASURES

~~~~~~~

Shipment Receiv't   Date: 7ᵗʰ 2' 453

Delivery for *Deulla Tremmel-Stchlz-Vanuuren*
At Address *23 Gargamel Lane*

Press **COMM** *to begin delivery*
Press **ABORT** *if you are not the intended recipient*

CONTENTS	ID#	Amount
Grounding Tiles (Square)	133	20
Grounding Tiles (Custom Cut)	135	8
Grounding tiles (Corner Seam)	134	18
Grounding Mesh (Floor)	141	16m²
Blackwell Soundstill Funnel	321	1
Blackwell Soundstill Coil	320	1
Focal Resonator	501	4
Cardioid Aural Dampener	504	1
Pathing Iron Kit	005	1
Grafting Interface & Materials	###	###

FRAUDULENT BEHAVIOUR OF ANY KIND WILL BE PROSECUTED TO FULL
EXTENT AND IS PUNISHABLE BY JUDICAR INTERVENTION UP TO AND
INCLUDING CLIPPING, WHEEL TURNING AND PURGE BY PYRE

As Purchased by

On the right-hand side of the creature's chest, where leathery pectoral became plated shoulder, there was a green button the size of a piggy coin. **COMM** was printed above it.

Meredith pressed it.

There was a brief tone and then the characteristic buzz of skyveil nodework connection. It was only a small wait until a chirpy voice emerged from the crawler's shoulder.

"Thank you for choosing Tremmel's Treasures! Is this . . . " papers shuffling, "Devalka Stohlz—oh, Val? Is this you?"

Meredith swallowed. This was not the same witch she'd dealt with at the emporium. That one had checked Devalka's license without even looking at it.

"S— speaking, yes." She reined in the panic and lowered her pitch, constrained her throat. "It's been quite some time. Hasn't it?"

"Soot and ash, your voice is so different through this thing. Perhaps Damra is right and an upgrade is well overdue."

"Damra, yes. I spoke to her earlier."

"I hope that rattleskull treated you properly. You should have come find me, I would have made you a better deal. I didn't even know you'd moved!"

"Oh, I, um. I didn't want to bother you."

"That's such nonsense! You're my favourite to haggle with, you know that. And this soundstill you purchased, a Blackwell? Whatever happened to your Galvanicat model? This is such a step down. I'd have never let you walk out with this one."

"Yes, I know, I—"

"Ogh, I'm so disappointed, how could you let me miss you like this?"

"I, uh. I was avoiding you, in fact."

There was a brief pause. "You were?"

Meredith cringed through the words. "I haven't moved. This is . . . it's a gift. For my new lover."

"Oh." Another beat. "That's . . . fine? I don't see—"

"You don't understand. I am very self-conscious about her, and I knew you'd ask about the address. I didn't want to talk about her. That's why."

"Ah."

Meredith could imagine What's-Her-Name sitting there, transceiver in hand, trying to figure out how to react. How out of character was this for Devalka?

She plowed ahead anyway.

"I need you to be discreet about this. I would appreciate it if you never bring it up. Ever. Having this conversation is mortifying enough."

"But— but of course! Of course. We have a good relationship, I wouldn't jeopardise it."

"I know I'm a mite of a gossip. I can see how it's hypocritical of me to ask, but I implore you all the same, don't breathe a word about it. You understand, don't you?"

"Val, say no more. I thank you for your trust, and this conversation never happened. Shall we get on with it, then?"

Meredith suppressed the relieved sigh. "Yes, absolutely. I need to set this up before she arrives. I'm quite tired, do walk me through it."

"Well then, before we proceed, you were provided with a random password for identification. You wouldn't want some other witch accepting this shipment, would you? Say the password now."

Meredith cleared her throat. "Bolegda."

"Good, correct." The repulsion fields dissipated. "Well now, do you want the goods to be brought indoors?"

"Yes."

"Marvelous, please verify everything can fit through the door before we proceed."

Meredith glanced back and forth a few times. "I think they can."

"You think so? Please make sure. You know how it is, we won't be responsible for any damage caused to your—to the living space."

"Yes, I'm sure, yes."

"Good, well then, command them to follow and show them where you'd like your goods delivered. It will help if you clear a wide path beforehand. Proceed when ready."

"Alright, hold on. . . ."

Meredith walked over to the Apprentice's Sofa and shoved it toward the hearth. After some consideration, she also rolled the rug and pushed it aside. Who knew where those hundred feet had been.

She cleared her throat again. "Alright. Follow."

The crawlers came alive as one, engaging their legs to mimic the smooth advance of a centipede. The cargo slid through the doorjamb undisturbed, thin limbs flowing around the frame like supple tendrils.

Meredith stopped in front of the door to the spare room. "Here is fine."

The speaker crackled. "Well then, tap first whichever crawler you see fit, then point to the floor clearly and say 'drop here.' Once the operation is complete, do the same with the other one."

"Tap. Of course."

After a moment of hesitation, she gave the nearest golem an uncertain tap to the shoulder and pointed at the area in front of the door. "Drop here."

The tapped crawler, the one that carried a large bulk of laminated foam-like material, turned around and backed to the desired spot. Its legs began retracting into its body, parts and gears and tendons clicking and whirring until the load was lowered to ground level, at which point its arms bent backward and pushed the detachable tray off the flatbed. The lip of the tray made contact with the floorboards with a faint *clack*.

The second crawler went through the same process, unloading a tray full of disparate parcels and bundles. The transceiver crackled again once the creatures had assumed their previous at-ease position.

"Inspect your merchandise carefully. Has delivery been completed to your satisfaction?"

"Yes, um. Yes, everything's here. I am pleased."

"Well then, go ahead and sign your name on the clipboard, down by the X. There should be a pen?"

"Yes, here."

The pen point hovered over the line for a while before making contact. How familiar would What's-Her-Name be with Devalka's signature?

With luck, not familiar enough to tell it apart from a forgery.

"Done."

It turned out indistinguishable from the real thing, to Meredith's eye. She'd practiced it long enough.

"Alright, so, let us know if there is anything missing. We'll collect the trays tomorrow at the usual time. If no-one will be home, make sure they're in an accessible location. I gather you are assembling this yourself? We provide assembly for an extra, very affordable fee, you know."

"No need. The trays will be outside, don't worry."

"Come now, are you sure? The price's hardly a scoop off the Froth for you, Val. I'd take care of it personally."

Meredith forced out a boisterous laugh, far louder than was warranted. "Ever the haggler, you are. Find yourself an easier target."

What's-Her-Name laughed in turn. "I had to try. See my guys out, if you don't mind. I would be appalled if they damaged something of yours."

"Of course."

"The marker should be outside. We'll gate in to retrieve them."

Meredith guided the crawlers as she had done before, all the way to the fence door—or rather, what used to be a door. Judging by the mess of broken boards and splinters, they'd plowed straight through on the way in.

"Ah. . . ."

"Is something the matter?"

"No. No, everything's fine." She stepped over the former fence and guided the brutes to the silver token on the side of the road. "They're in position now. Thank you for your help. And your discretion."

"I always look forward to dealing with you, Val. If there's something else I can get for you. . . ."

"Actually, yes, there is something you can do."

"Oh?"

"I agree with Damra, you ought to get these relics upgraded. You sound like you're at the bottom of a pit."

What's-Her-Name laughed again. "I'll take that into consideration. You're always welcome at Tremmel's Treasures. Ta!"

Meredith ran back inside before the portal opened, just in case the witch was standing right there in direct sight. There would be no flushing lights to obscure the view on an intra-Galavan gate. From behind the safety of her window blinds she watched as the rectangle to a well-lit warehouse popped into being and let the transports drum through.

The portal vanished, and the release of pent up breath became an involuntary moan. She swallowed past the hoarseness and massaged her throat. Why did everything have to be so hard all the time?

Her eyes lingered on the mangled fence. The door had been pulled off its hinges and crushed, reducing the whole section to a misshapen jumble. At least she had plenty of spare materials to make repairs.

She shook her head. "One thing at a time."

Meredith worked the entrance locks, walked past her purchases and selected a different key from her keyring. The door between bedroom and bathroom creaked open to reveal an L-shaped space lined with rudimentary shelves and bare wooden walls. The smell immediately permeated her nostrils: leather, bound pages old and new, dried spices, miscellaneous reagents. She strode around the bend, leaned over the busted sewing machine, unbarred the window and opened it. The heavy musk wouldn't be a problem once the room aired out.

Under the dim window light she surveyed the small area, mentally noting what needed to be pushed where. Plenty of space, if she got a little creative. She could always move the least incriminating shelves to the kitchen, things like books and preserves, while the more sensitive "merchandise"—the shinies, the assorted curios, the pilfered artifacts—could join the rest in the cellar. Her paranoia would rest just as easy knowing they were locked away down there, even if it would mean not walking among them as often.

Satisfied with her planning, Meredith made the small trek to Desmond's pen. Janette sat under the little window, diligently sewing under the pre-dusk light while listening to her soundmaker. Bricks had been moved from her abandoned fort-in-progress to accommodate her tush.

She looked up, plucked the one ear-wire and quietly smiled, the very image of dedication.

"It's all taken care of," Meredith said. "What are you plugging into your head, anyway?"

"This? I– I figured it was okay, you left it on the counter, so I thought I'd listen until it dies. Is it okay? I should have asked first."

Meredith spent a moment thinking about it. Was it okay?

"I don't see why not," she answered. "It helps you adjust, yes?"

"Oh, y– yeah, I suppose it does. That's a relief, I'm glad. Thank you." She considered the bud between her fingertips, then looked at her mentor. "Would you like to listen?"

Meredith recoiled as if she'd just been offered a puff of rolled noxbloom. Human music had been declared a mercy snare some hundred years ago, to be disdained and avoided by all. "Too endearing," judged the edict.

It was easy enough to acquire in clandestine markets, though. She'd always wondered, more so ever since Devalka had let slip her guilty appreciation for "The Beetuls," whatever that was. Accidental exposure was commonplace for travelers, she'd never heard of anyone being punished for it.

Curious fingertips grazed the nub. "Um, is it clean?"

"The earbud? Yeah, I think so. Well, let me. . . ." The girl used a fold of her robe to polish the rubber before offering again. Meredith took it, examined it closely, hesitantly brought it to her ear.

"This one is my favourite," Janette said while tapping the screen. "Dana and Bridget made fun of me, they said she's *so* last year, but I don't care. Her voice is so pretty."

Instruments she didn't recognize started playing. A voice joined them. Janette scooted to make room on her improvised brick bench and Meredith sat without thinking about it. For the next five centispan she listened to a terribly confusing little story about a young human princess—apparently they still had those?—trying to convince "Romeo" to stay by her side and do her bidding. In the end she seemed to succeed, bringing the boy to his knees and attaining proper offerings worthy of her station. It was all told at a peppy cadence, in pretty melodies and pleasant rhymes.

When the voice faded, Janette was looking up expectantly. Mentor and apprentice sat side-by-side, white cords dangling between them.

"I don't understand," Meredith said. "She says it's a love story, but there's no mention of sex at any point. I suppose it's implied? Is that what 'throwing pebbles' stands for?"

For some reason Janette's cheeks flushed a bright red before responding. "I . . . don't know, it could be? It– it's meant to be romantic."

"I see," she said without seeing at all. "Do you have more?"

Immediately the girl became bouncy with enthusiasm. "Yes, I have lots more! I downloaded all her albums and a lot of other stuff, you can listen to anything you like. Well, until the battery dies, at least."

Meredith looked at the device. She didn't know the first thing about it, but she was almost certain it ran on the same electricity on offer through her outlets. It should be fairly straightforward to find the appropriate transformer at Dreya's. Not that another trip through those shady side streets and alleys was particularly enticing.

"Don't worry about it." She gave the earbud back. "I believe I can work out a way—"

A gurgling sound rose inside the small enclosure. It came from

Janette's midsection.

Witch and apprentice looked down at the same time.

"Haven't you eaten?"

"Um. No, Mistress. I thought maybe I was supposed to wait for you? And, well, you said witches must be frugal, so I thought I better don't eat anything."

Meredith got an altogether unpleasant feeling at the bottom of her chest. It reminded her of the time she'd forgotten to let Desmond out for a whole day.

"I'm glad you're so dedicated," she said, "but you don't need to go hungry. Feel free to snack in moderation until dinnertime. Anything in the kitchen, and I'll even show you what's good for picking in the garden."

"Oh. Well, I'm not that hungry anyway. Don't feel bad."

Her stomach rumbled loud and long enough to be a full participant in the conversation.

"Um." The girl looked to the side. "It's just gas, honest."

Meredith snorted a chuckle. "Let's go put everything away and make dinner. After that, we're going to work on your room."

"Oh! Really? Already?"

"You won't be using it yet. But it won't be long until you do, if you apply yourself."

Janette nodded, very serious, very eager.

"Come," the Mistress said, and held the door open for her apprentice. "I've much to teach you."

CHAPTER NINE

BONDING

 ANETTE HELD TO HER FACE a strange contraption loosely shaped as a spiraling shell. It was the size of a large bread bun and partly translucent, catching and refracting the lamplights in myriad different ways.

"This is so cool. . . ."

"Be careful with it. There are very fine paths carved inside. You'll risk distorting them if you drop it."

The witch's apprentice reverently laid the instrument on its shipping cushion.

"That's the coil," Meredith continued. "It's the heart of the soundstill. It will process your infused words and imbue the intermedium with their conceptual essence. Then the intermedium is bound to the actual wordpaths in the trinket you're crafting, and to the trigger mechanism."

"This sounds so complicated."

Janette said it as if it was the most exciting notion she'd contemplated in a long while.

"Not too complicated, I hope, because it's *you* that's putting it together."

"Me?" Her voice climbed from excited to ecstatic. "Really?"

"Not any time soon, you need to know the theory first, and study the manual from start to finish. But all my apprentices go through this. It's very important that you gain intimate knowledge of how the sound distillery works. Because, clearly, everything you do here will help you in the future, when you become an independent artificer."

"I won't disappoint you, Mistress."

"I'll supervise everything, of course. I have extensive experience with soundstills, as you might expect. This one is fairly simple, but it's dangerous to get it wrong all the same."

"Could I maybe see the one you use, Mistress Meredith? I'd love to study an assembled one. This looks like an amazing machine . . . device-thing."

"The proper word is 'contraption,' and mine is, um—mine is at my workplace, in the lab. I work with several other witches, and you know the rules, I can't take you there." Meredith patted the girl's shoulder. Slightly less awkward, getting better. "But I will, once your apprenticeship is over."

"Aw. That's okay, I guess."

"Today," Meredith said, and gestured toward the large tray full of hard foamy sheets, "we'll work on insulating your room."

"Oh, it's cold in there? I don't mind the cold, truly. I could move in as-is."

"No, no." An involuntary groan escaped her as she pushed herself off the floor. "Magical insulation. Both to keep your presence hidden and to contain any terrible disaster we might brew in there."

Janette giggled, then noticed her mentor hadn't laughed. "Is it . . . is it that dangerous?"

"It could be. Let's get started. First, we have to make room. Follow me."

Mistress and apprentice spent the next half-span moving shelves and furniture, some to the center of the room, some to the kitchen so they could be later stowed in the cellar.

"These look so interesting," Janette had commented some time half-way. "What are they?"

Meredith had given the case littered with miscellaneous trinkets a final push to line it up with the others. "They are the product of an artificer's labour," she'd said, "and you'll have your own collection soon enough, if all goes well."

Janette had worked with even more enthusiasm after that. Once they'd moved every shelf, desk and container out of the way, one by one they unwrapped and arranged the foamy sheets marked with a W. The panels came up to Meredith's waist and were a fair bit heavier than she'd expected. Each one was carved with the same pattern of off-center spokes and jittery spirals she'd seen a thousand times over, engraved in every coin, watermarked in every note of currency.

"We'll start with the walls today," she explained. "Floor and ceiling tomorrow. Go fetch my ladder, will you? I'm sure you've seen it outside."

"Yes, right away."

Janette scampered off, and Meredith used the time to line up the sheets by the walls: two tall and one short to each pile, plus special ones for the corners. Getting them cut to fit the room's nonstandard shape had incurred a painful additional fee.

"Maybe I should've set her up in Desmond's pen after all," she muttered, already winded.

The clatter of wood on wood traveled from kitchen to doorframe. "Leave it right there for now," Meredith called without looking. Janette walked in after a final, careful thud.

"This seems like so much work. Do you need to do this every time you take a new apprentice?"

"I, uh . . . like I said, it's been quite some time since my last. So long, in fact, that I repurposed this room. Truth be told, I'd decided not to take on any more apprentices. But I changed my mind, clearly."

"Oh." Janette helped organize the rest of the panels, carrying them wherever the Mistress pointed. "Why not? Take any more apprentices, that is. I don't mean to pry."

"It's just . . . a complicated endeavour. Each one has been different, and it isn't always pleasant." Meredith chuckled as if remembering a particularly dismaying instance. "If you knew of even half of them, you wouldn't have asked."

The young apprentice winced like she'd just swallowed a bug. "I couldn't imagine anyone not being grateful for this opportunity, Mistress."

Another chuckle. "Why, I could point you to written accounts of young girls misbehaving so badly, they had to be boiled alive."

Janette almost let the last panel drop. "Witches do such things?"

"Oh, um, they used to, in olden times. It's not done anymore, of course."

The girl seemed to breathe easier. She let out a tiny snicker. "That's too bad. I knew some that would've deserved it."

"Is that so? Criminals of some sort?"

"No, just . . . mean girls. Stupid girls with nothing better to do than—well, you know." Janette shrugged. "They don't matter anymore. Should I go fetch some tools, Mistress? I meant to ask earlier."

It took Meredith a moment to react to the question. "No, that won't be necessary with these. Come over here." Meredith singled out one of the L-shaped panels and held it flush against a corner. Janette hurried to her side. "Now place your hands below mine and push. Like that, yes. As hard as you can."

The girl leaned into the piece and Meredith let go. "Now watch this."

Her fingers searched the top-left corner of the panel. There they found a small depression, a button just big enough for her thumb to press. She pushed it several times in a rapid succession of loud clicks, just like the instruction leaflet depicted.

The panel lit up with a barely audible whisper, a glowing string of symbols running its borders. Janette gawked, left eye open wide, right eye almost there. Then she gasped. "It's getting hot!"

"Don't worry. Keep pushing."

White light poured from the surfaces in contact and flooded the adjacent walls. The smell of seared timber wafted into their nostrils, mixed with a nose-tingling, chalky odor. The whisper grew a bit louder before stopping. The light faded shortly after.

"You can let go now."

Tentatively Janette stopped applying pressure, shooting glances at the line of contact between panel and wall. Wood planks and foamy material had fused together.

"The symbols," she murmured in awe. "They're gone now?"

"These aren't recyclable. Cheaper that way, no need to coil the words onto quality intermedium or carve the wordpaths before-hand."

"They were so cool, like Tolkien runes all smushed together! What did they say? Was it something about temperature? And something else, I don't know the word for it. Like . . . gather things up?"

Meredith's slightly smug expression dropped into stunned silence. Janette couldn't see it, as she was still facing the fused panel.

"Meld," was the belated reply.

"Yes, that's it! I wish I could've watched it for longer, I could hardly get a good look. Can we move on to the next? I want to see it again." She turned and noticed her mentor's grave expression. "Um . . . did I do something wrong, Mistress?"

Meredith blinked. Her mouth still hung open. "You read those?"

"Ah, well, not really? I just—I felt like I knew what they meant, if that makes any sense." She fidgeted in place. "I– I'm probably wrong. I'm sorry, Mistress."

"It takes entire moon cycles of study to grasp even the basics, but you just understood the conceptual sigils for *temperature*. You're not guessing, are you?"

"No, I—well, I don't think so, I just. . . ." The girl's hands wrung one sleeve of her robe.

"You're not in trouble, Janette. Just say the truth."

She licked her lips. "I saw the symbols, and I got this . . . feeling. Like I understood what they were about. The essence of them."

Meredith nodded slowly. She picked up the next panel and pressed it to the wall. "Watch closely, now."

The apprentice stared at the borders of the rectangular sheet. Her mentor activated the mechanism. Both watched intently as the commands lit up, executed and burnt out.

"Well?"

The girl glanced at Meredith. Her concentrated frown conveyed a fair amount of frustration.

"Raise temperature to some material's melting point? Something I can't understand, and then . . . 'meld,' as in– as in fusing something together." Janette only half-met her eyes, like a student guessing the answers to an oral test.

"Well, burn my robes and tar my ankles."

"What?"

Meredith had to smile. Continued exposure had rendered the girl's latent power an ignorable buzz, like an ever-present white noise blending with the background. But it was still there, as always, thrumming with the beat of reality. Possibly the girl's attunement was on par with that of Caterina Galvan herself.

"Yes. Yes, that's correct, for the most part." She was shaking her head in giddy disbelief. Was this the Universe itself, finally giving her a break? "Do you know what this means? You're so in tune with magic, this will shave so much time off my plan—I mean, the plans I had for your education, of course. I thought it would be several cycles before we got to artificing, but now. . . ."

Janette was starry-eyed by then. "Really? How soon?"

"Well, provided you grasp the basics and infusion doesn't give you trouble? You might cast your first spell within this moon cycle."

The girl had balled her fists with excitement, jumping in place. "Ooh, that's marvellous! I won't disappoint you, I swear it!"

"You've been telling me as much, and I'm inclined to believe you." Meredith gestured at the rows of unattached panels. "But of course, there's much to do before then. The faster we get this out of the way, the sooner we can work on *real* magic."

Janette quickly dragged the next panel within Meredith's reach. Both of her eyes glimmered with undisguised hunger.

"I can't wait."

MEREDITH SHUT THE BEDROOM door behind her at last. She tossed on the bed the wrist-thick tome she was carrying, disrobed, put on fresh underwear, donned her nightgown, undid her ponytail and brushed her hair. The weary stranger in the mirror fought to keep her eyelids from drooping throughout the routine.

She hadn't spent any time on the garden today. There were two orders pending, the curlstalks needed pruning badly and the taters were already overdue for harvest. Her hands itched for every gardening tool on the shelves whenever she caught sight of the dead husks and shriveled bushes.

None of it would get done any time soon, at this rate. The Circle meeting was happening next midnight, and they'd surely found out about the Four-Thirteen issue. What would Eleven say? Would they toss her out? The worry would help keep her awake, at least.

Maybe she'd postpone work on the home lab for a few days. Teach her "apprentice" some botany, and more recipes, and make sure all the chores were done just the way she liked them. Certainly spend more time in the kitchen—that might have been the worst tater omelet-become-mush she'd ever put in her mouth.

Janette had been *so* mortified. That girl sure was hard on herself. It had been a challenge to convince her it truly was alright to waste a few eggs.

It took several more brush strokes for Meredith to notice the fond smile that had snuck onto her lips. The smile vanished like a phantom caught in daylight.

Yes, she'd cover the basics now, instead of jumping right away into complicated, life-altering subjects. At the very least, it would give the all-knowing Mistress some time to study.

Setting down the brush, Meredith sighed a deep, deep sigh that morphed into a yawn. She shook her head in a vain attempt to clear it, lay face-down on top of the blankets and cracked open the manual for the soundstill.

CHAPTER TEN

EMBERS

 HE MANUFACTORY RESTROOMS were deserted early in the morning. It didn't stop Meredith from checking all four stalls for accidental witnesses before stepping into Devalka's Preferred Toilet.

Later, when Val huffed past her work station a whole fourth-span after seven, Meredith didn't ask what was wrong. Later still, when Val volunteered it all on her own, Meredith didn't offer to help. And after that, when Val enlisted her anyway to quietly scour every corner of the manufactory she'd visited the day previous—and, by the twice-charred corpse of Mergat, she better not tell anyone what they were looking for—not once did Meredith suggest to maybe look in the restroom.

They genuinely found it nearly a span into the search, while Meredith busied herself pretending to dig through the waste bin. She good-naturedly chided Devalka to maybe stow her wallet in her artificer lounge locker from that point forward, because at least then it would not get soiled on a bathroom floor all night.

Val was not amused. More importantly, at no point did Val express even a hint of suspicion.

And why would she? Meredith was as harmless as a baked turnip.

THE CEMETERY HIDEOUT was a cellar beneath the abandoned undertaker shack, and the walk there involved sneaking through tortuous paths by unkempt graves and looming stone mausoleums. The old cemetery was a bit of a tourist attraction in Brena, purposefully preserved in a state of vine overgrowth and bone-chilling neglect. A thousand dead stories thrummed in the stoneflesh, whispered in the rustle of dead leaves.

Meredith found it the most upsetting in the rotation by far, especially in the overcast darkness after dayturn. Eithday had just turned to Nynday, and so the dark clouds overhead had become a drizzle bound to drench every corner of Brena.

She carefully descended the ramshackle staircase, one gloved hand fast on the rust-eaten rail. Soot-encrusted pipes ran alongside her, now obsolete and dormant for decades after centuries of non-stop use, and as she advanced her shoulder bumped against a protruding valve as large as her head. Double wooden doors waited ahead, embedded at a slant on the wall and clearly leading further down. Meredith knocked in three sets of three.

A few moments passed, as usual. All other attendees would come in through the space-fold entryway set up inside. No-one bothered to stay posted by the door at all times for the one indigent that made the trip there on foot.

A small panel swung open at brow height, revealing soft light behind a metallic mesh.

"*The night is calm,*" Meredith said, vocalizing clearly to compensate for the mask, "*but the winds are changing.*"

"What? I didn't understand any of that."

Oh, bother. Thirty-Seven again. She cleared her throat and spoke the words louder, for all the good it would do.

"Alright," Thirty-Seven responded. "Who are you, anyway?"

"You know I'm Brena Sixty-Two. It's raining, please open the door."

"I don't know what you're talking about. You should leave, stranger."

"Must we go through this every time?"

"Only when you're late. So, yes, every time."

"It's not my fault, it's a labyrinth out here!"

"You got lost *again*?"

"*You* try to find your way in this horrible place when it's dark, it's not easy!"

"I don't have to. That's the entire purpose of the mockery, I thought it was clear."

"Can you please open the door?"

The padlock rattled, the bar clattered, the hinges complained in a sinister croak, and Meredith stepped back so the doors could swing all the way. A toothy Thirty-Seven smirked under her cowl, all other features obscured in the faint penumbra.

"Come in," she said. "Try not to make much noise, you cack-hand."

It wasn't Meredith's fault either that the mask and hood obscured her field of vision, making her constantly bump into things. She followed Brena Thirty-Seven as she heavily stomped down the steps, toward quiet voices and discreet glowstones. The meeting was underway, though it didn't seem to be far along.

" . . . Transport went as planned," Eleven was saying, "no incidents, not a whiff of chatter. It would've been quiet this week, if not for the manufactory issue."

"What issue?" someone asked, her voice tinny through concealment.

"*One* among us," Eleven responded as Meredith entered the room, "she felt compelled to venture into the cell blocks and provide one of the humans with supplies. Needless to say, the supplies were discovered. Our . . . *unwise* sister, who shouldn't even be present, may become compromised as a result."

Meredith tried to look perfectly innocent as she got to her seat. She lifted the fold-up chair before moving it so it wouldn't make noise, but every witch turned to look at her anyway, each one of them a faceless cowl in the faint glowstone light. Brena Eleven was on her feet at the head of the table, tall enough to tower even from all the way over there. Her gloved fingers were like raven claws spread on the portable table. Her eyes shone from deep in her hood, bearing down on Meredith with displeasure.

"Nina," she said, "carry on with the meeting, if you please." She side-stepped around the nodding Nineteen and gestured toward the space-fold room. "A cent of your time, Sixty-Two."

Meredith stood again, flushing hot under her clothes as the chair scraped noisily on the stone floor. Wordlessly they filed into the tiny side room. It was little more than an alcove, a minimal step up in privacy.

The moment they passed the threshold, the forewitch all but threw her against the wall. Eleven's voice sizzled through the delicately contoured mask concealing her features. "What in Grothgor's taint were you *thinking?*"

Meredith fought not to squeak under her imposing frame. "He'd done nothing wrong, I wanted to help—"

"You sent this man into an *interrogation room,* is that how you help?"

"I didn't mean—"

"And now you come *here*! They could have placed you under

surveillance, they could be out there staring at the front door *right now.*"

"No, I made sure they wouldn't, I got laughed off just by suggesting it—"

"Unless that's what they *want you* to believe. Do you think the Riven Circle has stayed in the shadows for so long by *taking chances*? Everyone here gets these impulses, but we all know restraint." Her voice lowered to a more confidential volume. "You are an informant on the Head of the Coven, *that* is how you help. You should've brought the matter to our attention and let those among us who are *qualified* take action, if necessary."

Eleven's penchant for dramatic emphasis had always unsettled Meredith, and this night was no exception. "Nothing would've been done about this—"

"Yes, *exactly,* because what you did helped *nobody,* and we could have *told you* as much ahead of time. This is why the Circle exists in the first place, do you not see? Rash individual action is unwise and short-sighted, well-intentioned as it might be. We plan everything. We assess risk and reward and move only when the time is right. *That* is how we operate to get results without losses. You made everything worse, instead."

Meredith looked away, lips pressed together. There was no arguing with the last point. She had a gift for abject failure.

"I'm sorry," she said. "I felt responsible."

Don't be sorry, Frau's voice hissed in her thoughts. *Be better.*

"You *are* responsible, now." Eleven's grip had become gentle on Meredith's shoulders. The harsh tone had mellowed, giving way to thoughtful lecturing. "Let it be a lesson. You gave in to our disease without a solid plan in mind, and it only caused more pain. Mercy is the burden we all share. Acting alone will crush you beneath its weight."

Her features were obscured, but the cringe stuck to her voice and mirrored Meredith's own. The defect that brought them all together was always an upsetting subject, best left unmentioned.

"I'm requesting a rescue mission," Meredith said.

The forewitch startled. "For this human? That is *absurd,* absolutely not."

"He's obviously loyal, he hasn't accused me. Isn't he a perfect candidate?"

"That only proves he's intelligent, he knows they'll wipe him hard the moment he points at you. That's not the issue. Even if he were fully vetted, he's extremely high-profile right now. What's more, he'll be kept in Block One for quite some time." She shook her head. "It's simply not worth the risk, not by far. Pure clodbait."

"We have to do *something,* I can't just sit—"

"Oh, you *can* sit, and you will. These are the consequences of your actions, and you'll hold the lesson to mind. Let us hope nothing *more* comes of this."

"You're not even going to put it to the table?"

"And say *what,* exactly? That we should place several field agents at extreme risk, out of consideration for your *conscience*?" Meredith could imagine the lips twisting around the word, the way they might around the word *parasite.* "Another brash action that would surely make everything worse, again. What you ask is *nonsensical.*"

Meredith lowered her eyes. As much as she wanted to argue further, she couldn't quite come up with an actual counterpoint.

"The Circle doesn't take such chances," Eleven continued, "so now you're going to sit in, and after half a span you will go back up there with Thirty-Seven. You'll take her in your arms in a *very* convincing manner out in the open before starting on your way back home. And after you're gone, you will keep away from us until the end of the next moon cycle, while everything settles down."

"You . . . you truly believe they could be tracking me?"

"I believe it's not a gamble I'm willing to make."

Meredith silently nodded. She could hardly fault someone else for being paranoid. Eleven sighed dramatically. "The matter is settled. I might as well get your report on Mifraulde while we're here."

"Oh, um. Nothing much, I didn't see her a lot. One issue did come up, quite important."

"Let's hear it, then."

"Yes, uh. She's very concerned about Selma Tarkai-Holtz-Grubber. The Tarkan prime gorgon? She's very vocal about—"

"I know who Selma is."

"Right, sorry. Apparently she's become a real threat to Frau. She assured me she has it under control, but she seemed rattled, honestly."

"Hm."

"Is there something we can do?"

"There is plenty. Silver is in charge of the Tarkis chapter, after all. There is a reason the Circle got started there. What's been happening in the swamplands lately is an abomination, the last thing we need is someone like Selma in control of the Coven."

"But what will be done?"

"I don't know yet. We'll put it to the table. Then I'll talk to Silver."

"I don't want this to hurt Frau. It's bad enough that I'm here shroudwise to her."

Eleven waved the concern away. "You needn't fret. Mifraulde is no ally, but knowing the alternatives, we want to keep *her* in power." She nudged informant Brena Sixty-Two toward the room's threshold. "We're done here. Sit with us, and remember your instructions. I expect to see you at Farshaw Alley in one cycle's time, if there are no signs of surveillance. Don't you dare come near, otherwise."

The prodding didn't move her. Meredith was stuck in place, back still pressed to what was left of the hundred-year-old wallpaper. Frau's words scraped against the insides of her skull.

You're done with them. Disengage *from those mercy-ridden fools.*

Meredith's lips puckered together. She looked into the forewitch's mask and nodded, once.

"Don't worry," she said. "I'll be there."

FOUR DIFFERENT LOCKS finally clattered shut. Raindrops spattered on the doormat. Bone-weary, barely awake and eventually drenched, Meredith had followed the most roundabout path back home there was, despite the well-established fact that nobody cared what she did or where she went.

She glanced at the sofa, concerned all the noise had disturbed Janette's sleep. She didn't even twitch. Not that it came as a surprise; she'd been pooped after barely a span of tater harvest. This girl was downright spindly, did humans simply not do anything outside nowadays?

After tossing the mask on her bed and hanging the cloak to dry, Meredith headed for the restroom with soft, deliberate steps. In retrospect, perhaps she should've curbed the girl's enthusiasm a bit. It had been indulgent to let her chase the flitglows and play "rip the sack" with Desmond. The sheer delight in her laughter had been . . . well, interesting. In a purely academic sense.

Meredith freshened up, cleansed all the street niff off her arms and face, swished rotnot for a good centispan and fastidiously flossed on top of that. Her concerns and anxieties drowned one by one as the prospect of passing out in bed flooded her mind. Finally, a weekend. At last, the chance to sleep in. Every problem could wait until she woke up.

Back in her bedroom she fully disrobed, put on fresh underwear, donned her nightgown, undid her wet ponytail and brushed her hair. The weary stranger in the mirror didn't even bother to wave hello. They'd met far too often, lately.

The voice reached her twenty-three strokes in. A sort of moaning, pitched low and drawn out like the growl of a cat.

Heavy eyelids widened, but not by much. Heavy thoughts struggled to process the sound, but only got as far as *it came from the living room.*

Meredith listened carefully.

She heard it well this time, a bit shorter, a bit louder. She got to her feet, taking a moment to keep her balance.

Another moan. Shuffling steps took her to the bedroom door. She cracked it open just a hair.

"Janette?"

The girl didn't answer. Only smolders remained in the hearth, shrouding the living room in red darkness and slow-thrumming shadows. Latent power permeated the room in a mouth-drying musk.

The next moan was long and anxious and angry, the impotent weep of an affronted ghost.

Meredith slowly approached the sleeping apprentice. She was restless on her back, fist balled on her blanket, fingers clutching the fabric with white-knuckled intensity. Her arms spasmed subtly, as if she wanted to move them but couldn't. Tears glinted on half-lit features.

"Janette."

The only response was another moan. Meredith neared the couch and placed a gentle hand on the girl's shoulder. "Janette."

She wriggled in her sleep, as if trying to escape contact. The stress bolstered her thaumaturgic aura to a troublesome peak, enough to have Meredith worry it might be noticeable from outside. She sat at the edge of the cushion and shook the girl lightly. "Janette, wake up."

The girl bared her teeth and slapped Meredith's hand away. The witch frowned.

"Apprentice! Wake up!"

Janette gasped as her eyes flew open. She looked around in a disoriented panic before focusing on Meredith's face. Her features relaxed after a moment of stupefied blinking, her body sinking into the cushions as the tension left her.

"Mistress," she breathed. Her hands gripped Meredith's arm and pressed it to her chest as if her mentor could disappear from one heartbeat to the next.

"You were having a nightmare. Moaning."

Janette didn't respond for a while.

"I'm sorry," she finally said, voice small.

"You're sorry?"

"I'm sorry I woke you."

"Oh, don't be silly."

Meredith felt a nigh on irresistible urge to brush the girl's hair off her forehead, but she refrained from it. Janette's breath slowly mellowed. Her desperate clutching subsided. Her eyes were cast down and her cheeks were red.

"I'm so sorry," she said. "This is embarrassing." She noticed her face was wet and made an effort to wipe the tears away.

"Here." Meredith handed her one of the napkins on the table.

"Thank you."

Janette breathed a deep sigh and worked on calming herself.

Meredith watched her, lips pursed, brow knit. The girl wouldn't stop shaking.

"Are you alright?"

"I'll be okay. I didn't mean. . . ." She left the sentence unfinished.

"Do you . . . want to talk about it?"

Janette winced, shook her head. "It's nothing."

"Nothing? You look quite upset."

"Yeah, but . . . I'll be okay. It was just a nightmare, I've had them before. It wasn't real."

"Do you often have nightmares?"

"No, well, not . . . really. I do, sometimes, but it's, um. It's complicated."

"How so?"

"Oh, it wasn't even the same this time, it was different. I dreamt I'd gone back, and everything we've done was just a fantasy, and I was back to that other life. I'll be okay, Mistress, I promise. Thank you so much for asking, and for waking me up."

Meredith sniffed with amusement at the obvious deflection. She shrugged. "Well, we better get some sleep. You'll probably be up before I am, try not to make much noise. There is much for you to study, still."

The girl smiled almost convincingly. "Yes, I'll get right on it."

"Good." Meredith started to get up from the couch. Looking at that smile, she hesitated. "Will you be alright?"

"Yes. Yes, of course."

The answer was suspiciously tardy. After some pondering, Meredith's butt remained on the edge of the seat. She looked at the embers.

"That's a lovely hearth, isn't it?"

"It's . . . very soothing, Mistress."

"It's been a while since I last enjoyed it. Do you mind if I stay for a spell?"

Janette breathed in as if to say something. She reconsidered at the last moment. "You don't have to do that," she said in a tiny voice.

"Do what? This is my home, I'll sit where I please. So, yes, you will make room for me to get comfortable, apprentice."

The girl gave a timid smile. She folded her legs to give her mentor ample room on the other side of the sofa. "Of course, Mistress Meredith."

"Good."

Meredith scooted down the couch and settled by Janette's feet. She rested a reassuring hand on the apprentice's ankle and watched the red and black wood as it smoldered. "Such lovely colours."

"I never knew how nice a real fire was."

"I'm positive the cold climate cycle was engineered into the system only so we could enjoy a good hearth."

The girl was quiet for a few beats. "All climate is engineered?"

Meredith nodded. "Caterina and her associates shaped this pocket of reality almost from scratch. Climate control was a matter of necessity. The system continues to get perfected even today."

Janette spoke at the end of a huge yawn. "How does it work? I'd love to know."

"Well, I'm no engineer, so I can't give you details, but all climate originates from moving air and water. Galavan is mostly a large valley, which makes the flow of water quite straightforward. The Coren mountain range traps the clouds, which is to say moisture, which trickles down until it all joins together to become the Froth— the river, that is. Tarkis Swamp, at the bottom, is controlled by a network of coil-furnaces that evaporate whatever is necessary for the desired cycle. It's always extremely humid down there, and the swamp-dwellers like it that way. You see, it's a very small closed system compared to Earth's impossibly large climate, so we can control every variable."

The girl's voice came in a drowsy slur. "That's . . . amazing."

Meredith continued. "Rainfall rotates all over Galavan. For Brena—that's the name of this area, did I mention that yet? I think I did—it comes every Nynday at dayturn. We're pretty far up, we don't get the kind of rain the crops do, closer to the swamp. I have to water from time to time, especially the hansels, they're greedy little imps."

"Mm."

"The furnaces make the swamp very warm, while the mountain range is kept close to freezing by the heat-eaters up there. So you see, to control surface temperature realm-wide, all you need to do is control airflow. That's why we'll often refer to the changing of seasons as the Tarkis breeze or the Coren chill. This is done through the flowlines. The Felling line passes close to my cottage, you can see the post from the garden. Conceptual runes drive the winds along pathways depending on the power fed into the lines. It used to be raw spark, but the whole system was overhauled to run on electricity. Feed more power into the paths you want and you create airflow in that direction."

No answer or acknowledgement came.

"It takes a lot of power to keep everything going, you know? Not just the flowlines or the Tarkan weather furnaces—there's also the gravitational mesh, and the skyveil nodework, and all these other fundamental systems that keep Galavan stable. It's quite complicated. I wasn't joshing when I said artificers are important.

"Anyway, I'll take the cold season any day, I don't much like the heat. Of course, it doesn't get *that* hot, nobody will be sweltering like it happens on Earth, but some chill makes for comfortable sleeping. Plus the ravens prefer the cold, they come down cheering from the Range. I like ravens, they make the funniest sounds. The garden does get better in the warm season, all the blussels will be in bloom, and the swarms of coraline flitglows come up from Devalen and light up the brush, it's very eye-catching. You'll like it."

Meredith glanced at the girl. Her breath had become long and steady. Her jaw had slackened and her lips were parted.

"Actually, I misspoke, the winds are created by invisible creatures called . . . gallyphants. Yes, they're invisible mammoth beasts, suspended in mid-air by magical harnesses. The gallyphants blow very hard through their trunks and flap their feathered wings whenever we zap them with cattleprods. Oh, yes, this is all one hundred percent factual."

The only answer was heavy breathing. Satisfied, Meredith wriggled against the cushions and rolled her shoulders until half her body had sunk in. It was hardly a step down from her own bed. To this day she scoffed at the silly crone who'd posted the sofa on the Exchange simply because her cat had ripped apart a chunk of the fabric.

Her mind drifted. For long moments she remained motionless, thoughts turning to the events of the day, to every word said behind mask and cowl. The coals chattered among themselves in their own quiet conversation.

"I don't know what to do," she confessed in a mutter. Janette didn't stir.

"I made a terrible mistake. I don't know how to fix it."

Well, she *did* know how to fix it, but she couldn't possibly pull off a rescue by herself. The Circle had resources, they'd been smuggling out duds and stunts for decades. How much harder could this one be?

"For all their talk, they don't *do* much."

Maybe it wasn't so bad. Maybe they'd release him over the weekend and by Firsday everything would go back to normal. There was no need to worry. She was a witch, she wasn't *meant* to worry about these things.

They would hard-wipe him, of course. Another empty shell ready for re-training. Or not even bother with the wipe and just. . . dispose of him.

Because of what she'd done.

Meredith chewed on her lip for a while.

"Let it go," she murmured. "Just let it go."

She stretched her legs, let out a murky sigh and watched the fire through half-lidded eyes.

The embers sure were lovely.

CHAPTER ELEVEN

MERCY

ELL 2-B, BLOCK ONE. A nightmare to reach undetected, but doable.

Firsday had gone by. And Seconday, and Thirday, and a whole week after that. A whole week without signs of Four-Thirteen.

Because of what she'd done.

It had surprised her, how heavy a weight the guilt was, how prevalent. It refused to let go of her, it grew heavier with each passing day. The guilt was an anchor lodged in her chest, pulling her ever deeper into the bog until it consumed her every thought.

Such a thing was not witch-like. Not in the slightest.

Meredith no longer felt that weight as she crept through the corridors of the holding pens, odor neutralizer activated, aural dampener masking her every sound. Large swathes of darkness separated what few islands of light there were, providing plenty of cover. Though inexpensive lighting had been available for centuries, administration felt it was important to keep the fusty dungeon feel. The smell of the place would've reinforced that notion for her, had the odor neutralizer not have been engaged.

The human was a black mound in the dark cell. He'd been there for three days, according to his entry on the log. It had been an ordeal all of itself to check as much the day before. Three days in the holding pens meant he'd spent the previous eight enduring Judicar ministrations.

Meredith deactivated the aural dampener. The patrol paths gave her a tenth-span window to carry out her deranged plan.

"Human," she whispered.

The mound stirred. She waited for a response or more movement, but neither happened.

"Human," she rasped, slightly more urgent.

He stirred again, lifted his head and saw her. Recognized her. He startled, bolted off the cot and moved toward the prison bars, but lost his footing in the process and fell to the stone floor, into the dim light. Meredith winced at a sight that was much like she'd feared. No wonder he'd tripped. They were not planning to wipe and reinstate this serf.

At least he was clean.

From one of her pockets Meredith produced a rolled-up strip of long, narrow parchment. "We don't have much time. Don't make any noise."

She knelt in front of the barred room and one after another she measured and ripped lengths of the strip, wrapping each one at the base of every bar in front of her. Four-Thirteen sat upright and repeatedly pointed away among angry groans.

"Keep quiet!"

She finished the bottom five, then moved to the top end, wrapping parchment slightly above her head. The two crossbars followed. The human grew more frantic, his guttural groans becoming louder.

"Are you mad? Be quiet!"

"Bee high yoo!" he sputtered. Blood dribbled down his chin. "Bee high yoo!"

On second thought, he wasn't pointing away in the general sense of the word. He pointed at a very specific spot behind Meredith.

Her eyes widened, and she jumped out of the way just as the beast pounced. It landed where she'd been standing only a moment ago, its claws scraping against metal and stone.

With a scream trapped in her throat Meredith took off running, shaky hands fumbling at her holster. The savage clack-and-grind of the cat's claws followed close behind; a heaving shadow swallowed her whenever she passed a lamp, getting larger with every spot of light. Vivid images of her entrails flying through the hallways crowded her thoughts and emptied her lungs.

Her crossbow clicked ready in her hand. Meredith whirled and didn't give herself time to stare at the maw of the beast.

A bolt the size of a pencil went into the hunter's mouth and buried itself at the back of its throat. The creature thumped against Meredith with a roar, pinning her to the ground, knocking out of her what wind she had left as her gear dug into her kidneys. The weapon flew out of her grasp and bounced on the nearby wall. Panic seized her as she fought against paws as large and heavy as cast-iron pans, her legs shoving and kicking desperately while the hem of her black robes ripped and tore under iron-vise hind claws. It was after an eternity of life-or-death struggle that she understood the beast was only twitching and convulsing without purpose.

She struggled to shove it off of her, but lacked the strength. For agonizing moments she squirmed and wriggled, slowly inching her way out from under it. From her position Meredith had plenty of time to notice the intricate patterns on the hunter's infusion-grounding collar. Even if a suitable spell had come to her lips at the right time, that collar would have rendered her magic as effective as a lullaby.

Good thing the nettlecap toxin she'd brewed didn't have a lick of infusion poured into it.

Meredith got to her feet, readjusted her hat, grabbed her weapon and ran back to Four-Thirteen's cell, free hand already digging in another pocket as shreds of robe fluttered about her shins. On the way she noticed a different human behind bars, sitting, staring blankly into a wall. She paid him no mind.

Reaching the appropriate cell took far longer than she'd expected. Had she truly run so far?

"You could've told me you were being watched!"

Four-Thirteen glared, or gaped, or both. There was a wild cast to his eyes that made all the sense in the world, considering what he'd endured so far.

Meredith's livid fingers clutched her kitchen firestarter as she brought its flame to the knots on the wrapped parchment. Her heart pounded, her breath collided against her teeth as it traveled in and out of her lungs at a rate that couldn't be healthy.

"Stand back," she needlessly said, her voice a high-pitched quaver. Four-Thirteen had already shambled well away from the exit to his cell.

Each section of parchment flared in quick succession, strings of words whispering and burning out with the medium that contained them. Every piece became a white-hot band around the metal, pressing inwards with sizzling intensity until the material was completely melted. Acrid fumes spread through the area as the dungeon's temperature dropped to an icy chill in response to the magical heat.

The new door sank and fell with a loud clatter. Kerchief held to her nose, Meredith quickly stepped through. With every care she could afford, she wrapped Four-Thirteen's arm around her shoulders. The serf groaned the moment his bandaged burns pressed against Meredith. The tell-tale welts and cuts of the Judicar wheel scored jagged paths down his back. His right leg was every shade of purple, swollen turgid from toes to knee.

Her left hand clasped his in a tight grip.

"Hold my hand. Do you understand me? Whatever you do, don't let go of my hand."

She couldn't have controlled the shaking in her voice even if she'd tried. Four-Thirteen eyed her like she was a raving lunatic, but still did as was told. Braced against Meredith, he did what he could to walk out of the cell without touching the molten nubs.

Three different halls converged at the intersection a few steps ahead. The cat mewlings already neared from every direction, heavy bootsteps heralding the swift approach of the juditor on duty. She'd be coming from behind, Meredith knew.

"We're going ahead, then left." She parted her mangled robe and pulled hard on a ribbon attached to her belt. Glyphs lit up around the belt's circumference, words flowing in a sinister susurrus. Witch and serf vanished.

"This thing is almost depleted, we have twelve cents to get out. Can't talk anymore." She held the aural dampener within its pocket, thumb caressing the knob that would activate it. "If you let go of my hand, we're both dead."

She switched it on and every sound died around them. They started forward, the human struggling to keep apace by painstakingly hobbling against Meredith's hip. It was extremely disorienting to walk without seeing her own limbs.

They waited at the intersection for the approaching patrols, pressing themselves against the stone wall just beyond the lamplight. Chest heaving with anxiety, Meredith held her crossbow in her free hand, ready to use it at the first sign of discovery. Though the optical camouflage was near flawless, she could notice a tiny rippling distortion any time she moved.

One hunter cat loped by, then another. She pushed forward without delay, bracing the wall as they rounded the bend. Another beast passed them at a canter, and its lashing tail brushed across Meredith's chest.

She froze in place. The cat slowed, stopping before reaching the intersection. It turned around. It let out a drawling whine, like an old, creaky door being slowly pushed open. It stalked toward their position.

Meredith stilled her breath, took careful aim down the invisible sights of her crossbow, and pulled the trigger not one meter away from the creature's face.

Blood spattered on the weapon and vanished as the dart pierced the hunter's eye and almost disappeared into its skull. The beast startled, stumbled, dropped to the ground with a muffled thud.

Meredith's throat lurched with nausea, and right away she averted her eyes from the twitching body. She put her every thought into moving forward as fast as they could go, nearly hauling the serf over her shoulder. Though no sound could outstrip the dampener's influence, his pained grunting rumbled against her chest.

A voice bellowed far behind them: "Human fugitive! Seal all the exits!"

That would be the juditor, finding a broken and empty cell and no trace of the escapee.

"Well, twaddlebag," Meredith whispered, though she herself couldn't hear it. "Plan B it is."

At the next intersection she turned right where she would've turned left, the dungeon's blueprints clear in her mind. Several more hunters rushed by without a glance, possibly heading toward the employee access door Meredith had planned to use. She plowed ahead, fervently hoping they wouldn't anticipate her alternative escape route. She didn't have a plan C.

A few turns later they arrived at an arched entryway as wide as she was tall. Dim lamplight let her read the sign above it, charcoal letters on dark wood. *Hunter Dens,* it said.

Four-Thirteen made as if to stop moving, but she goaded him forward.

The dens were a sea of thick shadows. Waning moonlight crept in through the multitude of second-story windows, wrapping every catwalk and pillar in silver contours. The catwalks interconnected in convoluted pathways all the way to the ceiling, where the prime lairs could be found. Giant fur-laden cushions littered the floor, strewn around load-bearing pillars wrapped in waist-thick rope. Several sections of rope were shredded to a mess of strings.

She stood at the threshold, terribly glad the odor suppressor worked both ways. There was no movement within: every beast was deployed, searching the dungeon, and none should remain. Who in their right mind would go into their den to hide?

The timer on her girdle precluded further caution. After evaluating the shady paths ahead, Meredith picked the sturdiest ramp she could find. Her breath ran ragged with exhaustion even before they started the climb.

Four-Thirteen leaned on her more and more, groans rumbling against her ribcage. Meredith's legs were ready to give out by the time she reached the second tier and turned toward the windows. Though no sound emanated from their position, the catwalk did vibrate with their every labored step.

They were almost to a windowsill when a high-pitched hiss came from directly above. They stopped immediately, standing as still as their level of exertion would let them. Meredith looked up with her heart in her throat and came eye-to-eye with a mouth full of fangs.

Well, there were only eight fangs, and fairly tiny at that. The rest of the cub's teeth had hardly come out. The creature hung from its perch upside-down, tail lashing behind it, paws extended, mouth open, nose sniffing the air not one finger-width away from the brim of Meredith's hat. The cub's black, fuzzy coat reflected the moonlight in pale blue hues.

She leaned back slowly, as far as her burden would allow. With glacial movements she raised the semiautomatic crossbow once more. Meredith's lips curled in distaste as her finger gradually pressed—

Another cub jumped out of the shadows and attacked the lashing tail in front of it. The first one yelled a startled meow and scrambled to a different platform, moving to chase its fleeing aggressor. They disappeared into the darkness among muffled fighting sounds.

Meredith exhaled her held breath and hurried to the window. It was shaped as a tall wedge, point at the top, and the glass was stained with a texture that cast moving shadows on the sill. Like all the others, it was sealed shut.

Wordlessly she motioned Four-Thirteen to lean against the wall, guiding his hand to hold on to the girdle. She pulled out the roll of igneous parchment and ripped two long strips, then a shorter one— all done by touch, as she couldn't see what she was doing. Meredith licked each strip in a few spots before plastering them all along the window's perimeter. The parchment materialized against the glass surface the moment she released it.

She dug through another pocket in her robe. "See? I knew all this stuff would be useful one day," Meredith told the serf between wheezing pants, conscious that he couldn't hear. "I wasn't just filching things for no reason all this time."

Her firestarter lit the end of each parchment. Soon after, heat ate into the glass with a high-pitched sizzle, prompting the cubs to start screeching and hissing—noises loud enough to resonate well beyond the den's confines.

So much for noiselessly propping the glass against the wall. The textured sheet came loose and turned invisible for the instant it was in contact with Meredith's boot. The kick sent it flying, spinning all the way to ground level outside, where it shattered in a huge spray of tiny fragments. Strands of molten glass stretched and waned like wilting stems all around the newly opened window.

Without a moment to waste, they gingerly stepped onto the narrow ledge outside. The dens jutted out in a dome from the holding pens. Meredith oriented herself based on the landmarks she could see: there's Galvan Tower, there's Broken Peak, over there is Sabrena's obelisk. They needed to go right, around the building and Distal-Tarkisward.

She reached behind her back, between shirt and robe, and detached from its harness the last tool they should need. It was a rectangular slab, as big as a large notebook, with an ovoid protrusion at its center. Meredith uncoupled the controller and dropped it in a pocket, then felt around the slab's contours until she found the corner notch. She pried at it and the trinket unfolded, once, twice, clicking firmly in place with each motion.

The former notebook had become a doormat-sized platform humming in her hands. She placed it on the ledge in front of them with the fervent hope that it hadn't been damaged during all the cat wrestling. It sure had damaged her back plenty.

The trinket, hovering over the wooden ledge, became visible as soon as she stopped touching it: a black dais, glossy once upon a time, with rounded edges chipped in places. Its surface was scored with sinuous bronze patterns of tiny glowing glyphs. Shallow indentations housing the appropriate directional knobs marked where her feet should go.

Meredith held the controller in one hand while guiding her rescuee onto the dais, struggling to fit together while correctly placing her feet. Once more the trinket became invisible. As the safety repulsion field engaged around them and the controller came alive against her faced-down palm, she was *almost* too frazzled to remember the accident that had seen her license revoked in perpetuity.

Almost. In quick succession the images flashed again, the tardy rush to the ceremony, losing control upon arrival, plowing through the banquet and the decorations and the row packed with dignitaries. Mifraulde, up in her high seat, horrified, livid, mortified.

The ground below started spinning. She squeezed her eyes shut.

"Nothing will happen," Meredith muttered. "It'll be fine. Nothing will happen."

She reopened her eyes and simply added *looking down* to the list of things she'd best ignore at that moment—noted right under the feline screeches and juditor stomps rising from the entrance to the dens. She raised the controller and tilted it forward. The dais took off just as a fireball the size of a grown hog shot under their feet. It rushed by close enough to make her legs feel like she'd just jumped into an oven.

"Don't look at it don't look at it don't look at it—"

Meredith fought the controller's inertia and pushed it to propel them as fast as they could go. The tilt necessary to compensate their sudden acceleration rendered them almost horizontal. In muttered gibbering she reassured herself she was not about to become an airborne hunk of charred flesh. As they picked up speed, Brena zoomed below them at a stupid rate.

Followed by lobbed fire and angry hisses, a transparent shade coursed under the moonlit skyveil, its flight swift like wind through the flowlines.

THEY CRASH-LANDED in a dark alley that ran along the crumbled city walls, behind Farshaw Street and a few intersections away from Blackened Square. The dais bumped a rooftop as they came in for landing, which made it wobble and ruin the orientation of the backthrust, which sent them rolling on cobblestones.

It wasn't too bad a crash, by Meredith's past record.

Their trip ended abruptly against the wall, and as if on cue the invisibility girdle whimpered dead. It took Meredith a good while to form coherent thoughts, and a bit longer to find her footing. Next morning's bruises were already blooming, while her stomach felt as if clenched in a fist.

"'Scuse me," she squeaked. She took a few steps to the side and retched. What was it, the third meal she spewed this moon cycle? At least this time she had an aural inhibitor to mask her abject heaves.

Not so for the human's groans, which had become dangerously loud. Four-Thirteen huddled against the brick wall, bracing a leg that had already been injured before landing. Meredith wiped a tissue across her mouth and switched off the aural dampener.

"Sorry," she slurred, but was interrupted by a coughing fit. Her throat felt like she'd swallowed sandpaper. Her belly still writhed with motion sickness and nerves. She tried again, nearly breathless. "Sorry, that was my fault. We're almost there."

Meredith stood upright and had to lean against the wall for support as the alley spun all around. Her field of vision shrunk to almost black; it returned over the course of several deep breaths. She goaded herself to collect the dais—which had powered off farther down the cobbles, perhaps damaged beyond repair—and folded it into its harness.

"Let's go. Only a few more steps."

There wasn't a whole lot of gratitude in his glower, but he cooperated when she draped his arm around her shoulders and hauled him up. He was clearly on the verge of screaming as they hobbled toward an unassuming metal door at the bottom of the alley.

"It's almost over," she said, mostly to herself. The door was a solid mass of gray, its only feature an indented rectangle at brow height. She'd almost knocked when she realized her face was plain for all to see.

With her free hand she tugged the floppy brim of her hat as low as it would go. The hood of her robe went over it, mushing it all down. She'd brought her mask, it was bundled in another pocket, but she'd need both hands to put it on. Four-Thirteen might not make it back to his feet if she dropped him again.

Meredith knocked in three sets of three and waited.

The indentation slid open, revealing faint light behind a metallic lattice.

"Can I help you? Are you lost?" A gasp sounded on the other side. "*Who is that?*"

Thirty-Seven again, hex the sun. Meredith scoured her brain to recall the entry code. "*The night is calm, but the winds are changing*. Open up quick, they could be after us."

"Are you mad? I'm not letting *that* in without approval. What's your number?"

"It's Sixty-Two, I said the words, let us in!"

"That's last cycle's words. Wait there, I need to ask about this."

Meredith pounded the door. "There's no time, this is sanctioned business, you'll be suspended if you delay any longer, *just let me in already!*"

There was a hesitant pause. After a lengthy series of rattles and clacks and opening bolts, the door swung inward. "No-one told me about this," Thirty-Seven said. "You'd think they'd let me know when a flaming *human fugitive* is coming."

"Just an oversight. Now, please—"

"You look terrible." She looked the newcomers up and down. "Sixty-Two. Since when do you go on field missions?"

Meredith shifted under her burden, head firmly downcast. "I've no time for your questions. Where's Ella?"

Thirty-Seven made a petulant pause. "What, you're a veteran now? That's *Eleven* for you. I don't like your tone. Last I knew you were only an informant, this seems dreadfully—"

"Where in the frothing gape of Shaglaroth is Eleven!"

The witch startled and stared as if she'd just seen the door spontaneously combust. "She's is in the meeting room. Assembly is still going."

"Fine, great, just what I needed." Meredith shoved past Thirty-Seven's girth and shambled down the narrow stairs, injured human in tow. The hallway leading to the meeting room had never seemed so long.

Someone came to the doorway as Meredith neared it, no doubt alerted by all the grunting and scraping noises. "What—"

Meredith thrust her burden at whoever it was. "This is Four-Thirteen," she said between pants. "Help me carry him to the table, please."

"*What?*" The stranger pulled her hands away from the load, the shift in balance nearly throwing Meredith and her charge to the floor.

"Hold on to his arm and help me!"

The stranger seemed too shocked to argue. The sound of conversation had died abruptly, and those seated around the large wooden table watched in appalled silence as the newcomers labored their way to the middle of the room. Two of the nearest witches quickly stood and got out of their path when Meredith gave no signs of stopping.

They laid down the battered serf as delicately as they could. She eyed his leg with worry. If it wasn't broken, it was close to it. His arduous breathing filled a meeting room that had fallen into a stiff silence.

When Meredith looked up—which, with the smushed hat, reached as far as chest-high—Brena Eleven stood at the head of the table, fingers clutching the wood as if trying to splinter it.

"What have you *done*, Sixty-Two?"

Meredith felt the heat of her glare and the scrutiny of every other witch in the room like a line of searchlights focused on her skull. "I—"

"Is this not the serf for which you requested help?"

"Yes, Eleven."

"And what did we decide, not even *one week* ago?"

"That it was too risky, but—"

"*Pure clodbait,* those are the exact words I used, before making it perfectly clear, *again,* that you were not to contact us for at least a cycle."

"Yes, but—"

"And yet you turn up here, bringing this *wreck* to our door, risking *everything* we—"

"Can't you help him first and yell at me later? Soot and ash, look at him."

The forewitch stalled, glowering at the interruption. Her stance softened at the sorry sight before her.

"Fifty-One," she said after a moment of consideration, "fetch Twelve, if you please. Tell her to bring tools to treat a broken leg and . . . lacerations, contusions, burns and possible internal bleeding."

The stocky witch who had helped carry Four-Thirteen disappeared through the doorway. A bitter tone entered Brena Eleven's concealed voice. "The Judicars spared no resource on this one, it looks like. Or were his wounds inflicted on the way here?"

"I found him like this."

"How long until they're tearing down these walls?"

"They couldn't follow me." Meredith drew back her shredded robe and showed the spent girdle. With her other hand she fished out her aural dampener and odor neutralizer and placed them on the table. Nineteen, to Eleven's left, made a scoffing sound, while a spindly witch Meredith didn't recognize let out an appreciative whistle. The chapter's leader leaned forward.

"How did you come by *these*? You're barely—" she caught herself and bit off the rest. Meredith rushed to fill the void.

"I know I took a big risk, but I went in prepared."

"Well, regardless, we *can't* underestimate the Judicars. We're moving two shelters forwards in the rotation, effective *immediately*. You can all thank Sixty-Two for the trouble. Let us *hope* that'll be the end of it."

A chorus of groans and displeased mumbling spread around the table. The large witch that had scoffed at Meredith's trinkets seemed particularly disgruntled. "Right now? We barely got started before this interruption. I lose enough sleep as it is."

Eleven was about to respond when Fifty, uh . . . was it Fifty-One? Meredith couldn't keep all the code numbers straight. Fifty-Something returned from fetching Twelve. She was followed by a short figure that moved with quick strides and swaying gait. Her robes were tan, with the saggy complexion of a swamp dweller showing on her exposed jaw and rolled-up sleeves. She carried an oversize leather bag in one hand and long splints under her armpit.

"Where's the victim?" she asked, then moved toward the prostrate human without waiting for a response. Eleven gestured at him anyway.

"Tata, do what you can and prepare to move him. We can't stay here."

"I'll do what I'll do and you'll wait if necessary, and that's it." Twelve had plopped her leather bag beside Four-Thirteen and was pulling out the tools she'd need. "Will you fair damsels make some room for me to work, or do you plan on spectating through the night from your front-row seats?"

The varied group of witches sitting closest grumbled to their feet. "Tata" didn't spare them a second glance, already busy inspecting every one of the human's injuries.

The forewitch sighed. "Gather your belongings and prepare to travel, everyone. Nina, you have the room. I need to make arrangements to deal with our new . . . *situation.*"

She walked toward the door, passing next to Meredith, who hadn't left the human's side.

"Follow me. You and I will have *words* about this."

Meredith swallowed and nodded. Brena Eleven and her dramatic emphasis, always unnerving.

A hand clamped on her wrist before she could start moving, and she looked down to see Four-Thirteen staring at her. He pulled on his grip, leaning closer through great effort. His gaze was intense, holding her in place more effectively than any fist around her bones could.

His iris was hazel, not brown. She'd never noticed before.

"Ghon gheev," he managed to say through bloodstained teeth.

"What?"

Past cracked lips she glimpsed horrifying gaps between molars.

"Ghon gheev me wiv-vem."

Meredith processed the garbled words until they fell together into an intelligible sentence.

Don't leave me with them.

"I . . . I have nowhere else to take you. They will treat you well. You're free now."

His fist tightened. Twelve put her hand on his chest and applied gentle pressure. "None of that," she quietly said, almost tender. "You won't be moving for a while."

He didn't seem to have the strength to resist anymore. His grip eased as he all but passed out on the table.

Meredith squeezed his hand before shuffling after the forewitch.

S HAKY FROM EXHAUSTION, Meredith sat by a foldable desk as the leader of Brena's chapter arranged Four-Thirteen's fate. Eleven could've made her wait outside the door, but she was probably making a point of how much hassle the incident had caused.

Silently Meredith witnessed comm spells she couldn't have hoped to cast herself, direct voice tunnels to counterparts in two other chapters. Together they rearranged the meeting schedule and coordinated for safe lodging and an eventual smuggling to Earth. It would've been much simpler to use standard transceivers through the skyveil nodework, but such comms were terribly susceptible to surveillance.

The shimmer from the last voice tunnel faded, and Eleven turned to face a properly contrite Sixty-Two. The forewitch stared for a while, her silent intensity dampened by the bustle outside the room.

"Pull back your hood, Meredith."

She said it one step above a whisper. With some reserve Meredith complied and kept her head down. Eleven leaned elbows on the desk and entangled her fingers. "You labour for a pittance at the manufactory. How'd you come by those trinkets?"

"They're Mifraulde's discards. Artifacts gifted to her that she didn't care for. She dumps them on my lap for 'safekeeping.'"

Silence.

"Are you *certain* you were not followed or identified?"

She met Eleven's eyes. They were two black dots beneath the finely contoured mask. "Yes," she lied again, "absolutely."

More silence.

"None of the proper steps were followed for this human," Eleven said. "He could be unstable or broken beyond hope. He didn't even seem all that grateful toward you. Whatever foolish spirit possessed you to do this?"

"He's not broken. He held out for a whole week without incriminating me."

"That's inconclusive. It could be obstinance, or pride, or madness. You're not qualified to make the call."

"I had to do *something*."

"Doing *something* and dropping him on our doorstep are two very different things. You chose to endanger us all."

"I couldn't—"

She waved Meredith's words away. "Save it. I'll consider suitable discipline later. For now you will sever all contact with us for the next six cycles. No reports on Mifraulde, no meetings, and *certainly* no requests for help. Understood?"

"But I want to be here when he—"

"No, this could all be traced back to you anyway and I can't take the risk if they place you under surveillance. At the very least they'll question you in some capacity due to your connection to the fugitive."

Meredith swallowed again. She hadn't thought about that. "What's going to happen to him now?"

"You ask as if there's any doubt we'll take care of him. He's a victim, we're not Judicar thugs."

"No, I just meant—"

"I know what you meant. We'll heal his wounds and evaluate his mental state. If he's viable, we'll soft-wipe him like we do to every human we rescue, and then we'll drop him on Earth."

"And . . . if he's not viable? What makes him 'viable,' exactly?"

"That's for me to decide. I'm not here to answer your questions, Meredith. I'm already affording you an unwise amount of lenience."

"Please. I need to know."

Eleven sighed. "Understanding of the situation. Willingness to cooperate. A number of other factors. Only from what little I've already seen, I've some doubts. And he's full-grown. The older they are, the harder it is to wipe their memory without touching anything else."

"So what happens then, if he's not viable?"

"You know what happens then. We'll have no choice."

Meredith's gut shriveled. "I didn't go through all this just for you to kill him anyway!"

"Lower your voice. We'll do what we can, but if he's too unstable, there are no alternatives. That's our reality. You know death is still a better fate than their former life."

"Shouldn't *he* decide that?"

"Humans in his circumstances don't make rational decisions."

"So return him to Earth anyway! Somewhere remote. One human alone can't undo the masquerade, they'd just treat him as a madman."

Eleven leaned back in abhorrence. "One exception is one too many, you should *know* that. You're distraught. I'll pretend you didn't even suggest it."

Meredith remained in her seat, head down and lips squirming. She shouldn't have brought him here. She should've found a way to hide him, to smuggle him out to Earth all by herself . . . somehow.

Just as before, she couldn't come up with a single alternative plan.

After staring for a bit longer Eleven leaned over the table, one gloved hand palm up. It took Meredith a moment to understand the intent. With unsure movements she reached out, and black-leathered fingers gently closed around hers.

"By brood and power," Eleven said, "I will do everything I can to see him through. That's all I can promise."

Meredith gazed into the sparkling darkness past delicate eyelid lines. "I . . . I believe you. Thank you."

Eleven squeezed, then let go. "Now, repeat back to me what I told you to do."

"Oh, um. No contact of any kind for six cycles."

"Which means no contact until. . . ." She gestured for Meredith to complete the sentence.

"The . . . the thirtieth day of Bloom."

"Good. If I or any of us get even so much as a *whiff* of you before then, the Circle will deem you a liability. You don't want that. Are you aware of how the Circle deals with liabilities?"

"Yes, Eleven."

"Call me Ella." The forewitch scribbled something on a piece of paper, tore it off and stood, motioning for Meredith to do the same. "You look awful. Twenty-Three will portal you home before we move out."

"That's not necessary, I can walk, it's not far. . . ."

"It's not a request, you seem about to fall over. More importantly, you must *not* be seen outside, tonight of all nights. No doubt the search has already begun. One glimpse of your shredded robes and it will be over."

Considering the issue settled, she walked around the desk and toward the doorway. Meredith followed, but instead of opening the door, Brena Eleven leaned back against the knob.

"One last thing before I go. Would you like to be a field agent?"

Meredith blinked slowly.

Meredith stared blankly.

"What?"

"You're surprised? You singlehandedly entered the holding pens, rescued a Block One prisoner and came out unscathed."

Meredith glanced down at the tatters below her thighs. "I, um. I wouldn't say 'unscathed,' exactly."

"None of the blood is yours, is it?"

"No." She checked herself, just in case. "No, I don't think so."

"An impressive feat. Though we all risk much doing what we do, facing danger so directly is a world apart. I didn't think you had it in you."

"I don't, I just . . . didn't have a choice."

"That's rubbish, of course you did. I don't offer this lightly, Meredith. You'll still have to be tested and vetted, of course, but the choice to pursue it is now yours to make. I'm offering you a chance to make a real difference."

"But I disobeyed your direct command. Endangered everyone."

"You did, and you've been temporarily suspended, pending further penalties. One issue does not preclude the other."

Meredith's eyes darted around the paltry room without focusing on anything in particular. In her mind's eye she saw herself slinking through dark alleys, infiltrating posh houses, freeing personal slaves, battling to stay always hidden from the Judicars. Foolishly she also envisioned freeing youths from the harvest pods and breeding dens, even though the Circle would never dare cross that line.

Then she saw her own capture, the extensive sessions on a Judicar wheel and her sobbing confessions. Mifraulde's outrage and disgust as they dragged her broken body to the Blackened Square. The searing torment of a fire-wreathed purge.

Her chest clenched with anxiety.

"I can't do it," she breathed.

"You just risked everything to rescue this human. It seems to me your convictions say otherwise."

"It's different. It was my fault. I was responsible, I owed him."

"We all owe the serfs. We owe it to ourselves to rise above Puritan doctrine and pursue a better society."

"It's different. . . ."

"Is it? If *that's* the case, you still owe this debt to the Circle, don't you? This wasn't *our* operation, yet it's *us* that will keep him hidden, now. One could argue you're *obligated* to do whatever I ask, if you're so concerned with repaying debts."

It's different, Meredith insisted in her thoughts. Her weight shifted in the seat. "Well, even then, I'm useless without trinkets. I can't afford to recharge or replace what I spent today. I couldn't do it again."

"Equipment would be provided. We'd hardly expect our field agents to expend their own artifacts on every operation. Your experience with magical items is in fact a boon. Haven't you noticed? The pendulum is swinging again, less and less witches rely on raw incantation alone, and who could blame them? Technology is so much more convenient. It's the way of the future, it always was. Don't you agree?"

"Yes. Certainly."

"Clinging to the old ways will only leave us at a disadvantage. Could you imagine, if we hadn't been so extreme after the Golem Revolts? Always the problem, this all-or-nothing approach. There are *some* that disagree, of course, and some of them sit at our own table. It's dismaying, how reactionary some of us can be."

"Yes, right."

"So from where I'm standing, *you* might just be ahead of the rest. You could be the next Silver, for all I know."

Meredith looked to the side. "That's . . . unlikely."

"Your self-doubt is unbecoming. In any case, you have six cycles to consider it." With her long arms she reached behind Meredith's ears, got hold of her hood and pulled it over her eyes as low as it could go. "Now, go downstairs and show this to Twenty-Three. You know your own coordinates, don't you?"

"Yeah. Yes."

"Good. You can input them yourself. Twenty-Three won't look, there's a reason she's in charge of transportation." She gave Meredith the torn piece of paper. "I must prepare for the move. Keep to yourself in the weeks to come and don't deviate from your routine. If they question you, bore them stupid with that routine. How good a liar are you?"

"I . . . I don't know, I've only ever lied to Mifraulde."

"It doesn't even matter. It's the simplest thing. On the thirtieth day of Wane you did what you always do. That is your story."

Meredith silently nodded, eyes lost in the middle distance. Eleven opened the door to the murmur and clatter that had taken over the building.

"What are you waiting for, then? Go." She nudged Meredith's back until they stood in the narrow hallway. Witches bustled up and down the corridor, many carrying personal belongings or portable furniture. In her daze Meredith started down the path, but stopped and turned shortly after.

"Ella!"

Eleven stopped at the threshold into the meeting room and glanced over the shoulder.

"You'll let me know, somehow?"

"He's no longer your concern. Go home, Sixty-Two."

The forewitch disappeared through the doorframe. Meredith looked on for a stupefied moment.

Operative Brena Sixty-Two, informant for the Riven Circle on the Head of the Coven, now field agent prospect, wordlessly shambled her way to the space-fold in the cellar.

CHAPTER TWELVE

SEEDS

 EAD STEMS FELL IN BUNCHES, one after another. They cracked and yielded to Meredith's shears like sun-worn wheat to the scythe. She cut without rhythm, aiming each shear with deliberate precision.

On her knees she raked every husk to small piles, and every pile to a modest mound. Into the sack they went, more refuse for the hearth, more carbon for compost. She cleared every bit, until there was nothing but dark brown around patches of wilted gray.

Trowel and glove broke the soil and dug out roots. The trowel was a bit rickety, loose at the wooden handle. She could've used a shovel. She could've been done much faster. Meredith remained on her knees through the task, earth and dry sap pervading her nostrils to the exclusion of all else. It was a lengthy process, and her hands felt the strain, yet they didn't grow weary. They had done similar things many times before.

It was all dead, all the way down to every tip. She might as well have left them in, they would never revive. She painstakingly sought each tiny root anyway, and dug them out until none remained. She hadn't meant for them to die. She'd never meant for *anything* to die. The plants were not dead by her hand, and yet the guilt lumped in her chest all the same.

Meredith raked more leaves and twigs and pebbles, left nothing but damp soil. In sweeping motions she filled in the holes and smoothed the bumps, plowed and fluffed it nicely into loose clumps full of breath. The soil didn't appreciate it at first, but she didn't listen to the complaints. She couldn't have new growth without pushing that big whiner out of its comfort zone.

From the compost heap she carted a good mound of rot and distributed it in orderly piles all through the patch, equally spaced. She tilled small holes, mixed in the little rot-piles, smoothed it back to soilbed, one after another after another. Her glove became soggy. Her nose was wrinkled. Every worthy goal required unpleasant tasks performed now and then.

The seeds lay on moist cloth, lined in parallel rows at the edge of the cobbles. The tiniest of sprouts poked their heads past the shells, each one with its own twist and bend, each one a bit different than the next. They seemed eager to break formation, eager to take root and feed and grow. Eager to fix the terrible wrongness upon this tiny parcel of land.

One by one the seeds went in, pushed sprout-down by a firm finger and a soft murmur. It helped them, hearing her voice before parting. They would try harder not to disappoint. It didn't need to be words, just a hum and an unspoken wish to see them again. With the right motivation, even the most timid of sprouts could surprise you, push through and thrive against the odds.

Once every seed was tucked into their new home, she laid out the temperature control mesh, adjusted the settings and switched it on. It was the end of Wither, several moon cycles away from the warm season. These wouldn't grow in cold soil; just making them germinate had been a challenge.

She straightened upright to assess her handiwork and give her lower back a much-needed respite. Her kidneys ached fiercely. The welts had been frightening to see in the mirror, but she would've had to be outright crippled not to come out to the garden. Too many issues in need of fixing. They'd constantly get in the way of her thoughts if they weren't dealt with.

Meredith readjusted the mesh *just so,* covering every bit of the patch. She didn't have a lot of experience with Earth strains, but she knew this one to be rare and fickle. It would take weeks to even see the first green. There would be uncertainty, and there would be worry.

They'd be worth the trouble, though. With proper care, they'd grow to be the most gorgeous thing in her garden.

The pruners called again from the cobblestone where she'd left them—they'd been calling for a while, now—and she finally decided to answer. With them in one hand and a bucket in the other she followed the short dirt path to the fence and the curlstalks taking over it. She nodded a respectful greeting at her one apple tree, who only bore fruit when the mood struck him, and as she passed it outgrowth of a variety of descriptions twined at her ankles. "Wait for your turn," she admonished them, "you're next." Secretly she had no intention of getting to them today. It was a small lie, just to make them feel better.

The curlstalks had seemed so bold from a distance, but they cowered up close. In the first few snips Meredith quietly apologized for thwarting their efforts, but her heart wasn't in it. Their advance had to be halted or they'd eventually claim the fence as their own, and that wouldn't do. The fence belonged to her. She had built it. It was hers.

In an unplanned bout of mercy, she spared a few upstarts. They could keep going a little longer. Let them enjoy themselves, there was no harm in it. She even cupped her hand around the snips, so the young ones wouldn't witness the carnage. The least she could do was protect them for as long as possible.

One by one the offending stalks were cut down and tossed to their mass grave. No-one would remember their names. Their sap stained the blades and made her glove a bit sticky, but it was fine, it would wash right off.

The bucket filled up, got dumped on the compost pile. Curly shoots that had reached too high and too fast for dreams they couldn't have. Meredith silently mourned them.

She continued to hide the snips, but maybe she shouldn't be so lenient with the up-and-comers. Maybe she should give them hard discipline and a clear view of what would happen if they continued on their doomed path. If she were in their place, what would she rather have? The awful truth or the hopeful lie?

It was the wrong question, of course. The right question was, what was more convenient for her? She was the witch, here. She was no plant. The plant's feelings didn't *actually* matter, as long as they did what she wanted. And besides, they might look innocent, but the curlstalks were known for being greedy and untrustworthy. They'd keep growing until the whole fence came down under the weight. Give them a toe and they'd crawl up your leg.

Another bucketful, dump it on the pile. It wasn't all for naught, one way or another. By the time she was done, plump leaves and supple stems made for another green layer of future rot all on their own. Life cut short to grow *better* life. Ruthless, perhaps, but such was the way of things out here.

Now that the fence was under control, the hansels got her attention. They'd been singing their usual tune, one dissonant note for every fruit ready to be plucked from its leaf nest. She walked past timid cakepetals and the few empty rows of taters. The lush little hansel patch was abuzz with green and golden-green ripeness.

She sat on her heels—gracious ravens, her thighs hurt to stretch— and listened closely, taking her time to pinch and nudge the fuzzy fruits this way and that. It was important to get the timing right, with hansels. Pick them too early and they'd never develop the proper amount of juice or sweetness. Pick them too late, and you'd regret it the moment you took the first bite. If only she could get a better look at the colors. When had it grown so dark out here?

"Mistress?"

As soft and tentative as the voice was, it still made her jump. Looking up, Meredith found her apprentice standing right there, a few steps from the kitchen door. At that distance her latent power was a subtle thrum barely in sensory range.

"Janette," she breathed. "It's proper to announce yourself."

"I . . . I did. Twice. I said dinner is ready."

"Oh."

Meredith looked around as if coming out of a trance. The sun had almost faded from the skyveil, dusk was almost over. No wonder the garden had grown dark.

"Any problems?" she asked. "You didn't burn the eggs this time, did you?"

"No, Mistress. It looks nice. I think you'll be pleased."

Meredith's eyes lingered on the ripe hansels. They were vociferously complaining, still. Or, well, it was more like begging. They wouldn't dare make demands.

They were right, though. It would be irresponsible to abandon them now.

"Did you cover it with a damp cloth and pat it down four times like I said?"

"Yes, Mistress."

"Good. Come here, then."

Tater omelets were better served cold, anyway.

With some reserve the girl strode into the garden. Meredith gestured for her apprentice to squat by her side. After wiping the stained pruners on her apron, she handed them over. "You're picking hansels for dessert."

"Ooo, nice."

"And some more besides. I'll point at them, and you'll snip right at the base."

"Okay."

"This one. See the colour, with the golden hue at the top? It nearly glows, yeah? Here, squeeze it. A bit harder. What do you feel?"

"It's soft, but firm inside."

"That's right. That's the way you want them. Get that one, over there."

Janette stretched to reach, winced and sucked in her breath.

"What's the matter?"

A self-conscious smile curved her lips. "I'm still sore from the last time, it's so embarrassing."

"Hah. I'm sore too, if it's any comfort."

"No, it's, um—actually, I've been meaning to ask. Last night, you seemed hurt. . . ."

Meredith pondered the issue for a moment. She had no recollection of getting to bed last night. Her one vague memory after the portal had faded was of endlessly fumbling at the door locks while fatigue bore down on her like a stone slab on her shoulders. It was all blank after that.

"Uh . . . I didn't mean to wake you."

Janette cocked her head, eyebrows knit. "You don't remember what happened?"

"No, I do. I was exhausted, that's all."

The girl kept her eyes down as she fiddled with the gardening tool. "Mistress, you walked in and collapsed on your bed, and you just wouldn't respond. You didn't even close the front door. I was so worried."

"Oh. I was *very* exhausted, you see."

"I thought you were sick, so I pulled off your boots, and your robe was all torn up, and you had this harness-thing strapped to your back."

Meredith clicked her tongue off her teeth. "My favourite robe."

"And everything had *blood* on it."

"Not mine. The blood, I mean."

"Yeah, you said that. I asked."

"But you just told me I wasn't responding."

"I *know*, Mistress." The girl had widened her eyes as if to roll them, but she seemed to catch herself at the last moment. "You woke up when I pulled on the harness."

"Are you sure? I don't recall waking up."

"You don't?"

"I don't."

"You slurred a lot, and you said loads of swear words, all while fumbling with your straps."

"Swear words? Doesn't sound like me, I don't like to curse."

"Well, I *think* they were swear words. I . . . I probably shouldn't repeat any of it, anyway."

In a poignant moment of clarity, Meredith remembered uttering the words *"shrub piddling pecker monger"* amidst pained moans.

"No," she agreed, "you probably shouldn't."

"So what happened? Were you attacked? Whose blood was that? Do we have enemies out there?"

"No, no no no, don't you worry about it. I simply . . . I had something to take care of, and it got complicated. It's nothing you should know about."

"But you were hurt! I mean, *are* you hurt?"

"Just a few bruises." She pointed again. "Get that one, it's ready. The leaves will tell you, too. See how they curl away from it?"

Janette didn't do it. She laid a hand on Meredith's, instead.

"Mistress, please. You looked *really* hurt. I saw. It's been on my mind all day, I didn't dare bring it up. I thought maybe you'd healed yourself, but I don't think you did. Shouldn't you go to . . . I don't know, a hospital? Do we have hospitals?"

Meredith felt herself get flustered under the attention. She gently patted the girl's hand, then just as gently guided it back to the pruners. "Healing house. And I don't need it. You shouldn't concern yourself with how much I hurt and what I do about it." She nudged the tool in the hansel's direction. "You only need to do as I say."

"But—"

"Don't doubt my word, apprentice. Concentrate on learning. I'll be fine."

For a moment worry clung to Janette's brow. The girl looked down at their touching hands. Her lips pursed. The soft crease smoothed out.

Snip.

"Yes, Mistress."

"Good. Your turn, now. Show me what you've learned."

Janette observed and nudged and squeezed with singular devotion, every concern put aside in favor of doing well on the current lesson. Together they harvested a good dozen hansels that were *just right,* went on to groom the arc of windthrobs and the whittlenut shrub, and carefully selected the best quality mellowvane for the order due tomorrow. Meredith reserved a particularly shrewd bud for Yurena.

Dusk became night and time flitted by under crescent moonlight and courtyard coil, witch and apprentice embroiled in tending to most of the rebellious growth—the garden wasn't all that big, but it was diverse and tightly-packed. Dinner was all but forgotten as Janette learned of proper watering procedures, selective pruning, optimal compost layering, differences between wane and wilt, healthy leaf-to-bud ratios . . . she learned, most important of all, that a thriving garden required dedication and attention to detail. Just like magic, the Mistress was keen to point out. She felt terribly clever for it.

All the while, Meredith's pain grew worse in spurts. When at last the time came to go inside, she straightened up with the fruit-laden bucket in hand, only to instantly regret it. The flare-up was intense enough to freeze her in place, a groan in her throat and a grimace on her features.

Without a moment's thought Janette was by her side, bracing her arm and shoulder for support. "I can carry that," she offered, voice only slightly anxious. With her free hand she gripped the bucket's handle like it was poisoning her mentor on contact.

"I can do it," Meredith countered. It was mostly a gasp.

"Y— yes, I know, but I should do it. You're the Mistress, *I* should do the labour, yeah?"

Meredith looked at her apprentice. The girl's corner-of-the-eye gaze was an undisguised plea. Clearly she'd only been pretending not to notice the abundance of winces and sharp inhales throughout the evening.

"Please let me carry this for you."

It was more reaction than decision: Meredith let go of the burden and leaned in. What was the harm in it, really?

Janette stuck close as they walked back into the kitchen, never withdrawing her support.

CHAPTER THIRTEEN

QUESTIONS AND ANSWERS

EREDITH BRENA-GALVAN-NEUMANN."

"Yes, that's me. W– what—"

"My apologies for interrupting your work, denizen. I am Inquisitor Bohm-Sajjan. We are in the midst of an investigation and your answers could help. Don't worry about lost work, your time has been cleared for questioning by the taskmaster."

"I . . . I'm not in trouble, am I?"

"No. Not yet. You only need to answer truthfully."

"Of course, yes. This is about that filthy stunt, isn't it? Did he truly escape? Please tell me you've caught him, I've been flinching at shadows since—"

"No, that is false. Who is spreading this rumour?"

"Uh . . . I overheard in the restroom, I don't know who said it."

"Escape from the holding pens is impossible, do you understand? The object of this investigation is none of your concern. Answer my questions and cease the spread of false information at once."

"Y– yes . . . understood. I'm sorry, I'm a bit nervous. I'll help in any way I can, Inquisitor."

"Good. First off, where were you a span after dayturn on the last day of Wane?"

"That's . . . last Naughtday? Or the day before that?"

"The very early morning of Naughtday, four days ago."

"Oh. I just . . . I was sleeping. Like any other day at that time."

"Hm."

"Last Naughtday . . . yes, I was home all day, I slept in late and spent the evening—"

"Quiet while I take notes. Answer only what you are asked, denizen."

"Right, sorry."

"What did you do before then?"

"Um. I worked here all morning until twelve, then I spent the rest of the day in my garden. I went to sleep at nineteen."

"Hm. I don't suppose you have a witness for any of this."

"N– no. Well, only work, Inquisitor. I live alone and the neighbours can't see through the fence. Someone might have seen me arrive at my doorstep."

"I see. This 'filthy stunt' you mention . . . number Four-Thirteen, is it? Describe the last time you saw him."

"It was walking out that door, after he had the gall to disrespect me and my coworker. He was mandated to report for disciplinary action. I hope you guys showed him who's in charge."

"I'm an Inquisitor, I don't concern myself with petty discipline. Incidentally, I did have the displeasure of interrogating him later, after he went from misconduct to crime. Your taskmaster informed me of your interest in the goods with which he was caught."

"Well, yes . . . I was concerned I might become a suspect since—"

"Your reasons were already noted and taken into consideration. Now, did Four-Thirteen ever approach you or try to engage you in any way while he was working for this station?"

"No, thank the ravens. I'd have reported him immediately if he had."

"Has a coworker or anyone you know promoted assisting the humans, making their workload easier, granting them freedoms or rights or expressed sympathy in any way?"

"I'd never associate with anyone who did, and I'd also report them immediately."

"Hm. Did anyone you know engage Four-Thirteen in a way not prescribed by your work needs?"

"No, of course not. Well, actually. . . ."

"Yes?"

"Please understand I don't mean this as an accusation of any kind, but . . . Devalka would often taunt and humiliate him for no reason other than her own amusement. I can't disagree with the sentiment, but it always struck me as a mite unprofessional. Personally, the less we interact with those animals, the better."

"Hm. Your coworker made no effort to conceal her sadistic abhorrence for them. You merely confirm her story."

"Good, I didn't want to get her in trouble, I just mentioned it since—"

"Fine, yes. One last question. Have you ever seen this before?"

"Huh. It's . . . some kind of fancy pen?"

"No. It's dart ammunition for a semiautomatic one-handed crossbow. Does anyone you know own one?"

"Not to my knowledge, Inquisitor. I thought . . . aren't all weapons registered and traceable to their owners?"

"Yes, all *legally purchased* weapons are, but not custom-made ammunition. The owner is obviously a criminal, denizen."

"Oh, yes, of course, that makes sense. I'm sorry, I wouldn't even know where to get one in the first place."

"Hm. Make sure it stays that way. These are dangerous tools only the proficient should handle."

"I couldn't agree more, Inquisitor."

"I suppose that'll be all for now. I might return as the investigation develops. Contact us through your taskmaster if you remember anything that might be useful."

"I won't hesitate. I wish I could be of more help."

"Stop spreading false rumours, then. One Coven, denizen."

"One Coven."

CHAPTER FOURTEEN

MAGIC

"ODAY," THE MISTRESS casually declared, "you will learn the basics of magic."

Janette nearly dropped the plates she was taking to the sink. She turned to look at her tutor, good eye nearly as wide as the dessert saucers she carried. "I'm ready now?"

Meredith couldn't hold back a smile. "You've been for some time, but there were other, more practical skills you needed to learn first. I've also been testing your patience and dedication. You've done very well, apprentice."

The pride and sheer pleasure in Janette's features filled Meredith with an altogether confusing warmth. In all likelihood it had nothing to do with the girl and everything to do with the jellybun indulgence she'd picked up for dessert on her way home.

"Come into the living room once you get those dishes clean. I'll be preparing for the lesson."

Her ward practically bounced with joy as she walked to the sink. Meredith left the kitchen with a glass of water in hand and pulled out a much-handled book from the shelf by her bedroom door. She reached for the satchel hanging on the doorknob and sorted through its contents.

A tenth-span later, Janette walked in to find her mentor sitting on the sofa, watching the newly-stoked hearth. An assortment of items rested on the table in front of her: the worn and aged tome; a thinner pamphlet, five pages clipped together; two ball-point pens atop a spiral-bound notebook; a black band of elastic fabric, with tiny clasps at both ends and many-shaped prongs protruding from a metal centerpiece; the glass of water; and a handful of glass beads, like flattened marbles.

"Come sit by me," Meredith said.

The girl gawked at the items with unrestrained wonder. Every trace of her increasingly sleep-deprived nights had vanished. Her breath was quicker than normal by the time she sat down.

"Relax, Janette. This will take some time."

"I'm sorry. I'm so excited. I've dreamed about this all my life."

Meredith chuckled. "It'll probably disappoint you, then."

"I doubt that very, very much."

"We'll see. Alright, let's start." She took a deep breath and let it out completely before continuing. "First I'll tell you what magic isn't, because I know you have a head full of fancy ideas. Magic isn't a cloud of energy you command with a wag of your fingers. It isn't throwing ingredients into a cauldron to curse your neighbours or spread the plague. It isn't rattling rat bones and pigeon entrails to predict the future, though some of the tribals might still tell you otherwise. Magic can't read your thoughts or sense your intent. It doesn't . . . you seem troubled already."

"Well, no, I just, I thought—what of all the witching lore? Like curses, and love potions? The flying broom and the bubbling cauldrons full of gross things. . . ."

"Thogwash, all of it, either apocryphal twaddle or exaggeration. Anecdotes run wild. Do you realise how difficult it is to balance yourself on a stick? And it's a horrible surface to run wordpaths on. We'll fly on a solid platform with safeguards, thank you."

"Oh! So you *do* fly about?" The girl appeared greatly relieved. "I've never seen you. I was afraid there'd be no flying."

"Remember the harness strapped to my back? That was the holster for my dais. I don't like using it, though. There are so many rules about it, you need to keep an up-to-date license, and I don't travel far, or much at all. I'd rather use my own two legs, they work just fine."

"You have to get a license?"

"Of course. You need to know the rules, mid-air collisions are a horrible thing."

"Of course, yes. That makes sense. And how about healing? Is there healing magic?"

"Hm, only to some extent. There's an alchemical compound that can be poured on open wounds to heal them much faster. Um . . . broken bones can be set and fused, too. Localised stasis is used instead of sedation, and sterilising surgical instruments is not ever an issue. Overall we rely on biology for the most part, though we do have excellent salves for pain and faster metabolism."

"Oh."

"What is it, why'd you ask? Are you sick?"

"N– no, never mind."

"You *have* to tell me if you're sick."

"I'm not sick, I swear. I was just hoping there'd finally be some way to fix. . . ." She vaguely gestured at her face. "You know?"

Meredith tilted her head and looked closely. "I don't see anything wrong. Fix what?"

The girl's cheeks were flustered red. "My eye, Mistress. You *must* have noticed. Everyone notices, even if they pretend not to."

The fold on Meredith's brow deepened. Her head remained cocked. "Whyever would you want rid of your witchmark?"

"My . . . what?"

"Your witchmark. The wandering eye? Oh, but of course you wouldn't know. It's a mark of prestige, apprentice. A sign of power, something to be proud of. Tremmel herself had it."

Janette stared blankly for a while, each pupil lost in a different region of empty space. She slowly brought fingertips to the skin below the half-lidded eye. "A mark of power. . . ."

"Indeed. Wandering, bleached or oddly coloured eyes, pointed teeth, deathly-white or dark-as-night skin, morbid corpulence, black tooth rot, pockmarks, blotches, hairy moles and warts and a number of other things—all witchmarks telling of a worthy brood. There's nothing wrong with you, quite the contrary."

The girl didn't seem to know how to take it. She just kept blinking, breathing sharply through her nose, eyes watery for some reason.

Meredith turned her attention back to the items on the table.

"Alright," she said, "if you're done with questions, we have our magic lesson to continue. And none of it will include a love potion or muttering over eyeball soup."

Janette's daze broke with a chuckle. She sniffled and dabbed her eyelids with the back of her hand. "It does sound quite silly if you put it like that. . . ."

"Are you *sure* you're not sick? I know for a fact humans are full of diseases and allergies waiting to happen. I don't know how you even survive."

"I'm not sick, Mistress. I'm . . . I'm better than ever." Despite her assurances, she sniffled again. "I'm ready to learn. I want to learn everything from you, I want to be just like you."

"Oh, well, um. That's exactly what we're here for, isn't it? Yes, indeed."

There it was, that warmth again. Probably just acid reflux, the stir fry had been rather spicy.

"Where did I leave off, again?"

"Magic isn't what I think it is."

"Aha, yes. Magic, *real* magic, stems from incantation, because magic is in truth a language: the language of the Universe. Each idea, each concept is contained in a specific Source word. You can write them phonetically, like in this book, or they can be written in Source glyphs, and that's what you saw on the insulation panels—it's the basis of artificing. Much like I chain the words of the English language to give you a command, we can chain these concepts to manipulate reality. It sounds simple, doesn't it?"

"So far, Mistress."

"Well, it's anything but. To cast a spell you need to understand language, infusion and sourcing. We're starting with language." Meredith gestured at the glass beads on table before them. "Now, suppose I want to use magic to move one bead, and only one bead, out of the pile and across to the edge of this table. How would you phrase that command?"

"A command? Like I'm talking to someone?"

"Yes. In plain English."

Janette pursed her lips, looking at the objects in front of her. Though her eyes were still a bit red, all of her attention had returned to the lesson at hand. "Mmmm. . . ."

"It truly can't be so complicated."

"No, but . . . I know it's a trick question, so I want to be clever about it."

Meredith laughed softly. "Just saying as much is clever enough. Simply answer, it'll move the lesson along."

"Okay. I guess, 'please move a bead to the edge of the table'?"

"Yes, that's a fine example to work with, thank you. Let's translate your command to the Source language. Here." Meredith used one finger to push the much-handled book until it rested in front of her apprentice. "You've used a dictionary before, I presume."

"No, not a paper one, Mistress." Janette was looking at it as if it were the holiest of scriptures. She ran her fingers over the in-relief lettering of the cover. *Concept Compendium*. The edition number was at the bottom-right corner.

"One hundred and thirteenth edition?"

"New concepts are discovered to this day. Our knowledge is always evolving. This edition is outdated by at least a dozen, actually."

Janette glanced at her mentor and reverently lifted the cover. After a blank page, she encountered the set of verses that Meredith had recited every morning of every day at Brena's academy:

Guard knowledge   Never let them know
Preclude freedom   Never let them go
Enforce silence   Never let them speak
Beware deceit   Mercy keeps the weak

"What does this mean?"

"Ah, just the tenets of the masquerade, it's not important right now. Get on with it, we've much to do still."

"Yes, of course, sorry." Janette flipped some pages. She passed a lengthy introduction and a few lists. "Where should I start?"

"It's in alphabetic order. There's a notch for every letter. The first half is for English to Source, look up 'move.'"

More pages flipping. "Goodness, this print is so tiny."

"I know."

"I suppose there's no such thing as the internet here?"

"I don't know what that is."

Janette chuckled as her index finger traveled down entries. "That might be the strangest thing I've heard so far. Here it is!"

"Read it aloud."

"'Move.' Um, I don't know what this stands for."

"That's just codes for compatible modifiers to this type of concept. Don't worry about it for now."

"Okay. 'Move:' code, code . . . 'reg.' stands for *regular*, I suppose? 'Relevant variants: displace, relocate, transfer.' Fff . . . *fen*? *Fen* is the translation? What are the squiggly lines?"

"They're called 'brogues' and denote the proper diction for every sound. They're *very* important. These tell you it's pronounced **Fĕṅ**." She muted the *f* to almost silent, subtly dipped the pitch of the *eh* sound during its second half, and finished with a hard, dry *n*.

"Goodness."

"It's of no concern at this moment, we're going to put it all down on paper first. Find 'bead' now, see what it says."

Janette flipped more pages. "Mmm . . . ah, there it is. Wow, it's so long. *Shal*, uh, *g– grah* . . . I don't even know, what are those symbols?"

Meredith had a knowing smile on her lips. "They need to be replaced by whichever qualities your particular bead has. You see, 'bead' is an indeterminate concept, and its Source translation has never been discovered. All we can do is approximate. For these, we'll say they're the size of your left hand's index distal phalange."

"Bosh."

"There are very few basic names left to find. If I'm honest with you, I believe 'bead' has been purposely withheld just so the classic lesson doesn't have to change. What are you waiting for, apprentice? Get to work on that translation."

They spent the next third-span converting the command to Source language, Meredith explaining grammatical rules as they went. Incantation clauses always led with an imperative and had to be nested in a specific order. Qualifiers apostrophed before nouns and should be combined in notation without spaces. Positional specifications like "beyond" and "atop" and "aligned with" apostrophed after their noun in headache-inducing sequences. A terminus clause always closed the incantation and the shape of it depended on the phonetics of the last few syllables.

"Nothing should be left up for interpretation," Meredith said. "Which bead, exactly? We don't want to move a bead that's three kilometres downfroth, but the one on this table in front of you—and there could be any number of other tables ahead, so you must specify a range. Also, we want the bead to move, but at what speed, and how far, and for how long? If you don't have it into account, you might create a supersonic projectile, or worse. And specifying these parameters isn't trivial, because what's a metre to the Universe? What's a gram, a quarter-span? These are arbitrary units, they mean nothing outside our culture. Everything must be denoted in relative terms."

"This is like word mathematics," Janette groaned.

"I warned you it might disappoint you."

"Oh, no, I'm not disappointed, I mean, there's apostrophes everywhere! There's nothing more magical than that. It's just . . . is this truly the easiest to start with? It's so overwhelming."

Meredith smiled. "That it is, and in fact that's a vital part of the lesson. Crafting magic is *difficult,* and this is why you'll continue handling brooms and washing dishes with both hands in the sink, even if you master every incantation there is. You will spend three span carefully composing a spell to move one and only one of these beads. . . ." She pressed her index finger onto one of them. "When you could just do this." She dragged it to the other side of the table.

"Guhh, three span?"

"Hm. You're quite bright. Maybe only two."

"But this spell is already researched, yes?"

"Of course. Your point being?"

"Well, we could maybe skip to the casting part. . . ."

Meredith was genuinely taken aback. "And what would be the worth of that? I thought you were willing to work for your magic, apprentice."

"Y— yes, absolutely! I was just hoping—"

Knock knock knock-knock-knock!

They turned their heads at once to the front door. It was only a moment later that the dead room clicked shut, and a quick glance verified that tome, pen and notebook were gone from the table. This girl was as fast as a flitglow scampering into the bush.

Meredith sighed and let whoever it was knock for a second time.

"Be right there," she called in sing-song. She groaned to her feet, one hand on the armrest, the other bracing her back. The bruises were slowly fading, but it was still a pain to get around.

A look through the peephole as she undid the locks showed Anna's small frame, fidgeting while she waited. Her sunken eyes were particularly dark through the distorted view, and her drawn-up cowl made her head look like a skull peeking from under a blanket.

Anna Brena-Jorel-Sauter got on her tip-toes and almost touched the glass of the peephole with her eyeball. "Has it ever been a criminal that knocks at your door?"

"There's always a first time." Meredith tried to swing the door open, but it only moved to a crack.

"I must be dangerous. I don't even warrant an open door anymore."

"Hold on." She looked down. Something was stuck under the doorjamb. A folded piece of paper?

Anna huffed. "Should I stick my hand in through the crack so you can prickle my thumb for a blood sample?"

"I should start doing that. The door is stuck, wait a mite."

Meredith bent down and pulled on the paper, wiggling it out with some effort. Somebody had pressed it in from the outside, it looked like, and must have done it after she'd arrived home. Puzzled, she dropped it in a pocket for later.

"There." She opened the door wide. "You didn't have to come, I was going out later tonight."

"I wouldn't have come if you'd managed to bring it to the manufactory like you were supposed to, hollowhead."

"I know, I'm sorry. But you still didn't have to come."

"I want it now. Hurry it up, I can't be seen standing here."

Meredith looked at the three pouches and jar on the doorside shelf and picked the pouch tagged "A.J." She handed it to the diminutive witch. "That'll be Eleven P and five."

"That's some fancy lettering there. Got too much time on your hands?"

She looked at the tag—at Janette's overly elaborate capital A and twisty, flowery J. There was an arc under the dots, mimicking a smiling face. "Just developing my artistic side."

"Yes, such a lover of the fine arts you are. How shrewd is this," she asked without inflection, holding up the bag.

"It's the shrewdest I have."

"It better be the shrewdest."

"It is."

"Here's the coin, and your old pouch." Anna shook it, producing a merry jingle. "And something extra inside because I liked what was in it."

"Oh. Joys and cheers to that."

"Joys and cheers, yeah. I heard you talking in there. You have visitors? Or are you losing your sanity already? Your brood has a history."

Meredith stared for a moment before pocketing the jingly pouch. "I was talking to my familiar."

"Your familiar." She stopped fidgeting long enough to look nonplussed. She rolled her eyes. "You mean your spoiled *pet thog,* don't you?"

"Desmond is an excellent familiar."

"Yes, I'm sure. Well, don't let me hold up that conversation any longer, you must have so many issues to discuss." Anna tucked the order deep inside her robe and turned to leave. "I'm gone. I didn't get this from you. I was never here."

"As always. Wary's worth!"

The witch waved dismissively without looking back, energetic steps taking her through the eerie garden and out the mangled fence. She turned her head and raised an eyebrow as she passed it, but refrained from yelling an admonishment. Anna mounted her gorgeously lustrous dais and flew off in a heartbeat.

Only then did it occur to Meredith that anyone flying over her house could have seen her "apprentice" tending the garden this past week.

She closed the door, leaned against it and blew out her pent-up breath. Quickly she stepped over to the cracked-open window and shut it all the way, rolling eyes at herself for all her careless indiscretions. "One day your luck will run out," she muttered.

The new weight in her pocket reminded her of the other item she'd stowed there. Meredith pulled out the doorstopper and spent an inordinate length of time picking at its elaborate fold. Why hadn't they simply used the drop-box?

I don't know what you've done to me.

I think about you constantly.

I must touch you again.

Make time for us. I guarantee you won't regret it.

You know where to find me.

-Y.

Her eyes were wide and blinking profusely by the last sentence. Meredith reread the creased note repeatedly, heat burning in her chest. She read it a fifth, a sixth time. Exhaling a tremulous breath, she folded the note, tucked it in one of her robe's inner pockets and walked away from the front door.

She unfolded and read the note a seventh time, standing by the lab's entrance. Her hand lingered on the door handle. Could she afford to cut the lesson short and make a trip to the library?

Meredith abruptly shook the idea out of head, crumpling the paper-full of temptation back into her robe. "Concentrate, you braden shlug."

She could sense Janette perking up, paying attention to her approach. Meredith knocked. "It's—" Her voice cracked. She cleared her throat. "It's safe."

After some muffled steps key turned in lock, and Janette swung the door open. The worn tome was in her hand, index finger wedged between pages.

"I hope you don't mind I took this," she said while getting out of the way.

"No, no, that's fine. Good initiative." Meredith stepped inside. "I do need to ask you not to be so creative with the pouch tags. Try to emulate my handwriting, it's a sign of efficiency and professionalism."

"Aw. Of course, Mistress."

"Also, we'll be having all lessons in here or in the kitchen from now on, and you're forbidden from going to the garden without my express permission. It occurs to me I've been careless lately. Over time, it's easy to forget you're not supposed to be sensed in any way. We'd both be in serious trouble if you were." She paused briefly. "I know it must seem like pointless tradition to you, but it helps keep history fresh in our minds."

"Oh, I don't think that at all. It's smart! Remember what's happened so it never happens again. I get it."

"Well, good." Meredith stopped by the bed, where pen and paper rested on white linen. Several lines of would-be incantations were written down, most of them messily marked or annotated toward refinement. "Wouldn't you rather use the desk?"

"Um. I suppose I should have."

She looked back at the girl. "But?"

Janette cringed and stammered. "I always did my homework on the bed, so . . . if I use the bed, it feels more like . . . like this is my room. I'm sorry, I know I must earn it, I was only fantasising."

Meredith kept her expression stern. She looked around pensively, eyes stopping on the feather cot in the corner, the lone bookcase half full with trinkets and supplies, the small writing desk and the wall-spanning workbench on the far end of the room that housed the assembled soundstill.

"You worked hard to put this together. Do you like how it turned out, apprentice?"

"It's lovely, Mistress."

"Lovely? I'm aware a young human girl would rather have a more colourful environment."

Janette shrugged. "I never cared all that much." A brief pause. "The shelf could use a dragon or two."

"Hah." Meredith paced about some more, wistfully regarding her surroundings. She stopped by the workbench and looked out the window above it for a good while. A part of her knew she was enjoying this a bit too much.

"We'll see what can be done about that," she finally said, "since you'll be spending most of your time in here from now on. You may move in."

The apprentice let out a delighted yelp and nearly tackled Meredith to the floor. "Thank you thank you thank you thank you thank you!"

Mistress Meredith broke out in laughter as she braced the wall with her one free hand. "Alright, fine, get it all out." She patted the girl's shoulder and fixed her hair. "You can let go now."

"Thank you so much, Mistress. I promise to always keep it clean and tidy, and I won't touch any of the stuff on the shelves without permission."

"We'll eventually get to many of those. You'll be taking apart some of them, even. For now, we need to focus on the foundations of your knowledge. Go fetch everything and move it to this desk."

Janette scampered off, so eager it was almost comical. Meredith took pen, notebook and tome to the writing table and reviewed the girl's progress.

"How in Tarkai's charred hovel did she work this out so fast?"

Near the top was their joint effort, a full paragraph that was the almost-complete incantation. Janette had kept going, carrying it to its predictable conclusion, though she'd used the wrong terminus clause. Meredith wasn't surprised the girl had figured out this much.

But then she'd crossed out the alignment clause and written a different one, realizing she could shorten the spell significantly by obviating the table's position. In the next line she'd worked around using the table altogether, effectively cutting the incantation in half. She'd shortened it further by omitting relative distances in favor of trajectory intersections—she'd simply have to point with her finger as she cast—which also let her imply which bead would move out of the pile, as opposed to pinpointing its location with words. There were a few misused terms, two flaws in the use of modifiers and a lot of misdrawn brogues, but the core concept of the spell was viable.

Janette walked in with arms full of items and a pocket bulging with beads. Her mentor looked up from the paper. "This is impressive. I was at the door for hardly a tenth-span."

"Oh! So it's good? I was afraid I might be scribbling gibberish."

"There are a number of mistakes, but you have the basics down. We can finish it later. Now come, give me the water and set up here."

Meredith leaned against the desk and took slow, deep breaths as she watched her apprentice lay the items in a neat line on the desk. The thought of embarrassing herself on this part was mortifying. She took a small sip, moistening a suddenly-dry throat.

"Knowing the language is vital," Meredith began, "but it isn't enough. In order to cast any spell, you need to know about infusion."

There it was again, that hungry shine in the girl's eyes. She looked ready to devour Meredith's next words like they were caramel-coated nuggets of wisdom.

"Infusion entails channeling your power into your voice so it resonates with the properties of reality. This is an oversimplification, but think of it as speaking in the proper volume and tone so the Universe will do as you say."

Janette took a moment to parse the sentence. "Like . . . a prayer? Is the Universe our god?"

"No, don't be silly. Well, *some* still indulge in eldritch worship, especially down in Tarkis, but it's all nonsense. Infusion is more like . . . taking your interaction with reality to a deeper level. Or maybe a higher level." Meredith waved her hand dismissively. "It doesn't matter, truly. I never concerned myself much with the philosophical side of things, and neither should you. Us artificers focus entirely on the practical application of spells. Let the self-important windbags at the conservatories talk themselves to sleep on metamagic."

Janette returned her mentor's conspiratorial smile, but she was still visibly curious.

"Maybe I have a book about it lying around here somewhere," Meredith added, "but you won't have much spare time to read it, I'll make sure of that. You can distract yourself with such things when you have a lab of your own."

The mention of the wonderful future to come brightened Janette's face. "Of course, Mistress."

"Right. Well. To pour magical power into your voice, you must learn how to draw it out. How easily you do so depends on your attunement. There are rigorous definitions for all these terms, but it's really all interchangeable—power, attunement, magical talent and so on. You know what I'm talking about, yes? You must be aware of it by now, probably you've been for a long time. There's this pent-up presence inside you that's like—"

"Like a fire that burns without heat. Ooh, I get it now."

Meredith quirked an eyebrow. "That sounds familiar."

The girl hesitated. "It's . . . from *Gallia's Burning Desire*. 'A fire that burns without heat, it yearns for release yet bows at your feet.' I found it in the sanctioned shelf," she hurried to add.

"Oh. Um. Yes, well. There are a lot of embellishments in that book, and it's all mostly fiction, you understand. Many artistic licenses."

"Ah, I see."

For some reason Janette's face had become dreadfully flustered.

"Are you well?" Meredith asked.

"Yeah, yes, I'm fine, I just thought. . . ."

"You thought?"

"It's kind of an adult book? Like . . . *really* adult." Her good eye wandered everywhere that wasn't up at Meredith. "I thought maybe you'd left it there by mistake."

"Hm. It's just a silly love story, I thought nothing of it. Oh, is it forbidden for human females to engage in such things? I'll admit I haven't kept up with your customs."

Janette's ears looked like they could've been used as hand warmers. "No, they do. Some do. It's just—there were lots of *details,* and I hadn't, uh . . . can we please get back to magic now?"

"Of course, yes. Drawing out your power, pouring it into your voice. That pent-up sensation, that fire you mention? It's scattered all over your body, in your flesh. You must gather it and push it forth. It's a matter of focus."

"But how? I've tried so hard, I truly have. Sometimes it felt like *something* was happening, but . . . I only got a headache."

"Ah, that's because there's another half to it. You must give your voice the proper shape. It doesn't come naturally."

The words *I don't understand* might as well have been written on the girl's forehead. Meredith's chuckle was painstakingly casual. "My, I haven't shown you, have I? I should have started with that."

She cleared her throat again and breathed deep until she felt ready. After a glance at the expectant girl she breathed some more, taking yet another sip of water.

"This is what infusion sounds like."

Breathe in. Breathe out. Breathe in, constrict and distend the throat in a very specific manner, channel forth her trickle of latent power.

She sustained a wordless note that reverberated beyond simple airwaves, as if her voice had folded over itself and split down seven different paths. She wavered slightly at the start, but remained strong for a good millispan. The expression of her modest power, raw and purposeless, dispersed around her in an intangible cloud that quickly vanished.

Janette gaped at her teacher in astounded reverence. "How do you *do* that?"

Relief and satisfaction swelled in her chest. Meredith slid the stack of clipped papers toward her pupil.

"*A Practical Guide to Infusion*?" Janette read.

"You'll need to study it thoroughly. I'll get you started with the classic initiation exercises, then it'll only be a matter of practice."

Janette was leafing through it. "I've never heard anyone do that with their voice."

Meredith nodded. "You need both the vocal cord training and the attunement channeling, otherwise it only comes out as a pitiful croak." She reached for the choker on the desk. "This will help, lift your chin."

With both hands she stretched the flat band around Janette's throat, ensuring the metal piece and all of its prongs made proper contact. The girl winced at the pinpricks. Meredith smiled, knowing exactly how unpleasant it was. She'd worn one of these for well over a year.

"Now," the Mistress said, "this is a test. I passed this test, as every witch must. I hope you are ready."

Never had she seen a face so quickly overtaken by anxious determination.

"It's quite simple," she continued as she latched the clasp. "When I tighten this, you won't be able to breathe anymore—not unless you channel your power forth. If you fail, you will die. Understand? Hold still, now."

Janette gasped and recoiled; even her lazy eye widened. "What—"

"It's a joke, I'm joking! It's perfectly safe, see?" She pulled on the elastic fabric, which snapped back to Janette's skin with a faint *pap*. "Nothing to worry about."

The girl touched it warily, though she was already giggling through quick breaths. "Mistress! That was so mean!"

"You looked about to faint."

"I believed every word! I didn't know you could be so mean. . . ."

"Ha! I'm a witch. I am wicked. And don't you ever forget it." She adjusted the metal piece, much to Janette's discomfort. The girl's pulse thumped under Meredith's fingers, though it didn't quite race. "Truly now, all you need to fear is a bit of a rash, if you wear it for long. How does it feel? You *can* breathe, yeah?"

She rolled her eyes self-consciously. "I can breathe, Mistress. Though it does press into my throat. It's hard to speak."

Indeed, Janette's voice now faltered to whispers in places.

"Right. It's supposed to. It helps your voice box take the proper shape. Incantations require strength and confidence."

Janette sniffed a short chuckle. "No wonder my magic never worked. It takes more than waving your arms and wishing for something really hard."

"Ah, and you benefit from centuries of research and terrible trial and error. Our version of magic is much more refined and formal than it used to be. Imagine how difficult it was in ancient times, with all the primitive ritual and dark worship—do you see why there's so much superstition around the craft?"

"I do, Mistress."

"Good. Now you know about infusion. Only sourcing remains, and it's fairly straightforward. You see, energy must come from somewhere. You can't simply create it at your fingertips."

Janette lit up like she'd found the way out of a terribly confusing maze. "I know about that, conservation of energy! That's funny, Ms. Jamison covered it in her last lesson."

"Ms. Jamison?"

"My science teacher. Well, she used to be my science teacher. She was nice."

Meredith frowned. "You didn't tell me you served a different Mistress before."

"Oh, no, no, teacher as in, you know, school? They put us all in a classroom and everyone listens to the lesson and so on?"

"Ah, an Instructor, of course, I see. Why was she nice? I suppose she didn't thump you as hard as the others?"

"Huh?"

"Maybe she spared you the scalding water. I had an Instructor that had a few favourites, and my brood-sister never got scalded."

"That's dreadful! Your teachers really did that?"

"I know, it was so unfair. Everyone should get scalded equally, they're not supposed to play favourites."

"That's not what I—"

Meredith waved the issue away. "We're never going to finish if we keep getting side-tracked. Like I was saying, every spell needs a source. You follow so far?"

"Y– yeah. Yes, Mistress."

"Good, back to the beads, now. If you want to push one bead with your hand, you will have to use your own energy to do so, correct?" Meredith demonstrated as she spoke, pushing a bead back and forth with one finger.

"Yes."

"There are only a few sources of energy I can use to move this bead: my own, that of some contraption, and little else. I have to touch it somehow, I'm limited by proximity, physical state, the laws of energy transference and so on. Yeah?"

Janette nodded, hanging on to every word.

"Magic isn't nearly as limited. The spell still needs a source of energy, but the laws are flexible on where it comes from. You can specify a nearby fire, the wind outside, the thermal reserves below, the biochemical stores of things around you—or your own, which could lead to a fatal thaumaturgic drain. And yes, you can source living things, animals, humans, even other witches whose attunement can't match yours. Attunement Duels are a bit of a sport, very popular in Tremmelton."

And dormitories full of juvenile witches eager to prove themselves at the expense of their peers, Meredith didn't add.

"Oh, wow. Isn't that dangerous?"

"No, no, the spell is minor, so the loser only gets very tired. But you're right to be concerned: weaponising sourcing against other witches is malfeasance of the first order. You'll become a Dire Criminal on the spot, regardless of context. The witches of old called it a drain hex. A truly horrific death."

The apprentice continued nodding, properly daunted.

"Glad you understand. Now, like any transference of energy, it needs a conduit. *You* create that conduit, you become it—and that's the bottleneck in the power of an incantation, given an infinite source. Many factors affect the efficiency of the transference, like distance and type of energy and conversion rates . . . a fair bit of mathematics involved." She smiled. "We won't be going into much of it, you don't need to make that face."

"Oh, s– sorry. I don't like it much."

"That's alright. I don't like it either. The basics are quite intuitive: closer is better, and the same energy type between source and target is most efficient. But no matter how much you optimise, there's always something lost along the way, because no energy transference is one hundred percent efficient. The seepage contributes to the aura you'll sense every time magical power is channeled."

"That's what it was, just now? When you . . . infused?"

"Mm, not exactly. What you sensed was my latent power, brought forth by infusion. It dispersed without being used, so you sensed it more strongly, differently than you would've if I'd cast a spell. Understand?"

"I– I think so? Yes. I think I do."

"Tell me if you don't understand, it's fine to ask questions."

"No, I understand, yeah."

"Alright, well, that's about it, then." Meredith reached for the notebook and placed it in front of her apprentice, pointing. "The source is specified at the very beginning of the spell. You could leave it out for something as minor as this, but it's always safe to include it."

"What happens if you don't?"

"Ah, I was getting to that. *Anything* could happen. Twelve times out of thirteen the energy will be sourced through the path of least resistance, but there's a significant degree of stochastash ... s– stochaseticy. . . ." Meredith slowed down to spell every syllable: "Stochasticity. Yes."

"I don't know that word."

"It's a fancy way of saying 'randomness.' Reality is connected in ways we sometimes can't predict, and a completely unexpected source might be tapped—from the stove, to the flowlines, to the fat under your skin. It's the same way for the wording of your spells: if you're not specific enough, *most of the time* the spell will work on whatever is closest, or most convenient. But not always, and that's why we're careful. It's part of why we isolated this room, it limits possible sources and targets to the confines of these walls."

"Oh. Makes sense." Janette looked to be re-reading the last iteration of the written spell, perhaps already puzzling out how to include a suitable source. She lifted her head. "So all those magical items you have—"

"Artifacts. Or trinkets."

"Those artifacts, do they all need a source when you use them?"

"Yes . . . yes, they do. In one way or another."

She hadn't planned to mention the spark just yet, but inspiration struck. Best to get it out of the way now.

"The cheap ones will require you to have a source ready," she carried on, "while the low-power ones can function through whatever environmental source is available, or your own body heat, and many don't even require you to know any magic to use them. Most powerful artifacts, though, especially the dangerous ones, will be built to obey only certain infused commands. And those artifacts, the ones that move mountains, and bend light, and shape reality? For those . . . you need the spark."

"The spark? Like, electricity?"

"No, no. Tell me, did you ever feel something odd when near some of your peers? As in, oddly attracted to them? A special kind of scent only *you* sensed?"

Janette's eyes widened. "Yes! Oh god, yes. Several times. Dana and Bridget always said I got the silliest crushes, but I knew that wasn't it. I thought I was mad."

"That's your nascent Hunger, and it will drive you mad,"

Meredith imagined saying. "Not at all," she actually said. "Only a witch can sense the spark. It resonates with our talent, they attract one another. It's stronger for some witches than others."

"This explains so much. . . ."

"The spark resides in all of us witches," Meredith lied, "and many humans, too. It courses through you, in your blood, every cell of your body, a source of magical potential without match."

"Really? But I don't feel it with you, why's that?"

"Oh, that's because . . . because I'm a grown witch, and I've learned to control it. Building powerful trinkets is my profession, I could hardly do that without my own supply, yes? Besides, can you imagine, going through life with that kind of craving in your mind? Insanity. No, we all have it in abundance. In fact, you could say it's the blood the runs through Galavan's veins. Everything would collapse without it."

Janette nodded at every other word, grave and thoughtful. Not one hint of doubt or suspicion at the questionable bits.

"When you say blood, is that, like . . . *literal* blood?"

Meredith pondered her answer. No way around this one. Janette would have to know sooner or later.

"Yes," she said, then amended, "well, not the 'Galavan's veins' part. That's figurative. But yes on using your spark for artificing. Empowering our creations is not without pain. I hope you're not squeamish."

The girl took it without distress, just one more piece of information to fit alongside the rest. She nodded one more time. "The price of power. That's only fair."

"It doesn't bother you?"

She tilted her head and considered it, as if being bothered hadn't even occurred to her. "Well, I want to be a witch, and that's part of what it takes, so. . . ." She finished her sentence by pursing her lips and shrugging one shoulder.

Meredith gave her an approving smile. "Exactly, yes. We do whatever it takes. I'm glad you understand."

Indeed, hard to find a statement closer to universal truth. A true witch did whatever was necessary in the pursuit of her goals. If there was a common trait to every lauded figure in the history of Galavan, that was it.

Pragmatic.

That was the word that best defined a worthy witch. Meredith held it in her mind and branded it onto her thoughts. She would do whatever it took.

"Sooo . . . what now?"

She startled. "Huh?"

"What should I do now, Mistress?"

"Oh! Well, now I give you the basic exercises so you can practice until bedtime. I have errands to run."

"Ah. Okay."

"What's with the look?"

Janette's disillusioned expression switched to an embarrassed grimace. "I just thought . . . well, at first I thought maybe I'd cast a spell before the day was over, but I didn't realise it would be so hard. So, since I'm not casting a spell any time soon, maybe you'd planned to finish by moving the bead with your own magic? It'd be great to see what I have to look forward to."

Meredith tried to hold back and not jump too quickly to the excuse she'd prepared.

"Mm, yes, that *would* make sense, would it not?" She drummed fingers on the desk. "But then you'd hear it, and you're smart enough to pick it up ear-to-lips. And I couldn't possibly have you cheating, now could I?"

Janette was properly horrified at the suggestion. "No way, I'd never cheat!"

"Hm, are you sure? You wanted to skip to the end earlier. . . ."

"Well, I just—I didn't think it through, I didn't mean it like that, I—"

"Alright, alright, calm down, I was only teasing. What I meant is, it would spoil the lesson if I cast the spell. Like me telling you the ending of a novel."

"Oh. Yeah. I guess that's fair. . . ." The girl looked down at her fingers as they pinched the fabric of her robe. "I guess I was really looking forward to seeing some magic at last."

She glanced up, one eye laden with enough heartbreaking disillusionment to make up for the other. She appeared so crestfallen that Meredith couldn't help but laugh. "I've a feeling that sad look of yours got you what you wanted more than once before, apprentice."

Janette's fluster made a fierce comeback, climbing all the way to her hairline. "I don't know what you mean."

"I'm sure you don't." She paused, internalizing a sigh. "You want to see some magic, you say. I suppose it's only natural."

She hadn't truly expected to avoid a demonstration. The promise of wonderful things to come could only go so far before the girl's trust and enthusiasm waned. Eventually the Mistress would have to prove herself on her own merit, without tricks or trinkets.

She'd prepared just the thing.

"You seemed concerned the other day fire and lightning wouldn't be possible with our magic," She walked to the door and opened it. "Let me show you something. Come into the living room."

The words captured Janette's full attention. Soon they stood side-by-side on the rug behind the sofa, mentor poised with calm concentration, apprentice expectant in wide-eyed reverence.

Meredith raised her hand, palm up. "Have you ever wondered what a fireball is made of?"

A hesitant beat. "F– fire?"

"Ah, but fire is not a material. It's a byproduct of combustion. To have a fireball, something must be *set on fire!*"

She launched into the spell without delay for maximum dramatic effect. Her fingers curled to conceal the ball of yarn that would soon become a small fireball hovering above her palm.

"**šhä'vēr cŏr Fæ į ŏṅ'ŷǎn'tħā ünđ Riṅ f̃r̃ēiŵṅ īlē'élųē ŏṅēş'ŷǎn'šųḷ vǎ'vēr úm!**"

Her voice wavered on the positional relative to her hand, pronouncing it *šũḷ* instead of *šųḷ*. What was meant as *above* come out as *ahead*.

With a loud *fwoosh,* the blooming jade in the corner lifted off the ground and burst into flames.

Janette gave a little jump as she faced the mystical burning plant. She didn't see Meredith's eyes widening to near-roundness or her mouth silently wailing in horror. For a few appalling moments Meredith watched the fire consume leaves and flowers, eat at the plant's stem . . . and continue to grow, fueled by the sourced hearth. It soon was licking the walls behind it, the wooden beams above it, devouring fuel of its own. She severed the link dribbling through her meager talent, but it was already too late.

"It's . . . beautiful. . . ."

Janette was as if entranced, unwitting or uncaring of the obvious danger. She took a step toward the floating fireplant. Meredith's voice-in-thoughts shouted through the panic: *Do something!*

Getting water would take too long, and tossing a blanket over the blaze would only set the blanket on fire. The only way to choke the flames quickly enough was. . . .

Her mouth bowed in dismay at the prospect, yet her thoughts churned on, trying to recall every word needed for the spell, trying to improvise together all the necessary clauses. "Ahead" was an easy enough *šũḷ,* yes. A rectangular prism would do, wide as she was tall, from floor to ceiling, from her hand forward. "Hand" was *ŷǎn,* and the word for "Oxygen" was . . . it was . . . agh!

"Air" would have to do, though this changed the effect from displacing a singular element to maintaining a vacuum. Was the *e* in "air" pronounced *ë* or *ē*? How in Caterina's twice-damned garments was "displace" translated? Would "move" work?

She took a wild guess.

"**Fěṅ'ēl kēħ'in val ŏṅ'tħā ŏṅ'rum'fħā pħā ŏṅēş'ŷǎn'šũḷ ārem!**"

A torrent of smoky air buffeted the room, sent robes flapping, tumbled books off shelves, folded the rug onto itself. The fire at the corner waned in an instant and vanished, leaving a shriveled ember to collapse in its wake. The wind died.

Before a moment's respite, the fireplace fizzled to a smoldering death, and the wind returned in the opposite direction. It nearly dragged mentor and apprentice along as air rushed to fill the unnatural vacuum. It blew upon the charred husk in the corner and scattered the ashes all over the walls. The ceramic pot thumped back down onto the floor.

Meredith blinked several times at the mess, panting and trying not to show it. In her haste she'd specified neither source nor duration, or a limit to the prism's depth, for that matter. Creating and maintaining the long wall of vacuum had consumed the hearthfire in one quick breath.

If the spell had drawn from her body, she'd have flaked apart into the ether in just about the same amount of time.

"That was the coolest thing I've ever seen."

Janette was gaping at the blackened pot that used to house a jade in full bloom. Robe rumpled and hair disheveled, she was the picture of ecstatic wonder, and not the least bit suspicious of her mentor's incompetence.

"Can I hear the words again? I think I understood some of it! No, wait, how about lightning this time? Should we go outside for that? Does it come down from the sky, or does it come out of your fingers, like a Sith lord? Oh, I bet you can do both. I bet you could zap birds mid-flight. Could you do that? Can we do that next? Plee-e-ease?"

Meredith's carefully measured gaze went from the giddy apprentice to the shriveled husk in the corner, the blaze-touched walls, the tendrils of smoke curling toward the ceiling. An acrid stink had already spread through the room, clogging her nostrils.

She absentmindedly fixed Janette's hood and hair, but stopped upon realizing how much her hands shook. "Maybe some other day." She gestured toward the insulated room.

"It's time to get to work."

MEREDITH WALKED PAST the front desk clerk and mildly curious nocturnals without making eye contact. She stopped for a hesitant moment at the stair-rest halfway to the first basement level, looked back up, and resumed her way down the steps. She knocked on the door to Yurena's quarters softly, almost bashfully. She waited, knocked again, waited, thought about leaving and pulled the string to the doorbell instead. A tinny chime sounded inside.

Yurena opened the door in robe and nightgown, glasses in hand, eyes squinted to white-glinting slits. They widened to almost normal upon recognizing her visitor. Faint smoke wafted past the threshold, and Meredith had no trouble recognizing the sweet scent of her homegrown mellowvane.

She raised a hesitant hand. "Hi. Sorry to drop by so late. I read your—"

She didn't have time to say more. Yurena had already dragged her inside and pressed her mouth to Meredith's lips.

They didn't say much else after that, either.

CHAPTER FIFTEEN

DEVIOUS

 HE SHEETS WERE SOFT and warm, so very warm. A heavy blanket covered Meredith from feet to nape, and as she lay there with her face buried in the pillow, half-awake in cozy contentment, the delightful warmth was all that mattered.

She stretched the best morning stretch she'd had in a while, toes sticking out from under the sheet. They grazed a leg, and in that moment she realized this was not her bed.

"I was wondering when you'd wake," Yurena muttered. She sounded amused and not drowsy at all.

"Mm," Meredith replied, trying to make sense of the situation. She'd planned to leave after . . . visiting. When had she fallen asleep?

Pleasantly cool hands rubbed her neck, shoulders and back. They deftly avoided the few lingering bruises from last week's deranged escapades—or rather, the utterly unremarkable fall Meredith took in her backyard.

Yurena leaned forward, whispering. "I was worried you'd disappear again. I'm determined to feed you that breakfast."

Meredith groaned in delight as the librarian's hands worked through dreadfully tense muscles. It wasn't a big deal, she thought. It couldn't be long after the sixth span, if that.

"You shouldn't make such tight ponytails," Yurena said affably, brushing Meredith's tangled mane over to one side. "They give your hair such a homely curl. You'd be surprised how subtly intimidating the right cut would look on you."

"I've tried," Meredith slurred. "My hair is terrible. It just flops down no matter what I do. So I stopped trying."

Yurena's weight shifted under the blankets. She moved to straddle Meredith's back, confirming her suspicion that neither of them wore a single piece of clothing, still. The sensation was. . . .

Well.

She could afford being a little late to work.

"I like the ponytails, don't get me wrong. Businesslike is trending in lately. You could easily go for that."

The fog in Meredith's mind was slowly clearing up. "I didn't know you had a mind for style."

"Oh, I'm only talking. Spread your arms," Yurena said, and worked her way from shoulders to fingertips.

"Gu-u-u-uhh. . . ."

"You're always so tense, like the skyveil is about to close on your head. I've wanted to do this for a long time."

The librarian's lanky fingers were surprisingly strong, kneading and massaging vigorously and methodically. The sweet scent reached Meredith's nostrils again. It came from the rolled-up mellowvane puffer cradled in the nightstand's ashtray.

"You truly like my herbs?"

"Oh, they're a gift from the Dryads. All the infused strains get to my head too much. They make the migraines worse, somehow. Yours blunt the barbs every time."

"You still get migraines?"

"All my life. I had it worse before. They considered termination back in early academy, did I ever tell you that?"

"You didn't. *Mmmh,* that's good, right there."

"You know how they are if they think a brood is defective. Which I suppose I am. Just not defective enough."

"Don't get me started on barely achieving 'good enough'—*gugh,* you're so great at this."

Yurena said nothing, but her pleasure at the compliment was clear in the way she pressed and stroked, kneaded and caressed. Her pointy fingernails sometimes grazed Meredith's skin in shiver-inducing ways.

And yet she couldn't fully enjoy it.

"What time is it?" she finally asked. "I can't be *too* late for work."

"It's after eleven. You slept a long time."

"What!"

Yurena used her leverage to hold her down. "It's fine! I already sent a comm that you couldn't come in. You are sick, and I'm tending to your sickness. Such terrible food poisoning, you've spent all morning in my bathroom, I've been mortified. You shouldn't eat the wild mushrooms in your backyard, Meredith."

"But—"

Yurena bent down so that her mouth was next to Meredith's ear, a cascade of hair brushing the arch of her back. Nails gently dug into her shoulders. "You're going to take a day off, and I'll make sure you enjoy it."

Her ministrations soon overpowered all resistance, leaving Meredith languid in the satisfaction of present-moment bliss.

"Speaking of work," Yurena carried on, "I've good news. Remember my offer? The opening I had coming up, with Martha leaving for Tremmelton?"

"Yeah. . . ."

"I might not fill it, after all. They finally approved my golem request, after I tried for so long."

"Oh?"

"That's right, it got through their thick skulls that no amount of basement tinkering is going to create another singularity, no matter how much Valeni blood runs through my veins. You wouldn't believe the amount of oaths they made me sign, it's ridiculous. Did you *ever* get a massage before?"

"No-o-ogh." Meredith's reply devolved into another satisfied grunt.

"I can tell. Anyway, I'm excited—I thought I'd never see the day I would have a golem of my own. I can't wait to crack it open, if only to look at the guts."

Golemancy was several branches removed from Meredith's haphazard spread into the tree of knowledge. Though she couldn't quite relate to Yurena's excitement, she did find it rather endearing. "I'm still sorry I couldn't accept the offer," she said.

Yurena snickered. "I must admit, I just wanted to get close to you."

"I don't know why anyone would," she mumbled.

There was no answer but for the meticulous knead of Meredith's every tangle and knot. Neither spoke for a while, the silence abated by elated groans, strong breathing, the arrhythmic whispers of rustling sheets and skin on skin.

Yurena's voice came faint and uncertain. "I shouldn't tell you this, but. . . ."

Her hands slowed, then renewed their vigor. Time went by.

"You were saying?"

"No, never mind."

A short while passed. Meredith prodded with a hint of trepidation. "You can say it, whatever it is."

A full centispan came and went before Yurena finally pushed the words out.

"I'm a little scared of how happy I was to find you still here."

Meredith kept silent, face hot against the pillow. The flutter in her chest wasn't alarm but . . . something else. Something exciting, and daunting, and lovely.

"It's never been like this for me," Yurena continued. "Gracious ravens, I'm the one being pursued more often than not, you wouldn't believe the kind of propositions you get at the front desk. But even when it was my initiative, it wasn't like. . . ."

She trailed off again. Meredith kept an expectant silence, nervous sweat itching in inconvenient places.

"Like?"

Fingertips rested lightly on both sides of her spine. She felt Yurena take a deep breath that trembled on its way out. "I'm doing a piddlesome job at not pressuring you."

Meredith's mouth opened and closed a few times, reason and yearning fighting at the back of her throat. *You're right, I don't want this,* she knew she should say. *I don't mind, we're past that point,* she longed to say. Neither came out.

Yurena made a frustrated sound, half grunt, half moan. "Burn it to the Hollow, I'm saying it anyway. I want more. I want a lot more of you. You're so different, I can't get you out of my head—and I feel stupid, because it's hardly been one cycle since our night together, and I haven't even seen you lately. I'm so ridiculous, I doubt I ever crossed your mind before we started this. I've watched you for years, you know? Ever since you applied. I started to find you interesting, and then it became something else. I wondered. I fantasised. And when we kissed the fantasies came true, and now it's become like . . . a siren's song. You call to me, all day, and eventually it turns into something I cannot ignore, and I have to go find you. I've tried visiting more than you know."

Her hands had stopped, listless on the small of Meredith's back. Her voice had quieted with each sentence. She sat there, silent, waiting for however Meredith would react.

Flustered beyond description, Meredith couldn't begin to sort out a reaction.

"Yurena," she croaked, wary and nervous and deeply touched but mostly wishing to buy some time. The impulse to profess her own craving battled the need to keep her atrocious secrets. How could she hope to hide Janette from someone that might want to spend nights at her cottage?

As if to grant her wishes for stalling, the intimate lighting of Yurena's room went out, leaving the basement dwelling in complete darkness. Both witches flinched in unison.

"Another outage," Meredith said.

"Yeah. . . ."

"I wonder if it will last long."

Yurena didn't respond. The lights came back on. Silence stretched further.

"I shouldn't have told you," Yurena finally said. She moved off Meredith's behind and sat next to her, knees bent, calves tucked under thighs. "This is so embarrassing. I shouldn't have told you." She shifted as if to get off the bed.

"No, please." Meredith turned and sought Yurena's hand. The librarian's dark mane flanked eyes that shone with moisture. "I just . . . I'm no good at this. I've never been close to anyone, not like this. I've had relationships, but they were always . . . abusive, in some way. They started it, they bossed me around, they got bored, and I simply went with it. This, what you're doing, what you just said, it's . . . it's all new to me. I don't know how to react."

Yurena frowned darkly. "Abusive?"

"Don't worry about it."

"I'll hunt them down and turn their flesh inside out."

Meredith squeezed her hand. "You're sweet to offer, but it was a long time ago."

They looked at one another. Yurena's frown transitioned into a cheerless smile. "What if I'd been forceful? You'd have gone with it too, I gather?"

Meredith raised her eyebrows and with some effort suppressed the impulse to deny the suggestion. She looked away. "Probably."

"Is that what you're doing right now? Going with it?"

She shook her head. "No."

"It's fine if you are. I told you it didn't have to be—"

"I've never felt this way for anyone before," Meredith said. "I want to be with you."

Yurena appeared startled. Her smile was sweet and genuine. "Is that the truth?"

"You're not like everyone else. I wish I'd known all this time. I only wonder. . . ."

"Yes?"

"Why me? You could do so much better."

Yurena didn't look pleased at the question. "I said it before. You sell yourself short." She repositioned her legs and drew nearer, her frown dissipating into a crooked smile. "You're smart. You're devious, Meredith. And I think you know it."

"Devious?" She laughed. "Whatever might give you that impression?"

The librarian's smile broadened. Sharp teeth gave bite to her words.

"Say, love. How is the youth progressing?"

CHAPTER SIXTEEN

✦

WICKED

TWENTY DIFFERENT LIES, all of them feeble, fought for supremacy over Meredith's tongue. Yurena spoke before any one falsehood could assert its dominance.

"Soot and ash, I can see the gears turning already. You've nothing to worry about. I haven't reported you and I've no intention to. Though I'd advise you not to have your lessons in the living room anymore, you never know who might have an ear to the door. . . ." She finished with a mischievous smile. "Or an aural augment trained on it."

Meredith found herself breathless. Clearly denial wasn't in the cards, and no lie could be big enough to justify what she'd done.

She stared back at Yurena, eyes slightly wide. "Why? Why wouldn't you?"

"Report you? I thought I just said. Lovers do foolish things for one another. Oogh, it was such a rush when I found out what you were doing." Meredith blinked with incredulity, which made Yurena laugh. "Reporting you would be a terrible waste! I could sense that youth through your walls, Meredith. Such a wonderful find, one of a kind, really. It's no wonder you kept her to yourself. So clever. . . ." She wriggled even closer, enough for Meredith to feel the words brushing against her lips. "So devious."

She found it hard to appreciate the intimacy. "I . . . I didn't mean to. I was desperate."

"Ogh, your breath."

"S– sorry."

Yurena reached behind her for a small box on the nightstand. She rattled the box, popped it open, picked a small mint and brought it to Meredith's mouth. She let Yurena place it on her tongue. The strong mint almost instantly cleansed the pasty bad taste between cheeks and teeth.

The librarian's thumb lingered on Meredith's lower lip, caressing it tenderly. "Much better."

"So . . . you're not horrified? It's a terrible crime, especially with the deficit. . . ."

"Pfah! Do you think every youth that's turned in is used the way it should? Who knows how many those Council crones keep to themselves. They'd rather let the realm collapse than give up the lifestyle. No, you saw an opportunity, and you seized it. And not just that—you could have been hasty about it, but you chose instead to build it up, to take the bigger risk and make the absolute most of it. That takes courage. That takes a special kind of witch."

"A special kind of fool, maybe."

Yurena chuckled and leaned in for a kiss. Try as she might, Meredith couldn't reciprocate properly. The librarian pulled back, seeming more amused than displeased.

"You're so tense. You're wondering what I want out of this, yeah? Will I blackmail you? Will I hold it over your head, demand favours, money?"

Meredith let out a high-pitched laugh. "Money? Won't get very far with that. . . ."

"I know. I only want to share, love. That's the price of my silence. When the time comes, share the bounty with me. I'm not even asking for half. Just a small bit. I'm not greedy."

"Yes . . . yes, of course."

"I could even help feed it and make sure it doesn't escape when you're not there. Is it getting fat? Is it complying with your lessons?"

"Yeah, she's—um, it's complying. But no, please, that won't be necessary. I couldn't bear making you an accomplice. You need to deny all knowledge if I get caught."

Uttering the words "get caught" made Meredith wince. She looked at Yurena with a knit brow.

The librarian crinkled her nose. "You look like you've a mouthful of rotten meat."

"I just can't believe it. . . ."

"What can't you believe?"

"This! You! What I'm doing is mad, and the Judicars will come after you if I get caught. You know they will."

"*If* you get caught. Are you planning on getting caught, love?"

"No, of course not, but—"

"But nothing, then." She planted another kiss on Meredith's lips.

"Yurena. . . ."

"It's worth the risk. You're worth the risk."

Meredith needed a moment to process the conversation. She felt her chest swell, with pride, with wonder, and found herself smiling. She squeezed Yurena's hand. "You . . . you truly think I can make it work?"

"Why *wouldn't* it work?"

"And you don't think I'm mental?"

"I'll admit it was shocking when I realised what you'd done. But I thought about it, and concluded it's brilliant." She pulled Meredith closer, legs tangling together, free hand caressing her face. "I do think you're mental. But I like it."

"I've been so worried about what you'd think of me if you found out."

"So you *do* think about me."

"Of course I do. It's hard to concentrate on anything else. So many times I've wanted to drop whatever I'm doing and just. . . ."

The corner of Yurena's mouth quirked. She raised a suggestive eyebrow. "'Just'?"

Meredith leaned in to demonstrate, all too eager to be rid of the tension pent up in the past weeks. The notion was so alien, and yet so inviting. Here was someone with which she didn't have to scheme and watch her every word. She could let her guard down and simply enjoy herself. In this corner of the world, in this bed, she didn't have to lie, to pretend, to keep hideous truths from spilling over.

Most hideous truths, in any case.

Yurena laughed between kisses. "So this is what it's like to have your full attention."

"I'm sorry. It's been so stressful. I've been going insane—" A concerning idea made her pull back. "This . . . this isn't a trap, is it? To get a confession out of me?"

"Yes, certainly. You've been entrapped, you foolish criminal, you. I'll turn you over to the authorities right now."

Meredith gave her a gentle shove. "Joker. Maybe this is *my* trap, hmm? I'm with the thought patrol, testing your loyalty, yeah? You've failed woefully."

"Ah! And do tell, does the thought patrol always sleep with their suspects?"

Meredith nodded knowingly. "It's required. No way to know someone's true self, otherwise."

"Well, we can both agree on that. I've no recourse, then." Yurena held her hands in front of her, touching at the wrist. Her voice lowered to a husky purr. "You must take me away, inquisitor."

It was enough to leaden Meredith's breath, but an urge of a very different nature could no longer wait.

"I, um. . . ." She swallowed. "I need to pee."

Yurena broke into laughter as Meredith scurried out of bed. "You're not afraid I might escape?"

She glanced at her crumpled red robe on the floor and decided to leave it there. Meredith held on to the bathroom's door and looked over her shoulder.

"I think we're both trapped."

The librarian smiled warmly. "I'll be making breakfast, love."

Meredith returned the smile and nodded. She made as if to shut the door, but her brow knit with worry. "Promise me you're alright with what I'm doing. I need to hear it."

"I am. I promise. It's such a smart fix to your infusion problems. A find like that, properly built up, it could last you for decades, maybe even permanently." Yurena stretched on the bed, quite clearly making a show of it. She spoke at the end of a contented sigh. "It'll be such a rush when we devour it."

Meredith tensed like struck by hideous cramps. With tremendous effort, she coaxed her head to slowly nod up and down, up and down.

"Yes," she said. "I can't wait."

She shut the door.

DEVOUR IT.

With mechanical movements Meredith performed her morning ablutions, the routine only occasionally broken by her unfamiliarity with this particular bathroom.

Devour her.

Why hadn't it even crossed her mind? It was the natural thing to do, the perfect solution for when she could no longer keep Janette— no, *the youth*—an unwitting captive. Much of the girl's unprecedented attunement would become hers for several years forward.

She continued splashing water from the basin to her face, rubbing her features far more harshly than was necessary.

And yet. . . .

Devour Janette?

The thought was sickening. It tied a knot in her chest and made her mouth involuntarily curl with disgust. But why? It was just a human child. Was this the extent of her merciful disease? Wasn't it enough to feel sympathy for the serfs? Wasn't it enough that she felt compelled to send the duds and stunts back, instead of damning them to a life of servitude, abuse and mutilation?

Maybe it was the girl's age. She was older than most specimens slated for harvest or consumption, hardly a few years away from sparkwane. The line between youth and adult had already started to blur.

"She's not just some youth," she muttered to her reflection. "She's a witch. One of us."

Was she, really? Not by current lawful standards. Perhaps in an alternate reality she'd have been brought into the fold, a reality where the post-Civil War purge hadn't criminalized the very notion. The girl would've spawned a whole new brood with that kind of latent power. It *wasn't right* to—

No. No, this was her shameful disorder crying out again. She couldn't let it get in the way of the perfect solution to her problems. Meredith had sealed the girl's fate the moment she'd lured her through the portal, and there was nothing to be done now but make the most of it.

She lifted her head from the towel, a determined frown on her brow.

"This is what witches *do*," she told her reflection. "Stop being a gutless sop."

Yurena's voice came from two rooms over. "Breakfast is almost ready!"

She carefully folded the towel and perched it to dry. Absentmindedly she browsed through the drawers, wholly without meaning to. Nothing all that interesting and she didn't have pockets, anyway. After a quick survey to make sure everything was as she'd found it, Meredith returned to the bedroom. The scent of fried onions wafted into her nostrils, along with the unmistakable musk of sautéed tips and piggies. Yurena must have been saving them for the occasion.

Meredith fought the revulsion starting in her gut, she quashed and pummeled it until it went deathly still. Once it gave no signs of revival, she stepped over her robe again and headed into the kitchen, feeling ravenous and not the least bit squeamish.

CHAPTER SEVENTEEN

ROUTINE

 HE MISTRESS WALKED into her kitchen and sat on her chair, following the new and improved morning routine. It had been in effect for hardly a moon cycle, but already it had assumed the comfortable rote of years-old tradition.

"Good morn," she said, pulling her seat up to the table. It was important to say it at the exact same moment every day.

She reached for a napkin, as she always would, and found none. Then she realized breakfast wasn't on the table yet. Then she realized her apprentice hadn't even responded. The girl was still at the stove, no robe over her hand-me-down night clothes, hair a tangled mess. Her movements managed to be both sluggish and abrupt.

"Janette? No 'good morning'?"

Janette muttered something that might have resembled the greeting, along with an apology. She dumped the contents of a pot into a bowl, brought the bowl to a fruit-laden plate, and brought the plate to the table.

Strawberries rolled haphazardly after she set the plate down. They still had stems attached and some dirt clinging to them. Meredith raised an eyebrow. "Did you not wash these?"

Janette looked at them. Her eyes, puffy and blood-shot, were squinted to slits. "Oh. Yeah. Sorry."

Without any urgency she got the bowl off the plate and took the fruit back to the counter.

Meredith glanced at the porridge. Just the brief look told her it was neither as thick nor as hot as she enjoyed it best. There was also no spoon with which to eat it.

She frowned and opened her mouth to point out the issue, but reconsidered before making a sound. Meredith watched her apprentice lean into the sink, scrubbing the strawberries clean under the tap.

"You don't look well," she finally said.

A moment passed. "Mm?"

"I said, you don't look well, Janette. You haven't for several days."

"Oh. It's . . . it's nothing. Trouble sleeping."

"Still?"

No answer.

"You don't seem to have slept at all. Did you just now get out of bed?"

Janette brought the fruit back, clean and neatly cut. "I'm sorry. Fell asleep in the end overslept. Didn't have time to bathroom."

"You're slurring. I can hardly understand you."

The girl squeezed her eyes shut a few times, abruptly shaking her head as if to clear it. An edge of irritation jagged her voice. "I needed to get breakfast ready for you. I didn't have time to use the bathroom."

"Well, go use the bathroom now."

"But I have to clean—"

"I'm *commanding you* to go take care of yourself, apprentice."

Color rose to Janette's cheeks. Every hint of impertinence vanished. "Yes, Mistress." Her eyes remained glued to the floor as she hurried out of the kitchen.

Munching on a strawberry, Meredith took the porridge bowl to the counter, poured it into the used pot and turned the stove back on. In silence she watched it cook, lips slightly pursed, eyebrows faintly drawn.

She was already enjoying a scalding-hot breakfast by the time Janette returned. The girl's hair was parted in the middle and held in place with barrettes at her temples, and while her eyes were still red and her eyelids puffy with exhaustion, she no longer looked ready to fall over. The apprentice stopped at the doorframe, headed for the counter and began cleaning, all the while carefully avoiding Meredith's gaze.

"Never mind that. Sit."

Janette let go of the pot and headed for her Mistress's table, movements quiet and hesitant. She sat as if afraid to break the chair and waited while staring at the hands on her lap.

"You're going to tell me what's troubling your sleep."

She glanced at Meredith, very briefly. "It's just dreams."

"Just dreams? You stay up studying and working all night, and I've seen enough to know it's not by choice."

"I . . . I do want to be the best, Mistress."

"I don't doubt it, but I can't let you work this exhausted. There's been enough incidents as it is."

The girl said nothing. She was fidgeting, fingers of one hand repeatedly pinching the skin of the other.

"Well?"

Janette looked to the side, moaning feebly. The corner of her mouth twitched down as she wrapped her arms around herself. Meredith's urge to give the girl a hug was awfully hard to ignore.

"I can't help unless you tell me what's bothering you," she said.

"It's really nothing. It doesn't matter anymore. . . ."

It was a thread of a voice. Mistress Meredith leaned elbows on the table, her stare as severe as she could make it. "No, it *shouldn't* matter anymore, but it clearly does, and it's only getting worse. You were *terrified* the last time I woke you. Maybe talking about it will help."

Janette grimaced, met Meredith's eyes, looked away.

"I don't want to."

"Janette. . . ."

"Please don't make me."

"Look, I know it's hard. I understand, there are secrets you think you need to keep to yourself. You feel they might be too terrible to share, that bad things will happen if anybody knew. You've kept this secret for who-knows how long and it claws at your insides, it's dug deep and it doesn't let go. It tells you, 'no-one must know.' It tells you, 'your life will be over if anyone finds out.' Am I right?"

The girl seemed struck by her mentor's insight. After some hesitation she nodded, silent.

"Well, sometimes that voice *is* right, and you shouldn't let anyone know. But right now, I'm telling you it's safe. It doesn't matter what it is. It's safe to tell. Believe me, it will be a heavy burden off your shoulders."

"I. . . ."

"Don't you trust me?"

"I trust you. Of course I do."

"Then?"

Janette didn't respond, and silence dragged on. It appeared she was on the verge of pushing the words out, but when she lifted her eyes to her mentor the pained expression transitioned to one of surprised understanding.

"You already know. You know, don't you?"

"What?"

"You said you'd been watching me before getting me out. You *must* have seen it." She blinked in mortified realization. "You've known all this time."

Meredith stared, features distant. She didn't have the first clue.

"That's not the point," she countered. "You need to say it out loud.

You need to discuss this with someone."

Janette's voice lifted with desperate hope. "So I'm not crazy? Two nights before you got me out, you saw it happen?"

The silence that ensued lasted for a little too long.

"You're the least crazy witch I know, Janette."

Panic joined worry in the girl's eyes. "That's not a 'yes.' Oh god, *please* tell me you saw, I'm not crazy, it wasn't just nightmares, I swear! There's no way—"

"I saw! I did, yes." Meredith, alarmed at Janette's agitation, reached across the table and laid a reassuring hand on her forearm. "It wasn't just nightmares, it really did happen, all of it. In fact . . . I rescheduled the recruitment day so I could get you out sooner. That's why I had to go report your retrieval that very same night."

Janette squeezed her tutor's hand and exhaled a tremulous moan, shoulders sinking down. She leaned forward until her forehead rested on Meredith's fingers.

"I knew it," she whispered. "I knew it. Lies, all of it, all lies."

An unpleasant feeling kept building in the pit of Meredith's stomach as she watched the girl unravel. She'd have done a great many things to make it go away.

Tears began wetting her hand. After hesitating for a moment, Meredith reached over and stroked Jane's hair. "It's alright," she said. "You'll be alright."

"I'm not there anymore. It's over, I *know* this. Why does it keep coming back?"

Unable to find a good answer, Meredith kept finger-combing the girl's wavy mane. After some time, Janette sighed and turned her head so her cheek would rest on her tutor's fingers.

"I worry about my idiot sister," she muttered.

Meredith let a few breaths go by. "I warned you about feeling homesick. It's normal."

"It's not like that. It's just. . . ." Janette shrugged. "She's so stupid, she didn't even know what was really going on. And mom's so damn useless. She's got too much to lose, so she pretends and goes along."

"I do wish you'd stop being vague about the topic. You will never grow past it if you continue avoiding it."

"What's there to say? You saw it. It's been going on for years, first my sister, then me. I knew it wasn't normal, I *always* knew. It was awful and gross and talking about it only brings it back."

Meredith internalized a sigh. Maybe if she knew more about human everyday life, whatever "it" was would become obvious.

Janette lifted her head and wiped at the tears with the ball of her hand, the gesture brisk and indignant like she resented their presence. She reached for the napkin nearby and gently patted until her Mistress's hand was dry. When she spoke her voice still faltered, but it had rallied some confidence.

"I can't just walk away from something like that, I guess. I need time. It'll get better." She lifted her eyes from the task and looked at her tutor. "It has to, right?"

Meredith sighed outwardly this time and ate another spoonful of breakfast. It had cooled far too much.

"I sure hope so," she said after swallowing. "I like my breakfast hot."

It got a rather satisfying chuckle out of the girl. "I don't know how you can eat it without burning your mouth. I do miss cold cereal, I'll admit. Honey Cheerios were the best."

"Yeugh. Your 'cold cereal' is an abomination." Janette's Mistress wagged her finger in mock severity. "You should abandon such base cravings at once."

"Ha! You've tried it?"

"There are many Earth goods available in Galavan's markets. On a whim I tried this *thing* called 'raisin bran' something other. Pfegh."

"Ew, that one's bad. You didn't try a good one, that's the problem. I'll make you a list of my favourites, you won't regret any of those."

"Hm. If you say so."

Witch and apprentice looked at one another. The subtle smile that curved their lips transcended the silly small talk. Janette's appreciation was plain to see. Meredith's sympathy was genuine.

Jane left her seat and without thought Meredith leaned forward to receive her hug. It felt natural, like it was supposed to happen. A harmless hug that neither slipped into awkwardness nor overstayed its welcome.

"You called me a witch," Janette said.

"I did? Funny that." She gently pushed the girl to arm's length. "Now, eat something light, clean up in here and go to sleep. I better not see a single component out of place on your desk when I get back, apprentice."

Janette's pleased expression fell. "But I don't—"

"Shush. I'll brew you something that will knock you out till I come back, and then we'll have a day off."

"What? But there's—"

"Magrat and Malkin, must I truly convince you *not* to work for a day? You haven't stopped since moving that first bead."

"But I can—"

"You can kill us both if you don't get proper rest, do you understand? We are not playing games here."

After a moment of pursed lips, Janette swallowed whatever further argument she was about to make. "You are right, Mistress. I understand."

"You better." Meredith leaned on the chair's backrest. "Now you'll eat this fruit while I eat my porridge, and then you'll clean up while I fetch some hagel and junleaf outside, and then you'll drink what I give you and fall asleep in your room. Is that clear?"

The girl sat back down. A crease of concern returned to her brow.

"You . . . you're drugging me?"

There was an undertone of deep-set horror in Janette's voice that gave Meredith pause.

"No, I'd never do that," she said with a dismissive gesture. "It's just herbs, crushed and steeped in water. Just like . . . a sleep potion? Completely harmless."

"Oh." The apprentice blinked a few times. "A potion. That sounds fun."

"As fun as dreamless slumber can be, yes." Leaving the issue as concluded, Meredith brought heaping spoon to mouth. Her lips twisted with displeasure.

"I can heat it up again," Janette offered.

"No, don't bother, I don't want to be late. . . ."

A playful smile crept onto the girl's lips. She pointed index and middle finger at the bowl.

"kĕḣ cŏr Riṅ f̃r̃ĕiŵṅ ēī'īlēth ėlụē ŏṅlēv'ŷăn'šūḷ vă'vēr úm."

A cool gust of air brushed Meredith's cheeks upon the last syllable of the spell. With Janette's infused speech came an alarming rush of spent power, pouring forth like roiling heat off a swamp furnace vent.

Hearty steam rose from the food.

Delight bloomed in Meredith's features before she could quell it. "Did you research that on your own?"

The apprentice nodded, pride clear in her every gesture. She'd cast her first spell not even a cycle ago, and oh how much she'd jumped and fussed, cherishing magic as the most wondrous gift instead of the dreadful chore it had always been for Meredith. She felt it again, the same she felt every time the girl made progress: her chest expanding with a sense of self-worth she couldn't quite explain.

It always brought to mind the way she was *supposed* to feel. She endeavored to purge out these emotions like they were a foul breath that had somehow filled her lungs. A severe frown overtook the wonder.

"I don't like you using magic lightly," she said, more stern than she wanted to be, far less callous than she should've been. "Remember what I said before? We value manual labour in this house. Magic cannot be cheapened with routine use and commonplace tricks. See, I could use it for half my chores or portal to the manufactory every day, but I don't, because using our hands and feet and tools is important. Do you understand?"

Janette's enthusiasm had shrunk with every word. "I didn't mean to . . . I mean, I just—" She pursed her lips. "I understand. I'm sorry."

The wounded look in her one expressive eye brought a tide of shame and guilt that wholly eroded Meredith's severity. It would all end poorly for the human girl, yes, she was well aware. There was no need to be unpleasant in the meantime, was there?

She smiled with encouragement. "Don't be so cross. Your spell was impeccable, I am very impressed. You just need to apply your talents more judiciously. Focus on artificing in the lab, and leave heating up porridge to more mundane tools." She pushed the plate-full of strawberries toward the girl. "It's what I do, after all."

Janette returned the smile, which washed away the bitter taste in the back of Meredith's throat. From there they ate their meals in pleasant silence, enjoying the morning as it should have always been.

Whatever was troubling the girl's sleep, it would pass. It was over.

It didn't matter anymore.

CHAPTER EIGHTEEN
❈
A POWERLESS PAWN

 HE NIGHTWOOD SIGN above the door read "Dreya's Goods & Curio." Deep in a seldom-transited alley within the Dredge, the door was painted a dark green that blended perfectly with the rest of the building. The "store" would have gone completely unnoticed if Meredith hadn't been looking for it.

She pushed the door and walked in, a subtle chime announcing her presence without broadcasting it to the entire neighborhood. Well-lit wooden shelves stocked with the most outlandish items met her eyes, but she suppressed the impulse to gawk and kept her free hand tucked deep in her pocket, lest it went wandering on its own. The last thing she wanted was to look like a tourist or be accused of shoplifting.

A sign stood to one side of the central aisle, next to a large mesh basket. In hand-painted black letters against white background, the sign read:

Juggling the parcel she carried, Meredith unholstered her crossbow and gently placed it in the empty basket. The smoke pellets in her pocket followed suit, as did the wrist-sheathed dagger she had no intention to ever use. Once properly weaponless, she went to the display case that doubled as a counter.

A witch stood behind the counter: short, wiry, gaunt, hairless. Her well-tailored robes were green with a golden trim and stylishly bound at the shoulder and forearm with black ribbon. She was looking Meredith up and down, a smile pulling at the corner of her paper-thin lips.

"If it isn't the cloaked stranger. That's more protection than before."

Meredith didn't comment on it. Making conversation didn't strike her as enigmatic. She approached in silence.

"What might you want today? Did that cheap converter blow up whatever Earth device you were trying to charge? I warned you about it, no refunds."

The converter for Janette's phone was working fine, much to her apprentice's delight. Instead of remarking on it, Meredith set the parcel on the glass counter and untied the packaging strings. The brown paper peeled back from Jane's work.

"How much?" she rasped.

The mask she wore infused her voice with a metallic reverberation, obscuring her words to near unintelligibility. The witch—Dreya, she'd always assumed—picked up the trinket and inspected it at first dismissively, then curiously, then carefully.

An itch prickled at Meredith's cheekbone and threatened to drive her insane as she waited.

"A pusher?" Dreya asked, though by her tone she hardly needed confirmation.

"Yes."

The old witch slipped a hand into the opening and felt her way around. "What's the power-up trigger? Standard specs?"

"Doesn't have one. Just press the index finger knob."

"An unlocked pusher? Not precisely Department-compliant, is it?"

"I prefer the term 'user-friendly.'"

The pusher switched on, muted celeste patterns whispering alive all over its gauntlet-like shape. She lifted a bare eyebrow.

"Shape and range?"

"Cylindrical. Range is adjustable, capped at seven metres."

"Strength?"

"Also adjustable up to a hard cap of twelve thousand vim. Without safeguards, it could probably go half over that."

Both eyebrows rose. It wasn't as much surprise as skepticism.

"I have the feeling," Dreya said thoughtfully, "that if I were to ask where you came by this item, I might not receive a satisfactory answer."

"It's mine. I made it. I wish to sell it."

"I see. What's the half-life?"

"Forty-three span at a hundred vim per mil, by my calculations. Refillable."

"Hah! What did you do, break and enter the spark harvest plant? If you had free access to that kind of juice, you wouldn't be looking to sell this here."

"Whose spark I used is irrelevant. This won't be the last one, if you are amenable."

Dreya switched the trinket off and looked up, inquisitive stare boring through the dark mesh covering Meredith's eyes. For an anxious moment she got the impression this sly shrew had always known who the "cloaked stranger" was and what she was up to.

"Roll up your sleeve," Dreya said, two fingers tapping the counter on Meredith's right side.

"What?"

"You wouldn't be the first overzealous inquisitor trying to strut their coif in my affairs. Roll up your sleeve or no transaction."

Meredith held still, trying her darnedest not to make a fool of herself. What would a world-weary, shady individual do?

"Very well," she finally responded, rolling up her right sleeve and offering her arm. Dreya grabbed it and closely inspected the crook of Meredith's elbow. She moved down to the forearm, looked just as closely and prodded with her fingers, as if searching for something under the skin.

"I'm not branded," Meredith said.

Dreya didn't look up. "Dermaturgy isn't the only thing I'm looking for."

"Hm," was the very stoic and world-weary response.

At last, Dreya nodded and let Meredith go. She rolled her sleeve back down. "Satisfied?"

The witch grunted. "For now." Her attention switched back to the artifact. "It's my policy to test all function-oriented items before purchase."

"I guarantee you—"

"The guarantees of an anonymous stranger aren't worth a dud's giblets. I carry out the tests after day's closure. Leave this in my deposit box, come back within the next three days and I'll have a fair offer for you. If it turns out you're wasting my time, I'll make you a rather forceful offer to get bent. If three days pass and you haven't come back, I assume ownership of all goods."

Meredith looked at the item atop the counter. It was the culmination of countless span of labor. Its painstakingly carved wordpaths represented almost two cycles of intensive lessons, practice, failed attempts, destroyed casings, shattered furniture, three small fires and one near-death experience. Parting with it for free, however temporarily, struck her as the silliest notion she could've entertained.

"Surely you're not doubting my integrity," Dreya said. "I've been in business for well over fifty years. I'd have to flog whoever referred you for not educating you properly. After I wring her name out of you, of course." She made a twisting motion with her hand as she said it. Meredith had no trouble imagining the old hag literally wringing her neck to squeeze every single secret out of her.

"No," she hurried to say, "I'm just . . . emotionally attached. It was a lot of work."

"Can't say I care. These are the terms. Accept them or go elsewhere."

Dreya's wry half-smile clearly conveyed her meaning. *Good luck finding a better fence.*

Meredith suppressed a long sigh. "How much, if the tests satisfy you?"

The storekeeper scowled at the question, yet soon the scowl turned to grave consideration. She rubbed thoughtful fingers on her lips, eyes glued to the trinket. "I have to check some of my data for the exact figure. *If* it does what you say . . . I'm willing to offer about thirty-two stem."

Meredith was thankful for the mask covering the goofy, slack-jawed expression on her face. The amount was more than she'd spent setting up the home lab.

After some very carefully controlled stillness, she slowly slid the pusher toward her new best friend in all of Galavan. "That seems . . . agreeable. Same time tomorrow, then?"

Dreya scribbled a few short lines on a piece of paper before taking the trinket in her hands. She held it with deliberate care. "As long as it's before day's closure, I don't give a rat's arse. Take your receipt."

The witch disappeared through a curtained doorway behind the counter, and soon after there were muffled metallic noises and keychain rattling. A rat was some Earth animal, if she remembered correctly. What might its arse look like? Why was it poorly valued? Such a peculiar idiom.

Alleged Dreya reemerged.

"You are still here. Did you want anything else?"

"Right, I mean, no. Until tomorrow, then."

Dreya shrugged. "You have three days."

Meredith nodded, turned and walked between elbow-height shelves and display cases. She was reaching for her basketed gear when something nearby caught her attention. It took her a moment to place where she'd seen a similar one before: Jane's Earth room, an eternity ago.

She turned. "Is this a trinket?"

Dreya was in the same exact spot, clearly watching Meredith's every movement. "What is?"

"This . . . creature." Meredith gestured without touching the winged figurine. It was as tall as her hand was long.

The storekeeper got on her tip-toes and leaned to one side. "That? No, just an Earth bauble. Yours for thirty-five P even."

"Um. How about twenty?"

"How about forty?"

"Right. Thirty-five it is."

Meredith cradled the figurine between forearm and chest as she counted coins out of her pocket purse while walking back to the counter. She stopped abruptly.

"Um." Heat rising to her ears, she held out the purse for Dreya to see. "How about . . . twenty-eight?"

The old witch glared, mouth twisted in disgust. She put out a hand. "Fine, give it here already. That pusher better be as good as you claim."

Meredith closed the distance and poured all seven coins on the wrinkled hand. "It's better."

"We'll see." Dreya produced tape and a roll of brown paper from under the display case and deftly wrapped the statuette. "It's almost closing time." She waved her hands in a shooing gesture. "Congratulations on your purchase, pleasure doing business, yadda yadda."

Package in hand and readily dismissed, Meredith retrieved all of her equipment and made her way outside. Upon stepping out she was surprised to see dusk was come and gone, the late sun replaced by a moon cycling toward full. The nighttime skyveil coated most of the cobbled passage in blue-tinged silver wherever the dingy, sporadic streetlights didn't reach.

She started down the alley, eyeing every shadow with suspicion. Juditors patrolled most of Brena's neighborhoods these days, but they rarely made it into the Dredge. Her free hand undid the latch to the crossbow holster, then dug in a pocket for the smoke pellets. Her fingers softly rattled the little spheres as she walked.

She was twenty steps away from the intersection when two infused voices descended from the roof above. The incantations mingled so that she only understood a few concepts from each: *gravity, void, ground, sphere.*

In a bout of panic Meredith crushed the pellets and threw them straight up. The pressurized hiss blotted out the back-end of the incantations, and as the thick shroud formed above her head she dashed toward the nearest wall, hand fumbling at the holster. Maybe she could get out of the way before—

An irresistible downward force bent her knees and threw her to the cobblestones. She fell on her left side much harder than she could prepare for. Her elbow thumped the ground, made a horrible crack and shot up against the shoulder joint to cause an explosion of pain.

"AAH!"

Package and weapon flew off her limp fingers and clattered beyond reach. They were upon her in an instant, one quickly wrapping something around her legs, the other rolling her over, planting a knee on her chest. Past the blinding pain Meredith saw a cloth mask, dark hood, dark ringlets, dark eyes.

"Scream all you want. No-one can hear you."

Meredith did just as much, unable to hold back. She struggled desperately, screams turning to sobs. The sharp wire around her legs bit into the cloth of her pants, tightening harder the more she writhed.

A serrated knife the length of her forearm flashed in front of her eyes.

"Stop that and give up everything you have, or I'll cut pieces off of you until what's left fits in a feed bag."

The knife quieted her sobs, though every breath still came with an agonized whimper. It was an inhuman struggle to remain still.

"Please, my arm, please. . . ."

Already the attacker's free hand was searching through pockets, patting for valuables. It deftly unclasped the concealed dagger from the wrist sheath and tossed it beyond reach. The pleas were thoroughly ignored.

"I'm certain you broke her arm," the other one said. She had a firm grip on Meredith's legs. "I keep telling you to change your blasted spell."

"It works. She'll live." She'd already found Meredith's purse and was rifling through it. "Is this a joke? Where's all the moppet? You go in with something, you come out with chud. Where is it!"

"I don't have any money, please, my arm. . . ."

"I can't understand a word." The mugger threw back Meredith's cowl and tore off the full-faced mask. The abrupt movements were like hot irons stabbing through her limb.

"Say again?"

"Aah!"

A rough gloved hand clamped on Meredith's mouth and chin, painfully puckering up her lips. "The chud. Where."

"I don't have any, I swear. . . ."

"Do you think I'm stupid?"

The other one peeked over her partner's shoulder. Dark hair in a tight bun. Slanted eyes, amber irises, ghostly skin.

"I've seen her face before," she said. "I don't remember where."

"Don't care. We'll just cut her up. Her parts will be worth something."

"Will you lay off with the cutting? There's no point in mugging someone if you're just going to kill them anyway!"

"You're the one bent on letting them live. Far more profitable—"

"*And* risky, *and* messy! Are we really arguing this right now, Cass? You're always—"

"Shhhush-shush-shush, you moron! You just gave up my name, what's wrong with you?"

No answer. Meredith's vision swam in stars, filling the alley with fleeting shimmers.

"We have to kill her now," the knife-wielding mugger concluded.

"It's only your first name, there are other Cassandras out there!"

"How many? All of three, maybe? No. Can't let her live." The serrated blade nicked the skin of Meredith's throat. "That's just too bad."

Meredith's voice was an asphyxiated squeal. "I can give you over sixteen stem tomorrow!"

The pressure on her neck eased. The thug's eyes narrowed.

"You really *do* think we're stupid, if you're hoping to walk away on a promise."

"Follow me home!" Meredith had to pause and take in a few choking breaths. "You'll know where I live, you can stalk me, she's paying me tomorrow, all yours!"

The cloaked witch exchanged a look with her partner. "Listen to this joshwag. She thinks we're—"

The thug cut off with a gasp. Close to the brick wall, the shimmer Meredith had mistaken for lack of oxygen materialized into a robed figure: short, wiry, gaunt, hairless. One of her arms was extended, at the end of which was a familiar artifact. It glowed with celeste patterns shifting all over its gauntlet-like surface.

There was a whispered string of sound Meredith had heard a hundred times before. She desperately braced against the floor with what strength she could muster, pressing herself flat to the cobbles.

The thunderclap of twelve thousand vim exploded from the trinket and blew in a cylindrical force tunnel against the attackers. Through squinted eyes Meredith watched the brutal compression and release of the space above her, the impact against the thugs, the displacement and disfigurement of matter in its path. One moment they were on top of her, the next they were by the alley's wall.

And on the wall.

And on the roof.

Spattering sounds filled the silence that followed.

"I need to learn some fine-tuning skills, it would seem."

Dreya was regarding the trinket with reluctant admiration. She approached the miserable witch in the middle of the street. "About time I dealt with those two. Elusive little rats."

Meredith tried to sit up and quickly desisted. Every breath was a groan. Dreya didn't seem to care, her gaze fixed on the grisly remains. "I suppose I owe you now, for keeping them busy long enough. Good job stalling."

She could barely push out an answer. "I had no idea . . . you were there. . . ."

"Ah. All the same."

Now free to cradle her broken limb, Meredith felt too afraid to try.

"Please, help me. . . ."

The wizened savior shifted her focus to the pitiful creature at her feet. Astute eyes seemed to absorb every detail—including every one of Meredith's features.

"I near glean you'd rather not go to the healing house to take care of this," Dreya said. It wasn't clear if she knew whose brood-sister she was talking to. Meredith wasn't *famous,* but her face had appeared on a trans or two. Usually alongside a terribly humiliating story.

She feebly shook her head. "No-one can—" She had to clench her jaw and just breathe through the pain for a short while. Her eyes were squeezed shut. "No-one can know I was here."

Dreya simply watched in silence, brow furrowed and mouth quirked. At last she left the pusher on the floor and moved to Meredith's side. She surveyed the wire around her legs.

"At least they didn't tie it off," she said, and lifted the bound knees as gently as she could so she could unwind the loops. Throughout the process Meredith sobbed as quietly as she could.

Once it was done, Dreya braced arms around her shuddering frame.

"We're going inside. This will hurt a great deal. You'll have to suck it up."

Meredith screamed through gritted teeth all the way to her feet. Cautiously they shifted weight from Dreya's surprisingly steadfast support to her own legs. It took a few attempts. She already felt bruised from toe to hip.

In faltering steps she followed back to the store, a world and a half away. Dreya detoured to gather the items scattered all over the alley.

"I have supplies and I know a thing or two about mending," she continued. "I'll set your shoulder back in place, fuse what I can, get you in a splint and transport you to your bed. I hope you have someone to take care of you after that, because I sure won't."

Meredith concentrated on getting to that dark green door among dark green bricks, thoughts entirely on her feet, one step, and another, and the next. Dreya watched her.

"Your bones better not be shattered. I couldn't do much for you, then. There's no blood gushing out, so it must've not broken the skin too badly."

"That's . . . comforting. . . ."

"I'm sure it is. You'll be paying for anything of mine that gets stained with your blood. The less blood, the better for your pocket. I don't think I need to tell you none of what I'm doing is free, do I?"

Meredith slowly moved her head from side to side, in very small movements. "Thank you, Dreya."

The old witch gave her a sidelong glance. "Dreya left long ago. My name is Wybel. What is yours?"

"Misha."

"And what's your real name?"

"Um. Meredith."

"That's what I thought. Watch your step."

Wybel pushed the door and waited inside. The jostle of going up the single step was enough to bring a dozen different curses to Meredith's tongue. She leaned against the doorframe with her good shoulder, panting.

"I'm also charging you for the cleanup outside. Fortunately for you, the pusher tested favorably."

Meredith looked up from her misery. Wybel was holding the door wide open. There was a frown on her brow and a reluctant manner to her lips.

"You got yourself a deal," her new best friend in all of Galavan said.

THEY STEPPED OUT of a portal onto the path to Meredith's front door. It was a three-meter trek to the landing, and she was out of breath by the time she made it. Then the locks didn't want to cooperate, it seemed. The keys kept jabbing everywhere but home. Wybel sighed impatiently when the keyring dropped to the doormat a second time, but still she made no effort to help or take over. Help opening the door was the last thing Meredith wanted, anyway.

It finally swung open, somehow. With haunted eyes she searched for signs of Janette, ready to "lose her balance" onto Wybel and push her back out, thus giving the girl a chance to scamper away. Fortunately, she was nowhere to be seen or sensed. The Mistress had given her very explicit instructions not to ever wait at the door for her.

"My room is right over here," she yelled despite the sore throat. She hadn't held back any of her screams in the last two span of torturous ministrations.

"I'm not deaf," Wybel said, helping Meredith forward, "much as you've tried to make that happen tonight."

"Sorry. I'm feeling quite . . . frazzled."

"You left a lit hearth unattended?"

"It's . . . very safe. Built right. And I wasn't supposed to be gone long."

"If you say so."

Wybel followed close behind on the way to the bed, watching every wavering step. Between the fall and the rough bondage, there'd been more purple than pale on Meredith's legs. Propping herself up on a mound of pillows was a sad ordeal full of regret-laden shifts and sucked-in breaths.

The older witch carefully adjusted Meredith's sling so it would rest comfortably on the cushions. She stood over her charge, one fist balled on her hip. "So where is your caretaker?"

"She'll be around . . . in the morning. I should make it until then."

The shopkeeper regarded Meredith with pursed lips. "Her name wouldn't happen to be Mifraulde, would it?"

"No, absolutely not. We don't . . . we don't talk these days. She can't know about—"

"Right, right. But you should have someone at all times. You will ruin everything I did if you take a fall."

"I won't move till she's here, I promise."

"Not even a trip to the bathroom, do you understand?"

"Don't worry about me. I'll wet the bed if I have to."

"That's a mental image I didn't need." Wybel dug out items from her satchel and placed them on the nightstand, one by one. "This for pain. This to sleep. Don't take more of either for at least four span. Here's your payment. Here's your weapons and your Earth bauble. You need water. Where is your kitchen?"

"Don't worry, please . . . I'll survive. Thank you—"

"Where is your kitchen?"

"It's . . . left from the door, across the front entrance. There's a jug on the counter. Cups in the cupboard above."

Wybel walked out without another word. Her steps grew fainter until the kitchen door swung closed. Then, silence. Meredith kept listening with caught breath and elevated heartrate, which made her arm throb even more. If Jane was anywhere other than in the lab. . . .

Dubiously she glanced at the crossbow, but discarded the idea off-hand. Even if she caught the eagle-eyed witch by surprise, there was no way Meredith could load and lock the weapon with just one hand. Besides, shooting someone who'd just saved her life was awfully rude.

She leaned forward and listened for the inevitable: a startled gasp, Janette's dismayed apologies, the furious stomps of an aghast old witch yelling at her face, demanding answers while berating her unparalleled stupidity. With a knot in her chest she envisioned the horrified look on Jane's face as she understood the kind of monsters that lived beyond their doorstep, the *monster* that slept one room removed—

The kitchen door creaked open once more, and shortly after Wybel's gaunt figure stepped through the doorframe. She carried a tall glass in her hand, full to the brim with water.

"Here you go. Drink plenty and often." She placed it on the small bit of uncluttered nightstand that was left. "I'm out of here."

It took Meredith a moment to calm her galloping neuroses.

"You . . . you saved my life. Thank you."

Wybel dismissed the words with an impatient wave of her hand. "You will bring your trinkets to me first, understand? That's what you owe me. No other venues, no striking out on your own. Not that you can do any of that for the time being."

"You were my only plan to begin with."

"Such a savvy haggler. Here is my comm channel." She left a small bit of scribbled paper on the corner of the nightstand. "Contact me if there are complications with your injuries or your caretaker drops dead. *No* talk of our deals over the nodework, understand?"

"Y– yes. Of course."

"One last thing. Where'd you get so much spark for that trinket?"

In her addled state of mind Meredith almost babbled, but she held on to her canned response. "That's a trade secret. I won't ever tell."

"Listen, if you're stealing from the harvest plants somehow, they *will* catch you."

"I'm not a thief."

She'd intended for a proper exclamation mark at the end, but she simply couldn't manage.

"Right," Wybel said without much conviction, and sighed impatiently. "Light on or off?"

"On. Thank you."

She stepped out without further words, and shortly after the front door banged shut. The low thrum of the portal outside died an abrupt death.

Janette's door clicked open. Meredith turned her head to see the girl standing at the door, sleeves rolled up, hands together in fidgety worry. Her eyes were sunken with deep-set exhaustion.

"Mistress? Who—" she gasped and rushed to the bedside, reaching for her good hand. "Meredith! What happened?"

The concern in her voice . . . all of that hoarse fear, the anxiety, sincere like nothing that existed in Galavan. It did something strange to Meredith's chest, like her heart was shrinking inside her ribcage. She felt her eyes water.

"It's nothing. I'm alright. Just a bad fall."

"How bad is it? Is it broken? Can I do something?"

Meredith patted her ward's hand. "You'll be doing plenty. I'll need you to help me get around the house. The ulna was fractured near the elbow, plus a dislocated shoulder."

"Is the ulna, um . . . which one is it?"

"The bigger bone in your forearm." With light fingers she sought Janette's own. "Here."

"Oh. Right."

Meredith leaned back on the pillows. Her deep breath had to be cut short before the pain became unbearable. The room seemed to shimmer in swirling stars all around her. She closed her eyes.

"Before this happened, the Head Artificer . . . she was very impressed with your work. She granted an advance, and clearance to produce more at will."

Janette fidgeted. "That's not important right now. Isn't there *something* I can do? As in . . . with magic, maybe?"

"No, what little can be done is already done. The bones are fused together again, but it's a weak bond until the body works around it." She tipped her chin toward the sling and splint, doing her best not to wince. "A few weeks like this, then just be careful for a while. I . . . I'll manage." She tried real hard for a reassuring smile. "Don't worry."

The girl kept quiet, uneasy eyes darting to Meredith's face. With slow movements Janette fished out a kerchief from her pocket. After a tiny start of hesitation, she gently dabbed the hollow of her mentor's eyelids.

"You must be in so much pain," she whispered.

Meredith's lungs sank at the words. The simple gesture of sympathy piled upon the fatigue, the stress, the nebulous painkiller haze, and it became too much. Something caved in her chest. Her breath knotted into sobs.

Tears flowed down Meredith's cheeks, and she just nodded, slowly, laboriously, lips pressed together and eyes shut.

"Don't worry, Mistress." The girl kept wiping, her voice as damp as the cloth in her hands. "I'll take care of you."

Meredith put her good arm around the girl's shoulders and brought her into a hug. Janette buried her face in her mentor's robe, holding on to the fabric as if it might float away any moment.

It was the last thing she remembered before passing out.

CHAPTER NINETEEN
❀
DYNAMICS

HE WOKE UP in pre-dawn darkness. Her whole side was throbbing, her legs felt like flour sacks attached to her hip. In a bout of panic Meredith tried to move them, succeeded, and promptly wished she hadn't. Paralysis might have been better than the stiff agony flaring below her waist.

"Ashen fool," she groaned at herself.

"Mistress?"

It was a tentative whisper, afraid to become too loud. A whisper previously uttered and gone unanswered.

"Janette?"

"I'm here. What do you need?"

Meredith needed a short while to parse the situation. This was her bed. The old witch had left her here, Wybel. Janette had rushed to her side. Then the wise and rigorous Mistress had broken down, blubbered like a cycle-old whelp and fallen asleep to her apprentice's comfort.

"Water," she rasped. "Please."

Clothes rustled. Gentle fingers guided Meredith's good hand to the glass of water. She drank in small sips. "Just switch the light on," she said.

"You should sleep more."

Despite Janette's protest, the bedside lamp promptly lit the room in warm orange. Through squinted eyes Meredith looked her ward up and down. "You're one to talk. You haven't slept, have you."

"I . . . I'll be okay. I think I did for a bit, on the chair."

"You're a bad liar."

"You're always there after my nightmares. It's only fair I'm here for you. Do you, um . . . do you need to go?"

"Go where?"

"You know, *go*. To the loo."

"Oh."

Yes. Yes, she certainly did.

"I'll help," Janette offered, eager and devoted and utterly red-faced. "Get you there, that is. And, well, with the . . . y'know, with the clothes and all. You don't seem—"

Meredith's denying gesture jostled her injuries in subtle yet awful ways, making her suck in air through clenched teeth. "No, soot and ash, no need for that. This is shameful enough, thank you."

"Mistress, there's no shame at all, you're hurt!"

"Yes, well. Regardless. And about last night. . . ."

"You don't have to explain."

"I was drugged, you understand? I was weak and emotional and it won't happen again. I want you to forget all about it."

Janette was quiet for a moment. She took her mentor's arm and draped it around her shoulders, ready to help Meredith out of bed. "Sometimes," the girl finally said, "sometimes you have to fall apart so you can put yourself together again. I understand."

"No. Maybe humans do that. I am a witch, and witches do not whimper. Witches do not cower."

As if to prove her point, the Mistress set her jaw, coerced her legs off the blankets and groaned upright. Breathlessly she half-stood, waiting for the pain to stop screaming inside her head.

Janette shifted under the weight, then stiffened. "Oh, god, Meredith, your legs. . . ."

She looked down in-between pants. Below the hem of Wybel's ill-fitting gown—loaned after she'd torn apart the Mysterious Stranger robes to get at the wounds—was a mess of purples, yellows and raw reds. They spread all the way down to her ankles.

"How can you even stand?"

"I'm . . . fine. Not that bad. Let's . . . let's go."

They limped into the living room, past the lab's door, toward the corner by the newly planted jade.

"Stop, I need to stop. . . ."

Janette patiently waited as her Mistress leaned on the bookshelf, puffing and gasping. Their eyes met.

"You shouldn't be seeing me like this."

The girl knit her brow, earnest gaze lowering to her toes. "Meredith . . . I only have admiration for you. More than I ever had. You are everything I want to be, and being hurt doesn't change that. It's an honour to help you through it."

There it was again, that upsetting catch in her throat. Meredith swallowed past it and wordlessly motioned to carry on. Upon reaching the bathroom's doorway the sight of the toilet felt like looking up from the bottom of a towering cliff. It crushed her battered spirits into a lump of acrid misery.

At that moment Meredith wished she could simply move time forward, past the pains and trials of her recovery, the indignities and constant need of assistance. Past the begging and groveling she'd have to do before Gertrude in order to keep her position at the manufactory. Best to keep her new source of income under wraps, at least until she could put a legitimate spin on it—which would be harder to do now, with Wybel's involvement.

Past the inevitable conversation with Yurena and the lies she'd have to tell to keep her away. Although . . . did she really want to keep Yurena away? She could meet Janette, be Meredith's hands while she healed, help out with keeping the girl hidden.

And also make Jane uncomfortable, and treat her like cattle, and probably end up tipping her hand about the abominable fate that would ultimately befall the apprentice.

No. Yurena would need to stay away. Maybe even . . . no, no, she couldn't end things for good, she just couldn't. Only a small break, then, a cycle or two. Things were going too fast, she needed time to think, that was it. Hopefully the crafty librarian wouldn't turn to stalking again, though it was rather clear she had a bit of an obsessive. . . .

Her train of thought trailed off in the face of a concerning realization. Meredith stood there at the threshold, left arm carefully shielded from any contact with the doorframe, right side leaning on the earthborn witch she'd been working with for nearly four moon cycles.

When had she started thinking of Janette's fate as *abominable*?

"I'll help you undress," the girl said, very matter-of-fact, very professional.

A beat went by before Meredith responded.

"No. No, I'll take it from here. Close the door, please."

"Mistress . . . please let me help, I'm begging you. I won't forgive myself if—"

"Close the door, apprentice."

Janette looked on for a bit, visibly swallowing any further protest. "I'll be on the sofa," she said instead. "Please call as soon as you need anything."

The door closed, and Meredith kept pensive eyes on it. She'd grown too close to this girl, it was plain to see. The charming enthusiasm, diligence and dedication had wormed their way into her heart, little by little.

The occasional laughing and dancing and singing together probably hadn't helped. Blasted humans and their jolly tunes.

She needed to cut it all off. This was a human youth, nothing more. She would die, like pets die, like cattle die to serve their purpose. There was only one way Janette's story could end, and continuing to get attached would only make it that much harder.

With a heavy sigh, Meredith ignored that irksome lump in her throat and turned to face her current nemesis. With careful steps she began the harrowing ordeal of getting on the blasted toilet.

T HE TEARS FLOWED AGAIN.
"Jane," the Mistress called.
The bathroom door instantly opened. Janette's head poked through, eyes glued to the floor. "I'm here."

"I can't do it," Meredith sobbed. She could deal with the pain, she knew she could, but it was the ashen *weakness* that had stumped her. Her legs wouldn't get her up by themselves, and the one lone arm could not find enough purchase. She'd had some bad close calls trying. One more try and she'd wind up face-first on the bathroom floor, she just knew it.

It was so small, so trivial and mundane . . . and she couldn't do it. She'd tasted defeat a hundred different times, but never as bitter as this. Never as humiliating.

With a trembling hand Meredith reached out to her apprentice. "Please help me."

PART II

CHAPTER TWENTY

WEALTH

 HE SNEER ON GERTRUDE'S FACE morphed into confusion. Her hand came down hard, and the pen cradled in it struck flat against the office desk with a high-pitched smack.

"You are quitting? What in Caterina's rotten flatulence does that even mean?"

Meredith kept her nerves in check, enduring the stare without flinching. "It means I do not wish to work here anymore. But I can stay for another week, if you need—"

"Some six cycles ago you were a cripple begging me to come back to work, and now you want to quit?"

"Yes ... yes, that is the case. I can't work here anymore, I'm sorry."

Gertrude blew out a dismissive breath, small drops of spit dispersing past her wrinkled lips. "A dud could have been doing your job all this time, Neumann. You are here only because your precious brood-sister personally asked a favour of us. I'll only be so happy to get rid of you."

Meredith pressed her lips together, but the words refused to stay inside. "It might have started that way, but I've earned my place. Serf labour won't match the quality of my work."

"That may be so, but it will cost me nothing, yeah? Don't flatter yourself. This has always been charity." The sneer returned. "Until now, of course. I'll be sure to notify the Head of the Coven that her worthless brood-sister will soon be asking for more favours. I'm sure Mifraulde will be all atwitter with excitement at the news."

"Yes, do tell Mifraulde. Tell her she inspired me to become the best I can be, and I'm doing exactly that. I'll be going into the business with my partner, as a freelancer."

Not one to disappoint, Gertrude only delayed for a mite before barking out a laugh.

"That's one fine joke! Who did you find to maintain you? Did that daft librarian finally take you in? I can see it, happily ever after in your abject poverty."

"It's not a joke, I've been working so hard, we've made actual discoveries—"

The laughter was even louder this time.

"Ah-ha! Yes, I'm sure you'll be successful against all odds." Gertrude stood and pointed at the door. "Get out of my sight, yeah? Don't even bother finishing for the day. You no longer work here."

Teeth gritted and lips clamped shut, Meredith restrained whatever poorly-thought-out response was bubbling up in the back of her throat. It didn't matter, it was done. She nodded demurely, turned around and stepped through the office threshold.

Quietly she closed the door behind her, took to the catwalks, held on to the rail. Meredith looked at her feet as she walked, pace brisk as though fleeing from danger while in polite company.

She stopped.

She drummed her fingertips on the rail.

She turned around and took off toward the Taskmaster's office. Gremlins brawled in her belly as she turned the doorknob and swung the door open.

Gertrude startled to attention. "I thought I told you to disappear."

"She's not daft."

"What?"

"Yurena isn't daft. She's far smarter than you are."

The Taskmaster's leathery cheeks took on a reddish-brown color. "Get out of my office this instant!" she thundered, but Meredith spoke under the words anyway.

"She's Brena's keeper of knowledge. In her hands are the keys to everything we are as a nation. What are you? A cheerleader for unwashed stunts, feeding off the dregs of real artificers. All you ever made were peep-a-dozen trinkets to be used and discarded in a week.",

Meredith's insides were curled and taut, limbs imbued with a nervous energy that made her feel as if she was floating off the ground. Her thoughts fought against one another, one side coiled in a disbelieving *this is foolish what are you doing,* the other poised forward and chanting *yes about time you stood up to the harpy*.

"You'll be dead in a few decades," she kept going, "and your legacy will be nothing but rubbish someone else made. You think so highly of yourself, but the truth is you're not worth the dirt Yurena Valen-Frost-Mergat walks on."

Gertrude's look had darkened with every sound out of Meredith's mouth. She stood slowly, knuckles on her desk as she leaned forward.

"Are you quite done?"

Breathing noisily through her nose, Meredith held her head up high. "I . . . I'm done, yes."

"Good. Now, I'd like you to understand a couple things, yeah? One, the only reason you're not dead on my floor right now is my high regard for the Head of the Coven. She will hear of this little outburst as well, make no mistake about that."

Meredith considered responding that Mifraulde had already written her off as a lost cause and cut all ties almost one year past, but perhaps now was the time to stop the reckless truth-telling.

"And two," Gertrude said, "I will be making sure none of my contacts, clients and providers ever entertain the idea of working with you. That list includes well over half of Galavan's market, mind you. Not that any of them would take you seriously in the first place. Now, relieve me of your burdensome presence once and for all, before I toss you out of a window myself. I hope coming back into my office was worth it."

Meredith considered mentioning the handful of high-end clients Wybel had already lined up for her—or rather, provided after a steep fee and sales percentage thenceforth—but she'd sooner exit the building on her own two legs. She had the sense of hurrying out the door before Gertrude changed her mind about the whole "dropping her dead" idea.

Tension bounced on her every stride as she navigated the catwalks, steps fast enough to almost become a jog. She suppressed the impulse to break into a sprint to the double doors leading outside. It was only once she exited the building that Meredith's quick, shallow breaths abruptly deepened, her lungs working to expel the sense of impending dread that had chased her out of her former workplace.

The stress unwound in shuddering eddies. It was swiftly overtaken by a swell of elation. Shaking, victorious fists. A triumphant smile.

Worth it?

She'd never before felt so proud of herself.

T HE ROSY SPARK'T WINE tasted like unnecessarily bitter grape juice. Meredith didn't like it, but she drank it anyway.
Yurena sipped from her own glass, by all accounts enjoying it far better. Her fingernails drew idle patterns on Meredith's hand while waiting for their dessert.

"I'm at wits' end," the librarian was saying. "We've been watching closely, keeping track of every book that comes in or goes out. I'd notice if someone was taking them."

"Maybe the library wards are faulty somewhere. Someone's using magic to steal your books for . . . some reason."

"The wards are fine, we tested it. Kestrel Library is a dead zone glyphed down to its foundations. You can't infuse a syllable without the walls soaking it up."

"Maybe it's your golem? Stocking the books under a rug somewhere?"

"No, we've watched her too. Betsy's a good girl. If she weren't so limited I could configure her for sentry duties, but I don't think she can go that far. It's enough of a challenge to have her dust and carry books where they need to go."

"You truly shouldn't give it a name, they'll repossess it if they hear—"

"Oh, shush. They'll only know if you whistlegab to them. Are you going to whistlegab?"

"I'm not going to 'whistlegab,' you boob."

"Good. You'd be on hot kindle if you did."

"I don't doubt it."

"I'm suspecting Martha at this point, as silly as it sounds. She was livid to have a golem replace her. She might have come back only to sabotage me."

"That seems . . . petty."

"You were going to say 'paranoid.'"

"Maybe."

"And you'd be right." Yurena took another sip. Many more had come before it. "So . . . for how long are you going to keep me wondering?"

Meredith gave her an innocent smile. "What do you mean?"

"You invite me to the fanciest eatery in Brena, show up *in a dress,* order us a meal worth a cycle's pay, and all through the night you act like you just scored the fattest tiddler in history. I have this bizarre feeling we didn't come here to prattle about my book thief."

Meredith laughed. "I was holding off till dessert. Speaking of. . . ."

Down the carpeted aisle a small cart rolled toward them. It carried a plate with enticing colors heaped upon it, red and amber atop rich brown. The dud pushing the cart, strikingly beautiful and impeccably dressed, stopped right next to their table and placed the delicate confection between the two witches.

"Caramelized tips and honey lids on chocolate and hazelnut fudge," it recited, its voice devoid of inflection. It placed two tiny forks on opposite sides of the dessert, turned with its rolling tray and walked away.

Meredith's eyes lingered on the female youth, noting its down-trodden gait as it shuffled past the other booths flanking the aisle. Normally its kind would just blend with the background, and yet. . . .

And yet, it was painfully noticeable the dud was around Janette's age.

"Ancient stones, look at it. This is grossly decadent, love. You better have a good reason to waste money this way."

Meredith focused back on the smiling witch sitting across from her. Despite her words, Yurena's delight was evident as she enjoyed the first gooey bite.

"But I do. I quit today."

Yurena froze with the tiny fork pressed between her lips.

"You quit?" she said around her mouthful. "The manufactory?"

Meredith nodded, pride returning to her features. Yurena brought a napkin to her mouth, forcefully wiping in a very unladylike manner. "So everything's ready, then?"

"The license is already taken care of. I'm making contact tomor-row. If half what Wybel says is true, we'll be in demand non-stop shortly after."

"Ogh, there has to be a way to get rid of that gourdmonger. Her cut is outrageous. She won't even be doing anything anymore."

Meredith shrugged the issue away. Wybel's leverage was indisput-able. There was nothing to be done about it, short of murder. Crossing her struck Meredith as a horrendous idea.

Besides, she'd grown to like the gruff old coot. Sort of.

"Are *you* ready?" she asked. "The questions will come sooner or later. You don't have to be part of it."

"Of course I do!" Yurena worked her fork into the dessert, arranging frosting and dudlets for the perfect bite. "No-one will believe it's just you, Merth. I have a background, you need me. Do you want me to recite the story of our research for the hundredth time?"

"No, no, that's quite alright."

"I'm not a loose end, love." She winked, fork halfway to her mouth. "I'm the knot holding you together."

Meredith chuckled, savoring the gentle jolt of desire brought about by Yurena's gesture. She was aware of her thoughts becoming a little more stupid every time the librarian licked honey-touched lips.

She picked up her own fork, intent on ignoring the nagging voice inside her. The voice (more of a squirming whine, really) had bothered her all evening, appalled at the dishes she'd ordered, horrified at the delicious, intoxicating mix of textures and flavors. It was currently throwing a fit in her stomach, but Meredith was determined to keep it all down this time.

It was her affliction, of course. It had grown steadily worse, but she took comfort in the notion that knowing was half the battle. As long as she could recognize what was happening, she could keep it under control.

She brought to her mouth a forkful of chocolate and caramel and honey, having avoided—purely by coincidence—the crunchy dudlets sprinkled on top. She couldn't help but close her eyes and moan her praise.

It got a soft laugh out of Yurena. "Utterly brilliant, isn't it?"

"Ogh. So rich."

"I'm so glad it's all finally happening, love." The sweet-toothed witch was already preparing another bite. "Just think, it won't be long until we finally devour you-know-who."

The words roused that nagging voice to an outraged yell, but with deliberate care Meredith continued chewing, continued playing with her fork, breathing, blinking. There was no outward reaction, no out-of-place movement to betray her visceral repulsion.

It was the affliction. That stupid, cumbersome affliction.

"It . . . won't be for a while," she replied, apologetic. Meredith looked around meaningfully and leaned in. "It's convenient to have her work for as long as we can. And I'm quite certain her spark won't wane for a few years, still. The more we delay, the better for the long term."

"Of course, whatever you think is best. Though we can't get *too* greedy. It needs to happen within the next year." Yurena gestured at the dish in front of her, by all accounts none the wiser to Meredith's inner struggle. "You've barely touched it, love. I'll eat it all by myself, at this rate."

"Go ahead and finish it. My eyes were hungrier than my stomach."

"Are you sure? I absolutely will."

Meredith forced a smile while leaning back on her seat, patting her belly. "I couldn't eat one more bite of this food."

Stifling her accursed emotions, she prepared to pretend her way through the next few span. Nothing she hadn't done before, she told herself. The feeling would pass, Jane's horrified face would fade from her thoughts, and then she could focus once more on enjoying her last night of anonymity.

Not that all the attention would happen overnight, but word would spread that the useless brood-sister to the Head of the Coven was useless no more—or at least was part of a worthy enterprise. If she wanted to bribe her way out of the youth retrieval lottery, it looked better to be a public mystery whiz than a shady trinket dealer. Both options were a risk, to be sure, but her revenue had to be legitimate or she'd rouse the worst kind of suspicion. The last thing she wanted was to have the Judicars break down her door after some overzealous, two-faced official tipped them off right after taking her bribe. They'd discover the whole operation, run straight into Janette, gag her, chain her, bring her to the harvesting plants, throw her into a breeder rig, and all the while she'd know, Jane would *know* what her precious mentor *really—*

Yurena's touch on her hand brought her back to reality. She'd reached over and squeezed Meredith's fingers, searching her eyes until they latched on to her full attention. The librarian held fast to her lover's gaze, and by the time she spoke Meredith already knew the path the quiet words would follow.

"You've grown attached to her, haven't you."

She tried to react with shock, maybe throw some anger in there. *Make a scene*, the rational part of her suggested. *Don't let there be the tiniest doubt.*

Shock and anger fizzled. She just looked away. "N– no, no, it's not like that. . . ."

Yurena brought Meredith's hand into both of hers. Her whispers went only as far as the confines of their table. "Love, I understand, I do. You have spent hundreds of span with it. With . . . her. She's diligent and eager to please, and she absolutely adores you. I don't know how *I* would feel in your position. If I'm honest, I've grown a mite attached myself. I've never seen anyone take so quickly to Golemancy."

Meredith looked back up, blinking in confusion. There was nothing but sympathy on Yurena's face.

"You try so hard to fight it," she continued, lips curved with amusement, "but you can't hide it from me. I wish you didn't try. I can help you, Meredith."

She got up and moved over to Meredith's side, who made room for her in silence.

"I could even take over for a while, if you feel you're getting too close. She basically teaches herself at this point, and the fantasy world you made for her is easy to uphold."

An outraged refusal immediately rose to Meredith's tongue. She held it back, just barely . . . and recognized the protective impulse as a terrible sign.

"I . . . I'll think about it. It's not as bad as all that, I know what's at stake. I have it under control."

"Then I can keep you focused on the prize." Yurena was leaning close enough for her breath to stroke Meredith's cheek. "I truly don't blame you for feeling this way. She's like Desmond, a pet far too adorable to butcher. Do you think every witch out there is immune to mercy? Do you think I am? It takes work, sometimes. Only the mightiest witches in the lore could ever do what needs to be done without reservation."

She closed what little space remained between them, lips caressing a temple, brushing the nook between jaw and neck. Her voice was a hot draught on Meredith's ear.

"It'll all be worth the sacrifice. I've been doing a lot of research on the empowering rituals for Council investiture. With the right preparation, we'll preserve the full boost for at least a decade—and yes, the spark will fade in time, but at least half her attunement should remain with you permanently." She kissed Meredith's neck, tongue-touched lips landing at steady intervals until they reached the exposed collarbone. Each one was a tingling shudder through her skin. "It'll be a different world for us with that kind of power. You could do anything you want. What gave Mifraulde the right, anyway? Why her and not you? A fluke of brood genetics, that's all that holds you back. We can change it, you and me. Is it not worth the sacrifice?"

Meredith found it difficult to concentrate. The room beyond voice, scent and touch had blurred behind a haze. She turned her head and pressed her lips against Yurena's mouth.

"Let's get out of here," Meredith breathed. Chocolate, caramel and honey lingered on her tongue.

Yurena laughed softly and kissed her again. "I'll go use the restroom. Meet you outside, you big stemhoard."

Meredith watched her walk down the hall. The librarian's tall frame, clad in vaporous white, cut a haunting figure in the dimly-lit ambiance.

Somehow, her stomach had settled. The squirming voice had vanished.

Meredith gathered the fancy clutch purse she'd brought and got out of the cushioned seat, careful not to mess up her dress by spreading her legs too far apart. She still felt ridiculous in deep green silk and fine embroidery, but Yurena had seemed to like it a great deal.

With measured steps she headed for the front counter, idly glancing into each booth as she passed them. It was in this manner that she made eye contact with the grinning Head of the Coven.

Meredith stopped mid-shuffle. They looked at one another in stunned silence. Mifraulde's features had spread in surprise, no doubt mirroring Meredith's own. Across from her, a coquettish Coren followed Mifraulde's eyes and encountered the standing witch. Her flirty smile quickly vanished, dark cheeks flustering to a deep crimson.

One blink, two blinks, and Mifraulde's face transitioned to calm control. She looked Meredith up and down and just . . . nodded.

Meredith belatedly returned a nod that morphed into a terrible curtsy. The Head of the Coven looked on for a bit longer, her serene expression betraying none of her thoughts. She broke eye contact and turned to her meal as if Meredith wasn't even there.

She stood in silent indecision. After the flustered assistant shot her an uncomfortable glare, Meredith resumed walking.

She'd been uncertain up to this point, but it was now clear beyond doubt.

The bond they'd kept since sharing a breeder's womb had been severed for good.

CHAPTER TWENTY-ONE

PRIVATE MATTERS

RINNING AND LIGHTHEADED, Meredith leaned her head on the front door. Though Yurena had already been late to opening time at the Kestrel Library, they'd stretched their goodbyes for a good while, kissing like lovestruck twits at an academy dorm.

Diligently she engaged every lock and chain and made sure the windows were shut, even if it meant the cottage would get uncomfortably warm. Thankfully the temperate season was winding down. In a few weeks Fallow would turn into Yearning, and after that Hallow's End would begin. It would be a matter of days until the Coren chill brought back the pleasant cool of Wane through Kernel.

Meredith headed back to the kitchen and its dishwashing clatter. Janette was there at the sink, cleaning up the remains of their breakfast—except, no, she was not. Instead, she'd engaged Squarepants and left, no doubt gone straight to her worktable.

"That girl has a work addiction."

"The dishes are done," Janette's voice declared at the sink, tinny and flat. "Powering down."

Squarepants' limbs folded upon themselves, transforming the automaton into a jagged cube latched upon the separation between sink tubs. Its dozens of minute wordpaths dimmed from neon blue to the dull steel of the golem's frame.

Meredith sighed and headed for the lab. It was possible Yurena had been spending too much time around Janette.

With slow movements she opened the door and went in. The musky smell of seared metal overpowered her nostrils as she neared the intermittent buzz around the bend.

Janette sat at her favorite chair this side of the Hollow, face leaning into a set of tinted lenses. The tip of the iron in her gloved hand flashed whenever it touched the artifact she was working on. White wires ran up from the phone at her waist to plug into both her ears.

Meredith went around her, nudged the dragon statuette and an empty spark battery off to the side, leaned over the workdesk and cracked the window open. A sliver of daylight sliced under the pane's insulating layer.

"Sorry," Janette said, a bit louder than necessary. "I forgot to open it again."

Meredith moved Janette's meticulous notes out of the way so she could half-sit on the sturdy wooden table. Currently held in place by the triaxial brace was the back of a metal-plated stretch-mesh gauntlet, from forearm to knuckles. Janette had peeled off the outer layer and was inscribing tiny glyphs on the inside. The three as-yet unattached mitt-fingers were in varying states of assembly, and much to Meredith's intense approval tools and parts were neatly arranged in parallel rows by the soundstill's inputwell.

"Back at it?" she asked. Janette didn't answer.

The Mistress patiently unplugged one of the earbuds and left it dangling off her apprentice's shoulder. "Working on Mark III again?"

"Mm-hmm."

"And your assignment?"

Janette waved a hand without looking up, gesturing at the floor by the side desk. Against the table's leg rested a bulky object covered with a white sheet.

"You finished it already?"

"Mm-hmm. Dried overnight."

The Mistress walked over, picked it up and removed the white cloth. It was a nightwood cylinder the size of a small drum, varnished and polished to mirror-like smoothness. The layer of varnish would give its red-tinted wordpaths a deep embersome glow when operational. Two buttons and a dial at the top, all clearly labeled and adorned with a golden trim, allowed for customization of the desired usage parameters.

It was just a spark't space heater, commissioned by some wealthy Valeni shrew that apparently couldn't appreciate a good hearth.

"Not worried one bit about your grade, I see."

"Uh, I wasn't until *now*. Should I be worried?"

"Depends on how well it works, doesn't it?"

"I tested it before you guys got up, I couldn't find any problems. . . ."

"Good. It looks excellent. There was no hurry, you know. This wasn't due until Sixday."

A small shrug, made smaller by her already-hunched over posture. "More time to work on the fun stuff. As long as there are no more outages, right? Do you think they'll be done upgrading the grid soon?"

"Maybe. Such things take time."

"I hate it when I have to stop right in the middle. I think I'll make a spark't lamp next."

"That's so wasteful, Janette." Meredith sighed again. "I shouldn't have let you work on your own creations. You need to rest more."

"Oh, but you *did* let me, and now you can't take it back." There was a smile in the girl's voice. "And I feel just fine. Fresh like dew on lettuce. Sleep is overrated."

The Mistress playfully bopped the back of her apprentice's head, mindful to do it between iron contacts. This girl truly had been spending too much time around Yurena. "I can take back whatever I please. Will Mark III at least work properly, Little Miss Hole in the Kitchen Wall?"

Janette was quiet for a little while.

"It should. It will. That won't happen again, I promise."

Meredith gathered the notes and leafed through them. The design was an exquisite refinement on their first work, far beyond the original blueprints she'd put together from library documents over half a year ago. It was always a challenge to conceal her awe at Jane's talent.

"The first pusher was good to begin with," Meredith said without much enthusiasm. "You could've just stopped there and worked on something else."

"Oh, but this is so much better! After the miniaturization lessons there was so much room for different modes, axis specificity, kinetic inputs—oh, the first one bothered me so much, I mean, why put it in a gauntlet if you can't make cool gestures with it?" Janette leaned back from the suspended set of lenses and tugged out the other earbud, excitedly looking up at her mentor. Her eyes were squinted and weary-red from prolonged strain. "You'll see, it's pretty much a juiced-up gravity gun at this point. Or it will be, by . . . I don't know, two days from now, hopefully."

"A gravity gun?"

"Well, a gravity *glove,* I suppose. Basically, it won't just push or pull, but let you grab an object and manipulate it in three dimensions. Should get eighteen thousand vim out of it at maximum capacity, up to a hundred metres."

Meredith snorted. "Are you building tools, or a weapon to destroy the whole city?"

"Aw, come on, we'll have fun with it! And I've learned so much making this. I could conjugate Fĕň and Fǽ in my sleep, backwards."

"Still . . . eighteen thousand vim seems too much, Janette. You were lightheaded enough after imbuing Mark II."

"This one has multiple smaller batteries, I won't have to do it all at once. I'll be okay, I swear. It's not like I do it every day—since, you know . . . you won't let me."

"I've told you several times. Every artifact must be crafted to its specifications. Pouring all of your spark potential into them regardless of their purpose would be" *terribly suspicious* "unprofessional."

"But they could be *better,* though."

"It's also dangerous for you. I'm not having this conversation again."

"But Mistress!" She brought her hands together and looked up adoringly, yet her smile was playful. "You'd always stop me before I bleed to death, wouldn't you?"

Meredith rolled her eyes. "I might not, just to save myself the headache of looking after you. Or I might dump you on Mistress Yurena's lap and retire from teaching altogether."

Janette winced and hid it behind a shakier smile. "I'll be good. I promise."

"What, you don't like her? I thought you liked her."

"No, no, I mean—yes, she's nice, it's just. . . ." She pressed her lips together. "I wasn't going to bring it up."

"Bring what up? What's this about?"

"It truly is nothing."

"What did she do, Jane?"

"No, she didn't *do* anything, she just—well, she looks at me funny sometimes."

"She . . . looks at you funny?"

"I don't know, like . . . I don't know. Intensely, I guess? I see it through the corner of my eye, and then it's gone. It's weird, to be honest."

"Oh. Hm. I haven't noticed anything like that. Are you sure you're not simply imagining—"

"It's *definitely* there, Mistress." The corner of her mouth was pursed and her good eye half-rolled.

"Alright, well, I wouldn't worry about it. I know for a fact that she likes you. She's doing her best, you are the first human she's ever interacted with, and she's just nervous. I'll bet you're catching her thinking about how to deal with you properly, yeah? She wants to impress me, you see—and she's doing quite well. In fact, I *am* impressed with her performance. She might be a natural fit for this job."

Janette was now looking up at her, mouth puckered in a restrained grin. Meredith raised an eyebrow. "What? What is it?"

"You go doe-eyed when talking about her, Mistress Meredith."

"Oh, don't you start."

"You know she talks you up all the time, right? She asks me about what it's like to live with you and your routines like she can't get enough. She's just as smitten, I can tell."

Meredith chuffled out a dismissive breath. "What do *you* know? I'm positive I read somewhere you're far too young to be noticing these things."

"Pfuh, maybe if I were *five*. It doesn't take a genius to notice your googly eyes." Mischief crept onto the girl's features. "Or to know what you were doing last night."

Heat rose to Meredith's cheeks, but she didn't restrain a smile. "I think it's time you got back to work and left my love life well alone."

"I'm not even teasing! I'm so happy to see you smile all the time now, after everything we went through. And actually, um . . . I've–I've been wondering about something."

"What is it?"

"It's a little embarrassing. Maybe I'm not supposed to talk about it."

"So let's find out, then."

"Well, I was just wondering, with the novels and you guys, I was wondering. . . ." Janette looked to the side, absentmindedly rubbing left hand on right forearm. "Is that all there is? I mean, *romance-wise.* Just other witches?"

"I'm not sure I follow. What do you mean, 'is that all there is'?"

"Well . . . I'm pretty sure I like boys? Like, human boys." Janette's brow was knit, like she was apologizing. "Not that I want anything *right now*, obviously, but, well, I was thinking about the future, and you have this wonderful thing, and I'll probably want something like that at some point, you know? But . . . I don't think I like girls that way, personally. I just *don't,* I try to picture it and it's like—*uurrgh.*" She coupled the groan with a very convincing shudder, dainty shaking fists and all. "So I was just curious, since boys can't use magic, do they even live in Galavan? How does dating work? I mean, we have to make baby witches *somehow,* right? Unless everyone is brought from Earth like I was, but that doesn't sound right to me. We fought a civil war over it, yeah?" She was mid-gesture when she looked up at Meredith. Whatever Janette saw in there made her start fidgeting. "*You* guys fought, I mean. You were born here, right? I feel so silly asking this, but there's still so much I don't know about Galavan, and you said I should ask, so that's what I'm doing right now—but going by your face I don't think I'll like the answer. . . ."

The prospect of feeding her charge a new fantasy swamped Meredith's good mood. She laid hands on the girl's shoulders and made a hasty effort to smile her displeasure away. "Alright, okay, slow down now. There's no need to be nervous."

"I know, it's just . . . awkward. And I don't want to make you feel

bad, if it's a choice between magic and having a boyfriend, well,"
Janette chuckled, "I don't even need to think about it."

Meredith stayed silent, thoughts fighting among themselves. But
of course Janette would wonder about these things, with Yurena
coming and going as she pleased, not reserved in the slightest about
her affections. It had been foolish to let her get so involved, but she'd
been so relentless after she found out about the injury that Meredith
had eventually caved. She could wager a kidney that, without all the
distractions, these questions would have never formed in Janette's
head.

Hadn't she told this girl enough lies already?

She found herself three words away from painting the grim
picture of reality. The history of Humanist debauchery, the inception
of the Puritan Department of Broodspawn Progeny and a civil war
that had outlawed any and all fraternization with humans. Doctrine
tenets oppressive enough to give rise to a rebellion, only for it to be
thoroughly crushed. The open abuse, the taboos, the ruthless
deviant persecution, the criminalization of mercy toward lesser
beings. How, over time, what was once normal had become
forbidden under penalty of torturous incarceration and pyre-
cleansing.

The truths roiled and bubbled and struggled to surface, like
trapped pockets of fresh air beneath layers of rot.

With much trepidation Meredith gathered up these truths, one by
one, and buried them as deep as they would go. She couldn't let
them out. Doing so would ruin everything she'd worked for.

What was one more lie tossed onto the mountain of deceit?

"First off," she said, "I know you're getting to that age, but you're
still too young to know what you like for sure. You might change
your mind, yeah?"

Janette's lips pursed, but she gave an accepting nod.

"To answer your question, no, that's not all there is. Witches
routinely mingle with humanity and forge relationships that way,
but it's done covertly. This is where the masquerade comes in.
Remember the verses on the first page of the Concept Compendium?"

Janette nodded again. "Never let them know, never let them go—"

"Never let them tell, yes. It's a call to caution. Humanity is
powerful, and open confrontation would be disastrous regardless of
who wins. But like you said, baby witches must come from
somewhere, yeah? Recruitment alone can't sustain a stable
population, because in fact, human apprentices are quite rare. We
don't go around the world abducting youths against their will, how
monstrous would that be?"

Instead of showing amusement, Janette seemed to weigh the idea
with serious thought. "But you offer *magic* in return. Only a fool
would pass up the chance. They'd learn to appreciate being chosen,

eventually."

"Oh. Um, you'd be surprised. It's happened to me a few times. They agree to stay, but then change their minds and never develop their potential. They were too attached to their former lives."

"Really?"

Meredith nodded matter-of-factly, fairly proud of her improvisation. Janette was frowning, head tilted to one side.

"So what happened to them?"

The question drew a blank for a response. Meredith coughed. "What?"

"What happened to them? You can't let them go anymore, they know too much."

"Ah. Yes, well." The Mistress leaned off the work desk and walked over to the bed, very consciously fixing up creases in the hastily arranged sheets. "I . . . turned them in. To the Reinstatement Department. So they could be placed back into their societies."

"They get killed, don't they?"

Meredith startled and whirled to face the girl. "What? No! Whatever gave you that idea?"

"I don't know, it makes sense? It's way more convenient than sending them back."

"Convenient? Absolutely not, no-one's getting killed, that's not an option."

"Oh."

"You sound disappointed!"

"Well!" Janette shrugged in a helpless gesture, gloved palms facing up. "It just makes me mad! There you are, giving some dumb girl the gift of a lifetime, and they turn it down? If they're that stupid, maybe they shouldn't be around in the first place. I can just see it, I bet they didn't want to work for it. Some privileged daddy's girls too full of themselves with their stupid hair and their stupid makeup to care about anything other than how cool their selfies look."

Meredith remained quiet. She was reminded of Mifraulde's rants, for some reason. The girl was shaking her head, a disgusted grimace on her face. "Idiots. It's not like they can never return, right? Grown witches can go back and mingle at any time. Is that right?"

"Y– yes, of course." She paused to restore her derailed train of thought. "Well . . . with some limitations. You need a mission statement, and it needs to be approved by the Coven."

"Really? But you brought me here through a space-fold. What stops you from using it any time you like?"

The Travel and Transportation Department and their carefully monitored nexus logs, for one.

"Um . . . nothing, I suppose. It's simply illegal. Interaction with Earth needs to be closely controlled. I'm sure you can understand the reasons."

"Yeah. Yeah, I guess. So you can only go there on . . . 'missions'?"

"You just need a good reason, like procuring goods for a certain market, doing research, scouting talent . . . you won't be able to permanently reside there, but you could stay for years at a time. Relationships happen in the meantime, I suppose."

"Ooh, that sounds like fun. Have you ever done it?"

Meredith recoiled in genuine aversion. "No, yeugh." She reflexively wiped her hands on her robe. "Once was one time too many. Never, ever again."

"What? You never told me about this, what happened to you?"

She didn't want them, but the memories came regardless. The first round of the field test to get an Earth travel license was meant to be a simple task: snatch an isolated youth in the black of night. In and out, quick and easy.

Whyever would a young stunt sleep with a wooden club at arm's reach? Why did it have to get up in the middle of the night, right as she was making her entrance? What did they *feed* these small creatures, for them to be so fulminating with their blunt weapon? Everything that followed flashed in her mind: the beating, the yelling, the arrest and horrible jail stay and the slaughter of witnesses when Mifraulde broke her out.

Meredith pushed it all away with a shudder. She'd never wanted to go there in the first place.

"Nothing happened," she said, voice almost steady. "Earth is simply dreadful. There are too many humans, and diseases, and mad weather. I'd suffocate within a day."

Janette snorted out a giggle. "Come on, it's not so bad as all that! Maybe we could go together? Sometime in the distant future, I mean."

"I don't know about that. . . ."

"Just for a little while, to scout a new recruit or whatever. Wait—" Janette seemed to be struck by a horrid thought. "Magic still works there, right?"

"Yes . . . yes, it does, of course. Though it is heavily discouraged. The masquerade, you see."

"Oh. Of course. So . . . what do you say? Yes? Please say yes."

Meredith found herself inclined to say *yes* and actually mean it. The impossibility of such a promise became a gaping sinkhole in her stomach. "No, Janette. I don't think so."

"Aww, plee-e-ease? We'll go somewhere nice and beautiful, and clean, and I could maybe meet a boy while we're there, and you could pretend to be my mum or my aunt or something. You'd worry about him not being good enough, and be all disapproving, and—and we could pretend to argue back and forth, but in the end he wins you over! It would be so much fun!"

Every word split the chasm wider. *We won't ever do any of those things,* she wanted to scream. *I'm using you and you're supposed to die.*

The truth of it stained her every thought. How could she let it get this far? How had she allowed herself to feel this way? She worked to hold back the anger, shut away her own treacherous longing for the future Janette envisioned.

"No," Meredith said. "None of that will happen."

"Well, there doesn't need to be a boy involved or anything, it just sounds like a fun adventure we could—"

"Stop talking."

Rage churned in Meredith's breast. Frustration, disgust, self-loathing, resentment, blame and self-blame—it all viciously gnawed through her lungs. The intensity of it caught her unprepared.

"We can't be friends, and you presume too much. You are an artificer's apprentice, and that is the extent of our relationship, do you understand?"

Janette flinched at the outburst, seeming to shrink in place. The sight made Meredith's insides curl with remorse, which in turn intensified the overpowering tide of vexation.

"I warned you at the start, did I not? Personal attachment and familiarity are liabilities. Yanetta's Folly, remember? I forgot somewhere along the way. Any other witch would be horrified I've let things slide this far. I am to blame, I've let this happen, but it stops now. It stops *now.*"

She was shouting by the time she got to the end. Janette had drawn her arms up to her chest, hands made into fists—like recoiling, like protecting herself. The look on her face was a knife plunged between Meredith's ribs.

"Don't cry. Don't you *dare* start crying. Do you truly wish to be a witch? Witches don't *ever* cry. We are ruthless. We are ambitious. We do what needs to be done."

She watched the girl struggle to keep her emotions in check. Janette's features scrunched up, her blue eyes watered and squinted. Meredith knew how deranged her rant must sound, how unwarranted and hypocritical it was after everything they'd shared. A flustered apology was ready to jump from her tongue, followed by the tightest hug she could give. It was an inhuman effort to wrest the impulses to the ground and squash them.

"I understand," Janette said in a subdued whisper. She closed her eyes and swallowed. "I understand, Mistress Meredith."

She couldn't handle it anymore. Meredith sternly nodded and headed for the door. She spoke with her hand on the doorjamb.

"Get some rest. You will have another assignment soon."

Without waiting for an answer, she stepped out and closed the door. Meredith headed straight outside and paced up and down the cobbled path to the gate.

Among crooked trunk and withered shrub she worked to calm her racing heart. Her breathing slowed. Energetic strides gave way to slow steps. Rage and remorse subsided, the resentment mellowed to a simmer—until only disgust remained. Disgust, caustic and rotten.

This needed to end. It had to end soon. She had to tell Yurena, it needed to end soon.

Otherwise, she might not be able to go through with it.

STANDING BY THE LAB'S ENTRANCE, Meredith stared into the gap of black between door and jamb. The moan troubled the darkness again, pitched low and drawn out like the growl of a cat.

Her nails had dug into her palms hard enough to make the skin raw. Only moans so far, but it had escalated a few times in the past. Screams. A broken lamp. It was routine to go in there and make it better.

This wasn't a coincidence. The night terrors got worse whenever Jane—whenever *the human youth* had a reason to be anxious. As was always the case, her raw power wafted through the gap like torrid fumes from a furnace. Meredith's hand was white-knuckled on the door handle.

Another moan, short and angry.

The Mistress blew out a mournful breath. She stepped back. She quietly latched the door closed.

She returned to bed, buried her head under pillow and blanket and shut her eyes tight. She let the sheets catch her tears.

It had to end soon.

THERE WAS SOME SOFT KNOCKING, and shortly after the bedroom door cracked a hairline. A narrow beam of light fell upon the rug and corner of the bed.

"Mistress?"

Janette's voice was a timid quaver. Even though dawn hadn't happened yet, Meredith had only been half-asleep. It took her a brief while to put a reply together.

The door swung slightly wider. "Mistress? I'm very sorry to disturb you."

"What is it, Janette?"

"I'm bleeding."

"Wh . . . what?"

"I'm bleeding. Down there. It's . . . kind of a mess."

Meredith pulled the covers off and sat on the side of the bed, rubbing at her eyes.

"Down there? Down *where*? Did you cut yourself?"

"No, it's, you know . . . my period? I think this is it. I didn't expect it to be this bad."

What in Caterina's condemned arse is a period, Meredith wanted to ask, but the memory of her studies came forth. The bleeding cycle had been tucked into a footnote on female youths concerning their breeder potential.

"It's a bit scary," Janette added, voice trembling with self-conscious laughter.

"Alright. Alright, let me . . . switch on the light, let me see."

The girl complied. Through squinted eyes, Meredith saw. The red stains on the white satin nightgown weren't widespread, but fairly noticeable. She quickly suppressed her panic as Janette fidgeted at the doorway.

"I went to bed early," the girl continued. "My belly hurt, I didn't sleep so well. And then I woke up and felt gross down there. I thought I'd wet the bed," she tittered again, "so I ran to the light switch, and I saw it. It's . . . it's normal, right? It's normal?"

"Of course, yes. Don't worry. Let's get you cleaned up."

"It's, um, it's still happening. It lasts for a few days, right? My sister complained for days."

"Yes, yes. We'll deal with it, come on. Let's go to the bathroom before you drip all over the rugs."

They walked in single file, Meredith's hands gently resting on the girl's shoulders, goading her forward. Janette's thighs remained glued together as she shuffled toward their destination. Once there, she stood by the toilet while Meredith busied herself around the room. "Here," she said, handing Janette a roll of toilet paper. "Stop the flow with this. Throw the dirty clothes over there. Don't let them touch the mat."

Tucking her bedraggled hair behind her ears, Meredith started the shower and flipped the switch above the faucet for the water heater to come on. After a small wait she adjusted the temperature until it became a pleasant lukewarm. She went to the left drawer by the mirror, pulled out a stack of rags and wet them, wrung them, neatly folded them atop the tiny table between toilet and bathtub. In the meantime a flustered Janette did what she could with the paper in her hand. Red fingertips trembled as they daubed pink off her thighs. There was a shiver from time to time.

She looked up and their eyes met. The girl drew a self-conscious mien that might have been half a smile. "I could have done this by myself. I knew it would happen sometime. I shouldn't have bothered you in the middle of the night."

I'm sorry I was so hard on you yesterday. I'm sorry I left you alone in the darkness. I'm so sorry I hurt you. I'm sorry, I'm sorry, I'm sorry.

Meredith clenched her jaw, taking a moment to swallow the words. She forced a smile that conveyed just the right amount of discomfort.

"Nonsense," she said, and began wiping her sleep-laden eyes and face with one of the damp rags. "I was going to have you use these, but that's more blood than I expected. Best if you step into the tub."

Poorly concealed fear showed through Janette's features. "More than you expected? You think there's something wrong?"

"No, please, don't worry. It will stop in a few days, like you said." She stood from the tub's ledge. "I'll get you clean clothes and plenty of gauze."

"Oh. Don't you have, you know, pads? Or I guess you might use those . . . things." She raised her pinky and wriggled it eloquently, mimicking the alleged thing. The gesture meant absolutely nothing to Meredith.

"I don't have any."

"No? I figured you kept that stuff in your room."

"Can't say I do. The water's running nice and warm, hop in."

Janette continued talking while gingerly moving into the tub. "Where do you keep them, then? I've looked everywhere."

"You mean you've *snooped* everywhere."

"I spend a lot of time alone in this house! I like knowing where everything is stored."

"I don't need those things, Janette. I don't get a . . . period."

"Oh?" Her eyebrows lifted in understanding. "Ooh."

Janette placed her hands under the showerhead, rubbing her fingers together. The blood washed off slowly. "I feel so stupid. You look young, it didn't occur to me you were past . . . you know. That stage. You've probably gone without it for over a hundred years!"

"Sure, yes," Meredith said. "I'll give you some privacy. I'll be back with clean clothes."

"I . . . I hate to insist, but I *really* could use some actual pads, Mistress."

"Gauze and cloth is all I have right now. Later I'll go out and get you something better, yeah?" Meredith didn't have the first clue how to fulfil such a promise, but that was a problem for the future. "Will you be alright?"

Janette nodded, eyes down to her belly button. "Are the cramps always so bad?"

"I don't know, how bad are they now?"

"It's not too bad right now. Earlier it was like someone taking a hammer to the base of my spine."

"That sounds terrible."

"Is it always going to be like that?"

Meredith considered it. "Probably."

"Soot and ash. . . ."

"Soot and ash indeed. Do you need anything else?"

Janette shook her head. "Thank you."

The curtain was drawn and the water still running by the time Meredith got back. She quietly left underwear, one of Janette's robes and appropriately-sized gauze on the little table, then turned to leave the girl to her own devices. There was no going back to bed, now. She might as well get her morning routine under way.

"Mistress?"

She stopped in front of the mirror. "Yes?"

"If a witch has a son . . . what happens to him? Would he be a wizard?"

"Wizards are an old myth. Didn't I tell you that on the very first day?"

"Yeah, but . . . what, we raise boys in Galavan, even if they don't have talent?"

Meredith considered a number of lies. She ended up picking a perfectly truthful answer.

"Witches don't have sons. It simply doesn't happen."

"Only daughters?"

"Sure. Witches have only daughters, yes."

She stared at her own lips moving. It wasn't *really* a lie, if it was interpreted in a certain way.

"Why is that? Is it because of the magic, somehow? Or just . . . abortions?"

Meredith didn't even know what that was. She began brushing her hair, pulling it back as tightly as she could. "Why are you asking me these things?"

"I'm just curious. Since, you know, I can have babies now." There was a short pause. "That's what this means, right? Obviously."

"Yes. Obviously."

"So it starts now, and it stops around fifty years old. Right?"

"That sounds about right."

"It's such a brief window, if I'm going to live for hundreds of years."

Janette's wistful musing was another needle to Meredith's gut. She simply kept quiet, lips pressed onto a hairband as she brusquely collected every loose strand and brought them above her nape. The sounds of falling water became wholly uniform, as if no part of Janette was touching the stream.

"Did *you* have children, Mistress?"

"No. I did not."

In the mirror she saw the shadow behind the curtain shift from side to side. "I'm sorry, that was rude to ask. You'd have mentioned it by now."

"I don't know if I would have."

Stretch the elastic and pull the hair through. Twist and pull again. Twist and pull a third time. The uniform shower stream broke and splashed around once more.

"I think I'd like to have a daughter one day," Janette said.

The hairband broke with a painful snap against Meredith's fingers. She dug her nails into the flesh of her palms. They were still raw.

"I'll be in the living room," she said, voice not all the way there. "Call if you need anything."

"Oh, um, alright. I've kind of been done for a while. It just feels nice."

Meredith fished another plain hair tie from the drawer and headed for the door.

"Mistress. . . ."

"Yes?"

"Thank you."

I know you feel bad, Meredith heard in the girl's voice. *I know you're just following the rules.*

It doesn't need to be this way.

We could still be friends, nobody needs to know.

I won't tell anyone, and you could pretend in front of Yurena, just like you've been doing all this time.

Don't you think I deserve to have a friend before you kill me?

"I have no choice," Meredith said, spine bent and breath shallow.

"I'm sorry?"

"Don't thank me," she said, louder. "It's only my duty, apprentice."

Janette didn't respond.

Meredith closed the door.

FRETTING AT HER LIP until it was chewed sore, Meredith stared into the swirl of colors within Wybel's space-fold. She watched for any sign of Yurena, just as she had for the last tenth-span. What had been mild worry had become twists and knots inside her stomach that relentlessly goaded her to take the plunge and go find her.

There was *no way* she was jumping through a portal to Earth, though—especially one for which the nexus would soon expire. So Meredith watched, and waited, and worried.

Wybel's voice drifted in from the storefront. "Are you done yet? It's nearly lunchtime and you two will not spoil it with your presence."

"She's still out there. Do you think she's alright? Is this normal? How long does it take to conduct business in a human market?"

"She is probably dead by now, go home."

"That's not funny at all!"

"Who's trying to be funny?"

Meredith fidgeted, and needlessly adjusted her robes, and sighed dramatically. She started pacing. Maybe she could get her mind off the problem by doing another tour around the workshop. It was modest in size, but efficiently packed with tool shelves, a workbench with a soundstill, a well-equipped crafting station, storage lockers, a medical supply cabinet and miscellaneous odds and ends. There was also a large fold-up table leaning against the wall, and the sight of it was enough to bring a painful twinge to Meredith's arm. Not even her visit to Earth could compare to the agony she'd suffered on that table.

Still darting fretful glances at the active portal, she neared the crafting bench and leaned over Wybel's incomplete project. Apparently she was skilled at something other than making a profit off the work of others. Meredith poked the metallic toes up and down, watching how the still-exposed joints and biomechanical tendons moved and reacted all the way up to the ankle. Proper mezzode parts would be intricate work even without miniaturized wordpaths and infusion to worry about.

She wondered what kind of rich harpy might be missing a foot out there, that they would commission something like this. Maybe another alchemy apprentice literally playing with fire, or perhaps some old witch tired of her arthritis and looking for a replacement limb.

"It's awful quiet in there. You're not touching my things again, are you?"

"I'm just watching the blasted space-fold!"

Yurena stepped through the portal in the middle of the sentence.

"Maryam's Ashes," she cursed right away, "humans keep getting fatter and fouler. It must be some kind of disease."

Clad in close-fitting T-shirt and jeans, she looked like an entirely different person. She wore a juvenile headband on her hair and a vexed expression on her features, and from her forearm hung several flimsy plastic bags full of colorful, cushiony packages. *Safeway*, the bags said in bold black letters.

Meredith exhaled her relief and hugged Yurena tightly.

"Oof!" She patted Meredith in the back, tense in her embrace. "Whatever got into you?"

She retreated to arm's length, still holding on. "You were gone for a long time. I was worried something might have happened to you."

"It takes a while to get places over there, and you have to deal with congestion and lines and so forth. Here." She passed the bags to Meredith, switched off the space-fold and began to undress, speaking in hushed tones all the while. "And the rudeness! Yeugh. Human males kept leering. One of them even *talked* to me." She shuddered. "The female I asked about period bandages looked at me like I was a halfwit, and the store clerk smirked and said 'I see you're good to flow, sister,' whatever that means. I had half a mind to bake her eyeballs inside her own skull. Aren't you going to pass me my clothes?"

Meredith snapped to the task, dropping the bags and grabbing the librarian's attire from the nearby chair. She withheld them at the last moment, looking Yurena up and down. "I don't know, I rather enjoy the view."

"Don't get cute with me, I'm not in the mood."

"Alright, alright. . . ."

Yurena perfunctorily put on her blouse, skirt and robe. She gestured at the bags. "That better be worth the trouble. I nearly got lost in that jungle full of savages, I'm not familiar at all with the eighth meridian band. You and your ashen emergency."

"Thank you so much for doing this."

"I still don't even understand it." She lowered her voice even more. "Are you *sure* she's not sick? It's so odd for humans to bleed at random, from *there* of all places."

"I told you, it's not random. It's once every cycle and it lasts a few days."

"That sounds horrible. Why wouldn't they fix it?"

"It has something to do with fertility." Meredith smiled impishly. "I hear there's a library somewhere in Brena with books that explain it, you should do some research."

"Oh yeah? And how would you know? You only ever cared about cookbooks, I thought."

"As far as you know, yes. I have to keep up appearances, the librarian there is a snoop."

Yurena tossed her discarded T-shirt at Meredith's face. "I hear she always gets what she wants."

"Sounds about right." Meredith reached for a hand and pulled Yurena close. The tall librarian let her. "She's dazzling, too. Have you seen her?"

"She's not my type. I like plain, bumbling and freckled. I must be a fool."

"Still can't disagree." Meredith got on her tip-toes, cupped her lover's jaw and softly kissed her. Despite her words Yurena wrapped her arms around Meredith's waist, squeezing tight.

"I hear lots of whispering," Wybel's voice came in through the doorway's heavy curtain, "but no footsteps getting out of my workshop!"

Meredith felt Yurena's irritation through the tension on her lips. The wizened shopkeeper swept into the room as their mouths parted. It was a warm day and lighter clothing was to be expected, but it was still strange to see her clad in silken blouse and long skirt.

"Alright, love-twits, it's time to disappear. You can carry on with your sentimental nonsense by the refuse pile outside, for all I care. Now, clear my floor of your illegally acquired rubbish and get out of here."

Meredith rolled her eyes. "Half your inventory is 'illegally acquired rubbish,' Wybel."

"This is what I get for doing favours for criminals, a mouthful of baseless slander."

"Favours? You *charged me* to exchange some measly currency and use your space-fold."

"A below-market fee of my *untraced* space-fold, and I'm starting to regret it. Why are you not leaving yet?"

Yurena's fine eyebrows were drawn down. "Are you this dismissive of everyone? Or only of Meredith?"

Wybel regarded her evenly. "I have plenty of sneers for you too, if you want them."

"So you treat all your associates this way?"

Meredith pulled on Yurena's arm. "She's always like this, it's just harmless banter. Come on, let's go. . . ."

Yurena didn't budge. "She's making you a fortune without you lifting a finger. Don't you owe her some respect, at least?"

Wybel snorted. "So that's your bone to pick. I've been wondering since you walked in the door. I'll have you know she wouldn't be 'making a fortune' without my help, hatchtwat. If there is a burdensome party in this venture, I would point straight at you."

"Hey now," Meredith said, but was interrupted by Yurena's shocked laugh.

"Me?" she said. "What do *you* know? *I* am involved every step of the way, enough to know you're an obsolete in-betweener latching on to a ridiculous cut you never deserved. You are blackmailing her."

"And you say this as you step out of *my* untraced space-fold, inside *my* workshop. Yes, clearly you need none of the things I offer."

"You don't *offer* anything, you just gouge her for every clip you can get your hands on!"

"I charge for every service, as any sensible business would. At least I'm up-front about being a gold digger."

Yurena clenched with anger at the unfamiliar insult. "And what exactly is that supposed to mean?"

"It means what it means, you ignorant wealth-latch."

"How *dare* you—"

"Stop it! Both of you!"

Meredith's voice was shrill and shaken, nearly strident. It made the warring witches turn in unison. She addressed Yurena. "There's no need for this. Wybel saved my life, remember? And she's right. We struck a deal and I'm fine paying her dues. She earned it."

She addressed Wybel. "Yurena is also right. She's part of my life, I wouldn't have come this far without her, and I could use a bit less mockery from you. I'd wager I've become a big chunk of your income, I'm quite certain you wouldn't be pleased to see me go."

Both witches stared at Meredith for some time. She looked at each one in turn, nervous chills wracking her core—yet above the anxious nerves reigned the triumphant empowerment that came with finally asserting herself. She could do it, she really could, just like she'd done in Gertrude's office. It was high time for her to start conducting herself—

"How *dare* you!" Yurena took a step toward her quarry as if Meredith wasn't even there. "I was with her before she ever made a single sale!"

"You are more of a fool than I thought, then. You are made for one another."

Meredith puffed out a breath, stuffed the bags and human clothes into the unassuming rucksack they'd brought and pulled her livid girlfriend toward the back door. Yurena kept talking over her shoulder all the way there.

"Oh yeah? Well, at least I *have* somebody, you decrepit gourd-monger. What will you do with all those riches when you croak? Leave them to the ravens picking at your carcass?"

Meredith successfully ushered her out the door, but it didn't close in time to block Wybel's sneering response.

"I'll leave them all to you so you can buy yourself a brain."

The door slammed shut. Yurena turned and kicked it. "Uurgh!"

"Calm down, Yune. Come on, let it be." Meredith kept pulling subtly, eager to get out of the back alley. Dark memories swam through its midday shadows.

"What an insufferable harpy! Is this what you've been putting up with?"

"It's not so bad. I just ignore it."

"You mean you just *take it*. You need to stand up for yourself!"

Meredith shrugged. "The more upset you get, the more she'll enjoy it."

"So she can simply walk all over you?"

"Only happens if I confront her. She has all the leverage and she knows it. I'm just culling conflict."

"Well . . . it wouldn't hurt for you to actually cull one now and then."

"I do. Believe me, I do."

Meredith's calm seriousness seemed to work on Yurena's temperament, smoothing some rough edges. The tall witch spoke after a stretch of walking in silence.

"I hate to see others disrespect you. They don't know your worth like I do."

Meredith smiled. She sought Yurena's hand and clasped it. The librarian didn't pull back, but she didn't squeeze, either. "That's because you're smarter than anyone I know," Meredith said.

"Right, sure. I'll take the compliment, despite the tiny sample size."

They walked hand-in-hand, not quite caring about Brenan decorum. The nameless alley turned into Magrat Street which would soon lead into Circe Street. The Dregs weren't so bad in daylight. On both sides brick residences messily fought one another for the streetfront, jettying above the geometrically perfect cobbles as if eager to crash upon them. Their walls were painted in a variety of pastel colors that had positively no regard for their respective neighbors. Foot traffic was sparse: a few cloaked duds running errands, a golem troddling by the wall, dragging its sweeper back and forth, a lone witch in a white cowl going who-knows-where. The sun shone brightly in the skyveil, as it always would in the last few days of Yearning.

Meredith glanced at Yurena. Though the worst of her ire had passed, there was still a bothered frown on her brow.

"Yune," Meredith said.

"Yes?"

"I kept thinking about losing you while you were gone. It was atrocious."

"Well, I should hope so."

Meredith stopped, pulling on Yurena's hand to get her full attention.

"No, I mean . . . I was *so* worried." She played with the ring on Yurena's finger. "I was crippled with fear. It caught me by surprise."

"Honestly, Meredith? 'By surprise,' after nearly a year together? Is this supposed to be flattering?"

"It is! You don't understand, I never . . . *cared,* before you. Not for anyone. But you . . . you're different. You are . . . real, to me."

"What are you scheming?"

"What?"

"You're trying to manipulate me right now. What are you scheming?"

"Nothing! I just wanted to tell you. I thought you'd like hearing it."

Yurena rolled her eyes. "Mm-hmm."

"Wait, are you mad at me?"

"Well, I went and did this favour for you because you're so terrified of going to Earth, and she mocks me and belittles me in front of you, and instead of getting outraged you go and stand up for *her*."

"But . . . you started it."

"Did I? I was *defending* you after she treated you like mud on her boot. I'd like to think you'd do the same for me, but clearly that's not the case."

"But I stood up for you too, didn't I? I just wanted to keep things running smoothly. She can ruin us, Yune."

"Don't 'Yune' me. She's not going to throw away all her precious fees and percentages just because you told her off."

"But you held your own so well!"

"That's not the point." Yurena resumed walking, barely looking at Meredith. "I felt like I was on my own in that room."

Meredith followed a bit belatedly. "I *did* try to say something, but you two were shouting at each other."

"And yet you had *no trouble* shrieking at me towards the end."

"That's . . . not. . . ."

She stumbled into a babble that went nowhere. Meredith could feel herself sinking into an ever-deeper pit. With each step flustered anxiety built inside her, the same kind of tension that had gripped her all through the mad caper in the holding pens. How serious was this spat, anyway? Could she defuse it with a few well-placed words? Could she simply ignore it away?

Silence stretched for entirely too long.

"I was only trying to be rational about everything," she finally offered.

Yurena stopped and looked at Meredith with raised eyebrows. "So I'm being irrational? Is that what you're saying now?"

"No? No, I didn't mean—"

"What *did* you mean? Because if you were only being rational, and I'm upset about it, then what does that mean?"

"It means. . . ."

"I'm listening."

"Maybe you *are* being a little irrational?"

She regretted the words before they were done coming out. In dreadful detail Meredith watched the change happen, a dozen minute shifts in Yurena's features: a small flinch and wince, eyelids that subtly widened above and narrowed below, a downward quirk to the corners of her mouth.

"You are unbelievable," she said, and stalked off with angry strides.

Meredith chased after her, the sack-full of pads bouncing on her back. "Yurena, no, wait."

"What for? So you can keep insulting me? I've had enough of that for the day."

"I didn't mean it like that, it came out all wrong. Please, stop."

"*You* are calling me irrational, you, with your compulsions and fears and twenty locks on your door! I'm *so* done with you for today. Have a fun walk home, tell your pet she's welcome."

"Yurena. . . ."

"*Stop*. Following me."

Meredith paced to a reluctant stop, watching her walk away. Yurena's fists were balled, her gait rigid and abrupt. She turned at the intersection and went out of sight.

Don't stop, chase after her!

She wanted to listen to the impulse, but indecision kept her glued to the spot. What if she made it even worse? Could it be made worse? Was she just being a coward again? What if Yurena *wanted* to be chased after? How serious was this, honestly? It didn't seem serious, it couldn't be *that* serious, right?

Her heart felt constrained to a tiny cage, beating against its bars without control. A trio of prattling crones had stopped to watch the scene. Their faces ranged from disdain to amusement.

She couldn't be bothered to care. Meredith leaned against the earthy-orange front of someone's house and stared at the corner where Yurena had disappeared. She continued staring for a long time. Truly, how serious could it be?

Eventually she started on her way home with slow, shuffling steps.

MEREDITH SHAMBLED into her cottage, dropped the sack in front of Janette's room and knocked half-heartedly. Without waiting she headed for her own room, closed the door and sat on her bed, numbly staring into the middle distance.

Every word kept playing over and over in her head, punctuated with fantasies of what could have been, what should have been. All the things she should have said, all the times when she ought to have kept her mouth shut. Throughout her walk home she'd fluctuated between dismissal and anguish, guilt and anger in turn. But mostly regret. Yes, definitely regret.

Surely this was all blown out of proportion inside her head, yes? A lovers' quarrel without much consequence in the long run. Every relationship went through this type of thing. It couldn't be blood-rain and fat harvest all the time, there had to be fights and disagreements at some point. It was even healthy, yes. One could say she'd done a service to them both.

But the look on Yurena's face. . . .

"You can be *so stupid,* Meredith."

In that instant the future became crystal clear in her head. The connections were so easy to make. Yurena would realize Meredith's *true* worth at last, come to her senses and go straight to Mifraulde. They'd come for her with gags and shackles and throw her into the dungeon, and mount her on the wheel, and eventually set her on fire, and take Janette to the harvest plants, to the breeder pods—

There was a soft knock at the door.

"Yes?"

Janette pushed it open wide enough to peek through. "I just wanted to say 'thank you.' I know you're only doing your duty, but thank you anyway."

"You are welcome."

She pitched the words in a way that she might as well have said "goodbye," but the silhouette at the door remained motionless.

"Anything else?"

"Is . . . is everything okay?"

"Everything is fine. Go back to whatever you were doing, Janette."

"Alright."

The door moved to close after a hesitant pause. It didn't make it all the way.

"You seem very upset, Mistress."

Meredith squeezed her eyes shut.

"That's because I'm very upset."

Saying it out loud brought an antsy sting to her eyes. Her voice had trembled a bit. She pinched her thigh as hard as she could.

Don't you start crying, you pathetic sop.

Janette walked into the room with tentative steps. She neared the bed as if afraid to disturb a single mote of dust and sat at arm's length from Meredith. There she stayed, hands on her lap, legs loosely crossed at the ankles. She didn't say a word or move to touch the Mistress in any way.

Meredith glanced at her. In her work robes, gloved as usual, long waves tied back in a puffy ponytail. She wasn't trying to make eye contact—Jane was simply . . . there.

"I got into a fight with Yurena."

She hadn't meant to say it. It just came out.

"Oh, no. . . ."

"It was my fault."

"I'm sorry," Janette said.

"Why would you be sorry?"

"I'm sorry it happened."

"Ah."

There was a brief pause. Janette tilted her head to look at Meredith side-long. "I've never seen you cross at one another."

"We've never fought before. Sometimes we get a mite peeved, but it always goes away in the same breath."

Janette smiled faintly. "Like that morning, with the buttered toast?"

The memory brought a similar smile to Meredith's lips. "Yes, like with the buttered toast. You don't put the butter on right away, it melts into an oily mess. You have to wait until the bread cools. That's just how it's done."

"Yes. Absolutely. It's uncivilised to do otherwise."

"That sounded like mockery, but I know you wouldn't dare."

Janette sniffed a soft chuckle. "She loves you, Mistress. Whatever happened, I'm sure she will forgive you."

"You truly think so?"

"Well, um, you didn't stab her or anything like that, right?"

"No, you boob, I didn't stab her. I just . . . I did the wrong thing and chose the wrong words."

"Oh." Janette daintily tapped her lips with her fingers. "Do you know the right words now?"

She contemplated the question. "Yeah. I suppose I do."

"Then . . . you should probably say them to her. As soon as you think she'll listen."

"Yeah."

"Don't worry, Mistress. Every time couples fight, they always end up closer together. It's like that in every story."

"That's why they're only stories. In reality, fighting just makes you bitter and loathsome until you can't take it anymore."

"Aw, maybe you feel that way now, but you'll see. Everything will work out for the better, I promise."

Meredith snorted. She would have voiced her skepticism, but the earnest confidence in Jane's face gave her pause.

"You . . . you really think so?"

"Oh, I know so." Janette scuttled closer, full of enthusiasm. She covered Meredith's hand with her own. "The way she looks at you . . . I can't even explain. It's fairytale stuff, I didn't think that sort of love could be real until I saw it here."

The words drew a self-conscious smile out of Meredith. She rolled her eyes, flustered. "I've never noticed. You're imagining things."

"You just can't see it, because you're not on the outside looking in. I swear, she adores you."

"Oh, shut up."

"I swear!"

Wrapped in their candid grins and open eye contact, both Mistress and apprentice seemed to realize at the same time the way they were speaking to each other. Meredith's smile became brittle. Janette looked down at their touching hands. The girl flinched and awkwardly withdrew the hand back to her lap, gaze downcast.

"I'm sorry," she said, "I got carried away."

"It's fine. Not your fault." Meredith fidgeted with her robes, rubbing the hem between her fingers. She stood. "Thank you for . . . um, thank you. You're dismissed."

"Of course, Mistress."

Janette left the bed and headed for the door. Her hand lingered on the knob.

"Mistress?"

"Yes?"

"You . . . you *do* like me, right? I mean, if it weren't for the rules, we'd still be friends?"

She seemed afraid to look back. Meredith put her rebelling

thoughts in order before responding.

"What I feel doesn't matter. This is the way it needs to be."

"It does matter, though. It matters to me."

"It shouldn't. Worry only about your studies and your assignments."

"Are we under surveillance? Do you have to say these horrible things, even in private?"

The hurt in her voice brought a lump of sick to Meredith's stomach. She swallowed past it. "I have to treat you this way because the rules dictate it. I thought you understood."

After a moment of quiet, Janette swung the door open. "I do, it's just . . . so difficult. I've been home by myself countless times here, but today felt like . . . like I was *really* alone. It was awful."

"Yes," Meredith started, cleared her throat, swallowed again. "Yes, it's been difficult for me too. It's my doing it got so far, and for that I'm sorry. But it doesn't change anything. I can't continue to get attached, it's not allowed."

"So you *were* attached? At least tell me that. It'll make it easier."

Meredith pressed her lips together. Her voice came out as a brittle mutter. "You're making this very hard for me, you know."

The girl looked back. For the twentieth time in recent memory, Meredith noticed the bloodshot eyes, the dark half-circles under them, the pallid shade to her complexion. She was starting to look outright gaunt.

"Were you?"

Meredith blew out a stormy breath. "*Of course* I was, Jane. How can you even doubt it? I'm so very fond of you—but it can't be, alright? I can't let it happen. Now please get back to work, before I start yelling like a scatterbrained whelp again."

Janette's melancholy broke into a grin that she quickly tried to hide. "Yes. Yes, um, Mistress." She hurried out the door and closed it, careful it wouldn't slam. Meredith stared at it for quite a while.

"You are so weak, Meredith."

She lay back on the bed with a deep sigh. Too many blasted emotions lately. In fact, this whole last year had been one big fat dramatic experience after another. At least, looking ahead, there were only a few more in sight. To wit:

Patch things up with Yurena.

Bribe her way out of the retrieval lottery.

Devour a sweet, innocent girl a human youth to steal her power, a youth whose trust she commanded without question.

As easy as can be.

THE STANDING CLOCK in the main hall of the library rang dayturn, and so Meredith pulled the doorbell cord. The conversation she was about to have kept playing in advance inside her head, each time having a more disastrous outcome than the last.

Yurena answered her door after a small delay. She still wore her glasses and hadn't yet donned her nightgown, dressed instead in the library's ochre cowl. She looked her visitor up and down and blew out a puff of fragrant smoke. A mellowvane roll-up was cradled between her fingers.

"Right after dayturn. Clever."

Her unimpressed tone wasn't the most encouraging.

"I was an idiot yesterday," Meredith began. "May I come in?"

"I don't know. It depends. You are off to a good start, keep going."

"I . . . I held back when I shouldn't have, and I made you feel bad for defending me. And then I got flustered and said the stupidest thing I could. You had every right to get upset."

The ready admission of wrongdoing seemed to chip at Yurena's defenses. Her brow twitched away from a frown, albeit briefly. "I've been thinking I was too harsh on you."

"No, I don't think so at all."

"I just felt betrayed. It hurt, Meredith—to put it in words you'd say, it caught me by surprise how much it hurt."

"I know. I'm so sorry. I didn't think."

Yurena briefly looked to the side. "I've invested a lot of myself in you. In us. Maybe too much."

Her stomach jumped off a springboard, did a flip and dove into a hole, but Meredith kept her outward reaction to a worried knit of her brow.

"That's . . . for you to decide, but I don't agree. I could never have enough of you in my life."

Yurena's mouth quirked at the corner. Almost a smile. "I could have handled it better. I shouldn't have expected you to go against your nature."

"N— No, you should! I *want* to go against my nature, I *hate* my nature. I want to say what I think and assert myself all the time. I want to be respected and never let anyone dictate my life anymore." Meredith took a short step forward and held Yurena's hand. She didn't pull it back. "You've helped me so much with that."

"I just want you to be who you really can be. It drives me mad to see others troddle on you."

"And I appreciate that." She edged just a bit closer, hope and anxiety fluttering in her chest. Could this really be so easy to fix?

"Do you forgive me?"

Yurena didn't hesitate much. She tugged on the hand and brought Meredith into a tight embrace. Eddies of smoke wafted into her hair.

"If you call me irrational again, I will stab you."

"That would be the most reasonable course of action, absolutely."

Yurena pulled her inside while holding on to Meredith's hands, lips trying to hide a reluctant smile. "I'm not joking. Don't you try me, Merth."

"I wouldn't ever." She brought Yurena's fingers to her mouth and kissed them. "My life's in your hands, remember? I was terrified you were fed up with me and went straight to Mifraulde."

"Hm. Is that the only reason you're here? Making sure I don't become a problem?"

Though Yurena's eyebrow was quirked in a teasing manner, Meredith could tell there was sincere concern in the question.

"No, of course not. I felt wretched, I had to make things right. You can ask Janette. She talked me out of my self-pity."

The librarian pulled back slightly, a hint of dismay in her voice. "You talked to her about this?"

"No, no, I didn't mean it like that. She just noticed how distraught I was, and happened to mention how much she likes seeing us together. It made me think outside the shame and guilt."

"Ah." After a pause that carried on for slightly too long, Yurena shrugged a shoulder. "In any case, you have me all wrong. I'd never go to Mifraulde, no matter what."

"Hah, you say that now, but. . . ."

"No, you don't understand, I truly never would. What a waste! If it came down to it, I'd much rather kill you in your sleep and keep the girl all to myself. It would be *so easy.*"

Meredith stared. Yurena's voice had been cheerful. There was a twinkle in her eyes and an impish crook to her lips.

Both witches broke in laughter at the same time, after which they looked at one another with renewed appreciation. A trip to the sofa and increasingly impassioned kisses naturally followed.

Meredith considered herself warned. It was a sensible plan. Pragmatic.

Yune was nothing if not rational.

CHAPTER TWENTY-TWO

SUCCESS

HE STALL DOOR next to Meredith slammed and locked in one swift motion that no doubt had been repeated hundreds, thousands of times. There was huffing and there was puffing, along with the rustle of robes and undergarments laboriously yanked and tugged out of the way, respectively. There was a toilet seat being severely mistreated as the witch found the perfect way for her flesh to rest upon it (sit, half-stand, sit, half-stand, sit, settle), and then the sigh, that profound, anticipatory sigh Meredith had learned to dread as the herald of desolation, should she choose to stay for what followed.

She didn't have a choice today. She knocked on the separator and whispered, "Devalka."

"Sosgh!" The stall shook with the startle. Hopefully she'd spasmed and clamped shut for the time being. "Choke on ash, who's there?"

"It's me."

"Who's 'me'? Is it—" Her voice dropped to a hush. "Meredith?"

"Yeah. I've—"

"What are you *doing* here? Didn't you see the signs?"

DO NOT allow THiS WiTcH TO ENTER THE PREMiSES

MEREDiTH BRENA·GALVAN·NEUMAN

IF YoU WiTNESS HER ATTEMPTiNG To GAiN
ENTRY, CoNTACT TASKMASTER GERTRUDE
iMMEDiATELY

"I saw the signs."

She'd found the artist's rendition rather flattering, though she could've done without the sneer. She wasn't known for sneering, was she?

"How'd you make it in here? Who even let you in?"

After what she'd pulled off in the past, sneaking into the bathroom had barely qualified as a challenge.

"Never mind about that, I've a question to ask you."

"Draw a line straight to business, don't you? I haven't seen you in over a cycle. You left without even a wary's worth, and the next thing I know is you're not allowed into the manufactory."

"I couldn't say goodbye, I was expelled as soon as I quit."

"And before? I even asked why you were so restless, and you claimed it was just gas. You couldn't tell me what you were up to?"

"I couldn't afford it, Val. You're the worst kind of rumour-monger, don't even try to deny it."

"I *wouldn't* try to deny it, but if you're about to disappear—"

The bathroom door thumped open, interrupting Devalka mid-sentence. Hurried steps shuffled closer, but their advance abruptly stopped. Whoever it was stood there for all of an exhaled breath before turning and fleeing the room.

A reasonable course of action, if Devalka's bespoke stall was locked shut. Meredith could relate.

Only the distant rumble of machinery disturbed the silence.

"So, anyway," Meredith said, "how've you been, Val?"

"Aggravated. Thank you for asking."

"Do you miss me that much?"

"I miss you *listening,* instead of Hilda's constant yatter. You remember Hilda, form the alchemy annex? She took over your empty space and let me tell you, she will not stop. You can't fit a word in-between all the prattle of alchemy principles and her shotel team and her precious cats. It's aggravating."

"Sounds dreadful."

"Thrice as bad as it sounds, swear by brood and power. I near glean the others encourage her only to annoy me. Brienne's been insufferable, too."

"What did she do?"

"Brienne being Brienne, that's all. You had a question for me, and it wasn't to ask me how I've been."

"Oh, um. Well. It's a sensitive matter."

"I'm nothing if not discreet."

"Right. Well, remember we talked about trading retrieval dates? I was wondering how you go about it. Is there a market, or a gathering, or some kind of message board?"

"Pfah! Sickeningly honest Meredith, finally doing what it takes."

"Yes. You could say that."

"It's very simple: you meet with this contact of mine, she gives you a list of available dates, you purchase whatever date you want from the list and you trade in yours. Prices are graded by desirability."

"That's all it is? A witch you know, and she gives you a list?"

"What more do you want? An office with a sign above the door and a cozy waiting room? The Harvest Department might look the other way, but that doesn't make it legal."

"Right, that's fair. . . ."

"Whatever made you change your mind?"

A convenient question. Meredith took a moment to adjust how she'd broach the subject. She leaned closer to the separation, hushed voice full of intent.

"Say I was interested in more than trading dates. Would this contact point me in the right direction?"

There was an equally long pause on the other end.

"What are we talking about, exactly?"

"Imagine a new friend of mine had a stroke of good luck, and she recently had an artificing breakthrough that lead to considerable fortune."

Meredith couldn't see Devalka's black-toothed smile, but she knew it was there. "Did she, now?"

"Imagine she did. Hypothetically."

"Hypothetically. Of course."

"Yes. If she were interested in perhaps skipping next year's youth retrieval . . . would your contact help?"

Another thoughtful pause.

"Yes, I believe she would know who to talk to. For a fee."

"Oh. Naturally."

Silence returned and stayed for a while. Meredith shifted on the edge of the seat. "So. . . ."

"So?"

"So perhaps you could set up a meeting?"

"Gertrude mentioned the reason you quit, you know."

Meredith considered the abrupt new direction through a few blinks and a rub of her nose. "Yeah?"

"I must say, I was surprised. You could never infuse a trinket worth half a clip for as long as I've known you."

"Yes. That is true. It's a partnership."

"Hm."

Not one to become a stranger, silence lied down and stretched on the bathroom tiles. It gave no signs of leaving until prodded.

"Will you set up a meeting, then?"

She waited for a reply. Silence climbed the locked doors, perched above the stalls and looked down intently. Meredith rolled her eyes.

"Just name your price."

There was a deep breath intake, followed by a long exhalation. "Answer me one question, and answer it truthfully."

"I've no other way to answer."

"Does your hypothetical new friend use a Blackwell soundstill?"

"That's, uh. . . ."

It was confusing for only a brief while, after which dread came swiftly.

There was only one reason Devalka would ask such a question.

"Val, I didn't—"

"Answer, Meredith."

Silence climbed down into the stall with her. It entered her lungs and pushed from the inside out.

". . . Yes."

Any other answer would've been spitting in Val's eye.

Devalka pondered it for some time. Silence took it upon itself to redecorate the inside of Meredith's ribcage.

"You'll get your meeting."

"Oh. Truly?"

"Give me a few days. You will hear from me. Now leave before Gertrude storms in and drives a hot iron through your skull."

"Alright, uh . . . yes, alright." Meredith stood, arranged her robes, used a kerchief to unlock the door even while wearing gloves. Her newly charged girdle hummed in anticipation.

"And Meredith?"

"Yes?"

"If there are lines that can be drawn to you going forward, make sure to actually erase them this time."

Meredith nodded and stepped out. "I'll do my best."

Val snorted. "That's what I'm afraid of."

There was no time to respond. Without any warning, desolation itself thundered into Devalka's stall.

Meredith jolted away and escaped with her life.

THE QUESTION "WHO do I need to bribe" was not a trivial one. The names of the four officials belonging to the Retrieval Lottery committee were not public knowledge. Only the Head of the Coven, the Judicar Magister and precious few other Councilors were privy to the committee's current roster.

Devalka's arrangements led to an encounter with a skeletal hag between stalls at the nocturnal market. This encounter led to a silent exchange through the slot of an unmarked door deep in the Dregs. The unmarked door led to a blind drop in a bin down Galvan Boulevard. One day after, Meredith retrieved a handwritten card from the underside of the one oakwood bench in the Crooked

Gardens. The card noted some needlessly complex directions and a passcode. The directions ultimately pointed at a narrow turnoff from Yawleth Road, right up to an unassuming shed behind Galvan Tower itself. Following her instructions, Meredith sat in the darkness of that shed.

A disembodied voice whispered in the darkness, a voice that reminded Meredith of a purposely-uncomfortable bench and a scratching pen eroding at her sanity. The voice sent the Cloaked Stranger on her way to the next rung in the ladder—for the appropriate payment, of course. And for the appropriate payment, the voice explained, this contact would reach out to this other contact who would reach out to *her* contact, who was known to have the ear of a Lottery official.

Not all of them would be bought with money, the voice had said.

What might they require, Meredith had asked.

"Favours," the familiar voice responded, and left it at that.

A THIRD OF HER SAVINGS, A thieving break-in and one as-yet-unreported account of arson later, Meredith stood under the shade of Yanwar's Loathing, smack in the middle of Devalen's Green. The centuries-old stones of the colossal arcade did most of the work keeping her upright, as she was still reeling from the flight to Devalen—a nerve-wracking non-adventure full of circumventions and over-the-shoulder glances. She was already fretting about the way back and the distinct possibility of getting caught without a dais-operating license. It was the eve of Hallow's End, and many juditors were looking to fulfil their quotas before the Five Days of Night began.

In a silence that only pretended to be casual she waited for the agreed-upon signal. It was hot at this latitude, more so under Meredith's wide-brimmed hat, but she'd be damned before fanning herself with it. The fewer witches that saw her face, the better.

Several of them milled about, enjoying meals together on the grass, reading under the sun, hanging Hallow's End decorations, making love, swaying or even dancing to the group currently clanging twin harpsichords on the half-circle. Over at the flaying posts, a small but jovial crowd had gathered to watch today's public punishments, and not far from there, in front of a modestly large wooden stage, a dud auction was taking place. The attending witches cooed and heckled, poking and prodding specimens with a critical eye. The Green was a noisy location at this time of the day, more so with the looming festivities.

Meredith averted her eyes from most of it. Her face had been red for quite a while now. Devalen was well known for two things: excellent manufacturing, and lax public customs.

She was busy ignoring everything around her when the familiar sense of vacuum of an aural funnel opened to her side. A barely noticeable distortion, like a sphere of roiling steam, hovered a few centimeters away from her ear.

"Don't move and don't talk," a soft-spoken voice came through. "Do you have it? Nod or shake your head."

Meredith nodded.

"Good. Behind your left buttocks there is a crevice between stones. Reach back as if scratching yourself until you find it."

It didn't take long to find the crevice in question. It was a vertical slot as wide as two of Meredith's fingers, cleverly disguised as a rough gap between the Arcade's eroded building blocks.

She nodded again.

"Drop it there without turning around. Then our business will be concluded."

"Wait, I—"

"Don't talk," the voice hissed.

"No, look, I need some kind of guarantee, this is everything I have."

"What is it you want, exactly? An official document assuring your unlawful removal from the lottery pool? Would you like it dated and signed?"

"Hm."

"Your *guarantee,* denizen, will be the absence of a retrieval window notice in your dropbox. It will be the fact your name won't be on the Retrieval Accountable list next year. You were sent by the right people. You are talking to the right people. Stop wasting my time."

Meredith held on to the fat envelope in her pocket. Three hundred stem. It was more money than she'd ever dreamed to have, enough chud to afford any tool she wanted and feed her for twenty lifetimes.

Did she truly *have* to? Yurena had been so enthusiastic about how much easier it would be once they consumed Janette. They needed to do it soon, before next year's retrieval window. Surely that had been Meredith's plan all along, yes? Devour the girl so that retrievals would happen in a snap. Quota fulfilled, get on with life. No bribes even considered.

Turn in human youths.

Every year.

With slow, deliberate movements, Meredith crammed the envelope through the jagged slot.

"Good."

"That's it?"

"Yes. It will be an additional one hundred next year."

"What? One hundred—"

"Now wait for a cent, look up at the skyveil, sigh in disappointment, and walk Tarkisward out of the Green. Farewell, Meredith Brena-Galvan-Neumann, resident of 23 Gargamel Lane."

The aural funnel collapsed. Meredith stared at the spot where it used to be.

"That last bit was unnecessary," she muttered.

Slightly disbelieving it was over, Meredith sighed and pretended to have been stood up just like she was told to do. She walked Corenbound, even if it would mean a much longer trip to the nearest exit.

That would show them.

S HE KEPT LOOKING AROUND constantly, watching for anyone that might see her arrive at the copse near her cottage, and this is what caused her to fly into a tree.

"Ghrkk," she said, and tried to correct course, and plunged through a storm of branches and pine needles. The repulsion field spared her from the savage whipping, but did nothing to stop a low branch from knocking the dais into disastrous wobbling.

She held upright, she flipped sideways, she yelped and wound up rolling at high speed through brush and dead leaves. In some prodigious alignment of far-off constellations, her tumbling avoided every girthsome tree-trunk and rock until a funneltooth bush snagged her to a reeling stop. A wild thog startled upon her arrival and scampered into a shrub.

Meredith spent the next tenth-span pawing through the brush, searching for her skull. In the end it turned out to still be attached. Not so the poor dais, which ended up lodged under a particularly twisted gnarl of root and mantle. Upon inspection, the extra chips and scratches added that much more character to its surface. She wasn't all that worried about it: if the crash through the alley hadn't shattered it, nothing would at this point.

As Meredith swayed through her third dizzy spell, she conceded that maybe it was a good thing she'd been officially grounded in perpetuity.

She emerged from the copse some time later, all belongings in place and almost entirely needle-free. Her hat had greeted her while hanging from a conveniently low branch, and the scrapes on her face and hands didn't even sting that much. She was so preoccupied with robe-brushing and hair-fixing that the cloaked figure pacing by her door didn't register until she was nearly upon it.

The unknown witch saw her down the trail, spent an instant properly identifying her and then left the porch.

"You!" she yelled, "It's all your doing!"

"Ah, twaddlebag." Meredith stopped walking, ill-at-ease on the loosely cobbled path. Her hand subtly drifted toward her waist and the crossbow thereabout holstered.

The angry witch stalked forth, her short frame comfortably filling out the contours of a duster. The cloth was thick and coarse, tinted the mute golden brown of dried wheat. Her hair was a messy shock of black, her skin was the shade of parched soil, and her dark eyes were sunk in the midst of twin charcoal smears.

"I should kill you where you stand," the stranger spat. Her voice was deeper than most, clipped around the edges by her close-mouthed Tarkan accent. "I'm sure you won't be missed."

Wide-eyed, Meredith drew, loaded a cartridge and aimed in a smooth motion. She'd practiced *a lot* since her arm healed.

The unknown tribal stopped her advance, though she didn't appear all that intimidated. She snorted. "No wonder Adribel put you forwards. She had a thing for shooters."

"Who are you and what do you want with me?"

"I'm a Tarkan operative. Take a shot at me and you *will* be dead."

She said it while holding up her left fist and briefly hitching up her sleeve. What Meredith had thought was a gloved hand was in fact a mezzo-mechanical limb from elbow to fingertips. A plethora of wordpaths glowed in dull silver all along its smooth metallic surface, far more than a replacement arm would normally need for motor and feedback functions. Meredith didn't doubt some of them operated a kinetic deflector of some kind.

"Circle?" she asked. The aggressive witch grimly nodded. Meredith lowered her weapon just a smidgen. "Prove it."

The stranger raised an aggravated eyebrow.

"Please," Meredith added.

"Your codename is Brena Sixty-Two, you brought a broken human to the Farshaw hideout, and you were our biggest mistake to date. That proof enough?"

"Oh. Well." Slowly she lowered the crossbow until it was pointing at the ground. "We probably shouldn't be talking in the open, then?"

The stranger looked at her as if she were a half-witted buffoon. "We are shielded, you can't tell?"

In Meredith's defense, all of her senses had been far too preoccupied to notice the ear-clogging barrier of an aural dampener.

"No-one around, anyway," the witch continued, "except whoever's squatting in your cottage. I was about to blow a hole through the wall."

Meredith kept a neutral face. "Why are you here?"

"Eleven is dead, along with over half the Brena chapter. All thanks to you."

A few beats went by. "What?"

"Four nights ago, murdered one by one after the meeting was over. I came in after Adribel failed to attend the forewitch conference. She'd never missed one without notice."

"I haven't seen any of them for over half a year, I thought they'd forgotten about me. How could it be my fault? What happened?"

"I intend to take you there and *show you*. You deserve nothing less."

"Can't you just tell me?"

The tribal closed the distance between them in three strides. A powerful musk wafted forward and hit Meredith's nostrils, a mixture of tanned animal skins and woodburning smoke. Somehow a black-bladed knife had appeared in the stranger's metallic hand. "You'll come see it for yourself," she said, "or I'll make you see it the way *they* did."

Meredith stepped back while bringing up a hand. "That won't fix anything, we're on the same side, there's no need for that."

She holstered her weapon as a gesture of cooperation. Under cover of the motion, she used her middle and ring finger to spring free the contact points of the shocker coiled around her forearm—a far tidier alternative to the dagger she used to carry.

"We're going to the Farshaw hideout," the stranger said. "You'll immediately start working on redemption."

It was difficult for Meredith to be properly distraught by the grim news while being bullied so. She considered electrostabbing the hostile witch as soon as she turned her back, but she quickly decided against it. If she was indeed a Circle operative, murder would lead to someone else showing up, and this time without the courtesy of a conversation.

She glanced at her front door, far more anxious to check on Janette than she cared to admit.

"Could I maybe make a trip to the loo first?"

"You're not leaving my sight for one instant, and you are not taking me into your lair. I'll follow you to the bushes over there, if you need to go that badly."

Maybe electrostabbing wasn't that bad of an idea. Meredith sighed. "I'll be fine. Let's do it, then. Seems like I have no choice."

"That's exactly right."

Soot-smeared eyes never leaving her quarrel, the nameless witch pulled a fist-sized cube from her many-pocketed satchel. She rotated a small knob until it was dialed to her desired setting, pressed it in with a loud *click* and placed the trinket on the ground between them.

Meredith had a hard time suppressing a reaction. She was intimately familiar with the design of this artifact. She knew, for instance, that the dial button was clasped by eight zero-point-two-millimeter pins within a rotating bearing that was a real bother to engage into the spring mechanism. She knew the retracting arms were hollowed out and engraved with miniaturized runes all over its inner surface. She knew the spark batteries were partitioned and embedded in flexible twin cylinders attached to the main casing underneath the copper-inlaid input panel.

She knew these things because she had worked on them herself. Janette had finished infusing this artifact about two cycles ago.

Exactly as intended, the portable space-fold unfurled in increments, first lengthwise, then toward Meredith, until it shaped a doormat-sized rectangle. The frame hummed alight, the desired wordpaths inputting the pre-programmed coordinates—you could save up to seven at one time. A grayscale rendition of the destination appeared inside its boundaries: a pitch black surface, save for one thin line of light.

The tribal squatted and touched the frame.

"Şæ rīd'ün vēr'vă'reth ŏnēş'ŷăn úm."

Her considerable power bloomed forth, and the thin line of light took on a yellow tint—the flat image became an actual *place,* somewhere's ceiling connected to soil and stone.

The stranger tossed in a pebble and waited for any kind of response. When none returned, she gave the contraption a gentle push. It sank through like lead on honey, leaving behind a perfectly delineated portal embedded on the ground.

She stood upright and eyed Meredith coolly. "Inside the entrance. After you."

"There is a gravity dampener on the other side, right?"

"Jump in and find out."

Meredith pursed her lips. "So what should I call you?"

"Madam. My patience is running out. Go."

Though her first impulse was to comply without question, a wave of indignation kept her jaw clenched and her feet glued to the spot.

"I don't know you. I won't be bullied by a stranger with a fancy story and an attitude problem. You could be an inquisitor luring me into a trap, for all I know—and even if you're not, I'm not going anywhere without at least knowing your blasted codename."

The stranger's expression darkened. Through the corner of her eye Meredith saw the tribal's flesh hand ball into a fist.

"I'm Silver," she said. "You'll swallow each one of those words when you understand the disaster you wrought."

Meredith blinked. "*You* are Silver? *The* Silver?"

"There's no other Silver."

"So you're the Tarkis *forewitch,* not just—"

"Go through, or I will stab you in the neck and be done with you."

They stared at one another, one impatient, the other mildly starstruck. Silver, co-founder and living legend of the Riven Circle, was far shorter than Meredith had imagined.

She let out a breath and sat on the path, legs dangling into the portal. A dreadful musk reached her as she leaned forward, like old sweat and spoiled milk.

Meredith winced and jumped in.

THE FIRST BLOODSTAIN was in the middle of the entryway, atop the staircase leading into the hideout proper. An expansive spatter, like a spilt glass that someone had poorly mopped, then dragged the stained mop all the way down. The *real* stench began halfway through the climb down the wooden steps.

Under the ghostly light of Silver's glowstone they descended into the first basement floor, each creaky step smeared in a dark trail. Meredith walked at the front, one hand covering her mouth and nose, the other white-knuckled on the railing.

"You got pine leaves in your hair," Silver whispered. She sounded mildly irritated by it.

Meredith wiped her hands along her ponytail. Several needles prickled her fingers.

"Thank you," she whispered back. It felt appropriate to whisper.

The narrow stairwell landed upon a small reception area before turning around and carrying on to the second basement level. This tiny room led off into three doorways, one for each side. More trails converged toward the left doorway.

Meredith looked over her shoulder. "This is hideous."

"Keep going. You haven't seen a damn thing yet."

"I . . . I don't handle dirt well."

"Don't see that as a problem of mine."

"What are we going to find in the meeting room?"

"Exactly what you expect."

Their steps turned slick and sticky going into the dark hallway. Between the two of them the sound was sickening, like a spoon stirring a bowlful of raw meat. Copper and rot and the stench of feces fought a messy battle inside Meredith's nose as they neared the solid wall of black at the end of the corridor.

"We could at least turn on the lights," Meredith said between shallow breaths.

"Tried earlier. Building's off the grid, and the generator is destroyed beyond repair."

"Look, I don't need to see it. They got found out, it's a massacre in there, I can imagine it well enough. Whatever example the Judicars made out of them, I don't need to see it."

Silver prodded her forward, hand firm but not particularly forceful. "Beg to differ."

Ghostly white illuminated the room ahead little by little. Meredith kept her eyes on her own shifting shadow, watchful of where and how her feet landed on the soaked wooden laminate. They got to the head of the meeting table. Silver raised her glowstone. Meredith looked around.

Six wire-bound bodies sat around a table that was more red than black. The wire held them up against the chair, mouths gaping grotesquely, eyes open wide. Every one of them had a suppurant gash across their throat. In the middle of the table, a centerpiece: six misshapen tongues in a tight line.

To the right, on the long whiteboard that still contained traces of work distribution, agendas, projects and assigned goods, three large digits had been written with bloodstained hands.

"Four-Thirteen," Meredith breathed.

Nausea hit her on the inhale, and despite her best efforts she couldn't hold it down anymore. She turned, leaned against a wall that was slick to the touch and threw up every last bit of the scrambled egg and toast she'd had in Devalen. Her heaves entered a vicious cycle of sound, smell, touch and thought, leaving her gagging and spasming long after her stomach emptied.

Eventually she brought it under control. Silver's voice came shortly after. "Oh, yes, you would make such an excellent field agent."

With a mien of revulsion Meredith tossed aside the kerchief she'd used to wipe her mouth. "Was it really him?" she rasped.

"The scene speaks for itself."

"Why? Why would he do this? *How* could he do this?"

"Don't know, *Sixty-Two*. You tell me."

"I have no idea! A single human against six paranoid witches, I can't even imagine how it's possible! Don't you think maybe it *was* the Judicars, and *that—*" she pointed at the numbers, "is just the reason they did this?"

"That a serious suggestion? The Judicars don't work like that. You've listened to too many horror stories."

Holding up the glowstone clasped to her wrist, Silver walked around the table to Eleven's corpse. She placed the light in front of the deceased forewitch and without hesitation began undoing the wire. Meredith noted with lingering queasiness how much Silver's fingers had to dig into the bloody flesh to separate the wire from it.

"They would've tried to take them alive," Silver continued, "and they wouldn't have mutilated the bodies like this. Your friend, however. . . ."

"But I rescued him, and they took him in. It makes no sense."

"Wrong. It would make no sense if he'd been vetted. That's what we do: screen every candidate to ensure they're not too far gone. Four Hundred and Thirteen was *not* a sound choice, what a shocking development."

"He seemed fine. Lucid."

"Sure. Reports also said for three cycles he was aggressive, mistrustful and uncooperative at the halfway house. Only seemed interested in the writing lessons to express more creative insults. The interviews were nothing but hostile. Several of your colleagues here advised termination over an Earth release."

"He was just traumatised by everything he'd gone through! If he'd had enough time—"

"Exactly what Adribel decided, more time to heal and adjust, despite the drain on resources." She finally pried enough wire loose for Eleven's body to slump onto the floor with a wet *thu-thud*. Silver watched it go down. "Might've worked, if he hadn't escaped the halfway house."

"He *escaped?*"

"Before he'd healed all the way. Just vanished, no witnesses, only things missing were a few books and a map of Brena. Don't know how he's survived this long on his own."

"They didn't try to get him back?"

"Of course they tried, he's a massive liability. You plan to just stand there and watch?"

"Wh– what do you want me to do?"

"Pry them loose, what do you think?"

"I don't . . . I don't have any gloves on me."

"You see gloves on my hands?"

"You have a mezzode hand, it's only half as gross."

"Feeling every bit, I assure you."

"But still—"

"Get over it. This is all your fault. You understand that? *Your* fault. These witches were special, working to make us all better. Adribel, here? I hand-picked her, a great forewitch, I liked her. Now they're dead because you were reckless. Least you owe me is taking care of the bodies."

Meredith looked down at the floor, feeling the shame build up. "I owed *him*. I tried to help him and he was disciplined harshly for it. I needed to do something."

"Should've taken him to your house and shouldered all the risk, if you felt so strongly. Instead, you dumped him at our doorstep. Stop with the excuses and get to work."

Taking him to her house hadn't been an option with Janette there. Maybe she should've tried the wooded area nearby, or been more forceful about staying involved, close to him. Maybe she shouldn't have risked so much to break him out. Everything had seemed so inevitable at the time, why did her decisions feel so questionable now?

With hesitant steps and appalled features, Meredith neared the closest body. She probably wouldn't have recognized any of their faces even if she'd actually seen them before, but this witch had a familiar stocky build. It was Fifty-One, who'd helped carry Four-Thirteen to this very table.

Her hands got smeared in red upon touching the skin-tight wire. Fighting down another bout of nausea, Meredith fished through a few pockets until she found what she was looking for: the thick handles of a pair of clippers, built tough and keenly sharpened. With some effort she wedged them between flesh and taut metal.

"You carry that with you?"

Meredith spoke without looking up. "You never know when you'll need to cut your way out of something."

"Hm."

The sounds of their grim work took over the room: wet squelching, grinding metal, the occasional snap and thump. It became unbearable. Meredith voiced her thoughts if only to get her mind off the terrible sensations on her fingers.

"How could he do this?"

"Told you. He's unstable."

"No, I mean . . . how'd he *manage?* He was just one beaten serf."

"And exceptional in the fight pits. What a barbaric pastime. We created this monster, all of us."

"Still, though. They couldn't stop him? With spells?"

Silver shook her head. "We all do *something* for the Circle, but most've never fought—and even then, no-one comes here expecting to get jumped by a lunatic. Don't know how he got in, but only Thirty-Seven over there saw him coming." She was pointing at the body next to Meredith's current project. "See the marks on everyone? Stabbed to the back of the neck, choked, caught by surprise. All except her. Stabbed in the chest, right up front, then got her skull bashed."

Despite her misgivings, Meredith forced herself to look. The visuals fit the words. As much as she'd resented Thirty-Seven's mockery, she never would've wished this upon her. "She's the only one without robes, too."

Silver nodded. "Large build, close enough for a disguise. Five separate trails out there, six distinct kill locations, no real signs of struggle. Just a cold-blooded stab right *there*, one by one."

Meredith pushed herself to look again. Along with several red blotches on the back, she found a puncture wound at the base of Fifty-One's skull. Something like her shiny new steak knives would gouge a wound just like it.

"Power to mold the Universe at our fingertips," Silver mused, not particularly speaking to Meredith anymore, "and so easily brought down by a gormskull with a sharp object."

A terrible thought startled Meredith. "Could he still be here?"

"I surveyed the place and cleaned up, but. . . ." Silver shrugged. "I suppose it's possible." She glanced up, noting Meredith's unease. "Calm down. The door's trapped."

She looked at the way in. On one side of the doorframe shone a faint reflective line, barely visible under the pale light of Silver's glowstone.

"Is that alchemy?"

Wordlessly Silver flashed one side of her coat open, showing three rows of small pockets holding smaller flasks. Slightly larger potions and elixirs were slotted or clipped along her waist and leg belts and many-pocketed bag. She let the coat fold back to normal, but not before Meredith noticed several knife hilts and a gun of some description holstered under her left shoulder.

Incidentally, Silver wore nothing but belts and beadstrings under her duster. How did she deal with chafing?

"I didn't see you do it," Meredith said while hooking a thumb at the door.

"Was hoping you'd walk through."

"What would happen if I did?"

"Very unpleasant, non-lethal things."

Meredith went from distressed to the beginnings of contrite. "I didn't mean for any of this to happen."

"And yet it happened anyway. They call it *consequences*."

"You know what? That's not fair. If he hadn't been a secret violent madman, I could've become a field operative. At the very least I'd have earned respect for what I did, so, yes, it's my fault, but it could've just as well not been."

Silver didn't respond. Meredith couldn't tell whether she'd made an impression or made a fool of herself with her flustered defense.

They worked in silence from that point forward, letting every corpse fall where it may, one after the other. Once her third one came down, Meredith found it curious how even the atrocious could become routine.

"Help me get them to this spot by the corner," Silver said once all the bodies were on the floor.

"What are you trying to do, anyway?"

"What do you think? They're evidence. They need to go."

"Oh. I thought. . . ."

"What?"

"Sorry, never mind."

"No, what?"

"I thought we were doing this so you could send them off in some way. What with your . . . creed."

"My creed?"

"You . . . you're a tribal?"

"Sure look like one. What exactly do you think that entails?"

Meredith hesitated. "Rattling a fistful of beads? Some kind of chanting and dancing ritual?"

Silver stopped her corpse-dragging and stood upright. Her head was tilted to one side, charcoal-laden eyes blinking in perplexity.

"Are you from three centuries ago, or only your preconceptions are?"

"I don't know, I've never been outside Brena!"

"That what they teach in Brena's academy, then? Every one of those primitive tribals down Tarkisward, all they do is bone rattling and Shaglaroth worship?"

"No, it's just. . . ." Meredith shrugged cluelessly. "I guess I've never bothered to learn otherwise."

Silver waved a dismissive hand. "Doesn't matter, who cares? Just get them over here."

They made a pile without much regard for poise or dignity. Silver did make sure Adribel's head was propped a good deal higher than everything else, square in the middle. Her hair, now free from the perennial cowl, stood out in a mane of wild curls. Her dark skin reflected the glowstone light with purplish hues.

Meredith stared. How imposing this witch had been. How intimidating and self-assured.

"Stand back," Silver warned. Orange flask in hand, she sprinkled the contents all around the pile, then reached in and dropped some at the very top of Adribel's hair. She poured the rest within the confines of the delineated cone.

She back-stepped to Meredith's position. "Shield your eyes."

From an inside pocket she produced a matchbox. It lit up on the first strike, and she cradled the flame, waiting for it to take. She tossed it at the center of the pile and looked away.

The match flew in. As soon as it touched the orange fluid, the entire room flashed alight. Through spread fingers and squinted eyes Meredith watched a cone of white churn and roar within its flawless lines.

Trying not to sound like an awed cave-dweller, Meredith raised her voice over the commotion. "What is it, exactly?"

"Bound Disintegration potion."

"You carry *that* with you?"

"Never know when you'll need to erase a mound of corpses."

As she spoke she brought out her weapon, which made Meredith take a reflexive side-step. It very much looked like a human firearm, yet it was made of white plastic. With routine movements Silver unclipped a small bottle from her belt and screwed it into a slot under the gun's barrel. Clear liquid sloshed inside the bottle.

The clamoring pyre blackened all at once, leaving the room in almost-darkness again. Silver pulled another flask from her coat, squat and opaque. She flicked a switch on it and tore off the lid. In one swift motion she sprayed her squirt gun on the cone, tossed the flask inside the churning black and jumped back a safe distance.

The liquid touched down, and the cone of darkness exploded into smoke for the briefest of moments—an ear-splitting hiss emerged from its depths, and the smoke curved and rolled unto itself, collapsing toward its center in a violent rush. In a short while, enough of it vanished to reveal the squat flask, spinning on its side, sucking in the soot with insatiable hunger.

The smoke spiraled in a receding cyclone until none of it was left. The flask continued spinning and hissing as Silver rushed back in, stepped on it, knelt to grab it. A wind rose at Meredith's nape, blowing her ponytail over her shoulder. Breathing became a tad harder, like her lungs had to fight an unseen force for air.

With decisive finality Silver twisted the lid back on. It locked with a loud snap.

The Tarkan forewitch seemed to let go of a held breath.

Meredith neared the area. In the pale penumbra the floor was a circle of pure shadow. The smell of charred wood wafted into her nostrils, quite subtle. Of the corpses, only black ashes remained.

"You came . . . prepared," Meredith said.

"*Returned* prepared."

"You craft those yourself?"

"Yes. Much rather use alchemy in the field. Incantations are so slow." Silver glanced at her, eyes lingering meaningfully on waist and robes. Her lips curved in begrudging approval. "You seem to have a similar opinion."

"Um. Incantation isn't precisely my specialty."

Silver grunted. "Whatever works." She kicked the residue all over the place. Sparkling puffs of dust rose around her booted feet.

"Wipe the board of every word," she said. "Including the numbers, obviously."

"How am I supposed to clean that mess?"

"Clean it, make it worse, don't care, think of something. I'm going to look for his trail again. He's using the old city tunnels. There must be blood smudges out there somewhere, leading to wherever he's hiding."

"How could an unbound and injured human get around without anybody noticing? How far is this halfway house?"

"Felling side of town, underground. Doesn't connect to Brena Below, but close enough. You underestimate him, much as we did." Silver strode toward the doorway.

Don't leave me alone in this place, Meredith almost pleaded. She stepped after the witch.

"Unless! Unless he broke into someone's house, and took over by force. Maybe we should look for signs of violence out there. Start knocking on doors."

"And say what? 'Good eve madam, we're looking for the killer stunt that escaped from our secret hideout'?"

"Well, no, we'd just . . . we'd just give some excuse and leave, or knock and run. The purpose is making sure there's someone answering."

"Hm."

White gun in her right hand, Silver spurted clear liquid onto the doorway—distilled water, if Meredith's rudimentary alchemy knowledge could be trusted. The only sign anything had changed was a brief ripple along the doorframe.

"That'd be inconclusive," she said. "If there's no answer, we'd have to enter every building to be sure, or use detection. Doesn't matter, I'm positive he's underground. Do you have any idea what's down there?"

"Just . . . tunnels. Broken tunnels full ancient rubbish."

"It's a mess. We tried using it for hideouts but stopped after a cave-in, too unstable. Anything below Old Brena is plain mad, a maze with a thousand exits and as many dead ends. If the trail goes cold I'll never find him. You can't even rely on magic detection, it's all tangled with foundation safeguards and all the holdovers from—"

Her explanation was interrupted by a loud boom farther down the passage. After it died down, it was followed by a yelled "Clear!"

They spent a precious moment looking at one another, eyes wide and bright in the pale darkness. Clomping bootsteps thumped down the stairs.

"We know you are there! Disable all your devices and dampeners! Come out disrobed and with a hand inside your mouth!"

Silver brought out the tin she'd just put away, flipped the switch on it, loosened the cap, hurled it outside and immediately closed the door. She slapped another vial to Meredith's chest before shoving her toward the right side of the room. "Get rid of that board, I'll make a way out!"

As angry yells and scalding smoke seeped under the doorjamb, Meredith stumbled toward her suddenly-urgent objective. She glanced at the glass container in her hands: murky black swirling with flecks of amber. *Kinofire,* read the label. How many kinds of explosions did this nutter carry in her pockets?

She looked over her shoulder. "What do I do!"

Silver was bent over her space-fold, placing it on the charred floor. "Smash it against the board! As hard as you can!"

Incantations rose from beyond the closed door. Without much thought Meredith wound up a throw, sprinted forward and chucked the flask at the wall, arm aching in protest. A deep amber blaze roared on impact, engulfing the entire half of the room in the span of a sharp gasp. The flame's black core, thick and tumultuous, spread onto the board like a splash of cannonballed tar and kept going, eating into the wall with violent hunger.

The blast slammed Meredith's shoulder and threw her onto a chair, hat taking flight while her robes flapped all around. Atop the chair she wobbled, wide eyes staring at the *disgusting* floor, frantic in her struggle not to dive through blood and char and who-knew-what filth.

Silver grunted and fell on one knee. "That was *too* hard, you mad bint!"

"How in blazes was I supposed to know!"

The kinofire collapsed as quickly as it had spread, leaving behind the dripping tatters of a former wall. Through it could be seen chewed-up weight-bearing beams and the neighbors' lower floor—some kind of abandoned basement dungeon. The incantations outside led to the swell of a high-pressure whistle; dark smoke rushed in through every seam around the door, adding to the fumes.

Meredith stumbled toward the forewitch, half-yelling, half-coughing. "What are you doing? Is it ready?"

"Almost!"

Silver was pouring something else in a wide semicircle around the entrance. Its pale blue shades fizzed and sizzled on contact with the dry blood. The pressurized hiss kept building at the door, now joined by loud cracks and pops. The smoke thickened, the hinges rattled.

Meredith had to bend down to Silver's ear, both to keep below the smoke and to make herself heard. "Use another of those black fire explosion things!"

"Are you daft? I haven't survived this long by killing juditors!"

Silver stepped back, raised her fist and threw something at the curved line of blue. Whatever it was, it shattered onto the substance one moment before the door exploded in a thousand splinters.

Icicles sprouted and bloomed in an instant, fractally expanding to form a barrier that soaked most of the deadly door fragments. The rest were deflected by the kinetic shield embedded in Silver's suddenly-alight mezzode arm. The black gale outside rushed the spiky ice wall and bounced back toward the hallway, off toward the ceiling. The roiling fumes created the semblance of thunderclouds overhead.

"Alchemist!" one of the juditors shouted from the corridor. "Forward watershields!"

Silver grabbed the wrist of a dumbfounded Meredith and prowled toward the unfolded portal. "They've yet to learn I exist," the Tarkan forewitch said, quiet in the relative calm, "and I'm keeping it that way."

She touched the device and recited the short incantation. Immediately she tossed Meredith through, pulling and pushing with effortless ease. Thoughts minced to pieces, Meredith found herself free-falling to an unknown place.

She landed heavily onto a bed of cushions, and after a bit of a bounce she had the presence of mind to climb down as fast as she could from the round pillowy platform, just in case Silver fell right behind. Looking up at a white ceiling, Meredith watched the space-fold sink through, reachable if she stood atop the cushions. She positioned herself to jump up and disengage the device as soon as Silver descended.

There was some kind of explosion on the other side, like the whole building was coming apart. Then, a hefty thump and ice shards raining through the gateway. A black-and-silver arm clad in pale gold denim flopped through and lifelessly dangled there.

"Drag her away from that portal!" someone yelled.

With a surge of wire-taut panic Meredith climbed on the precarious footing, grabbed Silver's hand and pulled. Clomping bootsteps approached fast as the head came through, the bust, everything above the hip.

There was a crashing noise of thuds and grinding armored robes. Meredith reached in, found one of Silver's belts and gave a hard tug. At the same time, a gloved hand clamped on her wrist.

The jolt of pure terror made her knees grow weak and give out, which was just as well: though the hand was exceedingly strong, it couldn't fight against two bodies' worth of gravity on such short notice. Silver's buttocks came through, and with them the face of a juditor. They kept dragging down until half the juditor's body was past the portal, one arm bracing Silver's thighs, the other exerting death's grip on Meredith's hand. Runescript glowed ice blue under the juditor's wristcuffs, no doubt suffusing her with increased strength.

For an eternal moment they stared at each other within their tug-of-war. The juditor's eyes were of a brown so dark it was almost black. She had an upturned nose and thin lips and a strong jaw, and pockmarked skin the color of Desmond's belly. Her horned jade coif had come off at some point, revealing a disheveled thicket of blond hair crammed into a bun. Sweat beads populated a soot-marked brow and her every feature was twisted with desperate strain.

She was no mere juditor. This was the inquisitor that had interrogated Meredith at work, all those cycles ago. She couldn't remember the name.

Staring into those near-black eyes, eyes that shone with the disbelieving spark of recognition, Meredith understood it was over. She was caught, right there and then. Every detail she'd noticed was another log to feed the pyre for her own execution.

And Janette would be worse than dead.

The prospect emptied out her brain, it purged every thought that could get in the way. Her hand dove into a pocket and closed around rubber handles. She used the judicar's grip for leverage, standing as tall as she could. Past Silver's calves, she reached for the portal device. Meredith didn't waste time with the off switch: she knew there were safeguards in place.

"Don't," the inquisitor said, voice choked by the effort of keeping a witch and a half aloft on poor purchase. She tried to let go and back out, but Meredith held fast. She jammed her wire cutters into the joint at the corner of the frame. She twisted and pushed. The frame buzzed and snapped.

The portal winked out like it had never existed. There were no sounds at all until a witch and a half crashed onto the cushions.

Then the screams started.

They lasted much longer than Meredith had thought possible.

SILVER SAT WITH HER BACK resting on the side of her unmade bed. After overcoming her daze, she'd cursed and quickly backed to her current position. From there she'd watched, transfixed, as the upper half of an inquisitor writhed and screamed and twitched until death.

She looked up at Meredith, who remained atop the cushioned stand, wire cutters still in hand.

"You're a jinx," Silver said. "Witchbane. Bad juju." She made a gesture over her chest as she said it, a short spiral crossed by a line.

There was no answer. It was a fair assessment, truth be told.

"You got any idea what this means?" Silver asked.

Meredith looked from the witch to the horrid mess on the floor. She blinked.

"You'll have to throw that rug away."

The rug in question was a lush thing that covered most of the large ceramic tiles from bed to cushions. Its feathery surface had become a mantle of dark red.

"What?"

"At least it's soaking most of it."

Silver scowled at the ruined rug and still-oozing remains. "Is that a joke? You find this funny?"

Meredith only responded after another stretch of blank silence. "No. No, it's just, your bedroom is so clean." Her eyes remained stuck on the Judicar's pallid face. "*Was . . .* clean."

There was nothing peaceful about that face. She lay on what was left of her back, mouth still open in a tortured wail. The eyes stared straight up, open far wider than death should allow. One of her hands clutched below the stomach, where an abdomen should have been, while the other was outstretched straight at Meredith, fingers curled like posing a silent question.

The empty calm inside her was filling up with something else. Something foul and gag-inducing.

She felt the touch of fingers on her arm. Silver stood next to her, at ground level, wearing a long-suffering grimace. Gently she half-held, half-supported Meredith's forearm, pulling her off the perch and toward the bedroom door. Meredith let herself be led, her gaze leaving the grisly scene to simply stare off at the middle distance. Silver's loose grip made her aware of just how much she was shaking.

The reluctant host took her to a tiny yet immaculate kitchen covered in pure white cabinetry and blue-flecked gray tile. She guided Meredith to the sink and pumped a large handle by the faucet. After a little while, water started to run. Meredith felt drawn to it like a tiddler to candy.

Silently they washed their hands, one rinsing while the other soaped, one soaping while the other rinsed. Sometimes Silver's limb would clack against the steel sink. It was mesmerizing, the way it moved. Fluid and dexterous, yet unnatural. A hybrid that was neither flesh nor machine.

"What happened to your arm?"

Silver's motions slowed for a tiny bit.

"Alchemy."

"Oh."

"Don't miss it."

The tub ran red and black and dirt brown. The shaking had considerably subsided.

"Never killed a witch before, had you."

Meredith scrubbed extra hard. "No."

"Didn't have much of a choice."

In her thoughts she relived that decisive moment, the sense of utter certainty. She looked for regret among the guilt, and found none.

"No," she said. "I didn't."

"Had to be done and you did it fast. The mistake was earlier, when you ruined everything."

There wasn't much in the statement Meredith could dispute, either. She worked on one finger at a time, digging out the filth. The maroon flecks under her nails refused to come off.

Silver followed her movements through the corner of her eye. "How in Yanwar's Purge did you manage to stay so clean?"

Meredith looked at herself, then at the Tarkan witch. She seemed to have just crawled out of her own grave. By comparison, only Meredith's hands were soiled to any noticeable degree.

"I don't feel clean," she responded. Silver sighed as she closed the tap.

"They'll tell you that's weakness, but hold on to the feeling. It's what draws us to the Circle. Puritan doctrine can't erase our empathy, no matter how much they try." She handed Meredith one of the rags that hung from a peg in front of the sink. "You were out of options, you know what would've happened. Be glad the rest didn't see you at all."

Meredith's drying motions were far more thorough and forceful than they needed to be. "How much *did* they see?"

"My arse, for one. Not my face, I don't think." Silver clicked her tongue off her teeth. "Might've let it go if they'd come out empty-handed, but now the Judicars lost one of their own. They'll scour the hideout and analyze every scrap of material they find, and we didn't clean up proper. One thing or another will lead them to the Circle."

"Why were they there at all? They went straight for our room."

"Good question, innit? They detected my dampener, that's why they went for our room—but they were *looking,* that's the disturbing part. Can't be a coincidence." She tossed her own drying rag on the spotless counter like she was disgusted by its very existence. "Hate to be caught flat-footed."

Meredith carefully folded the cloth and hung it back on its place. "You think . . . *he* led them there, somehow?"

"Who else? No-one escaped, no signs of struggle outside, no way for anyone to know what happened down there. Can't imagine how he tipped them off, but no-one else could've."

While she spoke, Silver fetched a pair of clear glasses from a cupboard and poured cold water from a jar she kept in . . . a refrigerator. An actual human-made refrigerator, plugged into a converter.

She also noticed the red smudges and tears on the back of Silver's coat. Silver didn't seem to be bothered by them. "Don't think we were the target. I think the Judicars were supposed to find what *I* found yesterday, and we simply happened to be there."

She offered the glass. Meredith took a polite sip that turned into avid gulps once she became aware of how thirsty she was.

"Maybe it's all good," Silver carried on, her own glass in hand. "Every other room was clean. As far as they know, I was some deranged mass-murderer in an abandoned basement."

"And the trails of blood? Won't they get samples and match them through the registry? And wonder what these witches from all over Brena were doing in that basement?"

"Hm." Silver put her glass down. She turned to face the counter and leaned elbows on it. "Hm."

"You didn't think about that?"

"I was *distraught*, don't know if you noticed! Haven't slept in two days. Should've finished the cleanup before getting you, but I got *so mad. . . .*"

"Well, they won't necessarily connect it to anything. Could've been friends gathering to play shotel, for all they know. Right?"

Silver kept silent. Finally she heaved a deep sigh, wincing on the inhale.

"It's done. Go home, Meredith. I've a lot of witches to warn."

"You seem hurt."

"Flesh wounds. Not the first, not the last. I've someone to take care of it."

"Oh. I should. . . ." Meredith glanced at the room with the cushions. What she'd done already seemed surreal. Was there truly half a body waiting in that room? "I should help you clean," she said, a bit of a tremor returning to her voice.

"No, just go. If the guilt is too much, think of the suffering that inquisitor had caused. They've no regard for the humans, none. Makes me sick."

The open mention of kindness and compassion was perplexing. Even among Brena's Circle meetings, mercy had always been more of an unwanted stigma than something to cherish.

She reflexively took a step closer so she could lower her voice. Hope cartwheeled off her tongue. "Isn't there something more we could do? Something to actually change things?"

Silver scoffed. "Been doing all I can without getting caught. You got some kind of genius masterplan I haven't considered?"

"Well, no, but . . . how about spark't youths? They're the most undeserving, don't you agree? Shouldn't we prioritise them? Shouldn't we . . . protect them, somehow?"

The bloodstained witch leaned back against the counter. Her mouth was narrowed to a line and one of her eyebrows was quirked. "That's Faedre talk. Lots of disciples burned for saying as much."

In any other context, it would have been the most dire of condemnations. Here, it only made her terribly uncomfortable.

"I'm only thinking out loud. . . ."

"Well, I've talked about it plenty with her. We want to work up to it eventually, but—"

"You spoke to Faedre? You *know* her?"

She waved it aside as if it was an unimportant bit of trivia. "Yeah, you could say that. Listen, we can't cross that line yet. It's failure, guaranteed. Look at every time witches mucked about with the spark supply." She counted with her fingers, one by one: "Mergat's Folly, Old Yanwar, the Civil War, the human rebellions—even the War of Succession, way back. Always escalates until a purge breaks out. I refuse to let that happen to us, there's a reason the Riven Circle's still around. We don't make a lot of noise, we don't take it too far, and slowly we grow in number. Until you ruined everything, that is."

Meredith's disillusionment compounded with every word of the screed, so much so that the final jab at her didn't even register. "So we rescue one human at a time, and that's it? What's the point, if nothing will ever change?"

"Didn't say that. I said we do what we can right now. What, should we behave like terrorists? Want to start another war? There's been enough of those."

"No, I don't want anyone to die."

"So it's complicated, right? Because Galavan needs the spark. Human technology can't power the core furnaces or the nodework— and forget the magical disciplines, they'd be toothless without it. So it's a thing we have to accept to some extent: the plight of the spark't is unfortunate, just like the life of cattle is unfortunate. Either that, or we let Galavan die, and witch magic will dwindle to silly cantrips without real power. Faedre thought that was a fine outcome, back then. Is that what *you* want, too?"

"N– no, obviously not," Meredith said. "I don't want to destroy anything. I just feel like there should be another way."

"Right. Right you are. All the pain and cruelty, that's what needs to stop, the ruthless Puritan doctrine and Progeny Department meddling. One day, we'll heal the Desolation. One day the witch broods won't be barren, we'll bring the Earthborn into the fold again and lift Galavan from the muck. And it'll happen without witches murdering each other."

Bring the Earthborn into the fold.

The words struck a chord of hope she wasn't supposed to feel for a possibility not meant to be contemplated, let alone proposed as desirable—but the volume of flagrant apostasy coming out of Silver's mouth, altogether more than she'd ever dared think in her life, gave her enough pause to keep her reaction in check.

"But . . . the Hunger," she objected. "It'll take over again, all the chaos and filth of Humanist times, it would all come back."

"No, of course not, don't be daft." The more Silver spoke, the more she paced and gesticulated. "That's some dire nonsense they feed you at the academy to make you docile, all the doomsaying of overpopulation and kidnappings and cannibalistic harvest. It's fear-mongering and indoctrination, it's to keep witches locked in a state of—"

"But those things *did* happen. Right?"

"Yeah, they did—over two hundred years ago, alongside wars and savage feuds, and not nearly as much as they hammer into your head. Like the Hunger. It can be managed, and that's a fact, like every witch manages their cravings, it's not the mindless tyrant they make it out to be. It's all about control, about the Puritans staying in power, it always was." She interrupted her pacing to look over her shoulder. "You've been to Earth, haven't you?"

"Y– Yes. Briefly."

"I've *lived* on Earth, and it's downright shameful how far behind we are. Complacent and stagnant, that's Galavan in two words. My mother saw it, I see it, it's been a hundred-year decline, we need all the new blood we can get—but no, here were are, stuck with this oppressive traditional mindset, *punishing* explorers instead of encouraging it. We already steal so much from human warehouses, it's not as if—"

"Did you say 'mother'?"

Silver turned to face her again. She seemed surprised at the question, like she was so far into her rant she'd forgotten Meredith was still there. "Oh. Never mind. Got carried away." She shook her head. "Too damn tired."

"You have a mother? You're not a broodspawn?"

"No, I said never mind, I misspoke. Listen, sure was nice, but I've had enough bonding over the disaster you caused. Time to go." She pointed. "The door is down the hall."

Meredith's eyes widened in dismay. "You're just tossing me out onto the streets of Tarkis? I've no idea—"

"We're not in Tarkis, you'd be sweltering right now. This is the Coren range."

Silver reached behind her and rolled up the blinds on the tiny kitchen window. Where she'd expected a mist-shrouded bog, Meredith found gold and faded green rolling down a crisp hillside.

"I'd portal you home," Silver continued, "but my new space-fold's broken." She gestured at Meredith's midsection. "With that, you should make it there by nightfall."

Meredith touched the dais in its lower back harness. It would've been stowed in her cellar if Silver hadn't caught her returning from the trip to Devalen.

She was eager to leave, but pressing matters demanded not to be postponed any further.

"Can I make that trip to the loo before I go? I've been out all day."

Silver rolled her eyes and pointed at a cracked-open door across the cozy little living room. Meredith hurried to it in as dignified a manner as possible, gaze firmly averted from the pool of crimson showing through the bedroom doorway. The reek that caught in her nostrils was the real challenge to ignore.

The bathroom was as spotless as the rest of the home, all around marble and smooth tile. It didn't quite match with the owner, a witch who'd just carelessly smeared dirt and blood all over the pristine kitchen without a single wince in the process. Meredith did her business with great relief, washed her hands again and left the towel exactly the way she'd found it.

While avoiding her reflection she noted the homemade bar of soap and the pair of toothbrushes on a stand by the tap, and the fine-toothed comb that would be completely ineffective at taming Silver's thick strands. There were also several products she'd never seen before, no doubt Earth contraband: a rubbery stick with a razor embedded in it, an oblong container reportedly full of "Old Spice," a squat glass bottle with a mountainous logo that read "aftershave lotion." She might've been curious in different circumstances.

When she came back out, Silver was still leaning against the counter. Her arms were crossed and her eyes had the low-smolder look of deep exhaustion.

Meredith headed straight for the door. "What will you do about Four-Thirteen?" she asked.

The witch glanced over and blew out an irked breath. "What *can* I do? Place is out of reach, now. He's as good as gone." She uncrossed her arms, leaned hands on the marble. "You're his prime target. You realise that, yeah? Wouldn't be surprised if he already knows where you live. Watch out for him at all times."

A cold lump clustered at the pit of Meredith's stomach. "Do you really think he could find me?"

"Who knows, at this point? He's obviously resourceful, and Brena Below connects to a hundred places. Not looking forward to hunting him down."

"When are you going to—"

"Farewell, Meredith." Silver gestured at the door with an up-turned hand. Meredith pursed her lips, twisted the door handle and swung the door open. A pleasant breeze blew into the cottage.

"I'm not done with you," Silver added. "If you're still alive when I find that lunatic, you'll be helping me."

Meredith looked back. "If you think I can."

The response was met with a snort. "I'll use you as bait if nothing else."

"At least you're upfront about it. . . ."

"Just go back to your life and try not to do anything foolish."

"What a novel idea. I'll try that for a change. Wary's worth."

She hurried to close the door before her sass could be rebuked. Meredith smiled inwardly at getting the last word, then remembered she had committed murder today. It sobered her up rather quickly.

Taking a deep breath of mountain air, she got her first proper look around as she fetched the dais from its harness. The cottage was nearly a cabin, its rustic look belying the sleek lines within. Silver had no immediate neighbors, though a few chimneys smoked in the distance. Only hermits and maintenance crew made their home in the Coren range. The view was one of cloud-cut peaks at her back and a sprawling valley ahead, green and gold and brown where towns or long-wrecked ruins didn't spread. Relatively close-by Tremmelton's burgs squatted on their walled plateau, with Brena's Tower across, on the Felling side. If she squinted hard enough, she could locate Devalen's Green, and the Ferris mills perched over the dam-bound lake. The Harvest Plants were an ominous speck atop the remains of New Yanwar, and Tarkis, all the way down at the bottom, was a misty blur of diffused light.

Perpetually mired in her day-to-day troubles, Meredith didn't often notice. Galavan was gorgeous . . . from a distance.

The Hunger can be managed, Silver's voice came back to her without prompting. A baffling thought. A troublesome thought.

"Beware the deceit of the merciful," Meredith recited out loud without a trace of conviction.

The sun had dimmed to the orange tint that marked a span before dusk. Even if she didn't get turned around avoiding other traffic, the best she could hope for was to get home at nightfall. At least this horrible day would finally be over.

It was only mid-flight, when she attempted to shade her eyes from the sunlight above, that she realized her hat was gone.

CHAPTER TWENTY-THREE

CLOSURE

 HE LANDING WENT SMOOTHLY, for once. It felt like a whole cycle had gone by since taking off for Devalen at midday. As she walked down the trail toward her cottage, Meredith wanted nothing more than to spend the next few days under the showerhead.

"It's only a hat," she muttered to herself for the twentieth time, fishing for her keyring. "There was nothing special about it, you didn't bleed all over it. Stop being paranoid."

The key grumbled into the deadbolt lock, and that's when she noticed the aura. Paying closer attention, she sensed unleashed magic seeping through the tiny cracks around the door, out the window seams. The otherworldly sense of spent power came from above as well, reaching over the roof tiles.

She hurried inside and locked the door behind her. "Jane?"

Jane didn't answer. The lab door was wide open, no-one inside. Meredith headed for the kitchen, alarm building in her gut. The aura grew stronger the closer she got to the swinging door.

"Janette?"

She pushed the door and looked. Dusk's dying light flooded in through the windows, illuminating a perfectly still kitchen with nothing but a single item out of place: a plate on the table, covered with a large cloth and a little off-center. Second Forthday's tater omelet, left out to cool several span ago. On the drying rack rested the day's washed pots and pans.

Meredith neared the door leading to the courtyard. The aura became thicker with her every step. Outside the window, a source of pristine white light.

A voice came from it. It was . . . manly.

"Jane!" She threw the door open and ran outside. The aura of unleashed magic was so dense here she could almost drink it; her skin crawled, her nostrils burned as if touched by sulfur. The scene she stumbled upon froze her in place.

A human manling trembled on his knees, hands held up and spread, colors swirling at his back. The source of light had been the backside of a portal—a manually-opened portal, bound only by glyphed stones hovering at the corners of an invisible doorframe. The man's feet were hobbled in place by the defective stasis trinket they'd finished for practice, nearly a year before.

Janette stood where Meredith always would when trying to retrieve a youth. She wore her satin-trimmed, gold-embroidered robes, hair falling in blond waves down to her bust. Her face was a mask of disdain and resentment.

She held Meredith's revolver in her hands.

"Nettie, please, listen to me," the man was saying. "This is some kind of cult. They kidnapped you and brainwashed you. Please come home, please. . . ."

"I *am* home."

Though Janette's voice quivered, the muzzle of the gun didn't. It was aimed straight at the man's chest. She noticed Meredith and her good eye widened, yet even then the gun didn't waver.

"Jane," Meredith said, equal parts awe and reproach. "What have you done?"

"You! You're the one that kidnapped our girl, aren't you—"

Janette took a step toward the man. "Don't you dare even talk to her! I *swear* I can do much worse than shoot you."

The man cowered. "Nettie, darling, come on, calm down, please. I came here with you, didn't I? I'm cooperating. Maybe you could put the gun down? No-one needs to get hurt. Let's just . . . talk. Can't we just talk?"

"You're good at talking. Everyone believes you when you talk, but I know better. I'm not afraid anymore."

"Apprentice," Meredith butted in, "explain yourself at once."

"*He's* the reason I still have nightmares. I'm putting an end to it."

The man's eyes darted from Janette to the revolver and back. "Sweetheart, please, this is a terrible mistake. Just come back with me, I'll drive us home. Everyone's been looking for you, we've missed you so much—me, your mother, and Abby. . . ."

"Mom is a coward! She doesn't want to see what you've been doing, she'd lose too much. Abby even *covers* for you, that's what you've done to her."

"Sweetheart, we've talked about this. They're bad dreams, it's all in your head. Please, I've never hurt you—"

"They were *not* bad dreams! Do you really think I'm as stupid as Abby? You made me doubt myself back then, but I know better now. The dreams are different. They're *different*."

"No, Nettie, you're sick, you need to get back on your meds—"

"Shut up!" Janette strode toward the man. He shrunk at her advance and shut his eyes tight when the revolver touched the side of his head. "You'll never drug me again, *never! You* are sick. I've had time to think, you know? Think with a clear head, away from you. A real doctor would've taken me to therapy, or run tests to see what's wrong with me. You just gave us pills and told us to keep it quiet. You *convinced us* it would destroy our lives if anyone knew. What kind of father—" Her voice broke mid-sentence. Janette swallowed, lips quivering with every breath. "You won't even say you're sorry."

"Janette," Meredith said in a soft voice.

"Look at me, dad."

"Janette."

"I have to do this, Mistress. Look at me!"

The man feebly swallowed and opened his eyes. "Nettie—"

"Apologise to me. Look into my eyes and say you're sorry."

"Darling, you have to believe me, you're my baby girl, I've never hurt you, please. . . ."

Janette pressed the gun hard against his temple. Her finger was on the trigger, so much so that the cylinder clicked and began to turn. "Stop *lying*. She *saw* you. She saw what you do, so she rescued me. She's good, and you're evil. Say you're sorry, it's the least that you owe me."

He glanced over to Meredith. Tears were streaming down his face. "Wh— what?"

"Say you're sorry! Say it!"

"But I never hurt you, I did nothing wrong. . . ."

Meredith spoke over the commotion, voice stern. "Janette."

The apprentice didn't look her way, but visibly restrained whatever she'd been about to scream.

"That's what he tells himself," she said instead. "That it's okay, as long as it doesn't hurt. It's so much worse now, looking back. Now that I can see it so clearly."

Meredith stared at the cowering man in the white coat. Wiry and bookish, he was shaking, paralyzed into inaction. Is this how she had looked to Frau the day before Janette entered her life?

"It's all I can think about. It's all I dream about. It gets in the way of my studies all the time, and I need to stop it. *This* will stop it, Mistress."

The man met Meredith's eyes with an earnest plea. "I don't know what she's told you, but I'm a doctor, she's not well, it runs in the family—"

"Stop. *Lying!*" She punctuated the demand with a forceful jab of the weapon. It would've been the perfect opportunity for a desperate attempt at disarming her, but the man did not fight back. He simply recoiled in terror.

"He's a liar, Mistress. We both know it."

Meredith stared on, thoughts churning with memories of overeager diligence, sporadic melancholy, bedtime wariness. Memories of a shivering frame in the black of night. Memories of soft words after night terrors.

Was this pitiful human the reason behind it all?

Formless outrage bubbled up Meredith's throat as she walked to her apprentice. The man watched her approach as if she bore scythe and black cowl. Lightly, she laid a hand on the girl's shoulder. "If I let you do this," she quietly said, "will the nightmares stop?"

Janette pressed lips together. Both her hands were on the weapon, gaze intent on the muzzle. "The fear will stop. That's good enough."

Meredith could relate.

"I just killed someone," she declared.

Father and daughter turned their heads to stare. Their expressions were oddly similar.

"You did?" Janette asked.

"I had to do it, I didn't have a choice. You cannot kill this man."

The human sagged slightly. The Earthborn witch tightened further. "Mistress. . . ."

"I can't let you. I wouldn't wish this feeling on anyone, you least of all."

"Listen to her, sweetheart."

"Would you keep quiet? She's not going to do anything you say."

"Mistress, I need this. It's the only way. Please."

Meredith spoke closer to her ear. "You don't want this on your conscience, Janette."

"No, you think I'll regret it? It's not like that." Her eyes were harsh. Her grip on the gun was a choke-hold. "I won't *ever* regret it."

"This is not an argument. I've made a decision, apprentice. You will obey me. Give me the weapon."

The scowl on Janette's brow deepened, but only briefly. After one darted glance at her Mistress, her face contorted to anguish.

"That's not fair. . . ."

"Are you disobeying me?"

"He needs to pay."

"And you need to do as I say. You're in enough trouble already."

A healthy dose of fear seeped through Janette's resolve. Meredith nudged her away from the man, and the young witch reluctantly stepped back. The gun lowered, if only slightly. "I . . . I can't let him go back to my sister."

Meredith extended her hand. "Give it here."

Mouth pursed and nostrils flared, Janette hesitated a bit more before carefully offering up the revolver. With a small sigh of relief Meredith held it firm and checked the load: five bullets, one empty chamber. Just as it was when she first found it.

Janette's breath quivered, tears gleamed on her eyelids as she continued to stare at the human. None of the tension had left her. The weapon might no longer be in her hands, but she didn't need it to tear this man apart.

"You can't kill him," Meredith repeated, "and you're certainly not making a mess. I mopped only last night, remember?"

Their eyes met for the span of a shallow breath. Whatever defiance was left vanished on the spot. She knew how particular the Mistress was about cleanliness.

"So you're just . . . you're letting him go free? After what he did to me?"

There was no reproach in Janette's voice. Only desolation.

The Mistress once more stared at the trembling man. "I didn't say that. Do you remember the verses on the first page of the Concept Compendium? The tenets of the masquerade?"

"Y– yes. I do."

"Then you know what must be done. Recite after me." Meredith pointed the revolver at the human's forehead. "Guard knowledge."

"What?" The man recoiled, his efforts utterly hampered by knee-to-foot stasis. Again he spread his arms in the air as if it would help him in some way.

Janette needed a moment to understand. The taut anxiety clutching her chest visibly eased. Her shoulders slumped as if a knot had been unwound. She nodded slowly, eyes closed.

"Never let them know," she whispered.

"You're mad! This is murder!"

"Preclude freedom."

Janette stepped closer, side-by-side with her Mistress. "Never let them go," she answered.

"I did nothing wrong!"

A delicate hand sought callused fingers. Meredith clasped it. "Enforce silence," she said.

"Never let them tell," Janette responded.

"You have to believe me!"

She cocked the hammer with her thumb, and her eyes narrowed. "Beware deceit."

"No, please, wait—"

Meredith pulled the trigger.

The sound was much louder and deeper than she'd expected from such a small weapon—the recoil nearly yanked the gun off her hand. Blood spattered out the other side of the man's skull and into the portal as the body jolted and fell. Only the head disappeared into the colorful swirl. The rest of the man slumped back on the cobbles, legs awkwardly bent within their trap.

Her stomach lurched and her ears rang, but Meredith focused only on what needed to happen. With measured steps she closed the distance to the man and flipped the switch to disable the stasis trinket. She guided the body to collapse into the portal, grabbed the feet and shoved. After a few groans she managed to make the corpse disappear completely.

With a troubled sigh she straightened and turned around. Janette gaped at where the body had been, lips parted and quivering, breath coming in sharp spurts after long pauses. Blood speckled her face like bright red freckles.

"You need to close the portal," Meredith said.

Janette didn't respond. Her hands were balled close to her chest, shaking.

"Jane." Meredith bent at the waist and looked up in an attempt to meet her far-off stare. She raised her voice so it would climb over the ringing in her ears. "The portal. Only you can close it."

Janette's gaze slowly focused. Her brow creased in anguish. "Mistress, I'm sorry. . . ."

"One thing at a time. Seal the portal, Jane."

The girl took a few more faltering breaths, closed her eyes, swallowed. She nervously licked her lips and infused a short string of syllables Meredith didn't understand. Power flowed around her like a torrid wind, and the gateway winked out of existence. The cornerstones fell from mid-air and clattered to a stop.

"Yes. Good. Are you alright? Are you hurt?"

Janette swallowed again and shook her head in short, quick movements.

"Good. That's good."

"Mistress, I. . . ."

The girl was looking at her mentor with unaffected dread. Irregular breaths became subdued sobs, and the first tears overflowed Janette's eyelids.

"Please don't be angry," she managed to say. "Please. . . ."

Meredith crossed her arms. "You should have talked to me about this."

The girl looked down and said nothing, patently striving to contain her sobs. A wet itch started in Meredith's nose. "You scared me senseless. I thought someone was attacking you."

"Sorry," Jane mouthed in a broken whisper. Meredith tried to uphold the stern look and miserably failed.

"Oh bugger it. . . ." She stepped close to Janette and brought her into a hug. The young witch buried her face in the hollow of her mentor's collarbone, hands clutching at her robe. Meredith tenderly cradled her head and shoulders.

"I'm not angry," she said. The girl's body seemed to slump at the words. Her slight frame shook with every gasp as she wept.

Meredith kissed the side of her head. "It's alright. It's over now."

"He deserved it," Janette breathed. No tears could douse the fire in her voice.

"I believe you. I've no doubt he did."

"He deserved much worse."

"I know, I believe you."

She pressed the girl to her chest, lightly rocking her from side to side. Meredith's own tears trickled down her cheeks.

"I believe you."

Janette cried softly in her mentor's arms, frail and helpless, nothing at all like a witch was meant to be.

S HE SLEPT ON THE COUCH, her head on Meredith's lap. She'd cried for so long that Meredith's robe felt soaked through.

Hand tenderly stroking Janette's hair, she was looking at the girl with dread in her core. Meredith had searched for regret or guilt inside and found none, unlike what the inquisitor incident had left behind. She felt a sense of grim pride, instead.

Looking at Janette right there, right then, it was so obvious. There was no waving it aside, no brushing it under a rug, no denial or delusion. What she felt for her was inescapable.

It would be so easy to choke her right now, the witch in her head suggested. *No more worry, problem solved. What's one more death at this point?*

What should've been a practical notion seemed utterly deranged to her—which crystalized a simple realization for good.

She'd sooner set her house on fire than bring any harm to this girl.

"What am I going to do?" she mouthed in a tiny voice.

Janette stirred and settled her shoulders more comfortably. With slow movements Meredith reached for the thin blanket on the sofa's backrest and pulled it over her ward. Janette breathed deep, a faint smile on her lips. "Thank you," she murmured.

Horror crept up Meredith's spine as she reveled in the warmth brought by that smile.

Her troubled thoughts kept churning deep into the night.

Chapter Twenty-Four

The Truth

 "I HAVE TO TELL YOU THE TRUTH."
Standing in front of her wardrobe mirror, Meredith watched her gaunt reflection pinch her lips in disgust. She tried again.

"Jane, I've been lying to you."

She clicked her tongue off her teeth and thoughtfully rubbed her cheek.

"I have bad news: the Coven has suspended my rights to tutelage. You're going back to Earth—egh! I'm sick of lying to her!"

She sighed and looked up.

"Hey, want to hear something funny? I'm a fraud, ha ha ha!"

Her flippant expression transitioned to a grimace. She flopped onto the bed, ran fingers through her hair and cradled the back of her neck. "She needs to know. Otherwise she'll want to come back. She'd find a way."

Meredith stared at the floorboards. A night of more worrying than sleeping had left only one option in her mind: quietly send Janette back to Earth. The prospect felt like cutting out her own heart and throwing it through a portal, but there was no other choice if she was to keep her safe. Somehow, keeping her safe had become The Most Important Thing.

"Maybe I can hide her until. . . ."

Until when? Until Janette grew into an adult witch and could blend in with everyone else? Even in her most delusional dreams she couldn't see it working out. She'd traveled this thought-circle several times now. Every trip led to the same place.

"You have to let go, you fool."

Soft knocking intruded in her whispers.

"Yes?"

"May I come in?"

Meredith made sure her eyelids were dry and her hair was somewhat dignified. "Yes, it's open."

The door swung inward. Under her slightly-outgrown robes Janette had changed into one of the all-black hand-me-down ensembles she'd "inherited" from her Mistress, cutting a svelte silhouette that these days could stand at eye-level with Meredith's chin. Her bust-length waves were pulled back with glossy black barrettes, yet her efforts in front of the mirror couldn't hide the fact she'd spent half the night crying.

She went no further than the doorframe. "Mistress. . . ."

"Janette, just call me Meredith, or Meri, it doesn't matter."

"Mistress, I need to apologise."

"Apologise for what? This is all my fault."

"B— but it's not! I was going crazy, and I went behind your back, I broke so many rules, I deserve to be punished. You trusted me, you . . . you've been so good to me, and I betrayed your trust instead of—" Janette broke off and swallowed. "I'm so, *so* sorry. I should be punished. I'll do anything you say."

Meredith creased her brow and waved a dismissing hand. The irony ground barbs through her chest.

"That won't be necessary."

"But. . . ."

"I need you to go sit on the sofa. I'll be out shortly."

Anxiety crept into Janette's tone. "Mistress, you . . . you won't send me away, will you? Please. . . ."

"I need to talk to you, Jane. Please go sit."

Janette stood there, one hand fretfully wringing the front of her shirt. She turned around and headed for the couch, but paused after only one step. Her voice came in a strangled whisper.

"You're everything I have."

Meredith's heart dove two leagues underground as she watched the girl walk away.

"You're about to find out how unfortunate that is," she said to the empty room.

She donned the plain cowl on her chair's backrest, sighing at the sight of the gear-packed robes strewn over the vanity. She hadn't even changed or washed since yesterday's unhinged adventures. She'd normally be driven to put everything back to its proper place, but the urge simply wasn't there at present.

Meredith shuffled into the living room. The girl was in the middle of the couch, head bowed and eyes cast down like a penitent soul awaiting judgment. Dawn's light would usually filter through the curtains, but it was the first day of Hallow's End, and the skyveil would be a solid slate of dark for one hundred and five span.

Meredith sat next to the armrest, back straight, head tilted up wistfully. Time went by in a silence she couldn't break. Her lips trembled as the damning words she needed to voice battled against the nervous jitters keeping her mouth shut.

"What you said yesterday," Janette began instead, "about killing someone. Was it true?"

Meredith closed her eyes, utterly vexed with her own dithering. "It was. It is."

"Would you like to talk about it?"

Sure. So Mifraulde—that's my brood-sister, the Head of the Coven—set me up to infiltrate the Riven Circle, yeah? But I ended up joining them sincerely, sort of, and I brought a deranged human prisoner to them so we could liberate him—because, you see, unspark't humans are used as slave labour in this realm, but I don't condone that—so then the human serf turned out to be utterly mad and murdered a lot of them, and the Tarkis Forewitch came over—

Meredith dug her nails into her own thigh. "I was protecting us."

A quiet moment passed. "Protecting us from what?"

"It's complicated. Jane, listen."

The girl looked at her mentor. Meredith breathed deep and kept her eyes glued to the spot where wall met ceiling.

"There are some things you need to know."

Janette kept looking at her—restless, fully unsuspecting of the fantasy in which she lived. Meredith inhaled and forced out the words that would unravel every single falsehood she'd spun.

"I've been lying to you."

She glanced over for a reaction, and saw Janette making a face like she'd just learned Galavan's moon was a glob of butter levitating in the skyveil. Gracious ravens, it was happening. Couldn't someone knock at the door? Couldn't a transmission come in? Couldn't the roof fall over their heads?

"What do you mean? Lying about what?"

Meredith waited. Nobody knocked. The transmitter didn't buzz or blink. It was just them and the mountain of lies between them.

"I. . . ." Which one first? How to unravel it all? Was it even possible? "I was never meant to take you in."

"What?"

"I've been using you, Janette. The witches out there, all of us, this whole realm, it's nothing like I've—"

The words were cut off by the booming thunderclap that blew the front door off its hinges.

They jumped and screamed in unison as the heavy door thrashed through bookshelves and slammed to a stop in front of the bathroom, crushing the blooming jade in the corner. White smoke rushed into the house and drowned the room in a dense haze that soon had them coughing and wheezing.

She pressed Janette to herself while trying to catch her breath. A dark figure strode in through the mist shroud, and Meredith felt her ribcage shrink upon recognizing her.

A severe Mifraulde stepped toward them, flanked by two other figures—tall, broad-shouldered, and wearing the unmistakable tri-horned jade coif of the Judicars.

The Head of the Coven met Meredith's eyes, then looked at the frightened creature in her arms. Never before had Meredith seen such loathing in her sister's features.

"What is *this*, Meredith?"

Smoke and anxiety barely let Meredith breathe, let alone give a coherent response. She felt Janette recoil from the strangers. "Mistress, what's happening!"

The possibility of escape passed through her consideration and was swiftly discarded: every trinket was either in the cellar, the lab or her other robe, as out of reach as the stars twinkling on the skyveil. Her thoughts raced to find some way to explain. Whatever had led them here, there had to be some magical words that would stay their hand and erase Mifraulde's wrath. Maybe a spell to turn back time and set everything right.

If such words existed, Meredith didn't know them.

"Frau," she heard herself say. "Please don't hurt her. Please."

Mifraulde's outrage had drained away, slowly replaced by stern detachment.

"Bind them, juditors."

Only the small tremor to her voice betrayed the gelid anger beneath. The images rolled through Meredith's mind again: the prison cell, the pyre, the pain, the screams—but all of it was trumped by what they might do to Janette.

She should have strangled her last night when she had the chance.

Meredith stood and stepped in front of her charge. "Frau, she's a witch, she'll be your greatest ally! Train her as one of us!"

One of the juditors drew near, restraints already in hand. "Cooperate, denizen. I will use force as necessary."

"Don't waste this opportunity! She's gifted, she can be the next Caterina, and she'll be in your service, think about it!"

Mifraulde's expression didn't change. The juditor stepped over the scattered debris, heavy boots crushing wood and glass into the rug. The other juditor wasn't far behind, watchful of any unexpected developments.

"This is your last warning, denizen."

Janette clutched at the back of Meredith's robe. "Don't hurt her! Mistress, don't let them hurt you!"

"Mifraulde, I'm begging you, she's one of us! Please—"

Meredith's plea was interrupted by a fist to the gut. She bent forward, straight into the juditor's gag. The contraption clamped shut at the back of her head.

"Meri!" Janette tried to get up but was struck by the juditor's brutal backhand. The girl cried out and crumpled on the couch.

"Nnmm!" Meredith threw herself at her captor, colliding with enough force to jounce the juditor off balance. She tried to drag the brute to the floor, give Jane time to—

It was only after two beats of expert hand-to-hand struggle that the juditor firmly held both of Meredith's arms at her back.

"How dare you even try," the juditor spat in a rasp full of contempt. Manacles closed painfully on Meredith's wrists, right above the shocker coil.

She'd completely forgotten it was there.

Mifraulde kept silent during the brief exchange. In a few unhurried steps she closed the distance to her immobilized sister, velvet slippers avoiding rubble and splinters with uncanny grace. Though at first glance she was impassive, her wrath showed in the details: the rigid set to her shoulders, the subtle flare to her nostrils, the foreboding darkness shrouding her blue stare.

Meredith begged in silent appeal, tearful eyes going from Mifraulde to the helpless girl in her care. What had led them here? Had it been the hat? Had someone followed her around? Had Four-Thirteen tipped them off somehow? Had Yurena betrayed her? Had they noticed Janette's adventure last night?

Did it even matter?

The Head of the Coven continued staring for a long moment—she drew back her hand and slapped Meredith's face hard enough for her teeth to shred the inside of her cheek.

"*My own sister,*" Mifraulde hissed. Her other hand shot out and gripped Meredith's jaw, forcing her to look up.

Meredith groaned. Unable to spit the blood, she swallowed.

"After everything I did for you, *this* is how you repay me!"

Once more she drew back her hand. Through the corner of her eye Meredith saw Jane stir on the sofa, face full of strain, blood seeping from the cut on her cheek and staining the cushions. She tried to call Janette's name, tell her to run, to hide, to use what she'd learned and escape, but only a moan came out. The next furious slap drove every idea out of Meredith's head.

You earned this, the voice in her thoughts reminded her through the daze. *You earned this.*

"Bind and gag the youth as well," the Head of the Coven instructed. "I could sense its power from the other side of the room."

Meredith moaned and sobbed as the other juditor pulled out her set of manacles and neared Janette. The Mistress struggled to break free despite the pain, but her captor held firm at her back, twisting until Meredith's bad shoulder felt about to pop out of its socket.

"*Stop* that," the brute said, "or I will *truly* hurt you."

Janette sat halfway up, still dazed. She saw the approaching juditor and her eyes widened in bewildered panic. She looked at Meredith, and saw the forced posture, the pained features and desperate thrashing. Her features shifted from panic to outrage.

Immediately she brought one hand to her chest, while the other pointed directly at her mentor. Her infused scream filled the room like shrieking thunder.

"Fǽr'vǎ'yunām ús!"

The words created a sense of vacuum around Meredith, of weightlessness—and then the room exploded. Mifraulde, the Judicars, the broken furniture, the walls, the ceiling; everything was caught in the simultaneous push-spheres centered upon mentor and student. The deafening clamor crashed upon Meredith's eardrums as her cottage splintered and flew apart, the intruders got thrown out like gale-swept leaves, the floor crumbled and gave way under her feet.

She didn't fall, not at first. In near complete darkness she had time to see Janette hovering in mid-air, just as untouched by the pandemonium. Their eyes met for a stupefied instant.

The spell ceased, and both witches tumbled into the cellar.

CHAPTER TWENTY-FIVE

HALLOW'S END

 EREDITH GROANED for a while. Her right foot had landed badly, the whole leg felt bruised from toe to hip. Her head had bounced into something during the fall and warmth flowed behind her ear.

Eventually she gathered the presence of mind to roll onto her stomach and wriggle until she got a knee under her. She'd never realized how hard it was to get off the floor without using her hands.

"Gah-neh," she tried to call out. Dust whiffed into her nose and started a coughing fit. With her mouth gagged shut, breathing soon became a problem. Between the coughing and the wound inside her cheek, her entire existence became not choking to death on her own blood.

A hand landed on her shoulder. "Mistress," Janette said in a whisper.

Meredith sagged with relief. She went to hug the girl but only succeeded in rattling the manacles. Janette had no trouble doing all the hugging.

"Are you okay?"

Meredith nodded. "Uomm?"

"Just my cheek, and I hit a shelf going down—oh, no, you're bleeding!"

The older witch gave a dismissive shrug. "Muh." She looked all around. "Mmmoh?"

"The others?"

"Hm, hm," she nodded.

"I don't know. I hope they're hurt. I hope they're dead."

Meredith tried to make out details in the Hallow's End dark. Some light reached them from the street lamps at the end of her little road, enough to see Janette covered in dust, hair disheveled, dirty face streaked by tears and darkened where she'd been struck. Her jaw and chin were messily bloodstained. Her voice trembled and both her eyes sparked with anger. "Who were those people? Why did they hurt you?"

Meredith couldn't have answered even without the gag. She shut her eyes and vigorously shook her head. "Mm-mm."

"Can I take that off you?" Janette extended a hand. Meredith raised her own and recoiled. "Nogh. Kghn." She struggled upright and looked around, wishing her eyes would hurry up and adapt. The dust settled enough to reveal a cellar full of debris and splintered floorboards. Damage was extensive where the ceiling had caved, but the shelves and miscellaneous items along the walls were mostly intact. There was no way to climb up through the jagged hole in her living room floor.

The sense of spent power was a flood all around her. Even though Janette had extensively studied spatial warping and gravitational manipulation in her quest for the perfect pusher, it was still baffling to witness her extremely word-efficient command of magic.

"Mistress, were those the guys you've been protecting us from? Will someone else come?"

Meredith groaned and urgently shouldered the girl toward the ramp leading to the exit.

The coded and padlocked exit.

"They won't budge," Janette said after pushing up against the double doors.

"Wuff wmm-mm," Meredith told her.

Janette stared, dumbfounded.

"Wuff wmm-mm!"

"I can't understand, I'm sorry."

Meredith made as if she was ramming something above and ahead of her, jerking her body upwards. "Wmpf! Bmm!"

"Hit it with my head?"

"BMM! WMPF!" She shook her elbows as if she'd just received an electric jolt. "BMMMF!"

"Blow it up! With magic!"

A high-pitched moan expressed Meredith's relieved approval.

"I just didn't want to cause more damage! Stand back."

Janette eyed the barred trapdoor while her mentor found cover behind a pile of debris. The girl coughed the dust off her throat, positioned her legs for a steady footing and spread her hands in front of herself as if holding an invisible cantaloupe.

"Fǽr'yunįdr."

The space in front of Janette's fingers warped, contracted and burst forth in the span of a heartbeat. With a crashing boom the distortion propagated into the locked doors and blew them off their hinges.

Immediately Meredith bumped the girl's back and prodded her up the ramp. Janette's aura was a cloud of plasma parting at their passing. They emerged into what used to be the back garden and nearly tripped on the mess outside.

Half the kitchen's far wall remained upright, guarded by three cupboards and a sink. The lab, insulated only from the inside, had caved in and was now a cracked shell full of litter. Everything else had been blown to pieces. Whole chunks of house were strewn all over the courtyard, the garden, against the partially demolished fences and beyond. Desmond's pen was a mess of bricks and wood— Meredith could only hope the poor guy had escaped to the trees. What was once a cozy cottage had become a disaster zone.

"Oh, Mistress . . . I'm so sorry, I was so scared, I didn't even try to control it. Oh, oh no. The lab, I'd just finished it. . . ."

Meredith blinked away the tears, shook off the grief. She surveyed the area, trying to focus on escaping unseen. One of the juditors was messily impaled on the broken fence. The other was a motionless mound, half buried under a pile of rubble. Any one of the countless dark shapes all around could've been Mifraulde.

"This is all my fault," Jane said. Her voice trembled. "It's all because of what I did last night, isn't it?"

"Mmuh." Meredith pushed her toward the trees. "Mmuh, nyuh."

"But . . . maybe something survived, we should search for a while. . . ."

Meredith kept pushing. As much as she wanted to sort through the wreckage, a house blowing up didn't go unnoticed. Probably there were eyes on them at that very moment. She could only hope Mifraulde was incapacitated, wherever she was, and would not give chase right away.

Even after what had just happened, the thought of her brood-sister being outright dead brought a painful twinge to her conscience.

Janette looked over her shoulder again. "Can I at least take care of your handcuffs?"

Meredith grunted and nodded absent-mindedly, trying to keep an eye on everything at once. The darkness would slow them down greatly, but at least it would keep them hidden. They slipped through one of the many gaps in the ruined fence and ventured deep into the copse.

Where they would go from there, Meredith had no idea.

A S SOON AS THE BACK DOOR opened, Meredith barreled through with Janette in hand. Wybel stumbled back and bumped the small desk by the entrance.

"What do you think you're doing? Who's this?"

Janette obediently kept her hood up and her eyes down. Meredith shut the door and leaned against it, breathing hard. Thank the furies for Hallow's End and its Market Square carnival. She'd felt like the nerve-wracking trip through Brena's deserted streets would never end.

Wybel looked a bit closer. "What's that around your mouth?" She walked up and pulled back the cowl obscuring Meredith's features. She came face to face with a gagged criminal on the loose.

"What did you—" She interrupted herself, grimacing like there was a bad taste at the back of her tongue. She looked at Meredith's companion. "Mergat's despoiled undercarriage, who in blazes are you?"

She threw back Janette's hood. Blue eyes risked a fretful look at the old witch before returning to the floor.

Wybel's face blanched. She looked from one to the other as she backed away, slack-jawed.

"Is *this* . . . are you. . . ."

Meredith stepped forth, hands coming together in a pleading gesture. The broken manacle chains clinked against one another. "Mmf. Bff."

"Get *out* of my house! Right now!" Wybel kept backing up from the youth as if she were plague-ridden. "I want no part in whatever this is!"

"Please help her," Janette said timidly, hands wringing her robes. "I'll go if I have to, but please help her. Please?"

"Nnuh." Meredith put her hands on the girl's shoulders. "Bff."

The Mistress tightened her grip and subtly pushed. *If it comes down to it,* she hoped to be saying, *you will make her help us.* Surely the resourceful shopkeeper would know of some way to get rid of the gag without Judicar intervention. If nothing else, they could use the workshop space-fold to get Janette somewhere safe.

Jane's fists balled at her sides, as if she understood. "I'm Meredith's apprentice," she said, "and I did something very wrong, so they came for her, and then . . . I attacked them. So now we're running."

Wybel was staring at the girl, blinking. Her hairless brow was creased in a pained expression Meredith couldn't decipher.

"I ruined everything," Janette carried on, "but no-one is going to hurt Mistress Meredith. No-one."

Her latent power pulsed in concert with her emotions, washing over the tiny foyer at the back of Wybel's shop. Meredith kept up an intent look that made every effort to say *I'm terribly sorry, but she will not hesitate to hurt you.* She wasn't sure whether it was a bluff or not.

The wizened witch closed her eyes, leaning back against the wall. She appeared breathless, haunted. As she shook her head, years seemed to pile onto her shoulders.

"It's not time yet," she said. "I can't get involved like this again."

Janette darted a dubious look back at her Mistress. Though Meredith made every effort to remain stone-faced, she'd have paid a fortune for an actual conversation. Tears brimmed on Wybel's eyelids.

"How did you find out? How long have you known?"

"Mmf," Meredith replied, wholly self-assured. She had no idea what Wybel was talking about.

"Figures." She pressed her thin lips together, looked at Janette. Her gaze softened, and she muttered to herself: "Horrors curse your bleeding heart, you should've tossed her out on day one."

Full of resignation Wybel started toward Meredith. Janette immediately stepped forth and pointed her index finger at the old witch. "Stop, I'm warning you."

She regarded Janette as if grieving the girl's folly. Wybel sighed. "I won't hurt either of you, child. By blood and power, I swear it."

Janette darted another look back. Meredith nodded. The girl reluctantly stepped aside.

Wybel neared the fugitive while tugging at her forearm. Below the velvety cloth of her robe, a wound strap of stylish wide ribbon became loose. She untied it with practiced movements that were clearly as routine as breathing. "Should've asked more questions," she whispered to herself, "should've tossed her out...." She pocketed the ribbon and folded up her sleeve.

There were minute scars on her forearm, like tangled claw marks arranged in rows. Meredith felt a dim surge of Wybel's latent power, the kind of surge that would come after infused incantations. A small string of runescript glowed blood-red down her arm. She pressed it to Meredith's gag while working the seam at the back of the head.

The gag easily came apart and fell to the floor.

Wide-eyed with shock and relief, Meredith breathed through her mouth like she'd come up from a long underwater dive. She moved her jaw this way and that, massaging it with one hand. She would've loved to spit out the awful taste on her tongue.

Janette let out a weak moan and hurried to fiercely hug her Mistress. Meredith pressed her against her chest, squeezing tightly, kissing her forehead. Why bother with pretense anymore? It felt good to care for this girl, to give her affection. It felt right.

Wybel was staring at the scene with a pained grimace, yet there was a measure of awe in her voice. "You care about them. You, of all people. How did I not see it?"

Whatever she was talking about, this stroke of good luck couldn't go to waste.

"We all hide our true selves," Meredith said with dramatic hoarseness, "and if we don't do it well, we're as good as dead."

"Yeah, don't you think I know that? You can't fight the Coven head-on. They made sure I learned that lesson. What's your plan with this girl? How long have you been doing this?"

"It doesn't matter, I just need to get her out of Galavan right now. You have to help us."

"Tell me how you found out who I am. Who else knows? Wait— are they chasing you? Did you lead the Judicars to me?"

"No, no, don't worry. I wasn't followed, and no– uh . . . I told one other person, for insurance. I didn't know how you'd react."

"Your love-bird. Of course."

"Right. Can we *please*—"

"How did you find out, Meredith? I need to know. I can't afford loose ends like this."

"Look, I wasn't sure, I simply had suspicions, I can tell you all about it once—"

"*How* did you suspect, exactly?"

"I'm just perceptive, it wasn't so hard! I'm not nearly as daft as you think."

Wybel stared without conviction, one hairless eyebrow raised as she closely studied Meredith's expression. It was a conscious effort not to fidget.

"We don't have time for this," Meredith said, "we need to—"

"You have no idea who I am, do you? I simply happened to be the only person that might help. There was not one whit of planning involved."

"Uh. . . ."

Wybel let out an infuriated breath. "And I gave myself away like the softhearted fool I am. A hundred years of work and still all it takes is an innocent girl in distress."

"Listen, whoever you are, I truly don't care. Help me out one last time and you won't ever see me again. I need to get her out."

"Only her? What about you? You can't stay in Galavan. At least for a few years."

"Me? Go to Earth? That's not, uh . . . there's no need for that, I'll think of something."

"Are you insane? You're the Head of the Coven's fugitive sister. If they catch you, Mifraulde will personally flay you alive before setting you on fire, just to make a point."

"I'll . . . I'll lie low for a while. Get a new life. Didn't *you* do that?"

"I did after years of exile. You've no idea what I had to do to disappear. Do you think my face looked anything like this? Do you think it's age that withered me so?"

"Look, I don't care, let's get her out and I'll worry about myself later." Meredith tried to walk past, but Wybel grabbed her elbow.

"You can't right now, you boob. It's Hallow's End."

"What does that have to do with anything?"

Wybel looked as if she was speaking to a particularly stupid thog breed. "Earth is locked away during Hallow's End. How do you not know this?"

Meredith stopped and blinked. "What?"

"What do they teach you at the academy these days? None of the nexūs are accessible while the skyveil goes through maintenance."

"What? No, that's . . . what?"

"Did you think Hallow's End darkness is all about tradition? You are stuck in Galavan for the next hundred span. Better think fast of a good place to hide."

Meredith spent a moment properly panicking, her mouth working on words without any sound coming out.

"If you ask me to let you stay here," Wybel finished, "I will slug you."

"What? No! We can't hide for five days, that won't work! There has to be something we can do, isn't there some kind of emergency nexus for dire emergencies? There must be *something*. . . ."

Meredith's outburst trailed off as she noticed the quiet sobs and sniffling noises at her back. She looked at Janette to see her leaning against the wall, head down and shoulders trembling. She was hugging herself like she wanted to fold into nothingness and vanish out of existence.

"Jane?"

The girl looked up dejectedly. She couldn't meet Meredith's eyes for longer than a heartbeat. Tears dropped off her cheeks onto the tiles. "I ruined your life," she said in an airy moan. She seemed barely able to breathe. "I ruined your life. . . ."

Her voice alone brought a lump to Meredith's throat. "Hey, no, no, don't say that." She closed the distance between them and gently squeezed her arm. "It's not true, you didn't ruin anything."

"Of course it's true." She sniffled and angrily wiped her face, turning away from Meredith. "I threw everything away. You gave me everything I ever wanted, and I threw it away for– for *nothing*, like I was playing a silly game."

"Listen to me, you don't have to–"

"You should hate me! Why are you still talking to me? I don't deserve any of it, your whole career is gone, your whole life, and– and now you're leaving Mistress Yurena behind, and it's all because of me, because I couldn't get over some childish thing that didn't matter anymore. How could I be so stupid? Stupid selfish idiot. . . ."

"Wait," Wybel said, alarm in her voice. "Your love-bird. She *is* secure, right?"

Meredith waved a dismissive hand. "I don't know, I haven't talked to her, why'd you even care?" She turned back to Janette. "This is all my fault, you hear me? All of it. I need you to stop feeling sorry and concentrate on getting through this. I'll explain everything when we're safe."

"What do you mean—"

Wybel raised her voice. "Your girlfriend will be the first person of interest when they go looking for you, dimwit. Exactly how long do you think she'll last in an interrogation? What will be the very first name she gives, considering our delightful rapport?"

Meredith blinked twice. A third time.

Yurena would tell them absolutely everything as soon as she understood what was happening. Probably spin herself into a blameless victim in the whole affair. In fact, Meredith could picture Yurena memorizing and rehearsing far ahead of time the exact words she'd say.

She was practical like that.

"We have to go," Meredith breathlessly said. "*Right now.*"

"Great. This is great. Thank you *so much* for ruining everything, numbskull."

Wybel took off and disappeared into a doorway, perhaps her bedroom. Meredith grabbed Janette's hand and dragged her into the workshop proper. "Just do everything I say, alright? We'll get out of this. That's all that matters right now."

She went over to the corner and wheeled the space-fold device to the center of the room. If not Earth, she'd need to take Jane as far away as possible, somewhere they would not look—at least not immediately.

Which meant. . . .

"Silver is going to kill me," Meredith muttered. She powered on the frame and got to work on the switches and dials, setting the gateway as local, one way. Wybel walked in hauling a large duffel bag she set down next to the portal device. It was already packed full.

"That was fast," Meredith said.

"I'm a Judicar defector with a mercy problem. You better believe I keep a bug-out bag ready." She pulled out a stack of small yet ominous-looking trinkets from a storage locker. "Among other things." She disappeared into the storefront's doorway.

Janette brushed close to Meredith's side. "Is there anything I can do to help?"

"Not right now. I only need to find where we're going and get the portal open. Just be ready to go."

"Even if we escape, how will you ever forgive me?"

"Janette, stop that. Aren't you listening? It's not your fault. I'll be asking you to forgive *me* soon enough, with some luck."

"Forgive you? You're everything to me. . . ."

Meredith held down a groan. "Actually, you can look through the workshop while I get this blasted thing aligned. Take anything that might look useful."

"Just . . . take it?"

"It's fine, she'll be glad you did."

"Alright."

Janette got to searching with her usual diligence. It would keep her mind occupied. Wybel walked through to the tiny foyer, gone again into the presumed bedroom. Meredith kept turning knobs and dials until what very much looked like Silver's cottage came into view, tucked away behind a rocky mound sparsely covered in mountain shrubs. She dialed the alignment as close as she could, lamenting her lack of actual coordinates.

"Is this a cyborg leg?"

Meredith looked up to see the girl nearly pressing her nose against Wybel's almost-complete mezzode limb. She was reverently running her fingertips over the wordpaths etched upon its surface.

"It's not useful. Focus on useful things."

"Y– yeah. Sorry."

"What is she doing?"

Janette startled at the voice and hurriedly turned around, hands tucked at her back as if caught stealing pastries. Wybel had stepped to Meredith's side, apparently done with whatever she'd been up to. A knapsack hung from her shoulder, and she'd just begun the process of checking every moving part of a human handgun.

"Keeping busy," Meredith answered.

The click-clacking noises of the gun paused. Wybel was staring at the portal's destination. "That's Silver's cabin."

"Oh. You, uh . . . you've met?"

Wybel snorted. "Yeah, you could say that. I don't want her involved."

"Well, I'm all for alternatives, but better come up with one fast."

"Hm." She was quiet for a while. "She's going to kill you for this."

"She won't, we're practically friends, you'll see." Meredith eyed the weapon. "Do you have more of those?"

"Not lying around here, no. Do you even know what this is?" She dismissed her own question with a wave of her hand. "You're protecting a human girl and you've been to Silver's cabin, I need to stop asking stupid questions. Are we done yet?"

"Yes, almost. Jane, come here, get ready."

"I don't know what to take, I can't tell what any of these are. . . ."

"Don't worry about it, we have to go." Meredith locked in the settings and set the reset timer for one cent. No-one should be able to follow.

"There's no need for a timer," Wybel said. "This place is going to blow when we leave."

"What?"

"Whether I like it or not, I've been your youth-minding accomplice all along. I have to go with you, and I'd rather not leave anything behind."

"But—"

"Wybel Tarkan-Fal-Drakari's life is over. It lasted far longer than I thought it would."

Janette winced at the words, but remained quiet. Meredith passed the command rod to the old witch. "Mind doing the honours?"

"Sure, whatever."

Meredith took Jane's hand and pulled her to one side, as close to the portal as they could safely stand. "Be ready to jump in when it opens." Noting the girl's harried expression, she gave the hand an encouraging squeeze. "Hey. Soon we'll go on that adventure we talked about, yeah? We'll live on Earth for a while, and you'll meet a boy, and I'll disapprove. Yeah?"

Janette gave her a half-hearted smile. "Yeah. It'll be great. Okay."

Wybel pointed the rod at the space-fold device. She recited the incantation like the routine bit of magic it was, and the black-and-white image of Silver's front door came alive in vibrant colors.

Meredith gently pushed Janette forth. "Time to—"

Another doorway opened between the witches and their escape route. Jane had barely taken a step when a hunter cat jumped in through the new portal, followed by its Judicar handler.

There were no words. The hunter immediately leaped forth and swatted Janette with its huge front paw. The blow brought her down with a loud thud and kept her pinned to the floor—Jane's cry was little more than a breathless gasp.

At the same time the handler raised her arm at the standing witches, all five fingers pointing forward. Her forearm glowed orange under the wristcuffs. Wybel had the presence of mind to jump out of the way, while Meredith simply stood, one hand still hovering where Janette's shoulder had been.

An invisible force hit Meredith's chest and threw her against the back wall, driving every breath out of her lungs. She collapsed to her knees, shaking and hunched over while bracing her midsection. She'd heard ribs crack on impact.

She couldn't breathe. Meredith tried to stand and move and *do* something, but the pain was blinding. She forced herself to move anyway, and got a foot flat on the ground, and stumbled, nearly falling on her face. Now the pain was *truly* blinding, white stars swirling all across her vision.

Janette cried an incantation Meredith couldn't even make out. The girl's power swelled and permeated the room immediately . . . yet no magic happened. Instead, the hunter's collar rumbled a deep bass, loud enough to send Meredith's teeth chattering. Janette cried out again, but this time it was only wordless pain.

In desperation Meredith once more tried to stand, leaning against the wall and dragging up her battered carcass, little by sputtering little. A gunshot rang. Wybel was yelling by the foyer, close to the exit.

"One step closer and the whole place explodes!"

Meredith had barely made it upright when an arm like solid granite wrapped around her neck. Her tortured scream was abruptly choked. Another arm was working quickly to shackle Meredith's hands together—in a flash of panic, she readied the prongs of the shocker coil still wrapped around her wrist and stabbed in the Judicar's general direction.

There was contact, a sparkling buzz, and her attacker began shaking uncontrollably. Meredith was thrown back to the ground in the resulting struggle, leaving her in breathless agony once more. The Judicar crumpled next to her with white foam frothing from the mouth.

"Stop! Everyone!" Wybel was yelling. "Or we *all* go up in flames!"

A voice seething with contempt answered not five paces away from Meredith.

"Go ahead. You would do me a favour. I need only step back and leave your smoldering remains behind."

Mifraulde stood at the portal threshold. One side of her face was stained red and bruised black and blue. Her robes were torn and filthy in places. She held one arm away from her body in an awkward pose, like it had been messily broken.

A second hunter slowly prowled back and forth in front of the Head of the Coven, black heckles roused in murderous aggravation. Its feline eyes were fixed on Wybel, who held up some kind of switch in one hand, a ready handgun in the other.

"We had an *arrangement,* Fal-Drakari," Mifraulde said, "and you've been keeping *this* from me?"

"The arrangement was, you stay out of my business and I make sure the Circle stays out of yours."

"You didn't think this was my business? My own sister hiding an Earthborn witch?"

"I didn't know that part until today."

As they spoke, Meredith dragged herself onto the frothing handler, teeth gnashing and breath rattled. Her hands searched frantically until her fingers closed on the blade sheathed under the uniform tunic. She pulled out the combat knife as quietly as she could.

"Stop pointing that thing at me," Mifraulde said. "Shoot me and they will tear to you shreds before you can fire again. Shoot them, and I'll make sure it will be the last stupid decision you make."

"Maybe. Or maybe, having a gun on you is the only thing holding them back. You shouldn't have left your precious medallion at home."

To the side of the room Janette was pinned under the massive weight of the first hunter. She was on her back, whimpering softly, too afraid even to squirm under the claw pressed to her ribcage. Blood flowed from a gash on her shoulder.

She was about three meters away. Meredith needed just one burst of energy, one decisive leap and stab. Set the pain aside and give it her all. It didn't even have to get the kill or avoid the claws—it only needed to create a distraction for Wybel to shoot and give Jane enough time to run through the good portal.

It was worth a try. The alternative was every nightmare becoming reality.

Mifraulde spoke again. "I don't care about you," she said to Wybel. "Leave now, and you have my word no-one will give chase. Or stay, and die with your fellow criminals. Is it that hard a choice?"

Dread clumped in Meredith's chest. Wybel scoffed. "I trust that promise as much as I trust my bladder these days."

"You can *trust me* when I say Silver will be hunted down and executed if you cross me right now."

The hesitation was brief, but noticeable. "I don't know how you'd manage it," Wybel responded, "when I'd be taking all of you with me."

"You *might*. Suppose you do. How do you think my replacement will govern? You know all about Selma, don't you? Won't that Tarkan savage hunt down each and every last one in your precious Circle and hang them from the Felling House balcony?"

"We got started in Tarkis. We've done a fine job staying alive so far."

"You forget who you're speaking to, don't insult my intelligence."

No answer came forth. The ensuing silence stretched for *far* too long. Every one of Meredith's muscles tightened until they ached.

Now or never.

Faster than she'd ever moved in her life, Meredith got on her feet and leaped toward the hunter, combat knife raised high. Her cry filled the room mid-jump: "Shoot now!"

Every person and creature present watched her soar through the air, close the distance, bring down the weapon—and immediately get swatted aside by the quick swipe of a claw. The beast didn't even have to lift its hold on Janette.

There were no gunshots. No struggle. Meredith was hurled into a workbench without contest, her head bouncing hard first against the desk, then against the tiles.

Every sound collapsed into a high-pitched buzz. She lay on the floor, face to face with Janette. The girl was reaching out to her, lips moving, screaming, but Meredith couldn't understand anymore. She tried to take Janette's hand, but Meredith's arm just . . . twitched. Her vision darkened around the edges while a white blot grew at its center, grew and grew until there was nothing but swarming white, and consciousness snapped.

She woke up. It felt like only a single instant had passed, but it was dark all around. Rough fabric touched her cheek. Her mouth couldn't move past a gag. Her head felt ready to split in two.

She was on a cot. She was in a cell.

She was alone.

CHAPTER TWENTY-SIX

MONSTERS

HEY DIDN'T BEAT HER. They didn't cut or boil her skin or even brand her. The cell was spotless-clean, they'd provided some basic hygiene utensils, and the toilet was in working order, thank the furies. Once a day a juditor came to feed her both food and painkillers, after which she'd be left tethered to a short rail by a shorter chain, alone with her pain and anxiety and low-burning desperation. Her days were spent sitting, lying down, staring at the amber light filtering through the door pane, all while she imagined in obsessive detail what might have happened to Jane after losing consciousness. The longer she waited, the more dread became pent up in her breast.

Three feeding times after Meredith regained consciousness, the Head of the Coven came to visit. The cuts and bruises on her face were already fading, except for the angry red gash above the eyebrow. Her arm was in an expensive-looking sling, hand restricted but useable. Two witches escorted her: Coren carried some foldable furniture, while a thoroughly interrogated Yurena held a large tray in her bandaged hands. Her eyes were vacant and downcast. She was not there by choice.

The delightful smell that wafted into the cell made Meredith's deprived stomach throw a fit. Coren set up a chair and a small table opposite Meredith. Yurena set down the tray and uncovered the meal.

It was easy to recognize. Yurena had explained it meticulously, unaware of Meredith's queasiness throughout. There were ways to prepare sacrificial flesh that would make the absolute most of its latent power. The dish fit the vivid descriptions in every detail.

Mifraulde sat and spent a moment staring Meredith in the eye. She stared until absolutely certain her brood-sister understood what was happening.

Meredith understood. She knew. She'd known all along what would happen in the end.

Mifraulde began eating. With each primly sliced and arranged bite, the Head of the Coven's latent power grew.

For three more days she returned, each day a different meal. Each day a different cut of meat.

And each day Mifraulde ate.

And each day Meredith wept.

PART III

CHAPTER TWENTY-SEVEN

PERPETUAL NIGHT

 HE SHUTTER OPENS. The tray slides in. The shutter closes.

Meredith swallows without much care of what she puts in her mouth. It doesn't matter. The pain doesn't matter. Nothing matters.

A simple serf brings her food, now. The gag is gone. Meredith chews on only one side, because the other side of her tongue always smolders below the painkiller haze. They only nicked it, a temporary wound with a lisp to match. It locks away what little magic she can work—not for very long, but that's acceptable. It will last for long enough.

In a way, she's impatient. Grief blisters her flesh more than flames ever could.

Her lungs are already full of ash.

* * *

The shutter opens. A flush of orange light pours through, cut by someone's shadow. There's a pause.

"Meredith."

She knows the voice. Yurena waits for a greeting and gets none.

"I was instructed to tell you—"

It starts out strong, but breaks six words in. She tries again.

"The Head of the Coven wants you to know you've been found guilty of all charges. She wants you to know. . . ." She pauses again, to gasp, to sniffle. "You will be publicly cleansed by pyre in three days' time."

The words could easily be the rumble of Meredith's stomach, the rattle of her breath. Another noise outside her control.

"I am to light the flame," Yurena says.

She waits for a response. There is none to give.

"Are you listening?"

A heavy boot steps forward. "Your task is done, let's go."

"No, wait, please. Can you believe this? She's mad at *me*, I can tell."

There's the rustle of clothes behind the door. A slice of Yurena's face comes into view through the shutter.

"What did you want me to do, Meredith? You know I didn't have a choice. You and your little fiend killed three Judicars, almost the Head of the Coven. How could you hide all this from me? How could you take it so far?"

Meredith's outrage blips for an instant. She imagines jumping off the cot, smashing her fist on the door, yelling the worst kinds of insults until her throat is hoarse. There's nothing stopping her—the tether to the wall is gone, for she is nothing even close to a threat.

The outrage dies in the same breath. What Yurena says doesn't matter. Their minds are warped, all of them.

More rustling, quick and angry. Unwinding bandages.

"See this?" Scarred fingers peek through the slot. Burns, cuts, blisters. "I didn't get out unscathed. I'm never to set foot in my library again. I'm an outcast."

She leaves the fingers in plain sight, as if their cragged surface could compare to the yawning maw in Meredith's chest.

"I can't believe you did this to me," Yurena says. "I wish I'd never met you."

The juditor clinks nearer. "That's enough, now."

"That's fine. I'm done with her."

The shutter closes.

Meredith remains still.

Three more days. Three days, and it will be over.

* * *

Standing by the lab's entrance, Meredith stares into the gap of black between door and jamb. The moan troubles the darkness again, pitched low and drawn out like the growl of a cat.

Without hesitation she walks in and sits on the bed. Softly she cradles Janette's hand.

"Jane, wake up."

It takes some time and a few tries. With patient fingers she brushes the hair off a damp forehead.

"Muh . . . Mistress?"

"Shh. I'm here."

"Oh, Mistress. . . ."

She grips Meredith's robe as if the witch could disappear from one heartbeat to the next. Meredith looks into those weary blue eyes and finally understands, she's awash with clarity. It's so obvious, how could it take her this long to figure out what truly matters? She easily finds the words she should've said cycles ago.

"I want you to gather all your things and get ready to go. We are leaving."

Janette struggles with it. She sits up. "Leaving? Where? Why?"

"I will explain later. I promise."

It's only a moment of consideration before she nods in acceptance. "Yeah, okay. I trust you," Janette says. "I always will."

In her smile Meredith finds absolution, and meaning, and a painful kind of joy she never knew existed. She clutches Janette to her chest without reserve, the way she should've always done. "You will know everything. I'm sorry, I'm so sorry. Please forgive me."

Meredith turns in her cot, face buried into the clump of fabric that passes for a pillow.

"I'm sorry. . . ."

* * *

The shutter opens. The tray slides in. The shutter closes.

Meredith doesn't touch it, despite the burrowing ache in her stomach.

The tray remains through hollow thoughts and fits of sleep. The next time she cares to look, it is no longer there.

* * *

She's bored.

She doesn't want to be. She doesn't want to feel anything. She wants to while away the rest of her existence in a catatonic fugue.

Yet as unwelcome as they are, thoughts continue to hound her. Span bleed into one another with nothing on which to focus but the throbbing aches and the caustic emptiness. Even this is changing, now—the void of loss and remorse is slowly filling up with pointless fancies of vengeance, of redemption. She knows these fancies to be hopeless and undeserved, and yet they come to needle her once and again.

In this instant of ennui, so identical to the next and the previous, Meredith decides. If the chance to escape presents itself, she will take it.

Her lungs are cinder, yet in her heart sleep embers.

* * *

The shutter opens. The tray slides in. The shutter closes.

Meredith looks at the slop and for the first time notices it for the gruel that it is. Sanctioned gruel to feed humans, all the nutrients and none of the will to live.

It's meant as an insult, she knows. A humiliation. Puritan hatred is mixed into each spoonful.

She eats the whole of it, scraping up every last drop.

* * *

A shadow clouds the door pane. The shape of a face peers through.

The door wails open, and the juditor escort steps aside to let Mifraulde into the cell.

"Leave us," she instructs.

The juditor hesitates. "Shall I restrain her?"

"No."

"She's a dangerous criminal, madam."

"And I am the Head of the Coven," she replies.

Mistrustful eyes level an appraising glower at the prisoner. "Madam," the juditor acknowledges, and steps out. She doesn't close the door all the way.

Other than to tense her entire body, Meredith hasn't moved from her sitting position. Warring emotions roil inside her—disgust first among them, revulsion, resentment. There's also awe, as always; respect, now begrudging. Fear, much to her frustration. And two layers of familiarity: one for Mifraulde, her brood-sister. Another for . . . Janette.

What having Janette near used to feel like.

Her chest tightens. In this moment, Meredith looks forward to the pyre.

Mifraulde stands by the door for some time. Something shifts in the tiny room, easily recognizable. It's the faint thrum of aural insulation.

She paces over to the wall across from the cot, close enough for Meredith to stretch her arm and touch the exquisitely embroidered hem of her robe. There she stays, casting silent judgment from all the way above her nose, or maybe working to curtail enough contempt to start speaking, or maybe considering another horrific form of punishment. Meredith doesn't know. She can't stomach looking up at her sister right now.

"Despite your betrayal," the Head of the Coven finally says, "I don't want you to die."

There are no hard edges to her voice. She speaks with her head down, shoulders bowed, good arm lightly cradling her sling. "If it were up to me, I know I would still spare you, even now. But there's nothing I can do. All of Brena is watching, all of Galavan. I need to send a very clear message." She pauses, heaves a big sigh. "My own sister, a spark-thief, a murderer, a youth-minder. If I didn't know of your tryst with the librarian, I wouldn't be surprised to learn you're a deviant as well. Maybe you are, and simply never had the chance to act on it."

Mifraulde isn't as much reproachful as she is . . . mournful. Defeated.

"Did you truly believe it would all go unnoticed? That I would somehow never find out what you were doing? How did you manage to delude yourself so? I could fill a room with the pile of evidence you've left behind, and that's without taking surveillance into account. How did your bile end up in that grisly crime scene? Why did I have to look at your hat and tell my inspectors yes, indeed, I've seen it sitting on your head? Did you truly think a retrieval lottery bribe from *the Head of the Coven's brood-sister* wouldn't immediately make it to my desk?" She brings fingers to her brow and rubs at the crinkle. "I don't think you're aware of how much mockery that alone has cost me. I could spend the day listing it all. Should I mention Gertrude's reports? The sightings of a youthful witch frolicking in your garden? The unmistakable disturbance of a manually-opened portal as it blew past the nodework? I can't decide what's more outrageous, the list of appalling crimes, or how thoroughly careless you were at it."

Without any of her regal decorum she blows out another breath, leans back against the prison wall, bends her knees to a disheartened squat.

"You bound us both to this path. How could you, Meri? I did so much for you. How could you betray me like this? I knew you might grow desperate after we parted ways, but I never imagined you'd go so far."

At this height, it's impossible for Meredith not to meet her eyes. In them she sees only sincere hurt. A genuine bid for an explanation to make sense of it all.

And in this brief connection, Meredith finally understands. She's known for a long time, but now she *understands*.

"We are monsters," she croaks past wounded cheek and swollen tongue. The lisp sounds as though she speaks around a cud.

"Louder, Meredith. I can't understand you."

"I'm surrounded by monsters."

"Oh, please. Monsters? I'm a monster for enforcing the rules, for punishing your betrayal? Are you even aware of what the Department of Mercy would've done to you if I hadn't interceded? You've enjoyed far more lenience than any other criminal."

"You don't even see it. You committed this atrocity, and you don't even think twice about it. Jane was . . . she was beautiful and brilliant, and you—"

She can't go on. The tears catch a spark of amber as they drop.

Mifraulde remains still for some time. Finally she leans back and shakes her head as if a long-eluding realization has just dawned on her.

"Oh, Meri. I see it, now. I chose to ignore the signs for so long, perhaps I simply didn't want to admit it, but now I see it clearly." She stands straight and lays a gentle hand on Meredith's crown— who recoils at the touch like the fingers are covered in infectious boils. With another sigh, Mifraulde lets the hand fall to her side. "You didn't betray me. Not on purpose. It's just this terrible illness that you have, you can't help yourself. Were you always afflicted so? Did you work to hide it from me, even at the academy?"

Meredith looks up through the blur. How absurd to hear this, how alien. Here is this witch whose worldview has been the bane of her life, whose presence hasn't ever brought anything but frustration and self-loathing. Here is this monster, thrumming with arrogated power, behaving as if she didn't rip Meredith's heart from her chest and feast upon it for days on end. For one wild flash she imagines the lunge for Mifraulde's throat, slamming against the wall, struggling to the floor. Squeeze and dig with her thumbs until the monster is dead.

Even if she succeeds in spite of her injuries and the guards and whatever protection the Head of the Coven might have against it—even then, there is no point. Thousands more monsters mill about their lives all around her, ever willing to preserve this vicious doctrine. To actually *fight* for it. How many of them would instead break free, if given the chance?

A glance at history easily gives her the answer: never enough.

"I may be in this cell," Meredith says, "but you are the prisoner."

Mifraulde sniffs at the words. "Is that so?"

"All my life I've tried to live up to something I loathe. I would make mistakes, I'd give myself excuses—I let go of so many youths, I lost count. The ones I did turn in . . . I won't have to live much longer with the guilt. It always felt *awful,* but I thought I had to do it. There was no other way."

Even now, scored by grief, scarred through every deranged plot, through pain, loss, hollow victories and bitter defeat—even after all this, the anxiety of confrontation still jitters in her core, it rushes through shaking limbs. Her thoughts are clear, her resolve steady, yet the tremor still clings to her voice. She knows this isn't something other witches suffer. She knows it won't ever go away.

In spite of it, Meredith juts her chin as she speaks. Her ribcage lifts, she sits up straight.

"Janette set me free, and I know this freedom is something you'll never have. When I die tomorrow at least I'll be free of Galavan, while you remain in this horrid prison." Her hastened breaths are as bellows to stoke her defiance. In the depths of her glare, embers flash ablaze. "I've envied you all these years, but now I have nothing but pity."

She notices the hand balling to a fist, the clench to her sister's jaw—she's about to be struck again, and in some perverse way she welcomes it. She *should* be punished for her failures.

Coiled with restraint Mifraulde leans in, eyes narrow. "Tell yourself whatever misguided nonsense you please. I've never expected you to repay me." She turns to leave. "I'm done with you. I'll remember this moment as the last time I spared you from pain."

If she could muster it, Meredith would laugh. "Why would you hold back now? Go ahead, hit me, do as you will. Tell them to treat me as they did Four-Thirteen. Nothing could compare to what you've already done."

Latent power surges to a thrum in the tiny cell, the sensation so painfully reminiscing of predawn mornings spent soothing Janette's night terrors. The Head of the Coven is looking over her shoulder. Her glower teems with baleful intent.

"Don't be so certain," she counters in a seething hiss. "She still lives."

Mifraulde strides out of the cell and slams the door without looking back.

The ringing echoes the sudden din in Meredith's ears.

"What?"

She bolts off the cot, rushes to the frosted pane. "Mifraulde! Is that true?"

Shadows shrink and disappear beyond the glass. Her fist bangs on the slab of iron. "Mifraulde!"

No answer comes.

"You're a liar! You hear me? You're *lying!*"

Tiny specks of red spatter on the pane with every muddled scream. She bangs the door until her hand is a shaking ball of pain. "It's not true. . . ."

The ringing dies down. The outrage burns to frustration. She's cradling her hand to her chest, forehead resting on the glass.

"She's lying," Meredith mutters. "She's lying to hurt me. They didn't, they wouldn't. . . ."

It is only now, looking down so close, that Meredith notices. A small strip of white stuck to the tray slot, wedged between hinge and flap. A folded bandage of the kind a thoroughly interrogated witch might conceal around her dressed fingers.

With mechanical movements Meredith plucks it out of its hiding spot, carefully unwinds each fold. In dead silence she stares at the line of black script that runs through it.

Somehow it's possible for her heart to sink lower.

"No."

Somehow it's possible for her lungs to empty further.

"No. . . ."

Every one of her fears has come true.

Her gift to Janette.

A fate worse than death.

PYRE CLEANSING

—EIGHTH DAY OF WANE, 454PE - ATTENDANCE MANDATORY—

This Most Dire Criminal Is Guilty of **GRIEVOUS TREASON**

For the **Crimes** of Serf Theft, Harvest Retrieval Fraud and Resisting Arrest
And the **Most Dire Crimes** of Serf Minding, Youth Minding, Grand Spark Theft
and **Multiple Accounts of Grievous Murder,**

Meredith Brena-Galvan-Neumann

=== Shall be **PURGED BY PYRE** as Befits Tradition ===

Ceremonies begin a span before dusk with **Disgraceful Pageant** from Galvan
Tower to Blackened Square. Rot will be available along Galvan Boulevard.
You are encouraged to bring your own. See guidelines below.

Brena's Council and your Judicar wardens call upon all denizens to unite
in their civic duty with **orderly conduct** for a successful and incident-free
ceremony.

Should an incident indeed occur, all attendees are expected to remain calm and allow the competent authorities to conduct their duties unhindered. Your intervention is likely to obstruct or complicate matters.
Toss Policy: Acceptable rot is limited to soft fruits, vegetables and mushrooms only. Foul concoctions must be innocuous and tossed in an adequately supple container. No flesh or animal waste allowed. No toxic, sharp or maiming projectiles allowed. **ABSOLUTELY no private excretions!** Failure to comply shall be immediately investigated and disciplined with fines of up to two(2) stem and possible incarceration.

DEPARTMENT OF MERCY

CHAPTER TWENTY-EIGHT
❈
THE PYRE

 HE JEERS WERE A TIDE of festive anger. They would surge and ebb as the procession rolled down Galvan Boulevard, and if it weren't for the occasional "traitor!" and "parasite!" climbing over the rest, the noise wouldn't have been much worse than the din of a Fifday daytime market.

The flung rot would have horrified some past version of Meredith, but the smell covering her matted hair and ragged prisoner gown was barely a concern in her present state of mind. The ordeal only registered when a particularly well-aimed throw would splat against the fresh bruises she wore from her escape attempt.

She'd tried, during a brief distraction as they moved her to the open carriage and custody passed from juditor handlers to ceremonial inquisitors. At the time, it hadn't been completely inconceivable for her to hobble fast enough to the open gate and find a hiding spot from there. "Not completely inconceivable" had been good enough to try.

The attempt was short and thoroughly unsuccessful.

Now she stood bound to the low-hovering carriage, neck and shoulder leaning against the standing post. Her head was bowed to protect her eyes from pelting projectiles, her stare was lost somewhere below the pavement—yet beneath the despondent veneer she kept track of the Judicars' position in the crowd, she noted gaps in the deployed fences, she picked out alleys and pathways that might give her a fleeting chance to lose possible pursuers. Meredith was determined. If there was an opportunity to escape, however small, she would not miss it.

Fists and mouths and pointing fingers leaned over the barriers ahead, earnest in their officially endorsed outrage. Devalka came to her mind, because she could easily picture her former coworker among them, stern and disapproving and woefully disappointed. She was no doubt here, somewhere. Would she cheer when the flames took hold? She always had, in the past.

Though everyone made a show of participating, rows further back were not so uniformly enthusiastic. How many of these witches would've rather been elsewhere, minding their own problems? How many regarded this spectacle as distasteful, even barbaric? Yurena hadn't cared about the supposed wrongness of Meredith's deeds. She couldn't be the only one.

At the bottom of the boulevard the crowd opened in a circle around a blemish of charred black. Erected at the center of the blot, a wooden podium. At the center of the podium, surrounded by tinder, a nightwood stake. A single raven perched at the top, momentarily victorious over all contenders.

Because ravens kept flying in, they lined balconies and rain gutters, they cawed and jockeyed for better vantage. They bore witness to the crawling parade, as they always would, and they waited.

The ravens remembered. They knew what would remain.

Above the crowd, in the one balcony free of corvids, the Head of the Coven watched the approach. The Judicar Magister stood next to her, one pace behind, clad in the thorny jade armor reserved only for public events. Brena's six Council crones sat three to Mifraulde's either side.

Loathing roiled in Meredith's chest at the sight of them, intense and tumultuous unlike anything she'd ever fathomed. The vicious tide all around her swelled as the parade entered the Square, but no heckle, rot or jostle could shake her steady glower as she neared the stake. Up in the Felling House balcony, Mifraulde met the stare with no outward emotion of her own, a perfectly poised statue dressed in pristine Coven regalia. Her arm was no longer hindered by the sling.

Thousands more watched from that balcony, peeping through the lens of the nodecast transmitter clamped to the rail and the efforts of the operator behind it. Thousands of witches, bearing witness all over Galavan in public assemblies, in rec rooms, sitting at home in front of their transceivers. Meredith could picture young apprentices gathered 'round the Instructor's desk at every academy, much like she herself had watched so many years ago. She had cried, that first time. She'd been punished for it.

Guided by inquisitors coiffed in ceremonial garb, the carriage hovered to a stop in front of the podium. One of the escorts climbed onto the transport and kicked through the tossed filth to reach her;

she unbound Meredith's wrists from the display stand and manhandled her off the carriage. Meredith's bare feet slapped cold on soot-scorched cobbles.

Blackened Square blared as they climbed the wooden steps onto the stage. Jostled without recourse, Meredith followed the narrow path around stake and kindling, prickly dry branches like skeletal fingers reaching for her rags as she passed. It was then, with her attention caught in the branches, with her nostrils flooded with the scent of fresh timber—it was then that her immediate future truly came into focus.

The robe, the kindling, her own flesh from feet to brow: everything engulfed in flames. Everyone would watch her burn. Everyone would hear her screams. Any attempt to escape her fate would only make it worse.

Despite her defiance, Meredith felt herself shaking. Her legs grew weak.

The inquisitor escort held her up. "Don't falter now," she said. "Almost there."

It was Silver's voice.

Instinctively Meredith turned to look at the face within coif and headdress, but rough hands goaded her forward. "Don't try anything!" the supposed inquisitor shouted, much to the crowd's enjoyment.

Meredith stumbled to the stake. Her thoughts struggled to find purchase. Was this a rescue attempt? Were the identical voices a simple coincidence? Had she gone utterly mad in the face of certain death?

With harsh movements the inquisitor roped her to the wooden post. The raven flew off. "The knot will give when you pull hard enough," Silver's voice said just above the racket. "Don't break free until the portal opens. Wybel will be waiting for you."

Meredith stared straight forward. This was real. She had to repeat it several times inside her head: they were trying to save her, it was real. But how could anyone carry out a rescue in the middle of this mess? There were three other ceremonial escorts in position around the pyre, a few dozen juditors spread all over the square, plus the entirety of Brena's Council in plain sight. Any one of them could dole out fulminating deterrents, not to mention the possible contribution of every single witch in attendance.

Possibly-Silver bowed to the Council and took her place at the foot of the stage. Meredith endeavored not to act any differently than she would have a moment ago, when a fiery death was a foregone conclusion—though she couldn't have stopped the shaking and the heavy breathing even if she'd tried. She just needed to remain alert. If a rescue was truly happening and a portal would open nearby, there would be a distraction of some sort. She would be ready.

The crowd all around continued to somehow get louder. Something slimy splattered against her shoulder and leisurely slid down her bust. Gremlins rampaged through her insides, anxiety and fear and the most foolish hope. Maybe escape was possible. Maybe she could find a path to the Yanwar plants. Maybe Jane wasn't lost after all.

Whatever was left of Jane.

In the Felling House balcony, the Head of the Coven stepped forth and raised one hand. It was like a landslide finally coming to a stop when the clamor died down to an expectant murmur. Mifraulde surveyed the square from one end to the other, letting the audience simmer in anticipation.

"Witches of Galavan," she began, her powerful voice made stronger still by the aural surger at her lapel. "Judicar champions, Members of the Council, sisters all. We gather here today to purge disease from our ranks once more."

The ensuing cheers and whistles bounced off brick walls, traveled down streets and alleys. Some of the younger ravens took flight, startled, only to return to their perch shortly after.

"Many of you remember a time when these gatherings were far more common. For decades we were a wounded nation striving to cleanse the wounds, to expunge the filth that had so treacherously corrupted our core. As I look out to you, as I regard my Council colleagues, I am all too aware of the scars we bear from those days of painful recovery—and yet I know, as *you* should know, how necessary it all was. How *necessary* it still is . . . for we all know that no wound can heal without pain.

"It was a trying process, but see how far we've come. Those days of weekly gatherings are now firmly in the past. With the policies instated by our venerable Coven, the diligent work of our Judicar wards, and the faithful vigilance of every one of us, all of witchdom has thrived beyond the dreams of our forebears: prosperous, pure and pristine under the unwavering guide of reason and pragmatism. After centuries of strife and discord, at last we embody their vision of a unified nation working together for the betterment of our kind!"

The shape of her speech rose up to another bout of cheers. Probably-Silver, up until then so officially stiff in the space between crowd and wooden platform, shifted her weight. Her head turned, ever so slightly. Her gloved hand became a fist and relaxed again.

"And yet," Mifraulde carried on, "some remain. Some who refuse to learn from past mistakes, who crave chaos, and conflict, and filth. Some who would place the lives of worthless humans before yours and mine. Some, who would work against the established order, who would assault, even *murder* those whose purpose in life is to keep all of us safe. These . . . anomalies, these ungrateful parasites, they plot and scheme to undermine the very foundations of what we are. Their actions are nothing short of treason. Their goal is nothing less than the destruction of our nation."

Probably-Silver seemed to grow more agitated as the speech progressed. Furtive glances at the squat clock tower Corenbound of the square became less and less subtle. She gradually transitioned from stoic guardian to wary prey, ready to bolt.

A quick look revealed equally antsy inquisitors to Meredith's either side.

"Let today remind you that they still dwell in our midst," the Head of the Coven continued. "Look beside you, and wonder. Look behind you, and question. So often we've heard the same claims during interrogation: 'we never expected this from her,' 'she never said anything suspicious,' 'we had no idea she was doing this.' Dissidence and deviance and *especially* mercy will hide and fester in the most insidious ways. Hold this lesson to mind, as I have: no-one can be free of suspicion." Her eyes stopped wandering back and forth through the crowd. They focused directly on the ceremonial inquisitor straight ahead. "The disease lurks beneath the most unlikely guises."

The Head of the Coven pointed. It was the signal for plainclothes juditors to surge forth from the audience.

Definitely-Silver already had her arm up in a defensive pose. Wordpaths flashed white under the sleeve of her ceremonial robes— a speeding entrapment orb smashed against Silver's kinetic barrier and got redirected into an oncoming juditor. The resulting scream cut abruptly as the stasis took hold and the chromeflow wrapped around her entire body.

Silver's hand blurred toward the ground, a glass vial shattered, and a cloud of black smoke instantly burst all around her. The juditors' own alchemy- and dermaturgy-based spells flung into the smoke before they too were engulfed: a plume of oilfire, aimed low; an ear-splitting cone of resonance that rumbled through the smoke in waves; a gravity shift that ballooned a section of the cloud toward the pyre. All disabling and possibly horrendous, but unlikely to be lethal.

There was no chance this was all part of Silver's plan, something had clearly gone wrong and there was no portal in sight—but Meredith wasn't about to ignore the gigantic distraction in front of her. She pulled as hard as she could on the binding ropes and immediately lurched free. Without a single clue on how to get through the stunned crowd unchallenged, she leaped off the podium into the expanding smoke, onto the black cobbles.

The world blurred before she hit the ground. She crumpled and stumbled ahead, no time to feel pain or cough out fumes. Already she could hear the roar of outrage closing in. Within the smoke there was an explosive snap that billowed fire and smolder in low-spreading rings, and through the black haze Meredith saw Silver shooting straight up to the sky, a trail of eddies spiraling in her wake as she contorted in mid-air to fetch the dais holstered at her back.

Resisting the urge to just watch and see what happened next, Meredith took off directly through the thickest cover. Her chest shriveled with every gasp. Searing heat scalded her feet as she ran.

Violent cracks and claps boomed all around, possibly juditors resorting to more lethal means after their ambush had failed. A witch-like figure appeared straight ahead, one of many coughing their lungs out, and for lack of a better option Meredith tackled her shoulder-first to the ground. The stranger's head hit the cobbles with a skull-cracking thump, audible even within the roaring chaos. The body went limp without contest.

Meredith grimaced in remorse, but it didn't slow her down one bit as she worked to quickly pull off the stranger's robes. It was desperate, deranged, but if she could get a semblance of a disguise going, if she could blend in with the rest and quietly slink through. . . .

Above the smoke, above the bellowing pandemonium and whatever battle was unfolding, above the hammering of Meredith's heartbeat and the spooked fluttering of a thousand raven wings, a singular voice poured upon the square. Vibrant through infusion, empowered beyond its natural means, Mifraulde's incantation reverberated into every recess of reality.

"ŏṅ cŏr Ḣæxxr vall sef'yaj'ẏun nox ŏṅ'reth élum!"

Every color drained away. All sound collapsed to stillness. The frantic thoughts slowed to a grind, and Meredith was no longer able to process reality. Kneeling on the floor astride a half-disrobed stranger, she learned what it felt like to be held in stasis.

Unlike what she'd always pictured, it didn't reach complete unconsciousness. It became an amorphous state of being, a dive into a featureless marsh where every endless moment drew a bit closer to drowning. She was remotely aware of the outside world changing around her, but none of it coalesced into patterns she could recognize. It was all deeply uncomfortable and vaguely terrifying.

Later—much later, only an instant later—reality came back all at once, though not so much her ability to understand it. Every sensory input was undecipherable, and she was only aware of the lull of her head as it loosely hung from a limp torso. Slowly awareness returned to inform her of the basics: she was roped to the post again, tightly this time. Once more she was surrounded by kindling. And a hand, not unkind, cupped the underside of her jaw, monitored her pulse.

"Meredith."

Mifraulde's face came into focus. There was strain on her features, intense concentration. At the same time, Meredith sensed the deluge of magical power that swamped the square.

"I must admit, I didn't expect you to inspire this kind of loyalty. I mean, it's more of a statement against the Coven, evidently. But they planned to rescue you all the same." Her fingertips gently tapped

Meredith's cheek, as if to wake her. "You must've made an impression."

Her voice punctuated the uncanny silence now blanketing their surroundings. For a short while Meredith pictured they were back in the cell, just the two of them in quiet isolation, but the notion faded as more of the new present became comprehensible.

It was a bizarre experience, with distant objects still obscured behind layers of blur and refraction. Two juditors flanked the Head of the Coven, looking none-too-pleased with their recaptured prisoner. Several more stood proud at the foot of the stage, facing the crowd.

They were the only ones free of stasis. Everyone else in Blackened Square posed in elaborate tableaus, yelling, coughing, cheering, backing away, surging forward. However the fight had unfolded, two of the nameless inquisitor infiltrators had become three unsightly mounds around the stage. Above the crowd, the Judicar Magister gripped the balcony rail in motionless dismay at Silver's imminent escape, while the entirety of Brena's Council stared in disbelief at the spot where Mifraulde had been, awed by her impossibly ambitious incantation. The ravens perpetually spread their wings in the stillness, as though painted mid-flight against the flashing skyveil.

The lighting seemed off. Desaturated, far too bright. Indeed, why would the skyveil flash? The reason became apparent as soon as Meredith could make sense of the scene as a whole.

Silver, frozen mid-ascent after whatever she'd done to escape into the air, caught halfway through fastening a dais to her feet . . . she was in the process of being struck by lightning. Jagged lines of white speared through the sky with no discernible origin. Radiant, near blinding, they converged in a crackling sphere around the airborne witch. In the midst of stasis they subtly flickered and vibrated, as if resentful of being captured.

Incredibly, the bolts didn't seem to actually touch Silver's flesh.

"She's impressive," Mifraulde said. She'd followed Meredith's eyes. "Do you see it? She flipped shields in time. Someone must've spent years engineering that arm of hers." She glanced over. "You'd count her as an ally, yeah? How much of the spark do you think she needs to be this formidable? How many youths has *she* harvested to get this far?"

Mifraulde beckoned at someone out of sight who promptly stepped to attention. It was the remaining ceremonial inquisitor. Her ornate headdress had come off, but she was otherwise unscathed. The Head of the Coven gestured in Silver's general direction.

"Proceed."

The inquisitor retrieved a glossy entrapment orb from her pocket and carefully lined up the trajectory, delineating a track with index and middle finger. Mifraulde leaned into Meredith in a conspiratorial manner.

"Do you think she'll deflect this one?"

With an ominous whisper the orb shot through the air in a straight path. It zoomed through the lightning in a shower of sparks and crashed into Silver's chest. The chromeflow deployed without contest and enveloped the static figure in lustrous grey.

"Nora, Vestat. Get in position to catch her and bring her down. Be careful with all that lightning."

The Head of the Coven watched as the juditors equipped their holstered dais and became airborne in order to carry out their instructions.

"You know," she said to Meredith, "I'm baffled your friends could be this bold. It's such a gross underestimation of our reach. Surely *you* didn't believe you were my one and only spy in their little Circle, yeah?"

There was no answer, but none was expected.

"They'd planned to blast apart the clock tower as a distraction, can you believe it? Centuries' worth of Brenan architecture destroyed, just like that. Disgusting. And your friend Wybel managed to escape us again, that venal old beldam. I'm not so worried. I did promise she could go free if she didn't shoot, didn't I? Such great friends you've made.

"It's a shame, honestly. Their trifling games were a harmless way to let dissention play out without much conflict. I've told you many times, it's healthier for the nation to give them some breathing room instead of stifling them completely. But today they went too far, so it's time for them to become another cautionary tale in history. I hope you understand we could've stopped this attempt at any time. I simply wanted their defeat to be as memorable as possible." Mifraulde took in a breath full of satisfaction. "So it appears you've helped me ensure I stay in power. No-one will question me after this." She glanced at her brood-sister once more without actually looking. "I suppose you *did* repay me, in the end."

"Frau."

It was a hoarse wheeze of a voice, muddled through a swollen tongue. The painkillers had long worn out.

Mifraulde seemed startled to be addressed directly. "What? What is it, Meredith? What do you have to say for yourself? Come on, let's hear it."

Meredith swallowed. Every sentence, every passing moment had made her fate as clear as could be.

She gathered every bit of herself that was left and poured it into her next words.

"Let Janette go. I beg you."

The Head of the Coven sniffed with disdain. "Soot and Ash, you're obsessed. These are your friends right here, are they not? Your allies, at the very least. Won't you beg for *their* lives?"

Meredith considered them briefly. "You wouldn't spare them. I was listening, this is . . . a great victory for you. And they chose to do this, we all chose our paths. But Janette didn't." She looked up at her brood-sister without guile or bitterness. Her pride was ash scattered on the cobbles. Her loathing was smoke dispersed into the flowlines. "You don't need her for anything, Frau. Please let her go. Please."

Though Mifraulde had borne a stare full of scorn with unflinching aplomb, she now looked away from Meredith's face.

"The youth is in no state to 'go' anywhere," she said.

Meredith shut her eyes. Just imagining the implication tore a gash down her throat.

"Then. . . ." She swallowed. "Then kill her. Set her free. Please. She doesn't deserve what you've done."

Frau turned her head, let out an impatient breath. Her mouth curled with resentment. "You're making it very hard for me to gloat."

Meredith couldn't quite sympathize. She stayed silent, earnest plea intense in her gaze.

"Do you expect me to simply indulge you? Such atrocious waste. The girl is already at Yanwar. Slated for a year of harvest, then handed off to the Department of Progeny."

"You could change it. You can stop it."

"Not without an unreasonable amount of effort. It would raise a lot of heckles, witches of influence that are squarely on *my* side now. And for what? To grant your irrational dying wish?"

"Mifraulde, I'm begging you, please. If . . . if you ever cared about me—"

"No, don't you *dare*. I *did* care about you, and you *betrayed me*. You could've come to me with your problem before all of this started. I would have helped you, if I'd known the extent of your illness. But you didn't, you did the complete opposite of that, and now you face the consequences."

"You shut me out first, Frau. You cast me away."

"I was testing you! I'd tried everything! I thought you might thrive under serious pressure. If you had failed again, I wouldn't have abandoned you—but look at what you did instead, look at what you did *just now*. You were free for barely a cent, and still you had time to maim a bystander in your bid to escape."

"I've made terrible mistakes. I accept my punishment, I do, I only ask—"

"You ask for nonsense. I will *not* indulge the rot in your mind, you could not be further from redemption. Now be quiet if you don't want to die with a gag stifling your screams."

She turned her back and strode to the edge of the stage. Meredith watched it happen with words still riding on her breath, words that withered on her lips and fell in eddies onto the pyre.

"It's time," Mifraulde declared. The Judicar forces, up until then conscientiously ignoring the sisters' exchange, readied in their stations. The Head of the Coven spread her arms in anticipation.

"noth'ŏṅ'Ħæxxt áx."

The quagmire of power sublimated to near-visible currents amidst the crash of thunder. Airborne juditors caught Silver's body as it dropped, raven wings fluttered to stay aloft, a murmur rose through the waking crowd. Brenan crones of all descriptions looked at one another in a struggle to piece together what had just happened.

As Meredith witnessed Blackened Square emerge from its collective dream into a new reality, her last effort collapsed into a void pulling from inside her lungs. Her shoulders crumpled, her whole frame sagged. The black abyss of despair yawned open once more, as wide as it could go.

Every witch in attendance focused on the juditors carrying Silver to the stage, to the Head of the Coven's feet. The murmur quieted, comment and conjecture awed to a reverent hush. Mifraulde, regal and terrible in her bearing, regarded the frozen body for a time. She looked out to the crowd.

"They are poison," she spoke into the silence. "These foolish creatures, unfit to be named 'witches,' they are a toxic parasite to be eradicated. This is the duty I've performed today, a duty we all share, as today they sought to undermine not only me or the Coven, but all of us. Look at them, and take heed. This is the outcome. *This* is where mercy leads. We must always remain watchful, for they must all be purged wherever we find them." She looked back at Meredith as she wilted on the stake. "Nobody is above the rule of the Coven."

The rapt audience seemed to draw closer, hanging on every word. It was an oppressive circle of desolation pushing in from all sides. Meredith instinctively shrunk inwards, sheltering her awareness as much as she could.

"Take the traitor to the Tower," Mifraulde commanded. "Her time will come very soon."

A pair of juditors carried Silver away from the podium. The Head of the Coven stepped to the edge of the stage and spread her arms in a grandiose gesture. "My dear sisters, we've delayed long enough. The turn of dusk is here. Bring forth the flame-bearer, let the ceremony begin!"

The square broke into whistles and cheers on cue, only emboldened by the awesome display of power. They grew ever louder as the victorious Head of the Coven was flown by her escorts off the stage, back to the Felling House balcony. For Meredith, it was a small relief to be rid of her dreadful presence.

Following Mifraulde's pronouncement, the double doors at street level groaned open. Meredith couldn't help but lift her head and look. She knew the name of this flame-bearer.

A raven-haired witch dressed in gossamer white stepped through the open gate, ready in her post despite what had just transpired. A path cleared through the crowd to allow her passage. Yurena walked with measured steps, eyes affixed to the middle distance, and with both bandaged hands she gripped a blazing torch. Nobody jeered or gestured at her. In fact, she faced no shortage of encouragement.

"Burn the traitor!" they would say.

"For the Coven!" they would say.

As dusk became night, as the moon lit up bright after Hallow's End renewal, Yurena made the cross onto black cobbles. Meredith watched with worn-out despondence, eyes sunken in smolder. Details became noticeable: the rigid set of her shoulders, the subtle squirm of her lips. The resolute way in which those cloudless white eyes avoided looking at her former lover. Perhaps it was projection, perhaps it was familiarity with her usual gait, but every step that brought her closer seemed to reveal one more layer of reluctance.

Deliberately her bare feet climbed the steps to the stage. She moved to stand where podium met kindling, front and center. As she raised the wooden torch above her head and turned in a full circle to the rabid chant of the audience, their eyes touched, wholly without meaning to.

Yurena's arms visibly trembled. They too were dressed in bandages.

How sincere had their time together been? How deep had their feelings run? Did Yurena's actions truly count as betrayal, given the horrid nature of the alternative to compliance?

Of all the things Meredith felt for her in the moment, resentment was not one of them. What was she in the end but yet another victim of ruthless Puritan doctrine?

"I bring this flame to cleanse the tainted," Yurena intoned in a quaver. The fire danced in her watering eyes. "May her sickness. . . ."

Her voice faltered. She struggled with a few shallow breaths, swallowed. When she looked down at the Most Dire prisoner, there was something close to remorse in her features.

These were all terrible mistakes to make at the center of a mob clamoring for death.

Yurena's floundering sparked something among the gloom in Meredith's chest, a fretful ache that pushed her to lean forward. Her bindings pulled taut.

"You monster," she cried for everyone to hear. There was no moisture in her mouth, but the mimicry of spitting at Yurena's feet was just as effective. "You're a monster, like all of them. I wish I'd never met you!"

The crowd shifted their focus away from the flame-bearer. Briefly they were taken aback by the outburst, but they soon reignited with vicious hostility. Perhaps for the first time, the outrage went from officially endorsed to sincere.

Yurena was properly stunned. Tears drew glinting lines upon her cheeks. "Merth," she mouthed below the rabble.

Meredith couldn't save herself. She couldn't free Janette. These were the truths she would die with.

But perhaps, at the very least, she could stop Yurena from jumping into the pyre with her.

"Puritan stooge, you ruined everything! Curse you to the Hollow!" She turned her head at the wider audience. "You're *all* monsters! Pox upon you!"

Most on the front row bristled, several farther back gasped. If the remaining juditors hadn't deterred the more enthusiastic witches from pushing through the barriers, the ceremony might have become a lethal pummeling instead of a traditional burning.

Within the distraction, no-one saw or cared about the look on Yurena's face, its transition from anguish to understanding, to gratitude . . . to grim resolve. No-one but Meredith.

Riding the new wave of indignation, the flame-bearer raised her torch high in riposte to the prisoner's insolence.

"May her sickness touch not the Coven!"

To a roaring cheer Yurena bent down and brought fire to kindling.

The flame caught on straw and twig, timid at first. Quickly it became hungry for more. It spread to the sides in a slow-going ring, eating through the fluff as it circled around the main course.

Yurena dropped the torch and backed to the steps off the platform. *Forgive me,* Meredith read in her eyes, right before she turned away and descended the staircase.

You're the one that must live with this, she wanted to tell her.

A few more hurried strides and Yurena was gone.

Smoke began to rise. As Meredith watched the white rivulets puff and dance all around her, the bellowing crowd shrunk to a distant buzz—matched, overpowered by the ringing in her ears. She'd attended three pyre burnings in her lifetime. There would be some coughing at the start, but a few well-placed trinkets embedded in the stage would vent most of the smoke away from the prisoner, making sure it was the flames that killed her. The screams were always the worst of it, those entirely unthinking screams that would overshadow the racket from the audience. They'd invariably go on for a long time, far longer than could be considered reasonable.

How long would *she* go? How early would she start? She'd singed her hand on the stove a number of times. She could see herself shrieking madly upon feeling that kind of burn and not being able to get away. It still seemed a way off, it didn't feel any warmer yet—or, did it? Yes, a little bit, maybe. It was taking a while.

In the stillness of her cell she had wondered what would run through her mind once the fire was ignited. She hadn't expected it to be this vacuous. In a surreal trance Meredith stared at the smoke, waiting for the heat to come.

A tongue of flame poked around the thicker branches, the first of many. She felt it in her naked toes, in her calves: an ominous warmth that threatened to become unpleasant. It was happening. Without her consent her chest heaved with anxiety, seized in a coughing fit. Soon it became a vicious cycle, a struggle in search of clean air to find only the choking fumes. She didn't remember the others coughing this much.

At least it took her mind off the encroaching flame. It would all eventually be over. As horrific as it might become, this was the last bit of suffering she'd ever have to endure. There was a measure of solace in that thought.

The hacking only worsened, she was utterly blinded by smoke and tears. Breath wouldn't come. Stars floated around her vision, and within the dizziness she considered that maybe this was Mifraulde's idea of a last kindness: she'd somehow arranged for the smoke to poison her before fire consumed her flesh.

She'd barely considered it when a strong wind swept into the square and pushed the fumes past her. It didn't stop the coughing right away, but it blew fresh air into her lungs whenever she could breathe it. She reflexively gulped it in as fast as it would come, even while aware of the far-worse alternative to suffocation.

Once she'd recovered enough Meredith blinked away the tears, squinted against the wind. Inside the barriers the juditors watched with sheer contempt in their features. As the tassels of their armored robes flapped wildly toward the stake, Meredith understood suffocation had never been an option: if the venting system hadn't kicked in, *they* would have intervened. They'd make sure this prisoner, this grievous Judicar murderer, would be properly punished for her crimes.

The fresh-air respite brought the fire's progress to the forefront. Now the heat was unambiguous, inescapable, a blooming smolder engulfing her from heels to chest. The sustained wind enlivened the flames, letting them jump dangerously close to her rags, and she became keenly aware that clothes catching fire would mark the beginning of true agony.

She shuffled from foot to foot to manage the pain, and it all seemed to worsen at once: the sweltering air blazed through her lungs, the soles of her feet became too painful to stand on, the hem of her tatters danced with windblown sparks. A desperate recess in her brain goaded her to search for Mifraulde and beg, but instead she clenched her jaw and shut her eyes tight, wishing for it to be over quickly, wishing for her skin to somehow turn to stone. A suppressed whine escaped through her lips as she squirmed in place.

Her flesh seared, there was no getting away, it was *searing,* couldn't push it back; the first scream tore out of her throat, shaken, wailing. At the height of her wail, the world split apart.

With a shattering crack, her whole being lurched upward. Splinters and embers flew alongside her, it all tore up into the skyveil. There was no making sense of it, this was the new reality

Meredith was screaming into: sailing through the air at high speed, stake still attached, firewood raining upward and hem of her robe aflame.

Within the shock she welcomed the rush of cool air in one gasp, one and a half—and then *true* chaos ensued. A turbulent distortion warped space from one side of Blackened Square to the other: straight lines wavered, patterns distended, the Felling House seemed to bend and stretch like taffy. One instant later the remainder of the stage, the crowd, black cobbles, *entire buildings* sprang sideways like so many weightless paper models thrown into a galeful burst of wind. Through the air it all flew, tumbling, flailing within this inescapable force.

Unlike paper models, none of it fluttered or folded upon colliding with one another.

Bloodcurdling screams rose from the Square, nothing at all like the jeers that came before. They were eclipsed by the cataclysmic crunch of exploding walls and buckling structures. All of the Felling House, from slanted roof to antique doors, from centuries-old emblems to fancy balcony full of dignitaries, *all of it* was torn from its foundations and toppled like a vanquished piece in a shotel match. Flung witches continued to smash into every part of it as it dropped.

Pulverized material bloomed in a cloud to cover most of the horror as Meredith's mad ascent slowed and flattened. The stake, so tightly attached at ground level, now wobbled loose at her back, ready to slide free. Her legs felt raw and sure to blister in places, but the wind and constant flutter had put out the fire in her tatters. In this tiny moment of weightlessness, soaring above broken roofs under the moonlight, watching most of Brena's population become a thrashing mass of limbs while she remained mostly unscorched, she could reach only one plausible conclusion.

None of it was real, of course. She'd been poisoned by the fumes and her last thoughts had been overtaken by hallucination.

Spooked ravens flew away at eye level, and then higher than eye level. The stake slipped loose and took its own path, slightly above. The hallucinated ground, a heap of flaming splinters and uprooted cobbles, grew closer and far more believable. Robe and hair lifted in a flutter with the increasing friction.

Would it be over when she hit the ground? Would she wake up and keep burning? Would she break her legs and have a nightmare within a nightmare? What was that glimmer, off to the side?

Like stars from rubbing her eyes too hard, a ripple between background and foreground that eluded focus, it zoomed toward her, overtook her—

Thud!

"Ga-ah!"

With the collision and under her yelp came someone's groan and an abrupt change in direction. Arms like taut ropes cradled her to a heaving chest. Breathlessly she looked down . . . only to see through her lap, through her own limbs.

She'd become a transparent shade coursing past roofs and ravens. Below, behind, Blackened Square was left mid-scream, torn to bits and painted red.

"What. . . ."

Within this nonsensical dream she lifted her head. If she squinted hard enough she could make out the contours of a jaw, the outline of a brow—but she didn't need to see a face to know who this was, not while pressed to a chest rumbling with deeply familiar grunts. She was wrapped in a distinctive scent she could've never forgotten.

Was it real?

How?

How was it possible?

Helpless even to hold on tighter, Meredith burrowed into Four-Thirteen and shut her eyes. The wind roused the burns on her legs and feet in horribly unpleasant waves.

She could think of worse dreams to have before the end.

CHAPTER TWENTY-NINE

BRENA BELOW

HEY CRASH-LANDED in a dark alley still within the ancient city walls, only a few intersections away from Farshaw Street and entirely too close to Blackened Square. As the dais hit the ground at an angle and they rolled off in different directions, Meredith could only conclude that her rescue had been, in fact, real.

She lay there for a while, catching her breath and generally returning to her own body. She couldn't blame him for landing poorly too fast. His controller hand had been encumbered by holding an entire Meredith aloft.

She'd skidded more than rolled, the hands at her back acting as a stop-wedge of sorts. She'd scraped her whole side and bruised in several places for sure—how very quaint, after almost becoming cinder. Once she was done finding a way back into her every limb, her only actual concern was being able to walk on the burns she'd suffered.

The groans farther down the alley rose from the ground and grew closer. The subtle shimmer became a solid body mid-stride. Four-Thirteen, so far removed from what she remembered: dressed in an ill-fitting robe full of old stains, steps ponderous in their century-old boots, gait decisive and self-assured and not coerced in any way. Notably devoid of filth, as well. He did limp on one side, either from the recent tumble or from an injury Meredith remembered all too well, and his former bulk seemed to have condensed into a sinewy frame.

And on his hand. . . .

On his right hand he wore one answer and five more questions, because he wielded Janette's most cherished pet project: *Pusher Gauntlet, Mark III*. Also known as a "Juiced-up Gravity Glove."

Meredith sat up as far as she could and paid no mind to how much the world tilted. "How'd you get that?" she rasped.

Now that she was paying attention, the girdle at his waist was familiar, as was the empty harness at his back. He walked over to where the dais had landed—and as he gathered it up she easily recognized its black surface, glossy once upon a time, rounded edges chipped all over.

No response was forthcoming, but Meredith's thoughts answered well enough: he'd raided the remains of her cottage, evidently. He must have done it before the Judicars could go back to the crime scene and sort through the mess. Which meant. . . .

It meant he probably had been stalking her when the explosion happened.

In a stunned silence she watched him come over, dais under his arm. "Gome," he said with a beckoning gesture.

"I'm still tied up," she replied, but already she was dragging herself to the nearby wall to prop herself up. Four-Thirteen stepped forward and offered a hand.

"No, I can do it," Meredith said. Laboriously she leaned a shoulder against the bricks and worked to get upright.

The blisters screeched madly as soon as she put pressure on her feet. She whimpered and squirmed and heavily leaned against the wall. *Grit your teeth and walk,* she exhorted herself. *First one foot, then the other, it's not complicated.*

She made it through three steps. She tried for a fourth, she truly did. Her limbs grew feeble from the pain, and she would've collapsed to the floor if Four-Thirteen hadn't been there to catch her.

"I can't do it," she moaned.

"Hm," he told her, and firmly sat her down by the wall. Past the waves of agony radiating up her legs she marveled at how easily he could push her around. Had she lost that much weight through this whole ordeal? Her kneecaps did jut out in knobs. They'd never looked so bony before.

He kneeled behind her and moved her bound arms so they'd be clear of her rump. With one unyielding fist he held the ropes away from her wrist; after some rustle and fuss, his forceful sawing motions rocked her body back and forth. He was cutting the ropes loose, presumably while wielding a knife not one fingerbreadth from her flesh.

At least they weren't manacles. Thank the furies for ceremonial bindings.

The tension at her back released all at once. She brought her hands around to her lap, and she had to peel the pieces of rope off her abraded skin. They left fat red-and-white imprints on her wrists.

Meanwhile, Four-Thirteen deployed the dais in front of her. It was still operational despite all the abuse. It had been a present from Mifraulde, after all, a present from a time when the newly invested Councilor regarded her brood-sister with more optimism than resignation. She wouldn't have skimped on a cheaply-made artifact.

"Goh," Four-Thirteen grunted, pointing at the platform. "I hepp," he added.

"That won't work, I can't stand."

"Foh." He patted his knees and pointed at the foot indentations on the dais.

"Oh. Alright, that might work."

She offered an arm and he picked her up like she was a sack full of hammers. Awkwardly they endeavored to position her knees well enough to be functional. It was not comfortable in the slightest.

He handed her the dais controller. "Hm," he elaborated, and beckoned her to follow again before nearing a grate embedded by the wall. The thing was encrusted with some three hundred years-worth of rust and disuse. It probably hadn't been touched since the War of Succession.

Meredith stared at the controller in her hand. It occurred to her she could simply take off at this point. It would be hard to do without proper foot pressure inputs, but doable.

She looked up at the man, the stunt Four-Thirteen, this tragic byproduct of Puritan ruthlessness. He'd rescued her. He'd also murdered several of her Circle colleagues for no good reason, and massacred a square-full of witches after that, easily thousands dead or grievously wounded. The enormity of it was only now dawning on her: most of Brena's population had been wiped out in one instant. The entire council was dead, Mifraulde was dead.

There was something truly broken in her brain, because the thought of a dead Mifraulde still brought a pang of grief to her chest. And Yurena. . . .

She'd rather not think about Yurena.

The grate clanged off its recess and lifted to hover in mid-air, held aloft by the gauntlet's grip. Four-Thirteen tilted his perennially hairless head toward the opening.

Meredith contemplated it. For all she knew, he was luring her into a very secluded, very private torture chamber. Was it wise to jump into *another* dark portal at someone else's behest?

"Hrm," he encouraged.

Without any more hesitation she pressed on the throttle and carefully tilted the controller forward. The transport painfully wobbled toward him. Every burn and contusion she'd earned so far was a constant wail at the back of her head, and the ribs that had cracked upon capture happily added to the mix with every breath. The tumble after landing probably hadn't helped that particular matter.

All of these were persuasive incentives not to strike out on her own.

"Thank you for saving me," she whispered while hovering over the edge. Four-Thirteen grunted.

Peering into the entrance to Old Brena Below, Meredith saw only darkness.

CENTURIES AGO, all the way from its clandestine founding on Earth, through the Conveyance and up to the War of Succession, Old Brena Below had simply been known as the town of Galavan.

The War of Succession culminated in Sabrena's rise to power. She later came to be known as Sabrena the Mad Crone, and for good reason. Meredith's memory was muddy on the details, but the relevant part was easy enough to remember: due to irreconcilable differences with the Eastern Cabal—which at the time threatened to claim total control of the town—she and her faithful crones had pooled their magical attunement together to literally bury Galavan under a mountain.

They were rather uncivilized times.

The newly-founded Brena thrived upon the ruins, and to add an extra dash of defilement, Galavan's former streets were repurposed as sewers. Eventually the portal-based system of pipes and septic tanks replaced such primitive means of waste disposal, leaving the remains of Galavan Town to forever decay within and below the perpetually-crumbling walls of Old Brena.

With this bit of history in her mind, Meredith found a number of her expectations immediately dashed. One, it didn't smell like sewage all that much. Only dank, rusty and earthy. Two, it wasn't as claustrophobic as she'd feared, despite the downward slope barely fitting Four-Thirteen without him hunching over. Three, it wasn't egregiously filthy. Most surfaces were only damp, since rainwater routinely filtered down the grates and courseways to be collected who-knew-where. The sound of trickling water was common, and already they'd passed a few paths flooded beyond traversal.

They progressed under the blue light of a glowstone that may have belonged to a defunct Riven Circle member, going left and right and sometimes up but mostly downward into the bowels of Old Brena Below. The cobbles under the dais glistened slick with moss, their roughshod surface a striking contrast to the perfectly sealed patterns of the streets above. Some paths had obviously been alleys buried long ago, while others were abrupt gashes into the earth, tunnels dug or cleared after the collapse for reasons Meredith couldn't guess. Sometimes they would go through the remains of someone's living room, someone's scullery, someone's picked-clean pantry. Despite the state of chaos and disrepair, it was still odd to find all furniture absent. Perhaps it was the result of looting sometime after Broken Peak's name change.

It was in one of these ghostly rooms, tucked inside a former closet, that Meredith noticed the first husk. It lounged on the floor as though taking a nap against the wall, this vaguely human torso of rubber and metal with four arms still attached, plus one rusted on the floor, and one more mostly missing. Obvious gaps were noticeable all over its frame where biological tissues might have been grafted once, and its midsection abruptly ended in a mess of dangling connections and golem guts. The long-extinguished wordpaths visible within the chassis were a hard-pack of miniaturized squiggly lines, far more intricate than Janette's work on the gauntlet. Its squat head tilted forward in the empty sleep of hollow sensor sockets.

"I thought they'd destroyed them all," Meredith had commented, glad to have something on which to focus besides the burns. She'd never seen one of these creatures outside of textbooks and propaganda.

Four-Thirteen had simply shrugged.

They came across others, husks full of forbidden technology, remnants of the most serious self-inflicted threat witchdom had faced since the Civil War. Some didn't even appear maimed. They were merely . . . dead.

Janette would've been entranced. Yurena would've committed a number of crimes for the chance to study them. How could they simply be littered down here for anyone to find?

Then again . . . where was "here"?

The longer they traveled, the more intricate the maze became. Meredith lost track of the bends, doors and tunnels, everything was a featureless blur as her focus narrowed down to following the bulk in front of her without surrendering to pain. She tried to consider her immediate future, to make some kind of plan that would take her to Yanwar in good enough shape, but no two ideas seemed to pair up coherently. The throbbing in her head didn't help matters any.

In this state of mind, she was startled when the tight confines opened around them. They'd gone through a crooked threshold much like any other, and suddenly the glowstone light could not reach half the walls. She found herself in the middle of a lopsided room packed with clutter of all shapes and sizes, and poorly arranged furniture, and more disfigured husks posed in curious ways all about. Unceremoniously off-center, a glyphed foundation pillar thrust down from the warped ceiling and kept going through the floor with uncontestable solidity, as if it had been impaled from above without any regard for the ruins.

Four-Thirteen left the glowstone pendant on the large desk by the pillar and beckoned her to a corner with some seven hundred cushions in various states of wear. "Foh," he pointed.

Not that long ago, Meredith would have recoiled in horror at a bed made of unidentified pillows. Now, the mere idea of lying down nearly brought her to tears.

"You'll need to help me," she mumbled while floating toward the makeshift bed. Her field of vision had shrunk around the edges. Her thoughts felt as though trapped in coiled wire. She'd had enough similar experiences to know she was at risk of fainting.

Four-Thirteen braced her underarms again, grunted and lifted. The move was neither forceful nor delicate, just this awkward dance to get her propped on the pillows without her burns touching anything. Once she was settled, he placed a number of cushions under her calves and draped a large piece of cloth over her midsection. With some imagination and a generous spirit it could've been called a blanket, though Meredith was certain it had been a tablecloth at some point.

"Thank you."

He walked off without acknowledgement, steps muffled by the eclectic variety of rugs all over the floor. Meredith closed her eyes and focused on her breathing. The pain was this raw, scorching beast, spitting fire up her legs. If only she could slip her toes into a nice cold water basin. . . .

The sound of copious water being poured from one container to another couldn't have been timed better. Four-Thirteen was tipping a large pail over a . . . well, it looked like a dresser drawer. A watertight dresser drawer, hopefully.

He sloshed to her corner and laid the improvised basin at her feet. She glanced at it a few times.

"Is it . . . is it clean water?"

He shrugged one shoulder. "Hm," he said.

"Burns get easily infected."

With another grunt he returned to the water bucket, grabbed a nearby cup and used a ladle to fill it up. He came back and made a show of downing it in one gulp.

"Alright. Sorry."

He moved cushions out of the way and let Meredith take her time. With a measure of anxiety she dipped in a heel, followed it with a lip-quaking shudder, followed it with the whole foot. It was like a scream made of frost wailing at her skin, and also somehow a bucketload and a half of relief. Gingerly she submerged her other foot and kept it there, working through tremulous breaths to bear the pins and needles stabbing underwater.

If nothing else, the new kind of throbbing helped her stay lucid. Despite her gratitude and Four-Thirteen's courteousness so far, she wasn't ready to pass out lost in the deep dark with only a historically ultra-violent man for company.

The vise clutching at her insides slowly eased, and she found herself able to lean back and relax to some extent. She looked up at Four-Thirteen, who had taken the time to bring her a cup of her own to drink. Meredith took it in her hands and endeavored to sip it judiciously instead of glugging it down the way she wanted. The faint taste of rust helped hold her back.

"You wouldn't happen to have whittlenut root or gambi sap lying about, right?"

He tilted his head to one side.

"Never mind. I couldn't possibly make a salve without some tools."

This prompted him to go over to the book-stacked desk, grab a notebook and pen and start writing.

On second glance, a lot of the clutter in the misshapen room was books. Books in piles, books in mounds, in pairs and by their lonesome; books on broken furniture, on precarious surfaces, strewn on the floor, teetering on their spines or flopped open for all to see. Yurena would have gone apoplectic at the sight.

Four-Thirteen neared once more and offered the notebook. She took it.

What do you need?

She looked up from the words to see the pen being offered. "What do you mean by this?" she asked.

He eloquently gestured at her feet. Then he gestured at the whole of her.

It was not a very flattering gesture.

"How could you possibly get anything from. . . ."

The words trailed off, because Meredith remembered again. Brena was now an empty husk. It was a bizarre notion, easy to forget from one moment to the next.

She hesitated a bit, put down her cup and brought pen to paper.

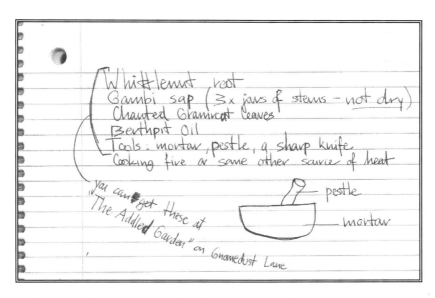

She considered her writing for a while, idly examined the pen. *Chlorinde's Ink & Page,* the barely-readable engraving said. It came along with the address, business hours and a moderate amount of grime.

Chlorinde was probably dead, now.

It couldn't hurt to ask.

Once more she contemplated the scribbles on the page. The directions weren't very helpful, were they?

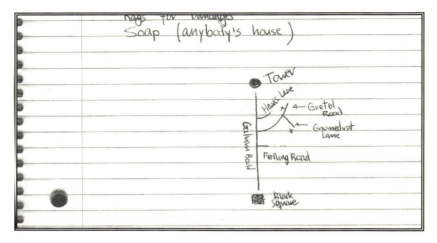

She was lightheaded again by the time she passed back the notebook. He studied it closely.

"Do you, uh . . . do you know what soap looks like?"

Four-Thirteen grunted. There was no telling what it meant.

"Well, if you're truly going back up there, stay under the rooftops. The pyre was nodecast."

He looked up and raised an eyebrow.

"It means every other town saw what happened. They won't, ah. . . ." She had to pause and wait for the dizzy spell to subside. "They won't take long to portal in, and you'll stand out. There will probably be survivors roaming the streets, as well."

Meredith could imagine the chaos as witches from all over Galavan flocked in. The Judicars would organize rescue efforts, they would bring in serfs and golems for cleanup crews. The Council would gather and start bickering immediately. Would they endeavor to restore Brena through migration? Would they sack it and leave the ruins for dead, as the Puritans had done with New Yanwar? Would they sift through the mountains of bureaucracy in Galvan Tower, appoint new officials and resume business as usual? With Brena's government body destroyed, Selma would seize the chance for all it was worth. If left unchecked she would lead Galavan to ruin with her deranged Earth domination plans.

Sinking into the cushions, Meredith couldn't afford to care. What mattered was: there would be a frenzy of activity around Blackened Square, but the rest of the town would remain deserted—and nobody would start hunting for the fugitives anytime soon. It was the perfect time to escape and mount a rescue, and yet here she was, broken and helpless. If she could make the burns heal quickly, or at least numb them enough to ignore them, she could get on with her trip to the Yanwar plants.

While her thoughts collided with one another Four-Thirteen

bustled all over the room, getting ready to venture back into danger. He spent some time staring at the desk, gaze going back and forth between whatever was on it and Meredith's writing. He ripped the list off the notebook, folded and pocketed it; he powered down the dais, folded and holstered it; he clasped the invisibility girdle, strapped a tattered satchel over his head and donned the gauntlet once more, stretching it to capacity so it would fit his hand.

Janette's gauntlet. Exquisite work and care had gone into its craft. It didn't sit well with Meredith for it to be handled so . . . *irreverently* . . . but she wasn't about to complain. How much longer would it last, anyway? She couldn't catch a glimpse of the charge gauge. Knowing Janette's overzealous nature, she'd probably charged it to the brim when the Mistress wasn't there to chide her for it. She wasn't sure how many doomsday explosions it could power.

In a thickening fog Meredith watched her savior prepare to leave, and without even meaning to she catalogued one by one the tools she would need for a Yanwar assault: a dais to get there, a juiced-up gravity glove to break in and deal with threats, a hopefully-still-charged invisibility girdle for a hasty escape. All of them with a new owner. Would he simply give them up?

In fact, would he show even one whit of sympathy for her quest to rescue a young witch from the harvest pods? What if he didn't simply refuse to help, but also refused to let her go?

What did Four-Thirteen *want?*

The former serf disappeared through the threshold without a parting gesture. He'd left the glowstone behind, because in his hand he'd been holding up a lamp Meredith would have recognized anywhere: opaque glass orb, ornate wire frame, overarching handle—perfect for comfortable reading without being a nuisance to others.

Yurena would've fainted if she'd known who her book thief was. Meredith made a note of asking him how he'd done it, if she ever got the chance.

Steps continued to drum for a while after he'd been swallowed by the darkness. Warily she stretched her toes underwater and winced at the cool nettles grinding into her flesh. The water had darkened with soot and dirt, but there didn't seem to be any red. How much worse would it be if he'd shown up even one scream later?

All on its own her tush wiggled deeper into the pillows. Her head felt too heavy to carry, so she put it down in a convenient spot. The ceiling, a mosaic of wood, dirt and stone, looked like it could cave if she sneezed too hard, and the prospect didn't seem as horrifying as it should have.

Soon her eyelids demanded too high a price to stay open, so she refused to keep paying. She could still find solutions to her problems with eyes closed, anyway. How to claim back all the artifacts she would need? How was she going to find Janette's exact location?

What would they do *after,* if she succeeded? Surely at least one solution would come to her.

Before her thoughts gave up on the waking world altogether it occurred to her that maybe she was a worthy witch after all. This man had saved her from certain death, and already she was planning to betray him.

S HE STARTLED AWAKE with a yelp. In her dream, a toothy little creature was clamped on her legs, gnawing relentlessly while she squirmed. She'd kicked at it, and the creature had chomped on her foot hard enough to make her jump.

For a few gasping breaths Meredith looked around in confusion, unable to figure out what was this blue place painted out of a horror story. Looking down at a mottled tablecloth and a dresser drawer full of dirty water, she remembered. The kick had made a mess of a splash.

"Ogh. . . ."

There was no telling for how long she'd been unconscious, but it couldn't have been more than half a span. Probably. Sucking air through her teeth, she lifted one foot out of the water. The skin had paled to near-translucent except around the soles, where big red splotches bloomed. She raised the leg and took careful hold of the foot, lips twisted in dread at what she might see when she turned it over.

It was red, ugly and wrinkly and some parts had indeed blistered . . . though not as horrifically as she had imagined all this time, it didn't look as bad as it felt. She only needed to resist the urge to poke at it.

A line around her ankles delineated the frontier between skin and dirt, driving home how filthy she was. To her mind came her cherished bathroom with its wonderful shower head and stubborn heater. She had laid those pipes herself, hacked into the walls and made every connection with her own hands and tools. How proud she'd been when the seventh attempt at running hot water had been successful, after only a few weeks of work and a negligible number of catastrophes.

"All gone now," she sighed. Would any of the flooded passages make a good wash basin? It didn't seem wise to mix stagnant water and fresh wounds. Meredith grabbed a corner of the "blanket," dunked it in the water and squeezed it over her legs, delicately patting over the raw lines where her thighs and calves had been singed. Droplets of soot trailed down her skin with every daub.

She did what she could to wipe clean these little corners of herself, gritting her teeth through the sting of a dozen scrapes down her arms and backside. She chafed at her disgusting rags, the state of her hair, the lisp in her tongue, the hunger pains in her gut and also the utter loss of everything she'd ever known. There were so many tragedies to grieve, she couldn't settle on any one. Even the drive for a successful rescue brought as much dread as everything else, because if she managed to pull it off, if there was enough of Janette left to save and they escaped somewhere safe, then . . . then she'd have to face her.

She would have to nurse her back to health, and explain why this had happened to her, and watch as she struggled to endure her atrocious new reality. Not in her most far-fetched delusions could Meredith imagine forgiveness.

No matter what she did, Janette was already lost to her.

In the still silence broken by the trickle-patter of her movements, deep in the blue darkness with only half-seen corpses for company, Meredith found her chance to fall apart under the weight of the world. The sobs took over gradually, a quiet swell that pulled at her chest until she was bracing her knees, curled into a shuddering ball.

She'd called them monsters. They *were* monsters, all of Galavan was teeming with them. Was this what they deserved, to be wiped out? Was it weakness to feel sorry for those who cheered while she burned? Head bowed into her arms, Meredith mourned all the lives she had destroyed.

Hold on to this feeling, Silver had said. *It's what sets us apart.*

Silver, who had tried to rescue her and as a direct result had become a captive in the Tower dungeon. The few remaining Judicars wouldn't have time to deal with her, now. She might remain in stasis for the next few decades. Surely her friends and contacts in the rest of Galavan would try to get her back—and Wybel had escaped, supposedly. Would *she* try to help?

Wybel will be waiting for you, Silver had said.

Waiting behind a portal, somewhere safe.

Where might that be?

"Silver lived on Earth at some point," Meredith muttered.

The dots connected. What she needed to do lined up in front of her like numbered steps in an artificing manual. None of the steps were easy or straightforward, all of them came with several question marks in-between, but there was a chance she could make it through to the end.

And then Janette would be safe, away from this dreadful place.

Curled over her murky dresser drawer, tears dragging soot off her cheeks, Meredith gave up on mourning. There would be time for it later, when all the death and destruction was actually over. Instead she considered how much whittlenut root she could shave into the salve without saturating the oil or giving her hives, and how much gramrout she could tolerate without making it lethargic or toxic—because she needed to shove her feet into a pair of boots and not pass out from the pain four steps in. Proper healing would have to wait until her mission was over.

Of course, none of it would be possible if her savior didn't return with the items she needed. Which brought her to the first step on the list, the first hurdle that could stop everything else from happening.

Deal with Four-Thirteen. Peacefully or otherwise.

Meredith looked around. Perhaps something in the room would tell her how to properly handle him. She might not be able to walk, but no-one could stop her from crawling.

Among lingering sniffles and strangled moans Meredith lifted her feet off the water and very carefully cloth-patted the raw flesh until it was dry. Her skin was swollen and tender enough to cast the entire plan into doubt. Regardless of her intentions, there was a threshold of pain after which she simply could not function.

"It'll be fine," she whispered. "You'll be fine."

She eyed the tablecloth critically. It seemed flimsy enough to tear with bare hands. Would Four-Thirteen mind? Maybe. He'd get over it.

Holding to her chest the thinnest patch she could find, she stretched and clawed and dug with her fingers. One managed to poke through, and it wasn't much more trouble to make the hole bigger, loudly tearing down along the grain of the fabric until the rip spanned half the cloth. Her arms were workout-weary by the time she'd ripped two long strips' worth of frayed bandages. Through whimpers and sharp breaths she looped them around each foot as best she could and tied them at the ankle in the shoddiest footwraps ever fashioned. Good enough to prevent air friction from driving her mad.

See-sawing on her behind, she gave herself a bit of momentum and groaned to her hands and knees. She resisted the urge to curl her toes while her ample collection of aches complained. It was a little while until she could hear her own thoughts again.

She headed for the big desk and the light perched upon it. Each rug under her fingers offered its own brand of dirty as she crawled around miscellaneous debris and scattered books. Meredith read spines as she went:

The Gorgon and the Shrew.
Human Armaments: From Spears to Super Sonic Missiles.
What Witches Want: A Guide to Modern Dating.
History of Galavan, Vol. 9: The Human Rebellions.
THE END OF ALL THINGS – A Novel.
Hexe Wardja – The Judicar Creed.

They carried on without much of a pattern, anything from fluffy novels through analytical non-fiction to heavily detailed historical accounts. Several of them had improvised bookmarks sticking out.

On already-sore knees she stretched to the desk, chin and arms resting on wood that might have lived through the Conveyance. Under the notepad, circled by more piles of books, Meredith saw what Four-Thirteen had been studying: a rather intricate map of Brena scrawled with barely legible notes and symbols. *Food, AVOID, safe, empty, clear*, a few lines routing through the streets. A number of other maps were stacked beneath: a big spread of the entire realm, floorplans Meredith didn't recognize, even a ragged lambskin parchment depicting the defunct town of Galavan. Next to all these, a notebook page with a mess of hand-drawn lines and figures. The shape of it was identifiable as Four-Thirteen's attempt to map Brena Below.

And beneath this diagram, clipped in a messy, crumpled and frayed pile, Janette's meticulous notes on the gauntlet's manufacture and operation. Only a few pages were missing. How long had Four-Thirteen spent in the Hallow's End dark, rifling through the ruins of her cottage? How long had the Judicars let the ravens pick at the remains? Long enough for him to scavenge at leisure, it would seem.

Unable to find anything immediately useful, Meredith looped the glowstone's chain around her wrist and returned to crawling. One corner housed what she could only describe as a pile of junk—a hoard of assorted items that might have contained something worthwhile, but she wasn't about to search through it. Heaped on an ancient lounger sat clothes much too large for her, all ragged, all dreary. Shelves were lined next to the exit, sparsely populated with everyday utensils and . . . food?

She would've run to it. Eagerly she sorted through what few items she could reach, some mundane like stale bread, oats, cured meats or dried fruits, but also several exotic finds such as boxes of cold cereal and wrapped candies from Earth. No Honey Cheerios, unfortunately. Meredith dipped her hand in the fruit bowl and stuffed her mouth with a fistful of dried apple slices, then more meticulously chewed through a strip of toughchop. Perhaps ransacking a host's pantry wasn't the best etiquette, but it wasn't so impolite considering every item must've been pilfered to begin with.

The murmur of trickling water registered while she gnawed on a hard chunk of bread. She listened. It seemed distant, without a specific source. Could it simply be the rain pouring down pipes and drains? Rain would mean it was the early morning of Nynday. Had she languished in a cell for *that* long? Had Janette been in their power for more than a week, now?

She resumed her search for useful information with renewed purpose. She couldn't afford to mishandle Four-Thirteen. Even if he'd been nothing short of heroic so far, there was no telling how volatile he would become when she broached the notion of leaving . . . let alone taking every artifact with her.

While the age-eaten panels of the far wall were hardly worth visiting, she could make out a closed door among the blue shadows. A notice of some kind was pinned next to it. Meredith crawled closer, raised the glowstone. She looked at the paper and her own face gazed back at her.

PYRE CLEANSING, the notice read, listing every one of her dire misdeeds. They'd reused that dreadful sneering portrait from the manufactory. A close enough likeness, but she'd never smirked like that.

What would Four-Thirteen keep in a room with her face attached to it?

She twisted the door handle. There was a click and a clack and the shift of unlatching, but the lopsided fit kept the door firmly—

Thump!

"Aah!" She startled away from the thud, lost her balance and fell back on her heels, which she very dearly regretted. The first door whack was followed by a constant rattle, as if someone was trying to shoulder their way through. Their voice was high pitched and muffled to unintelligibility.

Had Four-Thirteen kidnapped someone?

"Who's there?"

The rattling intensified as a response, but Meredith still couldn't understand anything. Maybe the prisoner was bound and gagged, unable to do anything but moan and bump against the door.

"Can you understand me?"

The rattling continued unchanged.

"Thump twice if you can understand me."

There were many more than two thumps. The moaning was this wordless weeping, desperate and urgent. What had Four-Thirteen *done?*

"I'm a friend," Meredith told the door. "You won't attack me if I open this, will you?"

The noises made no indication of acquiescence.

Her hand lingered on the handle. *Should* she open the door? She was in no shape for a confrontation if it turned violent. And who would be the better ally, anyway? Strong, capable, possibly deranged Four-Thirteen, or some random witch that might be beaten and feeble? This had nothing to do with her.

"Hold on," she said without much regard for the idea. Meredith twisted the handle and shoved as hard as she could. The door noisily ground forward but didn't budge all the way. She could sense the surprise on the other side.

"Get away from the door," she shout-whispered into the jamb.

The rattling ceased.

Meredith turned her body and threw her shoulder into the sturdy nightwood. Her ribs voiced a harsh complaint on impact, but the door made it a tiny bit further. She reeled back once more and *thumped.*

She collapsed into the threshold when the door flew open, and she was wholly unprepared for the blob of feathery fur that rushed at her.

"Wah—"

A wet upturned snout shoved its way right up to her mouth.

"Pfagh! What in the—"

"*Wheegh!*"

"What—"

"*Snrt.*"

Wispy ear floof tickled her nose in a deeply familiar way.

"Desmond?"

The barrel-bellied thog nudged her without mercy. He rubbed his ears against her jaw and excitedly clawed at her hands.

"What are you *doing* here?"

"*Snrt,*" Desmond said while licking Meredith's neck.

"Yugh!" Her hands could barely contain the relentless affection. "Alright, settle down, settle down already!"

As she struggled to hold back the uncharacteristically effusive fellow, Meredith became oddly aware of how wide her smile stretched her cheeks. It was such an unusual feeling. She scratched behind his ears with full hands. "You slobbering little mongrel, I'm so glad you're safe!"

"*Snrt,*" Desmond agreed.

"Did Four-Thirteen find you? Did he bring you here?"

"*Snrt,*" Desmond elaborated, and nudged her hands some more.

"He didn't hurt you, did he?"

"*Snrt,*" was the non-committal answer.

"Are you well fed? Do you need food? I saw oats. . . ."

Oh. So that was why the shelves stocked some dry oats fit only for animal feed or a desperate meal.

Mentioning food brought even more enthusiasm out of the fluffball. It was a trial for Meredith to get back on her battered knees. "Actually, you look *too* well-fed, Mister Saddlebags."

The resulting snorts seemed rather indignant. Steady petting kept her on Desmond's good graces. "I'm jealous, you're so clean. How have you kept so clean?"

The thog's response was inconclusive. Meanwhile, the sounds of trickling water had swelled to a downpour. With one hand still patting Desmond's bristly jowls, Meredith raised the glowstone and gave the room a proper look.

Torrents of rainwater splashed from messy fissures in the far wall ahead and pooled into a pond that somehow hadn't flooded the underground lair yet. The floor dipped more steeply in this room, keeping the turbulent puddle confined to its corner.

Close to the pond, along the wall, stood a narrow dresser as old as the centuries-worn floor tiles. It housed tissues, towels, a mirror on a swivel frame and (yes!) soap. A few unfortunate books had been wedged under one side to keep it horizontal in the cockeyed room.

It smelled as humid as her garden on a cold Nynday night, here, but it was also tinged with the fust she'd grown accustomed to through years of cleaning a thog's spoil-patch. A thick pile of rags and refuse in the corner farthest from her looked fashioned exactly for that purpose.

And across the refuse, up-slope along the wall, lurking in the shadows of the highest point in the room. . . .

A cloaked figure.

"Who!"

She would've jumped, had she been on her feet. Desmond startled, but the cloaked figure didn't stir. Meredith raised the light as high as she could and squinted.

Another golem corpse, far more humanoid than the average fare. It was propped with wooden planks and metal bars and stood surrounded by a diverse collection of items. It wore a thick red robe, brushed to a semblance of cleanliness. It wore a pointy hat that crumpled more than pointed. It wore an auburn mop-head for a wig and a piece of paper stuck to its face.

"Huh."

She didn't know exactly why, but her stomach shrunk with every knee-stride that took her closer. The hat seemed new but beaten on purpose to look the part. Holstered at the golem's skeletal waist hung a semi-automatic hand-crossbow, and she had no doubt at all she'd pulled that very trigger over a hundred times. Pasted to the metal forehead was the same portrait from the pyre notice, all the words carefully ripped around it.

The items circling the boots—and these looked like *her* boots, down to every discolored crease—all were recognizable. An ivory spoon. A dried rose, as deep red as old blood. The loose cobblestone that had one day disappeared from the edge of her garden, so recognizable in the shape of its jag. *Complacency of the Learned,* which served as the foundation for a tower of books that looked like they'd barely survived a trip through the flowline: *Concept Compendium, Non-Standard Transportation, Gallia's Burning Desire, Sparse Dining – 105 Recipes for the Frugally Minded.* A shattered-inside soundstill coil. A bloodstained, half-functional stasis trap. A raven-shaped hair tie. Janette's phone with all-new cracks. A pendant that needled at her memory, but she couldn't quite place.

This was . . . a shrine.

A shrine to her.

Meredith blankly stared at it, not quite knowing what to feel.

"*Snrt,*" Desmond suggested, and bothered at her hand until she was petting him again.

"Maybe it's here to keep you company, yeah?"

He didn't seem all that convinced.

The pendant perturbed her the most, of all things. She'd seen it before many times, but where? Meredith reached for it and let it dangle from her pinky.

It was the brass rhombus sigil of Vanuuren's brood hanging from a simple black cord. She'd seen this trinket around Devalka's neck from the moment they'd met. Val would compulsively touch it all the time while telling unlikely tales of its power.

There was no world in which she would part with it willingly.

Meredith's petting hand had gone limp, so more nudging ensued. She gave the thog a side-long glance. "Do you think he just . . . killed her?"

Desmond had no opinion on the matter. Unlike the situation with the Circle witches, Four-Thirteen had every motive to stalk, assault and murder Devalka in cold blood. Part of her was impressed at how very effective he'd been all on his own, the same part of her that was flattered at finding this disturbing shrine.

She slumped to one side of her calves so her knees could take a break, all the while careful not to put pressure on her feet. The grime and detritus encrusted all over her rags was a constant bother on her skin. "He's mad. I can't possibly trust him. Can I?"

For no apparent reason Desmond took off from her side. With her eyes she followed the thog's waggle, and this is how she noticed Four-Thirteen standing inside the room.

She froze. The rain-borne waterfall had masked his entrance. Within the blue shadows he glowered, ignoring Desmond's happy nudge-greetings against his leg. Was he angry about her wandering off? Had he heard her musings?

Best to go on the offensive right away. The pendant still dangled from her finger. She showed it to him in a silent question.

He took one deep breath, nodded, and stepped out of the room. Even in the dim light Meredith could tell his robe sagged heavy with rainwater.

She stayed there, belly full of tension as she tried to listen. The streams drowned out whatever he was doing out there. Desmond came over and flopped by her leg, exhausted by all the excitement.

Four-Thirteen returned wearing dry clothes—at once loose and tight, depending on where they'd better fit a witch's frame. In his hand he carried the notebook and a pen. He climbed the incline until he stood in front of her, just out of arm's reach. He wrote.

found everything

Meredith stared at the message, glanced at his face ever so briefly. "Thank you. Did you have to . . . did anyone see you?"

He turned the notebook and put pen to paper, but thought about his answer for some time before the words took shape.

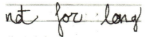

not for long

"Oh. I see." She considered the pendant still in her hand. Ten different questions came to mind, but at the same time, Meredith was all too aware she was wholly at his mercy. It would be foolish to start an interrogation in her current state.

"I have a lot of questions," she said anyway.

He nodded. He waited.

What do you want from me? How have you made it this far? Will you let me go? Am I safe around you? Just how unstable are you?

Her hand rested on Desmond's flank. "You didn't hurt him to bring him here, did you?"

He shook his head as the pen moved in small, careful gestures.

I watch your window many times

we become friends when you sleep

She pressed her lips together. Was he aware of how disquieting a notion that was?

"How did you find out where I live?"

you visit library at night

I lurk

I follow

Four-Thirteen listening by the door while she spent the night at Yurena's quarters didn't exactly put her mind at ease.

"But how do you get into the library in the first place?"

from below

everything ~~connects~~ connects

He elaborated by silently pointing up.

"Are we below the library *right now*?"

He nodded. The Kestrel library's rain gutters did merrily gush down a few waterfall-like grates. It would also explain the giant glyphed pillar spearing through the adjacent room.

"And you were never noticed?"

I was sometimes seen

never noticed

He let Meredith read the message. She raised the pendant again and spoke quietly. "Did Devalka notice you?"

His face went from somber to grim.

not fast enough

She grimaced. Devalka had almost been a friend. She also wouldn't have hesitated to report the slightest hint of youth-minding, had she suspected it. Dead one-on-one, dead in a mob at Blackened Square—did it even matter?

Meredith watched as Four-Thirteen turned to a new page.

"Did she suffer?"

His snort was packed with loathing. He spent quite some time scribbling his next message.

less than deserved

I watched her too

she was vile

all witches are vile and should be destroyed

She raised her brow with trepidation. "Including me?"

His frown deepened to a dire scowl, as if the question was profoundly upsetting. Meredith counted heartbeats while he wrote: seven, eight, nine, ten, eleven, twelve, thirteen, fourteen—

you live among them

but you are no witch

She read the shaky scrawl without much outward reaction. These words would've brought deep shame, once. They should've offended her. Now, looking up from the slanted floor of a rank underground lair, despoiled and maimed by vile creatures indeed, the statement only echoed her own inner struggle with identity.

Maybe that was the answer. Maybe she wasn't a witch at all. She certainly didn't *want* to be.

"Not all of them deserve it," she said. "The Circle witches were good. They would've taken care of you. Why'd you have to . . . to do that to them?"

Four-Thirteen was clenching his jaw and shaking his head, forcefully writing before she was done talking. He didn't so much turn the notebook as he thrust it in her face.

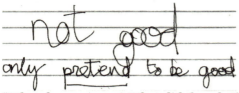

"What do you mean? What did they do?"
His pen hand slashed across the paper twice.

He was intensely staring again, exuding complete finality in his judgment. What had they done to him? Meredith could imagine a number of unsavory things—things deviants might do under the guise of altruism and kindness. She'd lived among witches all her life, after all. There was no shortage of stories.

She pursed her lips. "Was it all of them, whatever they did? Did they *all* deserve to die and get their tongues cut off? Do you know how disturbed I was to see that?"

It took a while, but his scowl eventually broke into uncertainty.

you saw?

"I was there when the Judicars came. I almost got caught."

He searched her face for some time, patently trying to understand. When he finally brought the notebook back up, there was an unprecedented degree of hesitation to his writing. He glanced at her before turning the page over.

sorry

He made this lopsided frown that perhaps meant to be contrite. The expression was entirely alien on his face. It was . . . charming.

Not in a thousand years would Meredith have anticipated such a thought, but there it was.

"Well, you did rescue me from a horrible burning death, so . . . it just about evens things out, yeah?"

She'd hoped for something resembling a smile, but his lips didn't even twitch, nor did his eyes crinkle in the slightest. He simply worked on his next message, which was lengthy enough for Meredith's wounds to come back into focus. The numbing cold had long departed from her feet.

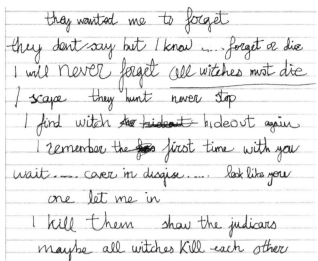

they wanted me to forget
they dont say but I know ... forget or die
I will never forget all witches must die
I scape they hunt never stop
I find witch the hideout hideout again
I remember the first time with you
wait ... cover in disguise ... look like you
*   one let me in*
I kill them show the judicars
maybe all witches kill each other

Meredith spent a good while interpreting the broken sentences, not least of all because the pains kept yelling improprieties in her ear. Silver had glossed over that *relentless hunting* part. Or perhaps some of those hunters had been juditors.

Constant persecution could drive anyone to take drastic measures.

"You wrote your number on the wall. With their *blood*. Why would you do that?"

He was scowling as he took the time to respond, though there was something decidedly self-conscious about the way he shifted in place.

not smart

I was angry
wanted them to know

He closely watched Meredith while she read—she'd barely had time to grasp it when he started writing something else.

you must heal now

He accompanied the reveal with emphatic nods. Her smile was more of a wince. "I wish. The salve takes work, it won't be ready for some time."

"Hm," he said, and wrote some more.

wash wounds first

dirt in blood

She looked at the perpetually splashing pond. The water appeared as cold as the Coren peaks and all the more inviting for it. Washing would be *delightful*. It could also lead to drowning, in her state.

"I don't know if I can, uh . . . I'll need help."

He nodded, tossed notebook and pen on the floor and without hesitation moved to pick her up. An apprehensive protest bubbled up her throat, but she was already being lifted. "Yalp," she said instead, and clung to his shoulders like they were handholds off a precipice. Desmond slumped to the floor and stayed there, unconcerned for her safety.

There it was again, that sweaty scent that made her want to recoil but not really. Somehow she wished for the trip to the pond not to be so short, even with the painful pressure of his arms on the scrapes and bruises. With strained care Four-Thirteen deposited her by the burbling shore before disappearing through the threshold once more.

Meredith stared after him, feet awkwardly hovering off the floor. Hopefully he was fetching a clean change of clothes. Anything would be better than this awful prisoner's gown, which . . . would have to come off soon, if she wanted to wash up.

In private. She would manage by herself, in private. Right?

Of course.

The subtle waves lapped at her hand. It was cold, but not as cold as she'd imagined it. Without much more thought Meredith undid her shoddy footwraps, pivoted on her tush and dipped her feet heel through toe into the chill. She closed her eyes and let the prattle of streaming rainwater soothe her through the barbs.

She sensed more than heard Four-Thirteen as he returned and dropped a cloth sack next to her. "Hm," he said. Clearly an invitation to browse through it. Crammed inside, Meredith found a thick white towel, a wide assortment of clothes that might possibly fit her, a hairbrush she hadn't asked for but dearly appreciated, a few medical supplies far above what she'd expected and a clump of life-saving undergarments.

She looked up at him. "Thank you so much for this."

He nodded but didn't otherwise act.

She could take over from here. There was no need for him to stick around. She could manage.

"I can barely move," her mouth said without permission, "will you please help me through it?"

There was a couple beats of indecision on both sides.

"Mm," he said with a nod. Four-Thirteen simply stood there, not quite knowing how to proceed.

"I'd like to clean the wounds first." Her thumb hooked on a frayed collar. The hand was mostly steady. "It's . . . tied at the back. Do you mind?"

He quietly stepped behind her. After some consideration, he fiddled with the knot between her shoulder blades. It wasn't long until she felt the gown ease loose. The rags pulled on raw skin, clinging to the dry blood.

"Alright. . . ."

She pulled the gown off her shoulders and very slowly disrobed, sucking in breaths as the torn fabric plucked off the scratches and abrasions on her arms and back. Flecks of encrusted grime crumbled here and there from the garment onto the tiles.

Meredith looked up through the corner of her eye. "Is it bad?"

"Hm."

He reached into the sack for the roll of gauze, tore off a patch, wet it lightly in the pond and knelt behind her. Cool, gentle pats started on her shoulder. Meredith did everything she could to relax her body and not flinch at the stings . . . or fuss at the touch of his fingers on her skin. Witches got minded by duds all the time. This wasn't so different.

Four-Thirteen worked his way down every small wound, white swabs getting discarded into a pile as they became soiled in pink and brown. Wordlessly she peeled away more of the prisoner rags until she was exposed from neck to waist. She might have held any other clothing to her chest for the sake of modesty, but repulsion won out. She just wanted it gone.

Her arms came free after some struggle. "Would you please undo the other tie?"

He fiddled and plucked at the cords on her lower back. The moment it was loose, she wiggled the gown free from under her buttocks and tossed it as far away as she could.

They exchanged a look. She couldn't help but blush, even if all the dirt and soot that remained could've been considered a layer of clothes in itself.

"Feels good to be rid of it."

"Hm," he seemed to agree—and of course he would, having worn similar scraps himself. He resumed his daubing without much of a bother. She watched his hands as he cleaned the lesions down her flank, to the side of her rump and on the outside of her thigh. The bruising was substantial, over there.

Meredith leaned forward to her knees and held on to herself. Her hair flopped by her cheeks in matted clumps. How did she look in this moment, bare and battered in a dark hole beneath Brena? Probably wild and grimy like a savage dud escaped from the swamps of Tarkis.

She turned her head and rested her temple on her forearms, looking at him. "I need to go in there and get clean," she said. "Would you please keep me from drowning?"

Four-Thirteen blinked a number of times. Perhaps it was reluctance. Perhaps he didn't expect her to be this forward. Perhaps he simply resented the request because he'd just changed into dry clothes.

He took a breath a bit deeper than usual and went to the mirror-on-a-swivel dresser. He came back with a clean rag and a bar of soap of the kind they might sell at the day market, paper-wrapped and hand-cut. He unwrapped it and offered it for her to carry; it was a pleasant white-and-purple swirl with a faintly sweet scent. Soap-making was a common hobby for many an alchemist.

Four-Thirteen removed his ill-fitting shirt, a perfectly natural thing to do before taking her to a waterfall. Under the blue light every blemish and scar was on display, every mark scored by years of laborious serfdom. How many of those marks were discipline for his rebellious streak? How many were reminders of vicious bouts in the fight pits? Pale lines crossed one another to tell the tale of a hundred-plus lashes. A claw had raked four distinct paths from shoulder to breastbone. His flesh rumpled in places where it had coped with acid or flame. This human, this man, he was a living monument to Galavan's cruelty.

And indeed he wasn't as bulky as he used to, yet every one of his muscles still stood out in statuesque definition. She couldn't help but stare. How different to a witch's body it was.

When he knelt by her side and braced her legs and back, Meredith let rag and soap fall to her lap so she could hold on to his neck with both hands. When he lifted her off the ground and pressed her close to his chest, she strove to do her part not to be an awkward burden. As they waded deeper into the turbulent pond, she rested her head on his shoulder and breathed deep.

"You never deserved all that pain," she told him. He didn't react one way or another.

Mist droplets sprinkled them like Naughtday dew here, knee-deep by the wall. Rainwater splashed merrily at arm's length. Though Meredith's face was flush with warmth, her skin roused to the chill. He lowered her slowly, squat-kneeling down into the water with her.

"Eee," she squirmed as the cold engulfed her rear-first. The memory of many cold showers flashed in her mind—but at least with cold showers she could control where the water went first. She'd have never chosen *that area* for first contact. She held on tighter out of reflex, but he kept going down until she was sitting on an underwater stool she hadn't noticed until then. It was placed on the perfect spot to lean back into the streams.

The water came up to her belly button, clear as glass where the rivulets would let it. The singed marks on her legs found much needed relief underwater. Abdomen taut from the cold, breath short and shallow, Meredith closed her eyes and tried not to think about how very exposed she felt as she leaned her head into the waterfall. Four-Thirteen's hand was a constant presence at her back, making sure she wouldn't tip over due to her inability to seek purchase with her feet.

A deep and long *Ooooouh* escaped her lips as fresh bliss ran over her scalp. Her fingers dug in, or tried to, combing through the mess in painful attempts to break clots and untangle knots. All the rot they'd pelted on her became this foul residue she had to constantly rinse off. It took quite some time to clear all of it, enough to let her become accustomed to the cold. Her arms grew weary from the effort.

She retrieved rag and soap from her lap, wrapped one in the other and worked a good lather against her breastbone. A mechanical routine took over as familiar movements fell into place, scrubbing paths from bust to fingertips she'd followed thousands of times—though she did have to deviate or retread to account for the unusual volume of filth. Mindlessly going through the motions, her hand paused when it was halfway down her abdomen.

Self-consciousness rushed in. He was watching. Not closely, not *intently,* but his eyes were on her without waver.

Meredith cleared her throat quite pointedly and waited. Four-Thirteen was right there at the corner of her eye, not averting his gaze at all. The cold water made the contrast with the heat on her cheeks all the more noticeable.

"Please look away now," she asked, somewhat strangled.

"Mm?"

Meredith didn't look up to study his expression, but he sounded genuinely confused by the request. "Hm," he concluded with a shrug, and turned his head to one side.

Thoroughly mortified, she rushed to make sure *all* of her was clean. She'd rather endure the sting of this relatively harsh soap than let a simple rinse suffice. Once that business was done she leaned on his hand for support and moved on to her thighs, pulling them out of the water one at a time. It was a laborious and terribly undignified task, but she was well accustomed to indignity.

Copious suds floated free as soon as each leg went back underwater. Meredith fiddled with the soapy rag for a bit before finally offering it up. "My back?"

He looked at it. Four-Thirteen grabbed the soap-rag gracelessly, as though unfamiliar with such a bizarre contraption. Maybe he'd been applying the bars directly on his skin all this time, he was rather new to cleanliness. Meredith leaned forward while keeping her hands latched to the underwater stool. "I'm ready," she quietly prodded him.

He made circular motions on her shoulder blade, building up lather like she had done. His other hand, so rough and heavy, rested on her shoulder more for the sake of his balance than her own. The slow quality of his movements—the sheer *concentration*—was intense enough to be almost comical. It was conscientious, serious work. It was . . . tender.

As the cloth glided on her skin in side-to-side patterns, as his hands covered the small of her back, moved over the bow of her spine, on to her shoulders, and nape, and as he leaned closer for the curves of her neck, for the nook behind her ear and the slight of her throat . . . a number of feelings stirred. Feelings a witch should never feel, unspeakable, abominable. Former Meredith would've pushed them down into a squirming little ball hidden somewhere between her spleen and her liver, never to be touched by conscious thought. The weight of indoctrination would've kept them well suppressed and abhorred.

As she watched the foam float in streaks toward a crack in the wall and disappear into darkness, Current Meredith acknowledged these feelings. She recognized them as real and valid and not particularly heinous. At a different time, in a different life in which she wasn't crippled and bereaved, she might have done something about them.

Here, this night, the path on which she crawled led somewhere else entirely.

"I'd like to do my hair, too. It smells." She looked up at him. "Doesn't it?"

He nodded without reserve.

"Like this." She gathered a floof of suds from his hands and squeezed it on a fat strand of hair, rubbing lightly on her way down. "See?" She did it again to demonstrate. "It's hard for me to reach it all."

He followed her lead with the usual impassiveness, letting her work the rag for extra foam. Methodically he covered every strand from one side of her head to the other, and without prompting he also massaged the lather into her scalp. It was a lovely feeling she'd have enjoyed better if his fingers didn't sometimes catch in the knots that remained.

"Guuh," she voiced her delight.

"Hm," he responded. Actual amusement, a small chuckle. It made Meredith feel safe.

She didn't realize it right away. It took the remainder of the wash and most of the rinse for the notion to fully form. She *wasn't* safe, not while being the most notorious fugitive on the face of Galavan since Faedre the Minder, not while stark naked under a broken ceiling, wholly dependent on a human with the strength to fold her in half twice over.

But she felt safe all the same.

Meredith leaned away from the wall, wiped the water out of her eyes and found his hand. She brought it to her chest, above the heart. Her body was far from elfin, her fingers were strong from decades of gardening, and yet they seemed like thin vines curled around his. She looked up and saw only a quizzical man raising an eyebrow. Not a violent former serf. Not someone to be afraid of.

"They were going to burn me alive," she started. Her voice was only loud enough to climb over the chattering streams. "For being kind to you, for looking after . . . someone else. A young human I took into my home. Janette. Did you ever see her?"

Four-Thirteen nodded. Of course he had.

"She was full of spark. At first I only wanted to use her, but . . . something changed. We grew so close, and I came to feel this—this *need* I can't describe. To care for her, to see her safe. I'd never felt anything like it.

"So I kept her with me. I could've saved her, I had so much time. But I was selfish."

The water seemed to get colder as she spoke. Meredith's shiver reached down to her bones.

"They devoured her while I watched. I will never forgive them. Never."

His expression darkened. The cold got to her all at once, she was shaking. Without waiting for an explicit request Four-Thirteen braced her legs and back, lifted her out of the water and waded to the tiled shore. Curled up and pressed to his chest, Meredith once more endured all her aches with grim acceptance.

"You're right," she whispered to him. "Sitting in that cell, I realised the same as you have. We're surrounded by monsters. All witches must die."

He stopped and looked down at her, grave, almost ceremonial. "Yes," he growled, slowly nodding like her words were a fundamental truth of existence. With delicate care he set her down by the dresser and wasted no time to fetch the giant towel from the bag. There was a sense of urgency in the way he wrapped her in it. She held it close to her body and worked to regulate her breathing while he walked off again, toward the Meredith-puppet standing by the corner. He came back with the thick robe and immediately draped it around her shoulders.

"I know how we can destroy them," Meredith said through chattering teeth. "And I know someone who will help us do it."

Now she'd captured his attention. His hands had stopped moving. His eyes were wide and intent.

"But we'll have to hurry."

There is someone imprisoned in the Tower dungeon, she told him. She knows how to reach Faedre the Minder, and you know who that is, don't you? The Judicar turncoat who led the human rebellions. I've talked to her, Meredith told him, she still lives. She wants nothing more than to end human serfdom, whatever the cost.

With her help and our trinkets (*our* trinkets) we can destroy the Yanwar Harvest Plants. Galavan cannot survive without them, the furnaces will die, the nodework will collapse and the realm will be crushed into the Hollow. I know this, she told him, because my sister was the Head of the Coven, and she said as much. The dwindling spark supply has been a long-coming crisis.

We need to get to that prisoner, she told him. We won't be able to enter and destroy the plants without Faedre.

And Four-Thirteen was eager to help her.

WITHIN A JAR floating in simmering water inside a hollowed-out golem head, berthpit oil was slowly instilled with all the whittlenut and gramrout Meredith could afford to toss in. *Complacency of the Learned* had finally proved useful by kindling the fire, which was facilitated by the kitchen firestarter Four-Thirteen had brought. The golem head hung over the bonfire by an improvised contraption of metal bars and wire hangers—the wire cutters she'd found tucked in the same pocket where she'd left them sure had been handy for the task. The fumes would rise to the ceiling and percolate through a thousand cracks to go clog somewhere else.

Still wrapped in robe and towel, hair thoroughly brushed and pulled back into a tight ponytail, Meredith watched over the instillment as if it could combust without warning. Too much heat, and it would. For his part, Four-Thirteen seemed fascinated. He sat forward on the creakiest chair to ever exist, closely watching as the gramrout flakes released eddies of blue into the oil.

"If it starts making tiny bubbles, you made it too hot," she continued explaining. "Don't let it do that or it'll boil away the active reagents. If I do this right, the chanted gramrout will take all the pain away, and the whittlenut will repair the tissue within a span. All scathe undone."

She might've embellished the healing properties just a mite. It wasn't *impossible* for the salve to be so effective so quickly, only . . . extremely improbable. She did expect the chanted gramrout to let her function until the mission was done.

Meredith shifted in place, trying in vain to get comfortable. Even though she knelt on the plush pile of rugs they'd pulled back to make room for the fire—well, Four-Thirteen had pulled them back—her knees still loudly protested their new role as substitute feet. As long as she didn't put pressure on the burns, all the pains merged into a variety of bother she could almost ignore. "We must wait until the shavings are brown all the way through," she said. "It'll be about another quarter span. You don't have to stay close if you don't feel like it, I won't need your help until then."

Four-Thirteen seemed content to watch it happen from start to end. She gave him a sidelong glance. "It's a good thing I'll be walking again soon, since . . . I'll need to talk to the prisoner alone."

He didn't react. He was watching the water simmer like it was a troupe of trained duds dancing on Devalen's Green. Admittedly, she'd said it in a murmur without meaning to.

She tapped his arm. He mildly startled. "Hm?"

"I said, um . . . I've– I've been wondering if there's a name I can call you. The number seems wrong. Doesn't it?"

He stared blankly before writing his response.

I have no other name

"Well, I think you should. You could pick any name you want, a proper name. Besides . . . if we make it through all this, we'll have to live on Earth. Every man has a name."

He very seriously considered her words.

I don't know any man names

"Oh."

Come to think of it, neither did she.

That's not true, her memory chimed in, and one after another rose names she'd heard during her time with Janette—names in the lyrics of songs they'd listened to, names in all the stories from Earth she'd shared. Meredith suggested them as they came, even the ones that didn't strike her as appropriate for a man of his presence and stature. How about Stephen?

Drew? Cory? John? Timmagraw? Don't give me that face, it's a real name, I've heard it.

Romeo is good. There are songs about it. No? Alright.

Mmm . . . Crisprat is popular, I'm told. Yeah, I don't like it either.

How about Spiderman? It has *man* built in already, very straight-forward. No?

Oh, I know. Ford. Short for Four-Thirteen.

"Fo-oh," he tried to say. He didn't look convinced. He was right, it was more a nickname based on his number than an actual name. It defeated the purpose.

Edmund. Peter. Rincewind. Gandalf. Frodo. Sam. Elend—

"Sam," Four-Thirteen interrupted. "Sam," he repeated.

"Sam?"

He said it a few more times and smacked his lips around the sound like he was trying to tease out the syllable's flavor. It was the silliest expression Meredith had ever seen from him. "Sam," he concluded with some satisfaction.

Was being able to pronounce it the whole reason he liked it?

"Alright, well. Sam it is." She mock-curtsied as well as she could while on her knees and in a towel. "Charmed meeting you, Sam."

"Pff," he responded, and got up from the chair. He went to the shelves and brought back the bowl of dried apple slices. His jaw already moved with shallow crunches when he sat again and offered the bowl to her.

Meredith took some out of politeness and chewed them one by one, glad to have an excuse to quietly ponder her next words. She longed to plop down onto the rugs and relax for a few meager cents, but she was too paranoid to take her eyes off the fire-brewed instillment.

While eating, Four-Thirteen . . . Sam . . . would tilt his head this way and that, directing the cud in his mouth by the only means he could.

"Sam," she began, and he paid attention to her this time. "This prisoner in the Tower . . . she can't know you're with me. She's a Circle forewitch, she wants you dead. I have to talk to her alone."

His chewing slowed and paused. It resumed. It paused again. "Hm."

She couldn't tell if it was a thoughtful *Hm* or a displeased *Hm*.

"In fact, I'll need to take her somewhere, and she can't see you at any point. I'll need to leave with her. Do you understand? Otherwise she won't help us."

After a good stretch of pensive staring and intermittent chewing, he tilted his head back and swallowed. He didn't eat any more slices.

"So, I'm asking . . . I'm asking you to let me do that."

Four-Thirteen frowned at that—Sam. He was Sam, now. He picked up pen and notebook again.

you alone very risky

"Yes, right, you're right. So I'll need tools. I'll need . . . you know. My trinkets. Otherwise I'll be defenceless if someone tries to stop me."

He looked over at the big desk, where girdle and dais and gauntlet lay. "Hm."

"I'm sorry to ask so much. We don't have a choice. This must happen tonight, or we'll lose our chance."

He sat back, eyes fixed on the items.

"There's no telling what all the outsiders flocking in will do with the Tower if we wait. I can go in unnoticed and fly off with her before anyone knows about it. And if there are guards, the gauntlet will let me deal with them without much trouble."

Four-Thir—Sam reached for the pen again.

I must think about all

The words to keep pushing the issue came to her, but Meredith held her tongue. The last thing she wanted was to be perceived as making demands . . . even if a significant part of her was rather fuffled at having to beg for her own artifacts.

The proceeding silence floated above running rainwater, it wrapped around the crack and crumple of flame-wreathed wood. The oil had tinted to a shimmery cerulean. The whittlenut root had browned considerably. As she resumed her watch over the nearly-done instillment, more sensible thoughts suggested all her artifacts would've been lost forever if it weren't for him. In fact, they'd be in Judicar custody. What a tragedy that would've been.

"Janette built that gauntlet. Did you know?"

Sam shook his head in very small movements.

"She was obsessed with the concept, I don't know why. She latched onto the pusher in *Basics of Artificing* and I couldn't keep up. I would barely know how it works if she hadn't kept all those notes. She was . . . she was so dedicated. And now. . . ."

She trailed off with a sigh. He was writing a new question.

she was a dedicated witch?

There was something foreboding about the curl of his scrawl and the shift of his frown. If Janette had been in the room, Meredith would have stepped in front of her.

"Not like *that*, she was no Galavan witch. I lied to her every single day. She would have wept if I'd told her the truth of this place. She would've wept to know your story, or that of any other serf."

Her bearing must've been more intense than she realized, because he brought up his hands in a conciliatory gesture. Indeed, she had to lean back from her forward stance and relax her clenched fists.

"Sorry. I'm sorry. I suppose I grew . . . protective . . . over her. Only too late. I think it's ready for decanting, will you help me?"

"Mm." Sam stood and hovered next to her.

"Please fetch me the red blouse."

Meredith moved the jar half-full of gambi sap to a convenient spot by the cushion. One of the blouses Sam had sacked—too small and too red for her to wear—was one-hundred-percent devilstrand weave, which was an ideal substitute for the fine-mesh colander in her defunct basement.

"I'm going to stretch the cloth over the jar. I want you to *very slowly* pour the mix onto the centre. You can still make out the opening, see? Right there. Make sure the oil doesn't get on your fingers, they'll go numb and you'll break out in hives for days. And don't forget to use mittens, it's hot."

She would've much rather been the one pouring, but she didn't trust herself to hold the weight steady in her current state. She watched him closely as he used a rag to pull the fat jar out of the simmering water and hold it over the blouse. He bent down opposite to her. She nodded.

"The mush will want to come out all at once," she warned as he began to tip it over, "go very slow so it doesn't splash everywhere."

A thin stream poured down, pooled briefly and dripped through into the jar. A sizzling whisper floated up as sap and instilled oil reacted together. The smell was syrupy sweet—sweeter still than fresh-cut gramrout leaves.

"A bit more. Gently. . . ."

The oily flake-and-shavings mixture dropped onto the blouse in wet plops. Scented waves of heat bloomed to Meredith's lips, brushed up to her cheeks. Gradually the jar tipped over until the stream became a drip that eventually stopped.

"Good. That's good. You can put it down. Be careful with the dregs."

She let it drain through on its own for a while. Very meticulously she puckered the fabric into a drooping pouch, always keeping the goop above the sizzling jar. "Now hold this up and don't move."

For lack of rubber gloves she used two broken boards to squeeze the pouch until no more oil oozed through. The golden sap and cerulean instillment were frothing together into a green lather that would quickly settle once stirred.

She reached for the nearby spoon. Meredith could flop down on the rugs at last. "The oil is a fel agent," she explained while stirring. "It's full of active elements, far too lively to be of use. You want to tame it with a mol agent, like this sap. Together they'll bond into a nice lotion."

It was fascinating to watch the froth smooth over and blend together. This was the real artisanal stuff, none of that highly processed cookery where equipment did all the work, or those fancy overpriced concoctions wealthy crones could simply pick off the shelves and forget all about the genuine. . . .

Her spoon hand slowed to a stop. She blinked several times. Only then did it occur to her she could've simply asked Four-Thirteen to bring *the salve itself*. Burns were common among alchemists and artificers. Plenty of ready-made balms on apothecary shelves, no need for all this time-consuming work.

She could've been on her way to the Tower by then.

"Piddle sideways on a shrub. . . ."

"Mm?"

Meredith glanced up and shook her head. "Nothing. Everything's fine. This is almost done, only needs to cool off now. It won't take long."

It better cool fast and work faster, because a new, deeply stressful urge was growing at the top of her bladder. She would *not* be asking for help on that front. There was a limit to how much humiliation she was willing to endure in one night.

"We might as well tidy up and put out the fire."

Sam crammed the gooped blouse inside the instillment jar and screwed the lid on, dumped the water on the fire—the resulting smoke had Meredith coughing for a while—dismantled the bars-and-wire tripod thing they'd rigged, gathered it all in a messy pile by his chair.

Meredith nudged the containers and the golem head so they'd all line up properly and ensured the metal bars were laid out in a tidy cluster. A fair distribution of labor. She was so preoccupied triple-checking the bars were perfectly parallel to one another that she didn't notice Sam's writing until he'd moved the notebook under her nose.

do you trust prisoner, witch

He looked particularly serious. Meredith considered the question.

"She tried to rescue me before you did. So . . . yes, I trust her, she'll help. As long as she doesn't know you're around."

"Hm."

More scribbles.

why need help?

we attack and destroy plants

no faedre

He gestured at the artifacts on the table like they were the solution to every one of his witch-shaped problems.

"I've never been there. It's not as simple as toppling the building, and there'll be magical wards. And without her we won't be able to escape afterwards. I don't have much to live for, but still I'd rather not die at the end of this."

Sam was thoughtful for a while. His head tilted inquisitively over the paper once he was writing again.

why do faedre need us?

Good question.

Yes, good question.

"She's been hiding for a very long time. Working in the shadows, recovering from all the terrible things that happened after she failed to bring down the system. That tome on the floor, the human rebellions—have you read it?"

He nodded, but qualified it with an ambiguous shrug. Skimmed it well enough to know how to spell Faedre's name, Meredith figured.

"Things are oppressive now, but not as much as they used to be. What little you saw, trying to get you to Earth? That's as far as the Circle can go without being destroyed. My sister was well aware of them. If they'd tried what we're up to right now, they would've been crushed. But now it's all different, with all the chaos up there, the Council in upheaval. Now is our chance, and we have the firepower to try, Faedre will jump in and give us the help we need, I know it."

The answer sounded disjointed and rambling even to her own ears. Sam took it in without further questioning, once more falling into a brooding silence.

Meredith blew out a tired breath. The pot full of creamy green had cooled to lukewarm. It was time.

With painstaking care she leaned back and shifted around until her legs were loosely crossed, feet easily accessible. She also made sure her back was turned from prying eyes, because she was still wrapped in a towel and the arrangement was precarious at best.

"This better work. . . ."

"Hm?"

"I said, I can't wait for this to work its magic. I'll finally be back on my feet."

She scooped out a dollop. Immediately her fingers tingled, but they'd be fine as long as she didn't leave it on for long. As gentle as cloud-tattered moonlight she smoothed it onto the ball of her foot and spread it toward the heel. The slight pressure on the wounds was instantly regrettable, but the pain allayed quickly once she was no longer touching the worst of it. The blisters were numerous, but they were small, and none of them were open. The salve cleared to a white sheen as she spread it on blotchy skin.

Once she'd treated the entire foot, she straightened the leg and brought up the other. This one was worse, with the big toe ballooning above the joint in a peculiar way and most of the midfoot swollen with inflammation. Meredith slathered it on thick to the whole mess. All through the process, her breath would come in tremulous bursts whenever she remembered not to hold it.

She'd worked up a cold sweat by the time she was done. It only took a tiny bit longer to cover the burn lines on her legs, which hardly warranted a whimper in comparison.

Her shoulders were tense as taut ropes by the time she thoroughly wiped her hands clean with Sam's rag. Already it felt like there was a difference down there, thank the furies. It was tender and tingly, a subdued reprise of the underwater pin-stabs from earlier—but it was also becoming . . . distant. Not so overwhelmingly immediate.

Meredith leaned back on her hands and closed her eyes. There was nothing to do now but wait.

Shortly after she felt a tap on her shoulder, and a flopping notebook followed. Meredith took it.

it is working?

She nodded, though she didn't try to hide the pain just yet. Best not to oversell it. "It needs some time, but yeah. I'll be ready to go within a span."

Not even a lie. She'd be ready to go whether the salve was effective or not.

She passed the notebook back. It didn't return. Time crawled forward in the rain-soothed calm of Sam's lair, deep breaths and stray thoughts lulling her into a rarefied sense of normalcy. Desmond bumped behind his door a few times, just to remind them he was there and very displeased at being excluded.

Eventually what used to be a raw scald in Meredith's feet became a mere sting, a smarting prickle that no longer throbbed. Wholly ignorable, with the right distractions. The gnaw of impatience already goaded her to stand and test her balance, but she held it in check.

"I'm ready to wrap my feet. Mind fetching the gauze and bandages?"

He didn't mind. Meredith scooted over to the chair and he helped
her up in the usual underarms-as-handles manner. Sam held the
items in hand and stood there, by all accounts ready to do the
wrapping himself.

"First," she instructed, "soak a strip of gauze into the salve. Not
too much, just make sure it's sticky with it. Don't worry about the
tingle in your fingers, it won't last after you wash it off."

She watched him do it. Meredith ensured robe and towel covered
every sensitive body part before extending her right leg.

"Now plaster it on. It's already numb, no need to be wary."

He was careful anyway, only applying the bare minimum of
pressure necessary. Her brow twitched, but her breath didn't shift or
catch. When he looked up, her expression was perfectly calm.

"Good. Now the bandage. Start above the ankle and go 'round and
'round down to the toes, then back again so you can tie it. Don't let it
slack, but don't make it *too* tight. . . ."

She trailed off, because he'd started before she was halfway
through the sentence. "You, uh . . . you seem to know what you're
doing."

"Hm."

His fingers were a bit clumsy, but progress was steady and
seamless down her foot. He even kept it light at the joint so it
wouldn't bunch up over time. As the pressure built on her skin,
Meredith's teeth remained unclenched. Her lips squirmed only for a
heartbeat before she got them under control. At least the swelling
had gone down considerably, she'd been afraid the boots wouldn't
even fit anymore.

He repeated the process with the left foot, and there was no
question this one was worse, but still she kept her throat quiet and
her face straight. It was manageable, she was fine, it would be fine.

"That's a fine job," she said. "Thank you."

"Hm," Sam nodded.

"I'll let this settle for a while." She smiled cordially. "You might
want to take care of Desmond. He'll *literally* waste away if you don't
feed him every single span, you know."

She was proud of her composure, relaxed by any measure. The
suggestion was casual and reasonable. She was certain none of her
intentions showed through.

Sam shrugged, grabbed the glowstone and the shelved sack of oats
and went into the lopsided wash room. Excited squeals soon
followed.

Her gaze fixed on the desk and the trinkets resting upon it.
Everything she needed, unattended. Would she have time to pull it
off? The door to the washroom was open, but he was out of sight.

There would be no better chance.

One antsy leg moved to lay a foot flat on the floor, wary like stepping on thorns. The pins and needles were indeed there, but now they prickled through a thick layer of gramrout-padded cotton. With both feet planted she death-gripped the armrests, took a deep breath, engaged her core muscles and pushed herself to stand.

The swell of pain was a muffled scream from a shallow grave, present and bothersome but ignorable with the right mindset. She tested a step, then two and three. It remained a dull bother, a voice that insisted *this is bad and shouldn't be happening,* but her feet kept her upright. The numbness felt like walking on stilts. Her toes were as glued-on pebbles.

A few steps later she was leaning on the table, panting. Her fingertips followed the grooves on the gauntlet mitts, grazed over the elegant little sigil on the backhand plate, the same sigil that adorned every Council signet. Jane hadn't known what it truly represented, of course. She'd just thought it "looked cool."

She slipped a hand in, wiggled and adjusted the mesh. It fit like it had been custom-built for her.

Meredith depressed the backhand sigil, and sparkflow hummed through the gauntlet in celeste patterns. The charge gauge beamed up to a dash over half. She adjusted the area dials at the wrist for a concentrated blast and flipped the little switch by the thumb joint from *grab* through ♥*auto*♥ to *push.*

Intermittent clatter came through the doorway now and then. Meredith steeled her resolve. Fairness didn't matter, gratitude didn't matter. She couldn't leave Janette's rescue at the whim of a cold-blooded stalker and mass murderer.

She only needed to call his name, put some stress in her voice. Make it urgent. He'd rush in to help without suspicion.

He trusted her.

"Sam."

It came out as a hoarse mutter, hardly loud enough. She looked at her gauntlet-clad hand, glanced at the door. Go on, she goaded herself. This is how it must be, this is the price of freedom. You told yourself you'd do anything. You said you'd stop at nothing.

Call him true. Do it.

Violently betray the man who saved you from burning.

The thought shut her eyes, turned her head to one side. A ball of disgust curdled in her throat.

Do it. Do it. Do it. If you let scruples stand in the way now, how can you hope to make it all the way to the end?

Meredith looked at the gauntlet once more. She took a trembling breath.

In slow, quiet movements she freed her hand from Janette's creation and reverently laid it to rest back on the desk. Sparkflow automatically ceased and dimmed, as if disappointed.

By the time she reached the threshold to the washroom she'd composed her features back to normal. Sam stood by the dresser, tossing a golem's severed arm for Desmond to go fetch over and over again.

She watched. Desmond had never fetched a thing for her in his life, playing or otherwise. Janette had taught him to do it.

"Sam."

He looked over with raised eyebrows, body tense like he would jump to her side at a moment's notice. She stepped in and leaned against the door, keeping it wide open. Anxiety was throwing its usual fit inside her chest, always so wary of confrontation, always so vexing and weak.

"I need to get dressed," Meredith said in spite of it. "I have to go."

He gave her the once-over and pursed his lips. After one long breath, he crossed his arms.

"I can't sit here knowing every mite I waste could mean failure. You know what I have to do. It's time I do it."

"Hrm."

He kept looking to one side, mouth twitching with his thoughts. Desmond sat by the golem arm and snorted. He was thoroughly ignored.

Meredith had made her choice.

"You know I can't fight you," she said. "But if you want to stop me . . . you'll have to hurt me."

Sam shook his head in exaggerated movements, raised a finger as if to say *wait a moment* and strode toward her. The spike of alarm at his approach felt rather silly when he simply blew past her into the main room.

It didn't take long for him to return with his notebook. He handed it over.

very chaos up in city
many fly everywhere

"Oh. Well, then . . . all the better, yeah? I won't stand out, just another witch up there."

He nabbed the thing off her hands like it could poison her. The scribbles were urgent.

your face everywhere
you must hide

"Y– yes, of course. I don't plan to talk to anyone, I won't get close to anyone. I only meant it'll be easier to blend in at a distance if I have to. If you'll remember, I've some experience sneaking around."

Sam didn't seem so convinced. He spent a good long while on his next message, glancing up often and puffing out reluctant breaths.

Over the burbling sounds of the pond came the stroke of his pen, drawn out as if it was a painful ordeal to shape each letter.

Meredith didn't shift on her feet even once.

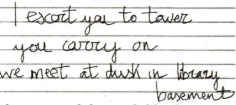

She processed the words like they were of no greater consequence. Like she hadn't been coiled with nerves she'd forever missed her chance at freedom.

"Yes . . . yes, we can do that. Although I think it should be elsewhere, in case they're already looking for me. They'll search the places I'm known to visit. How about. . . ." She tapped her lips with her fingers. "How about the old cemetery? There's a big monument to Tremmel right at its centre. It should be safe."

"Hm," Sam said. And then, "yes."

"Good, yes. At dusk. I'll be there. Well, I'll do everything I can to be there. You know how things can get . . . complicated."

He nodded and wrote.

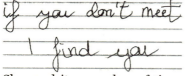

She read it a number of times and looked back at his impassive features. She was almost certain it wasn't a threat.

"I'm sure it won't come to that." She pushed herself off the door, head up, shoulders straight and feet steady on the lopsided floor. She didn't need to *feel* confident, she only needed to look the part. "I'll get dressed, now."

He shook his head again and made a big show of a long, resigned sigh.

"I hepp?" he finally offered.

"No, I can do it. I can fend for myself now. Thanks to you."

His grunt seemed doubtful, but he ended up nodding. Sam turned and left her alone with Desmond—who ran after the man before she could push the door closed. The golem arm clanked against the frame as he passed.

She gave herself a moment by the door, one brief moment to breathe and relieve the tension seizing her lungs. Why did everything have to be difficult all the time?

Conscious that Sam might be listening, she got busy without further delay. Meredith surveyed the room and every item in it, planning an itinerary for the most efficient path possible. The sack full of clothes, the golem effigy, the dresser and its mirror. Was there nowhere to sit around here? The floor would have to do.

At least Desmond was in good hands. They'd keep each other company. Too bad he didn't stay in the room with her, she'd wanted to say a proper goodbye to the little fellow. She'd never see him again after leaving this place.

As she pawed through the pile of clothes for a comfortable outfit, Meredith worked to shield her mind against woe and chunter, doubt and regret. This was the final ordeal, it had already begun. It would be a long time until she could rest.

No more complaints until it was done.

CHAPTER THIRTY

✵

SALVATION

ET'S HOPE NO-ONE HEARS THIS," Meredith muttered. She pointed the index mitt-finger at the stump where the door handle used to be, thumbed the hinge on the outer mitt-finger to adjust the power of the push, held her breath real tight and quickly released her thumb-hold.

The appropriate wordpaths in the gauntlet flashed from a muted glow to an icy neon, and the jolt brought back the memory of a revolver nearly snapping out of her hand. The push-blast struck the ancient door and threw it open; the metal slab screamed on its hinges, slammed against whatever doorstop there was and bounced back in a vibrating shriek.

The threshold had puffed with enough dust to choke a nation. Meredith stepped back, watching the door whine to a half-open stop.

"I suppose someone might have heard it."

Sam skulked into the dark, knife in hand and kerchief over his nose. It didn't seem cautious to Meredith, she'd rather have waited and listened, but he advocated for a more proactive approach. Hopefully he wouldn't trip on anything.

This was supposed to be the way into the Tower dungeon. Sam's homemade map said so, and who was she to argue? Galvan Tower was one of the few remnants from before Sabrena's Rift, and so it extended many levels underground. The door, grooved in squares and as grey as the stone walls around it, was indeed squat with the weight of centuries.

She waited in restless silence as billows of dust settled under the glowstone hanging from her neck. The gauntlet was an unfamiliar encumbrance on her hand, she kept wanting to fiddle with its dials and switches. Instead, Meredith depressed the sigil on the backhand plate to disengage sparkflow, because conserving even the tiniest idling trickle might matter by the time the day was done. The glowing patterns died to a steely black.

Sam's frame blackened the doorway. He nodded his all-clear go-ahead.

The room was an L-shaped hall crammed tight with empty cages, of the kind that might fit one body inside if squeezed hard enough. Tangles of chains and leashes hung from pegs along the walls. The stink of metal and rust burned in Meredith's nostrils as she followed the cluttered pathway and rounded the corner.

Against the far wall stood a ladder, and atop the ladder, a trap door. After briefly considering the issue, Sam made a fist at it.

"Boom," he said while opening his hand.

She raised an eyebrow at him. "We should see if it budges, first. I'd rather not make more noise."

He grunted and pointed all around the seams. No latch, no handle, no hinges. It didn't open from below. He mounted the ladder anyway, one dull shudder and puff of dust for every rung climbed. Upon reaching the ceiling door he pushed with one hand, pried at the seam, banged once, twice—

A crack like a log snapping in half, and *something* speared from above to stop one fingerbreadth away from his cheek. It hung there for an instant full of clattering metal and shattering glass—one instant for him to half-jump, half-fall out of the way before the trap door gave altogether.

They stumbled away as a steel-legged cabinet toppled through, shrouded in debris and followed by a deafening stream of pots, containers, beakers and jars. The drawers and cupboards burst open on impact, vomiting scales and spoons and miscellaneous alchemy supplies all over the floor. A strong and self-reliant plate, determined to survive, rolled in wobbles from the mess and came to bump against Meredith's foot.

The racket didn't completely die down for a good half-cent.

"Well . . . maybe there's no-one around to hear."

"Hm."

"You're not hurt, are you?"

Sam shook his head. The trap door had become a jagged black square on the ceiling. No dust rained down from it, surprisingly enough. He trod on the debris to get back on the ladder, but not before giving the gaping hole a wary look.

"They probably covered the door with shelves centuries ago and forgot all about it."

"Hm."

He reached the top and pulled himself into the gap. It might as well have been a portal to an Old Yanwar mass grave, because not even footsteps could be heard anymore. The restored stillness became oppressive in record time.

Eyeing the ladder with a healthy dose of dread, Meredith unclasped the gauntlet's wrist-guard, wiggled her fingers out of it and clipped it to the belt of her crossbow holster—one *could* grip things while wearing it, but it seemed . . . disrespectful. She tip-toed around the mess and held on to the ancient iron bars; she allowed herself one shaky deep breath before placing a foot on the first rung and beginning her climb. She was glad Sam wasn't there to see her eyes squeezed shut and her mouth puckered in a squirm. There was only so much salve plus padding plus boots could do for her feet.

She'd erased from her face every sign of strain by the time her head poked through the breach. A hand materialized in front of her and helped her up.

Another room full of clutter, shelves packed with a hundred different shapes, paraphernalia as worn and obsolete as the thousand steam pipes rusting all over Brena. Not one mote of dust clung to any of it, here, which meant the cleaning drones patrolled it regularly. The exit by the corner was wide open to an amber-lit hallway.

"That looks familiar," Meredith whispered.

It felt silly to creep to the door after thundering their way in, but they did it regardless. The hall was as old-fashioned-dungeon as it came, with chipped stone walls and centuries-worn cobbles. The only noticeable upgrade from ancient times were the electric bulbs in the once-upon-a-time oil lamp sconces, all properly screened so they'd give off the appropriate seedy candlelight glow. The room appeared to be at the bottom of a dead-end.

"Looks deserted."

He nodded, and seemed about to venture out, but Meredith laid a hand on his arm. "I can find my way from here," she said.

He frowned.

"Sam, she could be in any one of those rooms, and she might be out of stasis. This mission is over if she sees you."

He scanned the hallway once more and looked back at her. Sam gestured a message simple enough to understand: you go ahead, I watch from behind.

"But . . . that's not what we planned."

Sam shrugged and made the exact same gestures again.

"It truly won't work. I can't have you charging from behind the corner if it gets difficult. It could ruin everything."

"Ghmmh," he grunted in stubborn reluctance.

Meredith was halfway to a scowl, but it transitioned to a lopsided smile. Her hands slipped under his arms, around his chest. One careful step later she rested her chin on his shoulder, mindful not to let her hat bop his face. Her fingers met at his shoulder blades, and she squeezed tightly, without reserve.

Sam's confusion was present in his every muscle, but it wasn't long until his arms wrapped her in a tentative embrace. A few breaths later, he was actually squeezing back.

"I'm saying goodbye." She pulled back and looked up into his eyes. "You need to trust I'll be able to take care of myself. I rescued *you* first, remember?"

He groaned, but didn't let go. It was only a heartbeat of close eye contact, but it was everything her guilt needed to surge like bile up her throat. A confession pushed against her teeth, battled to spill out of her lips. There was a chance he'd want to help even while knowing the truth. There was a *good* chance he would let her go, regardless.

But Janette's life was at stake. *A good chance* was not good enough.

Meredith eased her embrace to clasp his arms with encouragement. "Meet me at the cemetery like we planned," she said. "I promise I'll be there," she lied.

Caught up in the moment, they didn't notice the little sphere that quietly rolled by their feet and into the room. The trigger was a droning whisper that gave Meredith only enough time to look down and wonder, *what's that sound?*

A pressure-cooker hiss enveloped them, a rush of wind that stole their breath in an instant and pushed it out of the room. Meredith's chest seized after her last exhale, no longer able to expand. All the air around them had been replaced by mouthfuls of panic.

They reeled away from one another, one hand to their respective breastbones, looking everywhere in a struggle to understand. Meredith's eyes felt like they would soon pop out of the sockets. She was choking in a vacuum.

She spotted the glowing artifact hovering off the floor. Some kind of suffocating trap. It had come from the hallway. She kicked at it, but her foot slid around its surface as though space itself disallowed her boot from going there. The resulting shuffle to keep her balance was a harsh reminder of her burns and a disastrous setback for her sudden need of oxygen.

Sam appeared utterly dumbfounded, back thrashing into a shelf, mouth agape in desperation. A trap like this would have a maximum range. *Get away from it,* she tried to say, but the croak that rustled in her throat found no air to propagate through. Already lightheaded, Meredith threw herself through the doorway in an attempt to get out of the area of effect before—

Wham!

Sparks gushed all over as she slammed hat-first into the barrier sealing the exit. She bounced back and collapsed on her behind, all of it eerily silent from within the vacuum; her battered ribs stabbed inwards, the dais harness painfully dug into her kidneys. Her vision was bloodshot and swarming with stars as her lungs filled with needles. Past the sparks and the roiling distortion, a figure now stood in the hallway, and it was pointing some kind of weapon at her.

Meredith recoiled in a mad scramble, enfeebled by the stifling clutch of suffocation. The gauntlet, use the gauntlet. Her fingers scratched and scrawled into the wrist guard, struggled to unclip the blasted clasp from the belt. Pressure built inside her skull with every heartbeat. Two nights and a day went by as she wiggled each finger to its proper place, all while her ribcage shriveled to the size of a dried plum.

She aimed at the wall to make an opening, but realized it wouldn't help unless she also jumped through to get far enough. Pushing or grabbing at the trap itself was useless while its warp field protected it. She aimed down, set her jaw, and hoped no bones would snap when she landed on—

Whoooosh!

The vacuum broke with a torrent of wind, and the influx of air scattered the frantic plan from her thoughts—along with anything unrelated to *breathe a lot right now*. She choked hard and spent time she didn't have coughing and thrashing on the floor, but still she strove to roll onto her side, on all fours, grab onto a shelf and get up to face whoever had—

"I thought it was you as soon as I saw that stupid hat. I can't seem to be done with you."

Her eyes would have widened if she weren't busy keeping her lungs inside her chest. Sam was similarly hacking, crumpled on the floor. The voice was familiar but just beyond the point of recognition. Meredith's vision was far too blurry to make out the features of the witch now standing in the doorway.

"I don't think you could've made more noise if you'd tried," the near-stranger said. "I almost killed you. I would've felt bad."

The pitch was different, but something about the cadence, the terse tone. . . .

"Wybel?" she managed to ask between coughs.

"Used to be. Last I knew, we failed to rescue you. How are you not dead?"

"I . . . keep wondering that . . . myself. . . ."

"That's a nasty lisp. Your new friend, is he going to be a problem?"

Meredith scrambled to make peace with the fact she'd almost died—what was one more time, at this point?—and adapt to the new development. Yes, Sam *might* be a problem. She stumbled toward him, slowly getting over the bout of choking. He was wheezing by a toppled shelf.

"Sam, are you alright? Are you hurt?"

He shook his head, which could answer both questions at once. Through the corner of his eye he was already staring at the newcomer. His scowl was foreboding and not at all friendly.

"She's on our side. Do you understand? Don't do anything rash, this is good, she'll help us."

"That's to be decided." Her weapon, a familiar handgun, disappeared into her cloak as she stepped in and closed the door. "Why are you here?"

Meredith hovered over Sam, perhaps a bit more attentive than she needed to be. It gave her some time to consider her answer.

"Same reason you are. I'm rescuing Silver before it's too late."

Wybel sniffed. "And why would you do that?"

Still blinking tears away, Meredith offered Sam a hand, but he waved it off. With some effort he clambered to his feet, eyes never leaving the old witch. For her part, Meredith made sure not to put any special emphasis on any one word.

"I need to speak with Faedre," she said, and very consciously moved between man and renegade crone. "Only Silver knows where I can find her."

There wasn't much of a reaction. Meredith could finally take a clear look at her former best friend in all of Galavan. This witch barely looked anything like Wybel: gone were the stylish robes, and the short stature, and the baldness—replaced by a leather cloak, thick-soled boots, black curls under hood and mask. Even her eyes, permanently squinted and circled by lines before, were now a lively gray that could've passed for youthful.

Or maybe . . . yes, that was it. She had eyebrows now, carefully painted. They made quite the difference.

She balled a fist on her waist. "And what makes you think Faedre wants anything to do with you?"

Meredith deliberately glanced to the side. Sam couldn't see it. "That's between her and me alone."

"I see." Wybel tilted her head toward the brooding man. "You weren't going to let Silver see him, were you? She would've flipped out."

Sam growled the way he might have at Devalka's antics. Meredith assumed *flipping out* was a terrible thing nobody should ever do.

"No," she said, "in fact, we were saying our farewells. Which you interrupted."

"Pfah, be glad it was me and not the two Judicars that stayed behind. I heard you from two floors up."

"Shouldn't we be worrying about them?"

"No. Not anymore."

"Oh."

Sam stood close enough for his chest to bump against her shoulder. She turned to address him.

"Sam. Sam, look at me." His glare at Wybel remained just as hostile. Meredith had to actually prod him with a pointy mitt-finger for him to dip his gaze. "She wasn't trying to kill us. She didn't know it was me. You should be happy about this, I'm not going by myself anymore, she'll be helping now." She looked over her shoulder. "Right?"

"Sure. As long as you stop wasting time."

"Yes, of course. I have to go." She unclasped the glowstone chain from her neck and cradled it in his hand. With barely a thought she stepped in and planted a kiss on his cheek. He seemed utterly befuddled by it.

Meredith adjusted her hat, cheeks hot and toes tingling. "We'll meet tonight, like we planned." She back-paced until she was ushering Wybel toward the door. "Wary's worth until then."

They went out into the hallway.

The door shut.

They stared at it for longer than they could afford. No sound came, nothing changed.

"I better seal it," Wybel whispered. She seemed actually concerned. Meredith caught her arm.

"No need. I'd rather trust him." Her voice was a bit louder— maybe just loud enough to be heard through a single door.

"And I'd rather 'Sam' didn't stick a knife in my skull."

"He won't do that. He saved my life. We're working together."

"Am I supposed to take—"

Something clicked and rasped around the corner. Wybel's gun was out and ready to fire in the span of Meredith's gasp.

A brush flashed at the bend, followed by a revolving arm, followed by the squat bulk of a cleaning drone. It detected the sudden lack of wall and turned into the dead-end hallway, scrubbing all over the fat plinths as it went.

Wybel lowered her weapon, but stayed focused on the golem. Once it was within reach, she kicked its stubby little dome.

"Off with you," she said. The golem recoiled in apparent confusion. A sensor flashed red onto their boots. The creature crossed over to the other side of the hallway and resumed scrubbing back toward the intersection.

Meredith raised an eyebrow at her.

"It would've gone into the room," Wybel explained. "I don't want your friend to get startled." After one last look at the door, she tilted her head as if to say *let's go* and started walking. She made no effort to hug the walls, but kept her steps soft and her voice low. "What were you doing in that closet?"

Meredith scrambled to follow and adjust to the abrupt switch in dynamic. "We opened a back door into the dungeon."

"No you didn't. You can't portal into this place."

"No, I meant an actual door. From Brena Below."

"Huh." She looked both sides before turning left. Meredith grabbed her sleeve.

"Wait, Wuh– Wybel. Are you still Wybel?"

"Just call me Faedre, I haven't settled on a new name."

"What?"

"You hadn't worked that out yet?"

"*You're* Faedre?"

"And here I was, thinking you might be somewhat smart after all." She pulled on Meredith's grip. "Keep walking, I don't know how long we have before someone else shows up."

Meredith pushed past the disbelief. One name or another, it really didn't matter. "Fine, look, I need your help. Janette is still alive, I need to take her somewhere safe on Earth—"

"Yeah, yeah, that's fine. First my daughter, then we'll see about yours."

"Dah . . . daughter?"

"Don't lag behind. This little detour has delayed me enough already."

They headed toward the staircase far down the lugubrious hall. Though Wybel . . . *Faedre's* gait was cautious, she seemed to know where she was going. Meredith had barely chewed on the so-casually-dropped revelations when the old witch spoke again.

"Can you explain what happened out there? Brena's a den of cats right now."

"Well . . . what do you know? Where've you been?"

"I was ready to portal you into my Suffolk safehouse when they came for me, so dealing with you has cost me two homes so far. I jumped through to Devalen and was told Silver was captured. I was also told you became a wailing banshee and destroyed the Square, they were outright spooked. What the hell happened?"

"Sam saved me." She raised her gauntlet-clad hand. "With Janette's latest tool of mass destruction."

Faedre grunted the way Sam might have. "You've a funny way to pronounce Four-One-Three."

She shrugged. "A free man should have a proper name."

"He didn't look free to me. Are you truly going to meet him later?"

"No."

"Then Silver doesn't need to know I let him go, yeah?"

"No. She doesn't."

The old witch glanced over. She seemed suddenly hesitant, fiddling with one of the several pendants around her neck. Her voice dropped lower. "I'm sorry about your girl."

Meredith didn't respond. The sudden burn in her eyes had become a well-known feeling.

"I choked on you," Faedre added. "I don't really have an excuse."

"What do you mean?"

"When they came for you, at the shop. I could've incinerated us all when you went down. I didn't. I saved myself, instead."

During her time in this very dungeon, Meredith had figured as much. She couldn't muster the will to be resentful, even then. She didn't expect anyone to immolate themselves for a cause they didn't choose.

"Janette is still alive," she said simply.

"That's not necessarily something you want."

"Don't you think I know that? I need you to get us out once I find her."

Faedre nodded. "Silver should have the portal beacon on her. You can take it once she's safe."

"Fine, good. That's a deal."

They fell to an uneasy silence as they carried on down the corridor. Faedre led the way, but Meredith had walked it all on a tour with Mifraulde and knew where they were going. This floor was largely abandoned, as these days the Tower dungeon only held the rare witch awaiting questioning or punishment for Dire crimes. There had been a time, long in the past, when the cell block had been crammed well over intended capacity.

It made the silence heavier, now—heavy enough to feed on their breath, thick and gravid with the centuries of screams trapped in every wall. The soapy musk that lingered in the air could never erase the smell of blood and filth soaked into the floors. Galavan's vicious history walked in the dark of their shadows.

They started up the stairs, eyes fixed upon the turnaround above. Each stone step was polished slippery-smooth after an age's worth of treading on their surface. Meredith felt the ascent dearly, though it wasn't as pointed as rungs on a ladder.

"You couldn't be Earthborn," she stated, more abrupt than she meant to be. Faedre didn't startle.

"I'm not."

"And you were hatched after the Desolation."

"Yeah. Of course."

"But . . . Silver is your daughter?"

The old witch chuckled. "She's as much my daughter as Janette is yours."

"Oh. So not at all?"

"You poor wick't recluse, you'd crack me up if you weren't so sad. Why are you here, what drives you? Is there anything at all you wouldn't do to get her back?"

I'll stop at nothing, Meredith's thoughts replied, primal as her heartbeat. Her whole answer was to press her lips together.

"Right, you're so desperate I can smell it. You couldn't stop if you tried. Why do you think that is?"

"It doesn't make me a breeder."

"A breeder. Such a lovely perversion. Blasted Puritans. . . ."

"Well, whatever you want to call it. It's not possible."

"No, but there's something in us, and no amount of doctrine or genetic tampering could ever cut it out completely. You took care of that girl and fell in love whether you wanted—"

"Fagh!" Meredith recoiled and lagged on the stair rest. "I don't *love* her, our relationship is nothing like that!"

"Keep your voice down. I don't mean *witch* love, you tool." She nudged Meredith's arm so she'd keep up. "I meant real love. Compassion, and nurture, and selfless sacrifice. Tell me if that isn't what you feel for your girl."

The indignation deflated over the course of ten steps.

"Only too late," Meredith said. Faedre nodded, pleased with herself.

"We can still love like humans for their young. I didn't need to give birth to become a mother."

Meredith processed it quietly, unsure of how to respond. Having a word for her feelings didn't make that big a difference. In fact, it didn't sit very well with her, considering what she knew of Janette's human guardians—what little was said, the volumes implied. Her eagerness to get away. What she'd done, in the end.

"Not all humans feel that way for their young."

"Sure, and not all witches can. . . ."

She trailed off as a tremor climbed up their feet, driving them to hold on to the railing. A distant rumble thundered somewhere above, like a mountain falling off another mountain. It lasted for quite some time.

"What do you think that was?" Meredith asked.

"Something massive, if we heard it from down here. Probably cleanup—"

She was interrupted by the crackle in her pocket.

"Tower guard," the pocket garbled, "Tower guard, respond."

Faedre fished it out. The device was a metal disk with a few buttons, a dial and a belt clip.

"Tower guard," it repeated, "this is urgent. We've reason to believe the fugitive will attempt to break into the dungeon. Respond immediately."

They looked at one another. The transponder crackled again.

"I know you're there, Jade. Are you still sulking? This isn't the time. Answer me." And then, quieter, after just about the length of a sigh: "Look, someone had to stay behind. I'll make it up to you."

Meredith gestured at the thing: *well, do something,* said her flapping hands.

"It's locked up," Faedre explained, "only the owner can speak into it."

"Jade? Are you there?"

The voice had gone from assertive to tentative. A beat later, there was another crackle in Faedre's pockets. "Judicar Lex, report."

"Just how many of those do you have?"

"Only two." Faedre threw them down the steps. The clatter was entirely irresponsible. "They know something's up now. Let's get to Silver and disappear."

"I suppose they figured you'd come for her?"

"They're talking about you, numbskull. *You're* the big fugitive, I'm nobody."

"Oh. Me?"

"Walk fast and quiet."

The relatively-modern sign above the next stairwell read *B02*. This floor was a replica of the one below, as far as they could see. They turned and kept climbing.

The steps widened to emerge into an arcaded hall spanning two stories-worth of balconies, walkways and windowed rooms. Darkest black pockmarked the looming walls, as the lone light coil remaining in the chandelier overhead could barely separate one color from another, let alone reach every alcove and doorway. Straight ahead, giant double doors barred entry to the clog of rubble pressing against the former entrance to Galavan Tower. The reflection of its elaborate reliefs twisted in odd shapes within the polished floors.

They quietly rushed through the pathways between fenced holding cells, single-prisoner cages and restraint-laden benches. A flogging post stood by its lonesome, chipped and scored with myriad lines but otherwise spotless-clean. The cages threw skeletal shadows after their feet as they navigated the room and passed the side of another stairwell, a wide spiral curling toward the actual ground level. The only path to the surface, as far as Meredith knew.

Processing, read the door to the small office-archive straight ahead. The double doors next to it, barred and meshed and barbed, would lead to their destination. The iron was more rust than metal— there had been reverence in Frau's voice back then, touting this ominous door as a relic from before the Conveyance.

Above the appropriately old-fashioned keyhole, a sleek rectangular box was fused into the seam. Faedre walked up to it, many-toothed key already in hand. After turning it thrice inside the lock, she pulled back her sleeve and pressed it to the box. She looked back as a line of sigils glowed bloody-red along her forearm. "How were you planning to move through this place?"

In all honesty, Meredith hadn't thought that far. She raised her gauntlet once more. "Destructively."

She sniffed. "Fair enough."

The rectangle whispered and buzzed, the bar retracted into the walls, the latch clacked open. The hinges were smooth and quiet in their swing, for once.

"They never changed the door codes after you left?" Meredith asked.

"Change the codes? You don't know how dermaturgy works, do you?"

"I suppose not."

"Best it stays that way. We're almost there."

Another set of double doors and a corridor later, they peered into an open threshold simply labeled *Stasis*. Behind them, a thick metal slab, shut and locked. *Interrogation,* it read.

"She better be in here and not back there," Faedre said while stepping forth. Lamps strong as midday sun automatically clicked and hummed. The transition was like entering a different building, all slick surfaces and rounded corners, stark and antiseptic. There used to be a tangle of pipes, dials and valves sprouting from hopelessly stained vats, here, but they must've renovated since Meredith's visit—everything was tidy and streamlined into one conduit at the top of every pod, five shiny pods to each side, all conveniently slanted at a forty-five degree angle from the floor. All but one quietly slumbered, their viewports dull and gray.

The one active pod droned by the corner. Faedre rushed to it, Meredith lagged behind. Another mountain collapsed somewhere above, fainter than the last.

The old-rejuvenated witch was fussing over the control panel. "Silly girl, the things you get up to, one of these days I won't be around to pull you out of the fire. . . ."

Meredith peered into the viewport. Silver was barely recognizable in her inquisitor disguise. Her mezzode arm was raised, her eyes were squinted in strain, her mouth was agape mid-scream. The layer of protective chromeflow was gone, already dissolved and retrieved by the pod's equipment.

The light brightened, and Silver went from perfectly still to slamming against the pod. "Aah—" her scream finished, right before she went limp. The light dimmed, and with a gust of steam the capsule door swung out to bop Meredith's nose before indulging a hydraulic slowdown.

Faedre didn't waste an instant to get an arm around the prisoner's shoulders and sit her up, free hand tapping her cheek. "Wake up, Tess," she said in a voice so kind it could've belonged to someone else. "No time to sleep, we have to go."

Silver was largely unresponsive. Her head would loll as though terminally inebriated.

"Tessa." Faedre shook her. Silver moaned. "Snap out of it. Come on, we have to get out of here. Stop standing there and help me get her up, will you?"

She hadn't turned her head, but Meredith gathered the last part was directed at her. She went around the door and grabbed an arm. "There's no way she can walk yet," she warned.

"That's why we're carrying her. Come on, I'd be surprised if they aren't inside the building already."

The awkward shuffle to get Silver out of the pod and on her feet reminded Meredith of hobbling around the house with Jane under her shoulder. She couldn't have fathomed back then those memories would become "the good times." Recovering witch between them, they limped and struggled toward the door while Silver's moaning worked to become actual words. They banged her elbow on the doorframe in their attempts to shamble through the threshold.

"Ow," Silver said, which had to be good sign. Her head rose to almost-aware level. Her legs would sometimes help along, mostly by accident. "Where we," Meredith was almost positive she heard.

"The Tower dungeon," said Faedre.

"Mam?"

"Yeah. It's mam."

"Whossit," Silver asked with a tilt of the head that nearly threw everyone off-balance.

"It's me, Meredith," said Meredith, strained. The extra weight did no favors to her feet.

"Huh."

Though her shuffle was becoming steps at a higher rate of success, it took her until the first set of double doors to put the question together.

"You're not dead?"

"I wish I didn't get asked so often."

"Never mind that," Faedre said, "can you stand on your own yet?"

"Getting there. . . ."

"Get there faster."

"Almost died, mam."

"You still might if we don't hurry. They know we're here."

"Alright," Silver said, her muscles tense in promising ways, "let go, I can manage."

They gingerly unbraced her, still supporting her with their fingertips as if she was a stack of books about to topple. Silver leaned against the wall for a few steps and stumbled occasionally, but she mostly did manage.

"How long was it?" she asked. "What's happened?"

"Still the same night," answered Faedre, "a span before dawn, the plan is to walk out the front door while all the Judicars are busy with the massacre at the Square."

"Massacre?"

Meredith flinched. "A friend rescued me when—"

"They're all dead and the Judicars are upset," Faedre cut in, "that's all you need to know, details when we're safe somewhere else. Stop it with the chatter and concentrate on going faster."

Meredith exchanged an aggravated look with Silver. "So she's like this with everyone?"

"Yeah. All a front, though. Mam's softer than pudding under the crust."

Faedre's voice became a growl. "I'll make *you* softer than pudding if you keep falling behind. . . ."

The antique door leading to the under-foyer remained wide open, just like they'd left it. The way out was up the giant spiral steps towering to their right. They crossed into the somber hall, Silver lagging behind only slightly.

Not for a moment had Meredith presumed they'd escape without hindrance. She'd lived inside her body long enough to know there would always be a problem of some kind. But she *did* expect a warning: yelling, an alarm going off, boots stomping, harried noises overhead.

She didn't expect the room to flash alight as beams of scorching white roared upon them from four different locations. They left no room for a reaction—she didn't even have time to recoil from the blinding glare.

Instead of plunging through her chest, the beams exploded into a wall of heat not one handspan away from Meredith's face, engulfing them in a dome of roiling light. In her shrunk stance she saw Faedre awash in white, glowing purple as two of her pendants blazed with blue and red wordpaths all over their surface. In the midst of the bellowing fireball, Silver's scream was a muffled whine at the edge of perception.

"Tessa!"

Faedre moved back and the dome moved with her, forcing Meredith to follow in order to avoid a roasted-black tan. Silver fell into their relative safety, if only just; her body shook and writhed in agony, her inquisitor robe was smoking like a doused hearth. Meredith crouched and threw hands at her until one found purchase. "Stay inside the circle!" she yelled, and did her best to drag her closer to the middle. "Silver, stop moving!"

She managed to hold her down. Silver was sputtering, wheezing, deathly pale despite all the effort. Meredith took a good look.

The fabric was scorched all along her arm, burned into the skin, and the smell was as grim as the patchwork of burns. A perfectly round wedge of flesh was missing from her shoulder. The white of the bone showed in the depths of the instantly-cauterized wound.

Meredith had to turn her head away to stop nausea from taking over. "You have to stay put," she managed to tell Silver, whose mezzode hand had clamped onto Meredith's robe as if about to fall into a pit. The wounded witch was panting through bared teeth, eyes sunken with strain, courage working hard to regain control.

"This is . . . a lousy rescue . . . so far," she blurted between breaths.

They traded glances. Silver was sneering through the pain, the daft nutter.

"Like you're one to talk!"

The conflagration died down almost enough to see through clearly—only to strike again, all from different locations than the first four. Faedre buckled this time, the air got uncomfortably warm. Her amulets flickered madly.

"We have to fall back!" she yelled. "This won't last and they know it!"

"We'll be trapped in there!"

Already Faedre was backing up slowly. "I'm open to suggestions!"

Meredith stood, panic rushing in and out of her chest. She raised the gauntlet and started adjusting dials. She couldn't see the targets, but it wouldn't matter if the blast was large enough. She didn't want to, it would spend a lot of charge she might need later, but better this than—

A firm hand pushed Janette's artifact down. Faedre had a wild cast to her eyes. "Are you sure you can use that and not bring the entire tower down over our heads?"

The question gave Meredith pause. She was almost positive the spiral staircase was one giant load-bearing pillar. It wouldn't do to topple it whole.

She lowered the thing. Maybe with a pendant of her own she could rush forward and aim, but she had no such protection. "Can't *you* do something?"

"There're eight of them, spark't out the arse and with all the initiative, there's nothing I can do! They won't let up until we fry!"

In blatant disagreement, the blast let up, and a pained scream replaced the crackling boom. A bang resounded across the hall, followed by another. Meredith's ears perked with shocked recognition. She could never forget the sound of that revolver.

"Ambush!" one of the Judicars warned. Another gunshot rang from behind cover. Meredith caught the flash of a muzzle, and an instant later the violent sparks of a kinetic shield deflecting the bullet. Chaos and barked orders ensued.

Here was a window of opportunity. A chance to break through.

She *did* have a pendant of her own.

Her mouth grimaced, her brow creased with worry and reluctance, but her hands didn't hesitate to fish out Vanuuren's sigil from inside her blouse. Meredith knew who had come to the rescue. She knew what would probably happen to him if she used it.

"Get her behind the door," she said to Faedre, "and close it shut."

If she had questions, Faedre didn't ask them. She immediately started dragging Silver away.

Striding toward the fray, Meredith depressed the knob and twisted the two halves of the amulet the way Devalka had so fastidiously demonstrated. It blazed alight, blue-white like a mid-Wither skyveil. She raised an arm, infused the trinket's trigger and hoped Val's tales weren't as tall and boastful as they seemed during her dramatic reenactments.

Sammeln.

In her haste, she didn't even have time to doubt her infusion before the word reverberated into the artifact. The trigger was accurate, Val hadn't just made it up, thank the furies. Like splinters, like thorns, like needles, shards of exquisitely pathed alloy peeled off each side of the sigil, breaking apart until only a die-shaped core remained. The shards spiraled up her arm in radiant pirouettes, their buzz like a hundred knives cutting the wind. They gathered as a swarm of hyper-energetic flitglows around her hand.

Some of the Judicars were dealing with the new threat behind them, rushing to their injured, but at least two had their hands trained on her. She saw them, one by the spiraling steps, the other by the flogging post. "The fugitive!" one barked, scorn and fury and above all *urgency* in her voice. Meredith watched their armor grow incarnadine from the underglow of dermaturgy. As the infused word-command made it past her lips, she knew it wouldn't be fast enough.

Suchen und zerstören!

The seeker swarm burst forth in incandescent trails. The Judicar melt-rails shot toward Meredith immediately after. She had just enough time to hope Faedre would carry on to save Janette without her. They owed her, now. They would try, they *better* try.

The first lance struck at her abdomen; she gasped as it engulfed her in a torrent of flames. The second one rushed at her forehead and glanced off the protective dome to scorch through the *Processing* sign, exploding into the room. The heat was near-unbearable, the light a pupil-bleaching flare all around her . . . but she remained unscathed.

Meredith shrunk in her bubble, mystified, and in luminescent outlines she noticed Faedre's tossed amulet dying down, melting away between her feet. The torrent of flame stopped abruptly. Ahead, all over the room, Judicars shrieked and howled among a slush of wet detonations.

She caught a glimpse of a couple seeker shards decelerating enough to bypass a juditor's kinetic barrier. They burrowed through her reinforced robe with a whirring hiss. A rumble built up in the span of a sharp breath—the blasts went off in reverberating thumps, followed by the spatter of several body parts hitting the floor in different places, at different times.

The trails each shard had followed still lingered in the air, glimmering paths coruscating as they faded over the most grisly scene Meredith had witnessed since . . . last night. As it turned out, Devalka's tales of Agnes Vanuuren and her devious artificing skills had not been exaggerated in the slightest.

Through ragged breaths she surveyed the hall. No-one was left standing, but groans remained. Death throes. Steps unsteady and lapel draped over her nose, Meredith walked across the aftermath.

The smell still reached her, a mix of seared flesh, ravaged metal, vaporized blood. And one other thing, a powdery pungence that clung to the air like bog miasma—motes of *something* raw and warpsome bubbling into her chest. It scratched at her throat and made her eyes water.

In-between cages and benches and torture implements her boots squelched through pooling dark. While watching where she stepped, her gaze kept darting to the one spot where she'd seen that muzzle flash, close to the staircase coming from the floors below. She immediately regretted leaning her hand on a desk to steady her gait. Her fingers came back red.

The glimpse of him was a weight dragging down her lungs, a weight that grew heavier as she neared. He was on his back, a juditor's body sprawled on top of him like a meat blanket. Her throat was cut. The knife lay in a mess of blood, not far. And there was the revolver, of course, resting where it had bounced off his hand, hot and spent and filthy. There was no visible wound on Four-Thirteen, but his skin was ashen, his eyes wandered and struggled, his breath was a saw-toothed rattle.

Meredith grabbed a lifeless limb and rolled the body off him. He didn't react, which couldn't be a good omen. It didn't take her long to see why.

"Oh, Sam. . . ."

A chunk of his ribcage was missing, an impeccably delineated wedge to the left of his stomach where the melt-beam had pierced through. Nobody should've been able to survive such . . . spillage. How he still drew breath, Meredith did not know.

She knelt by his side, cradled his hand. He tried to focus on her, he truly did.

"You couldn't help yourself, could you? You couldn't just stay behind."

It hadn't been her. He was already hurt by the time she'd sent out the swarm. They'd missed him entirely, he was already down and as good as dead.

The insight brought no comfort at all.

"You saved me again. You saved us."

It seemed to register. His gaze found her eyes and managed to stay affixed to them.

Hazel, not brown.

"Ghon . . . gheev me. . . ."

Blood spurted from his mouth with every word. Meredith shook her head. "No, I won't leave you, not this time."

Some of the strain eased from Sam's neck, from his face. Once again his eyes wandered and looked nowhere at all. His voice barely touched his lips on the way out.

"I . . . am . . . Sam."

Meredith watched through the blur, she watched as what was left of his chest stopped fighting. His cradled hand became an inert burden. His body unwound.

True to her word, Meredith didn't leave him.

Some time later, perhaps a long time later, two sets of steps neared in a labored shuffle. They stood over her shoulder and took in the scene, their presence full of tension.

"You are a beacon for disaster," Faedre quietly said. Somehow there was gratitude beneath the words.

"Who is this man?" asked Silver, though the jagged shape of her voice made it more an accusation than a question. It was hard to tell, with all the pain-induced strain.

Meredith looked up at them. They weren't leaning on one another, but seemed ready to do so if either faltered. Silver appeared as someone who'd just escaped a burning building and carried the wounds to prove it. A fiery crackle was taking over the deathly-still hall as the blaze in *Processing* continued to spread.

Meredith looked her in the eye. "His name was Sam, and he saved us."

"You mean *Four-Thirteen,* the murderer who—"

"Tessa," Faedre cut in, "just shut up, will you?"

"He slaughtered—"

"I don't care, it's done, it's over." She closed the distance to Meredith and lay a hand on her shoulder. "I'm sorry, but we have to go. I hope you're ready to keep fighting, they heard everything that just happened through their comm channel. There'll be more waiting at the exit, but I left a few surprises up there that should help." Her pull was gentle but urgent.

Meredith shrugged her off. She straightened up, feeling her now-wet trousers peel at the knee. With deliberate care she stepped around Sam—not *over,* how disrespectful—and reached for the revolver.

She checked it: five rounds spent, one left. Her thumb kept the last one in place while the empty casings fell. They tinkled above the fire like tiny wind chimes.

"That's a stupid plan," she said as she dropped the bloodied gun in a pocket. Faedre frowned at the lips. Silver continued wheezing through her pain. Black smoke drifted toward the upper floors.

"Follow me. I know a better way out."

MEREDITH STOOD by the Kestrel Library steps, portal beacon held firm in her pocketed fist. Under dawn's first light she watched them fly off on Faedre's dais, huddled and tied together to prevent a suddenly-unconscious Silver from falling. The rain should keep her awake.

Desmond swayed in his improvised belt harness, his panicked squeals quieted by the sock-muzzle they'd strapped to his mouth. He was *not* pleased in the slightest . . . but he'd survive.

"I was planning to go with you," Faedre had said, and she'd seemed wholly sincere, "but I have to take care of her. I don't suppose you can wait a day or two."

"Who knows how well-prepared they'll be in one day," Meredith had answered. It wasn't her main reason to hurry, but it was the rational one.

Faedre had nodded without question. "My last safehouse is in Melbourne," she'd said. "That means the nexus is open from midday to eleven. Give us until ten fifty before you use the beacon, we should be settled by then."

And off the pair went to continue their own adventure, to some lair somewhere to escape to Earth somehow—Meredith didn't care about the details, as long as they made it to the other side of that beacon-attuned portal. Hopefully Desmond would stay on his best behavior and wouldn't slow them down too much. She'd meant for him to keep Sam company, but now. . . .

Well, now it was out of her hands. With grim aplomb she turned back to the double doors, the desolate front counter, the pitch-black depths of the library.

Dread and hope brawled in her chest all through her search. Despite how unlikely it was, she kept expecting Yurena to pop around a shelf and call her name. "I left right away," Yurena would explain. "I couldn't bear to watch so I ran here before the destruction started." Meredith debated back and forth how to react, she wondered how they'd feel for one another, she considered an embrace and a scoff and a dramatic kiss all in equal measure. She'd already drafted a moving speech for their time of parting.

She'd also considered the *former* librarian might betray her as soon as she turned her back, because who knew the extent of her desperation? Perhaps violence on first sight would be the best option. Meredith wasn't sure she could bring herself to it. Not without giving her a chance.

Yurena never appeared. The place was deserted, dead. Meredith collected the floorplans she was looking for and left.

Maybe, some day, they'd see each other again.

But she'd probably died with the rest.

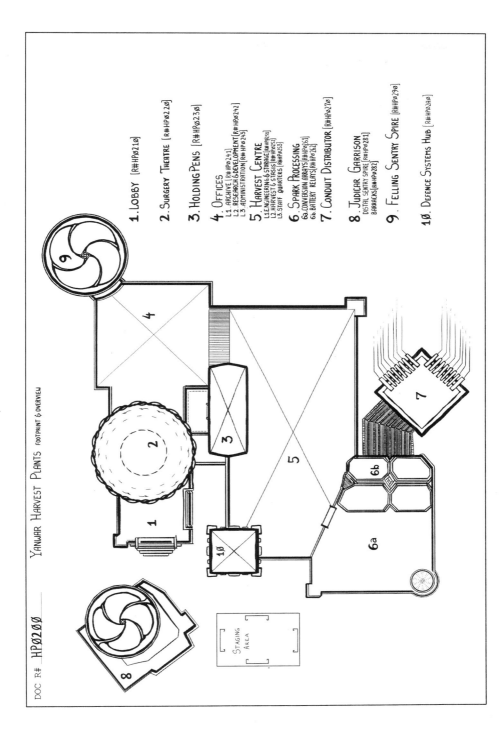

DOC R# HP0200

YANWAR HARVEST PLANTS FOOTPRINT & OVERVIEW

1. LOBBY [R#HP0210]

2. SURGERY THEATRE [R#HP0220]

3. HOLDING PENS [R#HP0230]

4. OFFICES
L1. ARCHIVE [R#HP0241]
L2. RESEARCH & DEVELOPMENT [R#HP0242]
L3. ADMINISTRATION [R#HP0243]

5. HARVEST CENTRE
L1. ENGINEERING & STORAGE [R#HP0251]
L2. HARVEST & STASIS [R#HP0252]
L3. STAFF QUARTERS [R#HP0253]

6. SPARK PROCESSING
6a. CONVERSION ARRAYS [R#HP0261]
6b. BATTERY RELAYS [R#HP0262]

7. CONDUIT DISTRIBUTOR [R#HP0270]

8. JUDICAR GARRISON
DISTAL SENTRY SPIRE [R#HP0281]
BARRACKS [R#HP0282]

9. FELLING SENTRY SPIRE [R#HP0290]

10. DEFENCE SYSTEMS HUB [R#HP0210]

STAGING AREA

CHAPTER THIRTY-ONE

BEYOND SALVATION

HE YANWAR HARVEST PLANTS were a multi-winged titan of ominous towers and black walls, a citadel-and-burg of stone, concrete and metal. The ruins of New Yanwar still languished in a broken sprawl all around them. It was a none-too-subtle display of consequence to opposition.

In boxy architecture every wing and building rose Distalside of the Froth, grandiosity and traditional wick't menace well prioritized over function. Each was shielded by a caustic regulator, a kinetic matrix, an anti-warp field, a network of heat-eaters and good old-fashioned thick walls reinforced with ferris steel. Galvan Tower in Brena was the seat of government, but here sat the beating heart of Galavan.

A pyramid-shaped hunk of mountain, sheared from the cliffside of Mergat's Fall, shot through the gathering clouds and descended upon the Spark Processing wing like an Earthly harbinger of extinction. Its sharpest point struck the building at full speed, exploding in shards and blazing sparks as the kinetic shield attempted to deflect it, stop it, chew through it—until finally, overwhelmed by the sheer magnitude of force and material, it gave out in a structure-wide hiss. Only half the pyramid remained by then, but it was enough to crash through the walls like they were made of marzipan. The air shook as the mountain demolished the whole wing into a giant cloud of black dust, conversion frames and battery arrays punctuating the chest-rumbling thunder with a smattering of explosions.

Janette's gauntlet seemed to exhale in relief at a job well done. Hovering in mid-air under the pale midday sun of early Wane, a mostly-dry Meredith checked the gauge on the artifact. Barely a sliver of charge left. Just enough, hopefully.

Her breath was heavy with effort as she waited for some of the smoke to clear. The gauntlet's haptic feedback was enormously helpful when manipulating objects, but it became unwieldy when the object weighed as much as a castle. She'd let Jane know, just in case she ever set out to design Mark IV . . . years in the future, in the safety of her Earth sanctuary, far away from this nightmare.

She maneuvered toward the wreck and hoped the Security Quarters were as empty as she expected. These were times of peace, and the Harvest Plants had operated without incident since the human rebellions. There was no full garrison on alert, no watch posts all around the perimeter or strict patrols looking out for saboteurs. In fact, most guards had probably left to help with the Brenan disaster.

After a deep gulp of air she dove into the smoke, rubble and incipient fires rushing below her. It was quite the challenge to identify the proper passage in the chaotic three-dimensional cross-section she'd just carved into the building. Several rooms and corridors were buried in an impassable wreckage, but the central arched hallway was clear enough. She sped toward it as the blare of a compound-wide alarm overtook the rumbling.

Her eyes watered to a deadly blur. The kerchief tied over her mouth and nose barely helped. The hallway floor was dim with emergency lights and heaped with debris. All these factors led to the inevitable bump and wobble and loss of control over her dais, but Meredith was a well-seasoned flight accident survivor. Instead of trying to regain control, she let go of the dais and jumped off toward the wall, hit it at an angle and slid all the way to the floor. She kept sliding forward for the length of a few steps.

Her robe dirtied up thoroughly, but didn't even abrade by the time she came to a full stop. She only stumbled a little bit getting to her feet—one of them hurt, the other was very close to throbbing. It wouldn't be manageable for much longer. She didn't even bother to dust off, what was the point? The teeth-chattering siren was a constant reminder there was no time to waste.

Meredith wiggled the gauntlet off and clipped it to her belt, eager to conserve what little charge remained. She fetched her dais and couldn't tell which dents were new. With practiced movements she tucked it into its harness, fished out the cord for the girdle and gave it a firm tug. After a whisper she couldn't hear, all of her limbs blended into the background.

Not a moment too soon, as the first witch rounded the corner and ran toward the disaster zone with the look of someone who'd just witnessed the moon sprout wings and fly off the skyveil. She was dressed in a tightly-strapped outfit that patently stated "I work in an antiseptic lab." Even with the sirens, Meredith heard her ululating wail as their paths crossed.

Another brushed past, close behind the first, but she was too distraught to notice anything besides the smoke and the fires. And they *should* be panicking. Meredith had just destroyed the power supply for half the realm. There were other harvest plants, other processors and batteries by Tremmelton and Tarkis—how silly it would be, for the system to be so fatally centralized—but this was a devastating blow. Coupled with the on-going spark crisis, it was possible Galavan wouldn't recover.

It should've been gratifying, but Meredith couldn't find any pleasure in it. To want retribution, she'd have to be blameless. To want justice, she'd have to be righteous.

She just wanted Jane back.

Meredith followed the parallel glow of emergency lights embedded in the wall plinths. Her anxiety kept anticipating a battalion of juditors and hunter cats around every corner, but she made it to the intersection without any more encounters. Her rational mind doubted there were more than a handful of Judicars in the compound. Her heart was jumping up and down her ribcage all the same.

One last look behind revealed a juditor hovering on her dais, surrounded by rolling smoke, talking to—yelling at—the Harvest Department staff. The juditor looked like she'd flown in the same way Meredith had. No doubt she'd been the one posted at the top of the Security Quarters' spire, perhaps now full of regret at not paying enough attention to the skies.

Meredith rushed ahead, following the path she'd traced on paper until she could recite it eyes-closed. Turn away from Distribution Conduits, down the hall, side door, find the staircase, hop up to the second floor, to the Harvest Centre—don't think about the squelch in your foot, it doesn't matter, keep going—now down the corridor around the Stasis Labs, (Jane might be there but probably not,) through the office spaces and the double swinging doors. In her journey she passed two more runners, a trio of witches frantically gathering documents and hand-held equipment, one juditor shouting evacuation instructions—*Stop pawing the gourd patch and get out!*—and several golems carrying trays and gurneys and doodads from one place to another as if nothing out of the ordinary was going on.

Through the swinging doors stretched another hallway, an intersection, a sign overhead: *Harvest Pods*. There was also an abruptly-stopping staffer who'd just seen a door swing open without anything to push it.

Her utterly befuddled expression lasted as long as it took Meredith to draw, load, aim and shoot. Not one syllable of infusion escaped the stranger's lips before the dart sank into her abdomen. Meredith had targeted the neck, but her aim was impaired by her wielding an invisible crossbow.

A burst of noisy words drowned under the alarm. The spell happened quickly after the stored incantations were done triggering. Here stood a human-shaped monster, posed in recoil, shock dawning on her masked features.

"Ghh," she said as Meredith passed her. Budget *Paralysis* couldn't be relied upon for very long, but it shouldn't matter. If she was still around by the time it wore off, it would mean she'd failed her mission.

She stood by the threshold below the sign, a threshold like the divide between a well-lit workshop and a cellar's gloom. Pods hummed and glowed in the penumbra, they subtly vibrated in long rows of glossy surfaces and daunting viewports. From inside came yelling angry enough to justify its volume without the sirens.

"We must evacuate, madam!"

"Absolutely not! That's exactly what she wants!"

It should've been a surprise. She should've gasped. Instead, hearing Mifraulde speak felt . . . appropriate.

Of course she was here. Of course it would be her.

They'd only been a few words, but they were enough to suggest Mifraulde was not her collected and calculating self. The air was charged with her outrage, which mingled with the throat-drying aura of a room full of spark-extracting devices. Meredith quietly entered and hugged the walls of the chamber.

Close to the middle of the room, the juditor appeared ready to break into a sprint. The coif insignia and armband designated her as the local prime. Mifraulde paced like she would during her most aggravated rants, and she was disheveled and filthy, the way someone might look after climbing out of a rain-soaked wreck and letting the mud cake for half a day.

"Where is the rest of your team? This youth needs to be secured immediately, I demand they be here this instant!"

"They're taking care of the fires, madam! I don't have anyone to spare! And if that banshee freak is here, I want everyone out before they become another trail of body parts!"

"You what? You want to flee? From *Meredith*?"

"I heard the report from the Tower, it was carnage, she's some kind of—yes, come in!"

The juditor leaned into the crackling device clipped to her shoulder and strained to listen. Meredith crept closer, crossbow in hand and ready to fire, eyes glancing into every viewport she passed—though she already knew Janette wouldn't be in any of these. Her brood-sister's pacing was consistently centered around a very specific pod.

"What?" The guard looked directly at the Head of the Coven. "Please repeat!"

The comms device warbled, but there was no way to make out the words.

"Yes . . . understood. Stand by."

"Well? Are the fires under control?"

The guard hesitated. "Madam, may I ask you to produce the Coven medallion?"

There was a subtle change in Mifraulde's stance, a tightness to her shoulders Meredith could read with ease as she skirted around the pair. For whatever reason, the juditor had just become a hostile party to her sister.

"What does that have to do with anything?"

"I apologise, but I must insist!"

"It's spent and vaporised after saving me from a massacre! Who do you think you're talking to? Why are you questioning me? I *appointed you* to this post, it's my signature on your certificate!"

Meredith hadn't noticed at first, but now the absence of tiara and council ring became acutely conspicuous. What had happened after the Felling House collapsed?

The juditor stepped closer. Mifraulde stepped back.

"Madam, I must ask you to come with me at once until we can sort this out!"

"I'm not going anywhere! A Dire Criminal is about to walk through that door, and I'm stopping her! She will *not* get away with this!"

"Please come peacefully, I don't wish any harm upon you—"

"Fĕn'vă ŏnēş'yunām ús!"

The prime juditor reacted, but not fast enough. As Mifraulde uttered the syllables her left hand slapped away the guard's suddenly-aglow arm, while Frau's other hand pointed fingers at the juditor's aghast face.

For one breathtaking moment the room drew into the incantation, it drained into Mifraulde's fingertips—and the spell exploded forth at point-blank range. The juditor's head whipped back with a horrid squelching snap. The body followed, lagging behind yet still attached somehow, limp as it crashed onto the floor and slid between pods all the way to the wall. It was a challenge for Meredith not to yelp.

She'd gone all the way around from the entrance, now edging as close as she dared to—presumably—Janette's pod. Meredith's laughable latent power could still give her away if she went too far. She watched as her brood-sister shook her fingers and breathed through her anger. This creature, who'd tortured her into an ashen husk, who'd cared for her and protected her for a lifetime. The disgraced Head of the Coven, here to stop the Dire Criminal from getting away with her nefarious rescue. Mifraulde, here purely out of spite, to deny Meredith's desperate attempt at redemption.

Words came unbidden to her tongue, so many she couldn't tell them apart. There should be a conversation, here. A resolution to all the grief and resentment, an attempt at getting some closure before the end.

Foolish, all of it. They'd gone a pyre and four meals beyond words. Meredith quietly aimed and pulled the trigger.

The dart thwapped forth and became visible. At the same time, Mifraulde happened to turn. The dart missed the nape of her neck by a finger's breadth.

Eyes wide and searching, she thrust her left hand in Meredith's general direction.

"Fĕṅ'vă ŏṅlēv'ẏunām ús!"

Half guess, half grasping at a shimmer, the spell struck Meredith's outstretched arm. An irresistible force walloped her at an angle, sent her weapon flying, tossed her spinning through the air and onto the floor until she rolled to a stop against a harvest pod.

"Meredith!"

The world was a starry haze all around her, the shoulder joint had made an ugly snap, but still she scrambled on all fours to crawl behind cover. Mifraulde strode after her, every step awash in fury. Meredith kept going, a blur in the darkness, crawling behind equipment and machinery to wherever she could hide. The sirens masked her labored puffs and scuffles.

"You've cost me everything," Mifraulde raged, "everything! It's all your fault! And you come in here and *attack me* without a word?"

Apparently, she wasn't as keen on leaving her grievances unaired. She rushed around the pod, weaved and bobbed around it for a glimpse of the sister-turned-nemesis.

"Do you know what you've done? Selma swooped in and took over, just like that! It was *humiliating* to be dug out of the rubble by her minions! But I knew it was you at the Tower, I *knew,* so I sent my most loyal, a last chance—only to be slaughtered! Disaster after disaster after disaster, because of you!"

You sound unhinged, Meredith nearly said, but she didn't take the bait, if that's what it was. She focused on staying out of sight, skulking on tiles that kept drifting askew under her hands and knees. Mifraulde was pacing back toward Jane, craning her neck over obstacles.

"Selma pretended to care, but she was doing cartwheels in her head, she gave this *insufferable* speech and then she *dared* tell her goons to place me into custody! 'Unfit to lead,' the nerve of that tub of maggots! 'Responsible for Brena's destruction!' As if she would've done any better in my place!"

No idea where the crossbow might have landed, if it was still in one piece. Jane could get hurt if she resorted to the gauntlet.

Clinging to the darkest shadows, Meredith dug in her pocket. The grimy revolver had stuck to the fabric. She had to work with both hands to peel it off.

"I've been working all my life, I've done more for Galavan than any one of those harpies! And you destroyed it all! How'd you do it? How? I know you, I've known you all your life, you're useless, you're nothing! You don't have the power to do this, *how'd you do it!*"

Meredith peeked around flexible conduits and vibrating metal. Frau was screaming breathlessly into the darkness, thumping the lid of Jane's torture device as a sort of podium. The pods were slanted toward the center walkway, meaning only half her torso was visible. A terrible target from this angle, at this distance, especially when the room was still spinning. She'd have to go across, but remaining unnoticed was far more of a challenge now that Mifraulde was watching for the shimmer.

"Nothing to say? You've *nothing* to say to me? No, you're sick, you only care about one thing, don't you! What if I switch off her life support right here, will you speak then? Let's find out!"

She fussed over the control panel. Meredith dashed across the center walkway, her stomach twisted in knots. Every part of her wanted to react, charge in and tackle this mad bint, but she forced herself to keep crawling, keep advancing for a better vantage. Jane wouldn't die instantly. There was time.

From her new position Meredith watched in quiet horror as the pod blinked red. Mifraulde must've expected immediate and dramatic results, because she chafed in record time at the lack of reaction.

"You realise I don't need to find you, yeah? I don't need answers, I only need your head! I'll take your head back to Brena and make that sallowbag choke on it!" She waited, watched. She couldn't spot Meredith as she prowled her way around. "Fine! We'll have it your way! Pox upon you!"

Mifraulde heaved, gathering her thoughts and her breath. A tiny corner of Meredith's brain noted, not entirely without sympathy, how exhausted Frau looked. She could relate.

Pointing one hand to her chest, Mifraulde launched into an incantation. Time had run out, Meredith couldn't afford to decipher what the spell might do. She aimed as carefully as she could and fired.

"Fǽr kĕh'ẏunām AAH!"

Aah was not a terminus clause. As Mifraulde jumped as if pecked by a raven, her channeled power dispersed without purpose into the already-saturated room. She leaned heavily against the pod, clutching at her side just below the hipbone.

Meredith had aimed for the heart. Invisible iron sights were far from ideal.

The recoil had lanced deep into her shoulder and jolted the weapon off her hand, but she stayed focused, because oxygen was no longer flowing into that sealed metal tomb. With throbbing limb and bloody feet, Meredith sprinted out of cover.

Mifraulde noticed her. There was this incredulous, affronted look on her face, as if even now she still expected her brood-sister to fawn and genuflect, as if surely this turn of events had to be some kind of mistake. Features twisted with resentment, she pointed a red finger at the approaching blur.

The approaching blur threw a phone at Mifraulde's forehead.

"Rĩṅ fr̄eĩ̇ẇṅ'ẏun—gah!"

The aim was true this time, but a flinch and a slap deflected it; the smack on her wrist thumped over the alarm. She couldn't deflect the Meredith ramming into her at full throttle, which wasn't terribly powerful in her current condition, but powerful enough to tackle her off their feet. Mifraulde was already invisible by the time they hit the floor. Every breath emptied out of her lungs under the hammer of Meredith's weight.

Meredith tried to take advantage of it but struggled to stay on top, not quite able to find purchase astride her writhing brood-sister, all while pawing and clawing at Mifraulde's mouth to stop her from vocalizing anything dangerous. It devolved into a conversation of groans and pained cries, a sightless brawl steeped in the smell of mud, the warmth of blood, the strain of overtaxed muscles at odds with one another. This was the Head of the Coven, she'd been trained in basic self-defense, but she'd also suffered an avalanche, a gunshot and over thirty span without sleep. Her strength was already waning by the time Meredith's hands found her throat.

They clamped on like a Judicar gag, hands closing upon her salvation, hands worn and hardened by decades of weed uprooting and fence pruning. Mifraulde scratched Meredith's face, but she didn't relent; clawed at Meredith's fingers, but there was no prying at them. The writhing became frantic, desperate. She rammed her fist into Meredith's arm, the arm attached to a shoulder with a torn *something* throbbing with every bit of exertion. Despite her best efforts, the pain rendered her grip numb on that side, weak enough for Mifraulde's flailing to shove it loose and shift Meredith's leverage. Mifraulde grabbed her sister's other wrist with both hands and shoved—what was a choke-hold became scratches at the throat, became a struggle to regain control of her limb. The abused invisibility girdle gave out then, revealing Mifraulde's blood-smeared grasp, ashen lips, a mud-crusted mane all over the place and eyes like windows into suffering.

The one moment of feverish eye contact brought a sort of confirmation, a mutual understanding between them that *yes, we are trying to kill each other and there is no going back*. Mifraulde now breathed in big gulps. Somehow she didn't cough or spurt, she simply filled her lungs and concentrated. With her grip straining on Meredith's forearm, she spoke.

ŏṅ'reth'vă cŏr. . . .

Dread like she hadn't felt in thirty years seized Meredith's breast. These words were burnt in her memory as herald of anguish and humiliation, words she would hear before every lost duel at the academy: the clause to designate as source whatever object was in the caster's grasp. Already the link pulled at her core, it reeled her into Mifraulde's attunement with inescapable finality. Once the spell took hold, she wouldn't be able to resist the drain any more than a raindrop could fight the Froth.

And Meredith could bet her life on the drain pulling far more power than a harmless duel cantrip.

Innervated above the pain, she coerced her free hand to obey. She dug through her robe as each infused word tore out of her sister's lips.

. . . Ḣæxx. . . .

Her fingers closed around a handle.

. . . ēl. . . .

Her fist rose above her head.

. . . ús!

The spell engaged, a stasis command at a realm-wide scale. Not even Janette could've powered it—and this was its purpose, an overwhelming drain hex, malfeasance of the first order. Their attunements matched against one another to control the flow of energy, and Meredith drew every bit of her latent power to put up a fight, delay Mifraulde's pull for a moment, half a moment. It was a pebble standing tall before a boulder rolling downhill.

It might have made a difference. It must have. The drain felt like Meredith was deflating from the inside as she plunged a pair of wire cutters into her sister's chest.

Mifraulde screamed inward in a gasping wail. Meredith collapsed on top of her, her every limb enfeebled beyond control. The blade wasn't long enough to stab through the heart, but it sure was long enough to break anyone's concentration. The tether between them snapped as if the clippers had found it between Mifraulde's ribs. The drain inside Meredith relented, though the weakness lingered.

Their link was severed, but Mifraulde had cast the spell, she was the conduit. A number of sources could've been tapped at this point, from the pod-bound youths undergoing harvest, to the nodework above, to the walls around them . . . reality interconnected in unpredictable ways.

Twelve times out of thirteen, however, a spell will source its energy through the path of least resistance.

Mifraulde became taut like a prisoner raked upon the breaking wheel. Her breath stopped, her cries choked to a rattle. The blare of the alarm collapsed into stillness as the realm froze in place.

Then the convulsions started. Meredith half-rolled, half-fell to one side as the shaking grew more violent, the eyes rolled back, the mouth spurted with froth. Mifraulde's body shuddered as if the very bones wanted to escape from under her skin.

The flesh started ripping and shriveling, caving in. In her throat gargled agony itself as every part of her was ravaged for magical fuel, layers peeling back, organs shredding and dissolving to appease the insatiable hunger she'd conjured. Her body flaked into eddies that spiraled into the ether. Mifraulde couldn't fight it any more than a raindrop could fight the Froth.

Meredith watched for an impossible eternity, numb and helpless in their snug bubble of relative timeflow, as her brood-sister ceased to be.

When it was over, only a mass of bloodstained clothes remained. The spell died with the last sparkling mote, bringing back the blaring alarm and the screaming colors of the Harvest Centre penumbra.

Meredith lay there not by choice, awe-struck, in shock, but most of all *feeble*. She would've mourned her sister, she would have, even after everything Mifraulde had done and everything she'd done to Mifraulde, but one concern kept shouting at her to get off the floor and *move*.

"Jane," she mumbled, fingers groping for purchase on perfectly flat tiles, "Jane. . . ."

She couldn't tell how long it took to scrabble up to her feet, using the pod for support all the way there. The sirens abruptly stopped, which meant the emergency was under control, which meant there was another timer chasing her tail. She had however long it took for the Judicars to come running.

Meredith panted onto the lid, anxiously looked into the viewport. It was dark as the inside of a coffin. She fumbled with the controls, nerves biting at her ribs; every breath restored some of her vigor, it brought her mind closer to normalcy . . . and allowed the dread to take hold once more.

The lid depressurized and smoothly opened with hydraulic lethargy. Meredith prepared herself. She knew the extent of the butchery. She knew the rituals. She'd seen the meals. All she could hope was for whatever was left of Jane to be *breathing*.

The lid swung past Meredith's face. A moan seized her throat, her knees nearly gave out as her eyes traveled from one horror to the next: the clamps, the needles, the sealed incisions. The empty spaces. No, nothing could've prepared her.

Monsters. They're monsters.

It was Janette, she was here, she was alive, that's all that mattered. Her body floated in the pocket of null gravity. Intravenous conduits pierced her skin in several places. A pronged contraption bit into her temples. Her muscles twitched every now and then, her brow was the picture of stress.

This was by design. A distressed subject produced a better yield. The Department had worked out the optimal balance between efficient harvest and long-term detriment.

Meredith swallowed her tears and got to work. Her every impulse was to wrap her arms around Jane and run, but it wouldn't be so easy, they needed to get well clear of the no-travel zone glyphed down to the foundations. She deployed the dais (Frau's gift, reliable, sturdy) and shrugged out of her robe. Among grunts and frustrated mumbling she tied the sleeves to the straps of the dais harness to fashion a carry sling, shoddy but serviceable. Lastly, she donned Jane's gauntlet and properly adjusted the dials. It better have enough charge left to make a tunnel out of the facility.

Her hands trembled as she worked the controls to release the patient. *Patient,* the black-and-green display had the gall to call her. *Yes,* she nearly shouted at the dialog questioning her, *I am sure I want to do it.*

The IV latches decoupled. The stimulus circlet clacked off. The null gravity field propped her up for easier access. Janette gasped, her eye opened, Meredith's hands were there to soothe her.

"Mistress?"

Her voice scattered in chattering fragments, just like with the night terrors, so much worse than the night terrors. She was wide awake, overstimulated, exhausted, one eye looking up at her and understanding nothing. Meredith pressed her close to her chest and lifted her out of the nightmare.

"Mistress, I dreamt— I dreamt, I dreamed—"

"It's over now," Meredith managed to say.

Jane was so light in her arms. So light. . . .

"Where . . . what's happening, where, why can't, I can't. . . ."

Jane was vanishing, shallow breaths growing further apart. Who knew for how long she'd been kept in a permanent state of tension? Meredith cupped her head and gently tucked her into the crook of her neck.

"Rest now, love. You're safe, it's over. It's over."

"My legs . . . I can't . . . move. . . ."

The thread of a voice frayed away. Her body went limp in Meredith's grasp.

She still breathed. That's all that mattered.

"It's over."

Meredith cradled her as snugly as she could. Jane had become slight enough for the holster belt to strap around both of them. By the time she was done securing her, the girl's bare skin peeked out of the robe-sling only from shoulder to cheek, with the rest of her face covered by her mass of unkempt flaxen waves.

As Meredith had worked the clasp and the cloth, her gaze

wandered over the room, over all the contraptions chugging along unperturbed. Among the hundreds of pods, well over half were active. Spark't youths, boys and girls as young or younger than Janette, twitching and whimpering in their own little bubble of torment.

Sickness and guilt crept up her throat. How were they any more deserving of this fate? Was she going to simply ignore them and leave?

They are not your business, the witch in her prompted.

True. Many were in a state beyond rescue at this point. She could never save them all. No-one ever would.

That certainty seared into her thoughts like scalding tar on a convict.

No-one ever would.

She made a choice.

Features like grim death, Meredith readjusted the dials on the gauntlet. There should be enough charge to do this, just barely enough. She didn't know if it was the right decision, though she was aware it would haunt her for the rest of her days. However few there might be left.

She mounted the dais and maneuvered to the room's threshold. The extra weight was excruciating on her feet, she could barely work the balance plates. The tied robe sleeve was a hot iron digging into her shoulder. It was almost over. Noises and shouts roamed the hallways, getting closer . . . and they were about to get much louder.

Blinking tears onto her cheeks, Meredith held out the gauntlet as if cupping the moon in her palm. She would've destroyed every harvest plant if she could, she would've erased Galavan from existence, but this was the extent of her power here and now. She could give these tortured prisoners a semblance of freedom.

She grabbed the ceiling and drove it upon Galavan's stolen lifeblood.

Jane's gauntlet flared to pull a massive hunk of third floor onto the middle of the room. An avalanche of living quarters followed, a cascade of walls and support beams and beds and mirrors collapsing through in an ever-spreading chain that pulled everything above, crushed everything below. The dust and debris forced her to take shelter behind the entrance and carefully shield her charge from the cloud blooming into the hallway. She felt more than heard the gauntlet's whine as it dimmed for the last time.

The sirens came back on after their short break. Dust rained all over, cracks webbed through the ceiling, but thankfully the corridor held. There she waited for the worst of it to pass, face buried against Jane's as they skimmed shallow breaths from the depths of her robe. Her mask had been torn off during the fight. She could smell Sam's soap underneath the blood and dirt.

Meredith waited, and watched, and lightly coughed. The building layout sprawled in her mind with daunting clarity: the harvest chambers were at the center of the facility; all around, multiple rooms and connecting corridors with a hundred variables before the nearest exit. She couldn't afford another encounter. Going back the way she'd come was the last—

The swinging double doors slammed open. Two soot-coated juditors barreled around the intersection.

They saw her and stopped. They recognized her right away, they knew who she was. Meredith, the Dire Criminal, the vengeful banshee that left a trail of body parts wherever she went. They knew whose blood stained her skin.

Caught in the open, utterly bereft of options, the Dire Criminal ferociously bared her teeth and thrust her gauntlet hand forward. The guards didn't know it could do nothing at all. They tripped over each other to dive back into cover.

The bluff actually working was hard to process, but she knew it wouldn't delay them for long. Immediately she swept into the ruin, holding her breath, squinting through the devastation, looking, hoping—yes, there, there it was! A glimmer of silver upon the clouds of wreckage, a shaft of daylight pouring through the broken roof.

Meredith flew above the ravaged harvest operation, toward the light. The center of the room had caved and crashed upon Engineering, one floor below. None of the pods appeared even remotely salvageable.

She couldn't pretend it was a good thing. It was only the least horrific option.

They zoomed through a gap circled by jagged roof tiles and sheared pipes, and all at once they were awash in daylight. She kept climbing, eager beyond words to get as far away as possible, but then realized how easy a target she was up there, a dark dot against the overcast skyveil. It was certain they'd give chase, the only question was whether she'd have time to hide and activate the beacon before then. Meredith dove toward the ruins of New Yanwar across the Froth. A hundred hideouts to choose from down there.

The sirens waned from bone-rattling to distant annoyance. It felt like half a day had elapsed since she'd crashed a mountain into the facility—and what a sight it was now, with half its profile leveled to rubble—but the eleventh span rain didn't even look imminent. The nexus window should still be open. Faedre better be ready on the other side.

Her cargo was too precious to risk an accidental landing, so she avoided the scorched bones of houses and structures in favor of the plaza in front of the former Tower grounds, uphill from the river. Even this open space had plenty of perils, with debris and boulders and charred market stalls scattered all over. Rust ate away at a giant pipe strewn across one side of the square, detached from who-knew-where, brought all the way there by any number of violent means during New Yanwar's civil war.

A clearing by the central statue-fountain seemed safe enough. She descended without incident, slowed to a stop smoothly. Much to her surprise, the dais came to placidly hover a handspan above ground, letting her step off at her leisure.

It would've been the perfect landing if she hadn't led with the wrong foot, the one that felt like it was about to fall off. She yelped as it gave out from under her, forcing a knee hard to the floor. She would've fallen all the way if the fountain's ledge hadn't been there to keep her balance.

Jane stirred in her harness, but didn't rouse. She wasn't as much sleeping as she was unconscious. Meredith held on to her for long moments she could not spare, eyes squeezed shut, just trying to block the pain away for a little while longer. The statue's broken torso silently witnessed her labored puffing from where it lay.

The plaque at the disembodied feet was still legible, translated beneath the original warble into modern English at some point before the war: *In Honour of Sabrena Ariedna Stohlz, Bane Exalted of the Dastardly Eastern Cabal. Hers Be the Flame what Stokes Our Immortal Phoenix.*

Meredith pondered it in the midst of her struggle. The inscription had aged about as well as everything else around it.

Soon it became evident her feet weren't up to hiding anywhere else. Meredith clipped the gauntlet away, then tore into her blouse pocket—she'd sown it shut, anticipating her tendency to tumble through the floor—and brought out the portal beacon. At the same time, she noticed two figures taking to the skies above the Harvest Plants. Three more followed. And then, outside the walls, in the staging fourway, a portal opened to let through a legion of assorted Judicars.

Word must've reached the rest of the realm that a place far more important than Brena was under attack.

She should be long gone by the time they found her. The plaza was relatively exposed, but she didn't stand out in her muted colors and dirty hair. Meredith twisted the little cylinder, placed it on the ground under cover of the statue's hand and watched it blink.

And watched.

And watched.

The airborne figures scattered in five different directions: one to meet the arrivals, four to comb through the dilapidated city. How much did they know? Had they seen her flee into the ruins? What kind of detection did they carry? Could she move at all without being spotted? Anxious questions kept piling up as the portal beacon failed to do anything at all.

It wasn't too late, she knew as much. Was it too early? They might have stalled, for whatever reason. They could've been caught. They could be dead.

Why had she let them go alone? Why hadn't she ensured they made it out of Galavan safely? She should've waited a few days, like Faedre had suggested, should've helped them, shouldn't have simply *assumed* they'd make it. But she'd been so eager to get going, so desperate. . . .

Desperate.

Oh.

The thought seized her racing mind. She dangerously wobbled with light-headedness. The truth shivered into her heart and pumped frost through her veins.

It was so obvious. They hadn't been caught at all. Faedre had escaped just fine.

She simply had never intended to help.

And how easy it had been. She'd used Meredith's desperation, told her what she wanted to hear so she'd fight in earnest, all while fully intending to dispose of her without fuss. A veteran like Faedre hadn't survived so long by risking her life on a whim. She was pragmatic, ruthless. She'd done to Meredith what *she* had done to Sam.

What a rube. It was no-one's fault but her own. She'd made a deal with no leverage. She should've never relied on a *witch* to provide safety in exchange of nothing.

No time to stew in her betrayal. As Meredith considered her surroundings and the expectant dais with a bleak sense of urgency, more figures took off from the facility. Staying put wasn't an option. Flying off undetected was impossible, an attempt to outrace them would be short-lived. Maybe crawl into a hideout with Jane, bury herself somewhere, wait until they gave up. She had to *move*.

One hand on the fountain ledge, the other over her mouth, she forced her feet to sustain her. One did, the other didn't. Her already-battered pants tore through when her knee hit the ground once more.

Come on, she pushed herself. *Come on.*

In squirming shudders she tried again, but the pain was breathless, her limb could not function past it. Go around it, then: raise the dais and use it as a crutch. She picked up the controller from where she'd dropped it and crawled on her knees. If she could—

Bwash, went the sliver of space above the beacon, creating a perfect rectangle of swirling colors. Faedre jumped through. "You barely gave us thirty minutes!"

Her clothes were torn, her face was filthy, her helping hand was bloody. She was a wondrous sight. Meredith reached for that hand with her last shreds of strength. She didn't know how long thirty minutes was, but she was ready to learn all about it.

There was a whistle and a yell somewhere above: "Over there!"

Her best friend on Earth grabbed Meredith's arm and draped it around weary shoulders. "Come on!"

They swarmed to their position, she could feel them, swooping in from all directions. With Faedre's help she screamed upright, her other arm cradling Jane's frame in an iron grip. They limped together as a chorus of incantations rose at their backs.

The flushing rainbow crackled at arm's reach. The ground exploded beneath their feet.

Meredith plunged into the portal to Earth, never to walk on Galavan again.

CHAPTER THIRTY-TWO

THE LAST OF THE WICKED

 HEY CARED FOR JANE as nurses would. She was vacant, like a shattered doll, like a mind broken. Her eye would open sometimes, but would not focus. Meredith helped through her own injuries, much to Faedre's annoyance, but the pain was as pinpricks compared to the uncertainty and worry. For three days, there were no signs of life behind the veil across Jane's gaze.

On the fourth day, she wept. Silent and motionless, at first; just tears streaming down her temples that Meredith dutifully patted dry. Then Jane turned her head to the side, covered her face, and sobbed in quiet whimpers. She squirmed and pushed when Meredith touched her. Even her sleep was like mourning.

There was no telling what Jane had seen, heard or suffered prior to the harvest pod, but one thing became obvious during this time: she knew just how much of her was missing.

On the fifth night, she spoke.

"Tell me what happened," Janette said, voice as tatters.

With tears on her tongue and a stone in her chest, Meredith told her. "I lied to you from the start," she began. "Galavan is a monstrous place."

Nothing but truth followed. Who she was, why they'd met, everything she'd done to become a dire criminal. Every reason why

Janette now paid the price of her Mistress' folly. Meredith didn't burden her with excuses, she didn't ask for understanding or forgiveness. She only spoke in quavers of her mistakes and misdeeds, of her regrets, her struggles and her love until nothing remained unsaid.

"I wish I'd seen it sooner," were her closing words, "I wish I'd understood it all sooner and escaped before they hurt you. If I could change one thing, that would be it."

Yes, nothing unsaid... except the impending sparkwane and Hunger. She didn't *want* to skirt around it, she wanted Jane to know everything, but she decided there was only so much the poor girl could handle all at once.

Jane's usual barrage of questions would've made the topic much harder to avoid, but she took every confession and revelation in silence. There was no sign she understood, no acknowledgment she was even listening. What had she heard during her captivity? How much had she already worked out during her recovery? How many of Meredith's confessions did she doubt, now that she knew her Mistress was a cheat and a liar?

Any reaction at all would've been better than her blank contemplation. Meredith reached for her hand, but stopped halfway. Jane's thumb, shaky and restless, kept going over the nubs, over and over and over.

"We'll fix you," Meredith whispered, "I promise we'll fix you."

Janette turned her head. The perfectly sealed wound in place of her witchmark made it impossible to withstand the stare.

"Fix me?"

"Like Tessa. Over there, in the bed. Have you noticed her arm? Wave at her, Tess."

Tessa waved.

"See? A new arm, just like that. Faedre's an expert. And your legs, even your fingers, you'll walk and build things again."

Her expression didn't change. The back of her head returned to the pillow. "Everything hurts," she breathed.

"It hurts? I have just the thing." Meredith reached for the little bottle on the bedside table. The contents were unlike any painkiller she'd used in her previous life, but she couldn't deny their effectiveness.

Janette shrunk at the rattle of them. "No. No pills."

"But. . . ."

"No pills."

Meredith deflated and set the bottle down. She fiddled with the lid. "Water?"

Jane nodded. She let Meredith tip the cup, wipe her chin— mundane gestures that felt alien in the context. For long moments the girl stared at the pleasant shade of green on the ceiling, thoughts buried deep under twenty layers of trauma. Silence saturated the room.

During all her anxious hours, Meredith kept returning to the same questions now choking the space between them. How could anyone recover from this? What could she possibly do to guide this girl back to a semblance of normalcy? She wasn't delusional enough to think replacing limbs would repair all the damage.

You'll have to be patient, Faedre had said. She'd rescued her share.

She'll need something to live for, Tessa had said. She too was Earthborn.

"Meredith."

"Y– yes?"

Janette was still looking up without seeing, lost in the maze inside her head. The name sounded so different in her lips, now. It had lost something. There was no cheer, no reverence.

"You told me magic still works on Earth," Jane said. "Was that a lie?"

"No. No, that's the truth. I understand infusing is a mite harder. Why?"

She didn't answer. Her thoughts quietly churned on.

Maybe a minute later, she tentatively raised her hand. Her fingers were spread among wary tremors. She drew the kind of expectant breath Meredith had learned to recognize.

The words of the incantation came laced with Janette's power, they reverberated in the confines of the little safehouse like spirits vying for freedom. Right away Meredith could tell the girl's talent wasn't as obscenely strong as before, but still significant.

The simple spell was cast, and warmth rolled into the room, snug and homely like heat from a good hearth. Meredith exchanged a look with Tessa.

"You could've just asked me for a blanket."

The words went unnoticed. Jane was considering the outcome with bated breath. The difference was immediately apparent: her chin had lifted, her shoulders had unwound. Her chest had loosened as though the weight of her fate was not so crushing. She leaned back into the pillows, visibly spent from the exertion.

And here was the path to follow. Here was the map to Jane's maze.

Meredith leaned as close as her own wounds would allow and took her hand. It was a conscious effort to ignore how different it felt in its current state. "You still have magic," she told her. "You're a powerful witch, they couldn't take that away from you."

Janette looked at her. Beneath the grief, beneath the pain and desolation, her eye flashed a hint of its old spark. It was there only for a moment, quickly giving way to the deep exhaustion of the convalescent. Her gaze lost focus again, her features slackened. The effort had been too great and she was going back to sleep.

"Pull through this," Meredith whispered, "and you'll be the best that ever lived."

Feeble fingers curled in Meredith's grasp.

A swell of hope ached in Meredith's chest.

In the shallows of her slumber, Jane smiled.

EPILOGUE

EREDITH TOSSED THE KEYS in the little plate by the entrance, set down the bag of odds and ends she'd picked up before work and headed straight for the bathroom.

She let the shower run and worked on peeling off the coveralls and shirt and pants and sweat-drenched undergarments. There were lockers at the shop, but it didn't feel right to leave her work clothes where anyone might tamper with them. What if they had spare keys to the padlocks? What if they'd recorded her number combination? Humans had an unnerving tendency to point cameras at everything. She couldn't risk it.

And, well, there was also Joel. He'd expressed . . . an interest. Removing any piece of clothing in his presence felt like encouragement.

Looking back from inside the mirror, her reflection seemed resigned to the sights on offer. Red-and-white blotches glistened wherever her clothes had stuck, and the grease stains always found a way, despite the mask and gloves and fastidious care. They drove her crazy, but they were worth the trouble. She'd developed something close to an obsession over the last two-years-and-change: the different components working in unison, the interconnected puzzle under the hood, that bone-rattling roar when they ran properly—and all without a single hint of magic! No wonder Earth was full of them; she was hooked the moment she sat behind a wheel. If only they weren't so damn *dirty* on the inside.

Antsy to get on with the scrubbing, she worked the clasps above the ankle and let her foot drop in the corner. The plastic step stool she kept on the shower plate would prevent her from tipping over.

As always when she fiddled with her prosthesis, she thought of Jane. She hadn't been around for almost a month. Their dinner should've happened two weeks ago, but she'd cancelled at the last minute. Similar to Meredith's guilt, worry had become an ever-present companion in the back of her head, a flux with erratic peaks and valleys that never went away. *Motherhood,* Faedre had called it. She liked to throw that word around.

Tonight was still on, though. For now. The steaks had been marinating all night, it would be a good meal, Jane would like it. This was important. On the list of Janette-related sources of dread, their fortnight dinners becoming a chore for the girl was near the top.

Meredith deftly limped into the shower. First the grease stains, always first, they'd ruined so many sponges before she'd figured them out. Her kit was ready: sugar, dish soap and water, mix them to suds in their dedicated bowl, rub and rub until the mix did the job, rinse and repeat.

Step under the stream, wet, lather, scrub and rinse. Lather and scrub scrub scrub till all the miscellaneous filth was gone. Repeat all of that, just in case. The comforting routine let her mind wander, and she rehearsed a few topics of conversation throughout: the spray hose anecdote at the shop, Auntie Fae's latest gripes, new music she'd discovered. It could be hard these days to get that girl talking. Jane lived in a different world, a world someone her age should have nothing to do with. She should be going on dates, worrying about her social status among her peers and getting good grades. That's what the magazine in the break room had said, anyway.

Janette didn't care about any of those things. She fiercely cared about her "renegade family," as Faedre would put it. She cared about power management, discovering new shortcuts and pushing at every magical boundary. She cared about windows of opportunity, captive youths and hunting down the wicked. She didn't tell Meredith much, of course she didn't, but Tess and Fae kept her updated. Sometimes, she wished they wouldn't. Knowing of Jane's tireless undertaking only made the worry that much worse.

Meredith understood. She even supported it, in the way a proud parent might support their son going off to war. But she didn't have to like it.

She finished up in the bathroom, stopped by the bedroom for a shirt and some strictly-indoors shorts, and made for the kitchen. Desmond looked up from his cubby, found nothing worth getting up for and returned to dignified snoring.

Oh, no. A message blinking on the machine. Ruefully she pressed the playback button, already getting used to the idea of another cancellation.

"Ya shameless bludger," a voice crackled, *"I got you a cell phone, stop chucking it in a drawer!"*

Just Faedre. Meredith sighed her relief. She listened while donning her daisy-print apron.

"See if you can stay the weekend with me at the halfway house, yeah? Tess will be out and I need some peace to focus on actually solving the problem. Finding where these kids belong wasn't supposed to be so hard. I'd tell our girl to slow down, but," she paused, *"you know, she thinks she's got that deadline like the world is ending.*

"Anyway, I could do two kids at a time, but three is too much, at this rate you'll have to room one just to get them out of my soup. Come by and we'll talk. No, it's nap time, put that down. I don't care, put it down—"

She abruptly hung up.

The whole weekend. A bit daunting. She'd take Desmond, they always loved Desmond. He didn't even stand out among Australian fauna.

Having one of the rescued kids stay with her, though? What was Fae thinking? She couldn't, she wasn't ready. She *shouldn't*, not after what she'd done to Jane.

Then again, it would be nearly impossible to screw up as spectacularly as the first time.

A problem for another day, she had dinner to cook. Meredith told her voice-activated golem servant to play her favorites—it had a very limited scope, but humanity was getting closer to the real thing—and off she went, occasionally bopping hips to the beat as she chopped and sautéed and fussed for a good hour and a half. She even sang along a chorus or two.

I'll ruin, yeah, I'll ruin you, I will ruin you

I've been doing things I shouldn't do, things I shouldn't do

The doorbell rang exactly on the o'clock. She wiped her hands clean, turned down Marina's impassioned wailing and walked as briskly as the limp would let her. She didn't need to look through the window. There was only one person Desmond bothered to receive at the door.

She turned the knob and opened wide. "Hullo-o-o!"

"Hey, Meri."

There she was, standing tall, smiling that fond-yet-reserved smile Meredith had learned to cope with. Sheathed in a coat and gloves despite the scorching weather, gaze inscrutable behind big reflective lenses. She'd recently gone through a questionable short hair phase, but now she'd let it grow into a chin-length bob, very flattering on her.

"I like the hair." Meredith turned and raised a hand in silent invitation. "You know you can just use your key, right? It's never barred when you're coming."

"Yeah, you always say." Jane hurried inside. The sun was shooting to kill today. "It smells delicious in here. Hey fluffball!"

Her smile widened without reserve as she squatted to muss Desmond's floof. Not as awkward or gangly as she used to, she'd grown into her legs. She puckered up Desmond's snout and baby-talked at him. "Who's a good boy? Have you been keeping Meri safe? Yes you have. Who's the ugliest boy? You are, yes you are." She broke into a giggle under his relentless nudging.

"He's so bored of me. He's only like this when you're around."

"He knows who gives him all the treats." Whatever she brought out of her satchel disappeared into his snout without Meredith ever seeing it. She casually wiped the slobber on her pants, straightened up and unclipped her bag to get it out of the way. She shrugged out of her black canvas longcoat with visible relief. "Don't know how you handle this heat. Like stepping into an oven as soon as you clear the portal."

Meredith closed the door and quietly watched as the teenage girl hung the coat, pulled off the gloves and stuffed them in the coat's big pocket. She raised her glasses and weaved the temple-tips into her hair, like a tiara. The sight of her arm never failed to be striking, those lean contours of black alloy, the lines of rust and gold like mineral veins through obsidian. Her sleeveless top revealed the whole shoulder joint, where the limb seamlessly connected to the socket. The intricate transition into flesh was in full display.

This was new. To say Jane's usual wardrobe was conservative would be an understatement, even while in the privacy of her close-knit circle. None of them could fault her for it. The straps didn't even cover the long claw scar that arched from shoulder blade to clavicle.

"What."

Meredith startled. She'd been staring. "Oh, nothing. You look great. It suits you, I mean it."

She seemed flustered, but it could've been the heat. "I'm just trying it out. It's not a big deal. I'm not letting the normies see me, don't worry."

"Honestly, after walking through a few of your cities, I don't think anyone would even notice. And if they did, they'd just say you look *cool.*"

"Hah. Maybe." She grabbed her bag and they headed for the kitchen. "I'm just tired of hiding myself, you know?" Jane stopped by the table. "Wow. No wonder it smells good."

"Take a seat, I'll get the rest."

"I can help."

"Shush and sit down. I hope you're hungry."

"Haven't eaten all day."

"Shame on you."

Meredith busied herself moving plates and silverware to their appropriate places. Jane watched from her chair, still clutching the bag.

"So I cancelled last time. . . ."

"Mm-hmm."

"And I didn't even tell you why."

"I figured you got busy."

"Don't you want to know why?"

"I don't pry into your business."

"It wasn't business. I finally worked up the guts to meet with my sister."

Meredith was leaning over with napkins in hand. She stopped halfway, gave the girl a quizzical look and slowly sat down in front of her, elbows heavy on the tablecloth. "And how did that go?"

Janette shook her head. "I chickened out and lied to her."

"Love, no-one would expect you to just tell her you're a witch."

"No, I lied about father. I pretended I had nothing to do with it."

"Oh."

The former Mistress imagined for a moment being introduced to this older sister. *Hello, this is Meredith, she kidnapped me and then shot our dad in the head.*

Not the best first impression.

"If I'm honest with you," she said, "I'm not sure you should tell her. What would be the point?"

"I know, thank you! I was going back and forth with it, and it's like . . . he was mugged on the way to his car, that's it, why make it any harder for her? Right?"

"Right."

"They're still living off his life insurance, so it's not like I ruined them or anything. . . ."

Meredith didn't fully understand the concept of *life insurance* yet—it didn't even keep you alive, it made no sense—but asking about it didn't seem pertinent to the issue at hand.

"And how about you disappearing one day? What did you tell her?"

"That I ran away, what else? I couldn't take it anymore and all that, I roamed around 'til a kindly old lady took me in. She didn't question it once."

"Not even about . . . " She vaguely gestured at the silver scar across her eye socket, "the missing eye?"

"I put on a band-aid and told her I had an infection." She sighed dejectedly. "Abby's so pure and wholesome. She's like a puppy. It was nice to see her, but I feel so dirty."

"I think you'll believe me if I say I can relate to that feeling."

Jane chuckled without mirth.

"But," Meredith added, "it's not the same, I don't think it's cowardice on your part. Telling her the truth would hurt you both, and there isn't much to gain from it. I suppose the question is, which will hurt you more, the truth or the lie?"

The girl was quiet for a moment. "It's not so simple. There's a good reason I wanted to tell you about all this."

She was quiet again, long enough for Meredith to prompt: "Yeah?"

"A while after I disappeared . . . her nightmares came back. Such a coincidence, isn't it?" Anger touched her voice, but it was the smolder of dying embers. Not once had they spoken about the night terrors since the day everything collapsed, two lifetimes ago. Her tone was mostly cynical, jaded.

"She went straight to him for help, she always believed every word coming out of his mouth. I guess gullible runs in the family. I used to hate her for it, the way she'd try to *convince me*—she felt sorry for *him* having to deal with our 'mental illness.' She's why I never dared tell anyone else."

Meredith listened like the words could catch fire if left unattended. Jane's gaze was fixed on the salad between them. Her fingers idly pinched at the tablecloth.

"It went on for months, 'worse than ever,' she said. And then we did . . . what we did, and he was found dead in the hospital parking lot. What do you think happened next?"

"Her nightmares stopped," Meredith said, soft as Janette's breath.

"Yeah. After they put him in the ground, her nightmares stopped. She said it still took her a while to piece it all together. So after telling me this. . . ." Her voice thinned. Her mouth twitched at the corner. "She . . . she apologised to me. And gave me a hug, and told me she wished she could take everything back—" Jane briskly dried her eyelid with the ball of her hand like she took offense at the moisture. "And then she gushed about how toned my arm felt under the coat." She rolled her eye, but a smile fought through.

Hesitant only on the inside, Meredith laid a supportive hand on Janette's fingers. The tactile coat on their surface felt a bit like rubber, a bit like velvet. Jane neither squeezed back nor pulled away.

"I thought you should know," she continued, "since, you know, when you pulled that trigger, you had no idea you were doing the right thing. You just wanted me to stop being upset."

It was hard to tell whether the tone was bitter or simply matter-of-fact. The more the girl progressed into her teens, the harder it was to gauge her thoughts. Some cursory research had confirmed this was a fairly widespread problem across humanity.

"I don't regret it," Meredith said.

"Yeah. Neither do I."

"Did *your* nightmares stop?"

"No." Jane shrugged a shoulder. "But it's better, now. Different. I can deal with it." She blew out a big breath, eager to move on.

"Anyway, you can probably guess I was a bit . . . emotional, after all that. I didn't want to bother you with it, you've had enough whinging from me."

"How can you say that? You *know* such a thing would never bother me."

She made a face. "Yeah, I know, I was an absolute mess, I wasn't ready to deal with it. She even said we should move in together so she could take care of me. It was adorable." She leaned back in her chair and seemed to take notice of where she sat. "I'm sorry, I keep blathering and the food's getting cold."

"Think nothing of it."

Despite her words, Meredith eagerly grabbed knife and fork, prompting the girl to do the same. Jane hadn't even prepared her first bite when her phone started buzzing. One eyebrow raised, she reached into her satchel and glanced at the screen.

The change was sudden and uncanny, from vexed and apologetic to dead-eye somber. The Janette looking into the phone was a different person altogether.

"I have to take this."

She stood and strode off. Only the first sentence was clear before the back door closed: "You're hours early, this better be important."

For the next one hundred and six seconds, Meredith managed her urge to snoop by ensuring every plate, glass and utensil was properly parallel and equidistant to its ordained match.

When she returned, Jane couldn't have been gentler with the door. Her step tarried as if the table was an open casket. Meredith concealed her disappointment as well as she could, because it was obvious enough: it would be dinner for one, after all.

"Meri—"

"You can't stay. I know."

"I'm so sorry, I wish it could wait. I thought I'd have plenty of time for you, but. . . ."

"I understand. You're a huntress. You get your chances when you get them."

"It's a lot bigger than that. Things are going to change, there has to be an end point somewhere, and this is it." She shook her head and waved her hand. "We'll talk about it next time we meet, I promise."

"Of course." Meredith stood from her seat, ready to roll with it without a fuss. "Tomorrow?"

She pressed her lips together, contrite. "I wish, but I can't, I'm sorry."

"Ah. Well, don't worry about it, Desmond won't let anything go to waste."

"Desmond? You know, you *could* invite someone else. As in, on a date? They'd be truly impressed with this."

Meredith winced. She'd tried it. Once. After endless meddling by riven witches.

It turned out Earth dwellers asked far too many questions, and she had a terminal shortage of answers.

"Alright, okay, it was just a thought." Janette sighed, glanced at her bag. "I have a present for you. I was going to wait 'til after dinner."

"A present?"

It came out of the satchel wrapped in brown paper and tied with yarn, a parcel about the size of a pigeon. The shape was lopsided on the table, narrow on one end, thick on the other.

Meredith looked up, eyebrows raised. The girl's face wasn't as much *I hope you like it* as it was *I'm ready to argue with you about this.*

"Well? Open it."

Meredith pulled on the string. The loop came undone, the paper fell away.

A foot. Every toe in place, every contour smooth. Every surface black, coursed with lines of rust and gold.

"Jane. . . ."

"It's simple, it had to be, but it's a big *step up* from that lump you have now."

"You made this?"

"With a bit of help, I'm not that good yet. Auntie Fae agreed to fit you with a socket, she's ready for you—I won't lie, it's painful to get through, but it's worth it. I promise."

Meredith picked it up like her touch could shatter it to pieces. It was solid in her hands, slightly supple, appropriately heavy, a gorgeous feat of mezzocraft. If she weren't holding it, she wouldn't have believed it was real.

"You're mad. How long did this take?"

"Oh, you know, a few hours here, a few days there, I didn't keep track. Come on, don't you like it? I'm sure it's the right size."

"Jane, you know I can't—"

"Don't worry, it's not spark-drain, it's battery. I infused it myself, it's very efficient, it should last a few lifetimes. You won't ever have to recharge it."

The former Mistress put down her gift. Ten more protests lined up behind her lips, all feeble. They were offshoots of the real reason for her reluctance, her inadequacy. It took her a moment of self-conscious squirming to push it out of her mouth.

"You want me to have this? After everything I put you through?"

Jane's brow creased. Her head tilted. Her gaze, so often guarded these days, became gentle as forest-bound sunlight. She fidgeted a bit, one hand rubbing her neck. Then, against every boundary she'd established over the years of grueling recovery, she closed the distance between them and came in for a hug.

Meredith was surprised at first, but soon she held tight. Perhaps tighter than she should. Jane's breaths were shallow, the only way her breaths could be with the lung she had left. She still had plenty of recovery ahead.

"I know I've been distant," the girl said, her chin pressing on Meredith's shoulder with every word. "I needed time to figure things out. And you know what? As far as I care, you'll always be the one who rescued me and taught me magic."

Meredith's throat tied in knots. While the worry would ebb and surge alongside her other thoughts, her guilt was a steadfast companion. It listened to every conversation, it shared her every heartbeat, it hovered over every decision and judged it harshly. It stood at her back that very moment, casting shame, *reminding her,* and there was nothing Janette could say or do to make it disappear.

Over time, the guilt hadn't quieted or relented, because no amount of atonement could erase past deeds. But Meredith had learned she could often bargain with it, and now and then earn a respite for her battered conscience. She'd felt good about herself for a whole afternoon the day Jane had walked again.

This moment, this embrace, Janette's words of absolution . . . they were damn good leverage.

She was so moved by the gesture that the obvious difference in Jane's aura didn't immediately register. More suspicious than alarmed, Meredith brought her to arm's length. "Jane, the sparkwane, is it—"

"I'm sorry, I really have to go." She drew back, cheeks red, and started gathering her things.

"You can talk to me about it."

"I know, there isn't anything to say, it is what it is. I just need to hurry."

She was already going for the coat.

"W— wait, at least take these, you need to eat." She reached over to the counter and offered the package she'd prepared. "Picked fresh."

Jane looked at it. "Hansels?"

"Mm-hmm. Six, individually wrapped."

The girl bit her lip. "I can make room in my bag. . . ."

Tessa had brought the pits one day. They had marked the start of the new garden. It went to show there were still some things worth saving from Galavan.

Jane bashfully crammed the ribbon-draped parcel into her satchel. "Thank you."

She wanted to insist, drag her into a conversation, find some way to help, but Meredith swallowed it all. "It was great seeing you. Please take care of yourself."

"I'll figure things out." She stuffed herself into the coat, pulled her glasses back on. "Don't worry about me."

"You might as well ask the sun not to rise. See you in two weeks, yeah?"

The half-hearted nods weren't precisely reassuring. She fetched from her bag a rectangular device that at a distance could've been confused with a tablet. "Can I use your wall?"

"Go ahead."

She got in position while her fingers busied themselves with dials and knobs and switches. Jane held it up like she was taking a picture of the wallpaper's vine design. Laser dots demarcated the four corners of a door-sized rectangle.

She infused a couple words Meredith didn't know, some trigger she'd made up. The portal device came alight, whispered its minuscule wordpaths and opened a gateway to somewhere else. Somewhere beyond a spiraling rainbow.

A portal to the mess that was left of Galavan.

"A nexus from here, at 6PM?"

Jane didn't even try to disguise the smug smile. "Travel's far more flexible if you bypass the nodework." She waved a final goodbye and strode forward.

"Janette!"

She stopped and looked, eyebrows raised.

Don't go.

I'm proud of you.

You don't owe anything to anyone.

Don't get hurt.

Finish what I started.

"No matter what happens," Meredith said, "no matter what you do or the choices you make, you'll always be welcome here."

Jane regarded her from behind her big tinted lenses. Her mouth tucked to one side. She nodded in understanding.

"I know," she whispered, and turned to the portal. A swirling blend of light and color reflected on her glasses. "Love you too."

Jane plunged through, and the portal was gone.

Meredith leaned against the table and stared at the wallpaper for a long time. Jane had never said such a thing to her. It felt good, it did, but somehow it made her far more concerned than before. It was like . . . like she didn't want to leave anything unsaid before leaving.

She'd sensed a significant difference, without a doubt. Sparkwane. In time, the well within the girl would dry up, and Hunger would follow. According to Puritan doctrine, it could not be ignored, it *had* to be sated. According to Tessa, it would be difficult but manageable.

How Jane would cope, it was anyone's guess.

She heaved a sigh as large as her worry. It was out of her hands, she'd done what little she could. No sense obsessing over it.

Meredith returned to the front door and pushed the knob-lock, turned the deadbolt, slid the chain nub in place. Her shuffling papped through the short corridor to the kitchen, closely followed by the clacking of Desmond's feet.

Along with her new foot, dinner languished on the table.

She drummed fingernails on a chair rest. Invite someone else, she'd said. A date, she'd said.

Meredith glanced at her bag. Joel's number was on a sticky note in there, he'd given it to her after their almost-year of apprenticeship and banal conversation. *A woman without a cellphone,* he'd laughed, *and she loves to work on engines. You must be from another world.*

She hadn't accepted his lunch proposal, but taking the number was harmless enough. She liked him. He'd be pleasant company. And she had to admit . . . she was curious. Tessa was, reportedly, rather happy with her Earth man.

Meredith reached for the phone on the counter and gave it some serious thought. The memories were served as they often were, with minimal prompting and no discernible pattern: Frau, tittering alongside her as they snuck out of the academy commissary, pockets heavy with fistfuls of sweets. Yurena, drawing patterns with her fingernails, grinning like a lovely imp who'd found a new pet to torture. Sam and the one and only chuckle he'd ever uttered, chest touching her back and fingers entangled in her hair. Mifraulde, eyes like icicles as she stared from a balcony. A hundred tortured souls, buried under the grasp of her gauntlet.

More memories joined. Her hand shook a little bit, it was barely noticeable.

Meredith put the phone down.

"Desmond, how'd you like a special treat?"

She cut it up for him. Desmond's teeth these days weren't what they used to be. She even placed the plate right there in the living room, next to her seat.

"Pace yourself, now."

He didn't listen.

She rolled out the little tray reserved for her absolute laziest three-minute meal-in-a-box dinners and wedged it in place against the sofa. It wobbled a bit when she set down the full plate and cutlery, but it would do. She had to carefully wiggle around it until her tush was properly established.

Meredith cut a prim little bite, then forked her way through a tater cube, an onion flake, a carrot slice and the morsel of beef, strictly in that order. She slathered it through the juices and then closed her mouth around it.

"Mmm."

Yes, very good. Jane would've liked it. Her loss.

Desmond flopped at her foot, belly full and grunts content. The channel-shifting rod was easy within reach. Whatever came on didn't matter much, there was always something good enough to entertain. How did anyone ever get bored in this world? As she feasted on carefully crafted food towers, Meredith settled down to enjoy the recorded antics of eccentric human beings.

Earth wasn't so bad, after all. She could get used to it.

She had no need for magic.

THE END

APPENDICES

Appendix A: Valeni Calendar & Timekeeping

Shrewd Valen, Founding Fury, First Engineer, Architect of Realms, chafed at the arbitrary nature of human timekeeping. Her initial drafts of a new system were far more radical departures with strict decimal constraints, but compromises were made for the sake of easy adoption and conversion from one system to the other, as witches routinely traveled back and forth between realms. After all the bickering, the outcome was a system just as arbitrary, which continued to bother her to her last breath.

A day is divided into twenty **span** (1 span = 72 minutes). Common fractions used are the centispan (1 cent = one hundredth of a span or 43.2 seconds), millispan (1 mil = one thousandth of a span or 4.3 seconds), and mites (1 mite = one ten-thousandth of a span or 0.4 seconds).

The year is divided into twelve moon cycles, thirty days each (further divided into three weeks of ten days each) for a total of 360 days. **Hallow's End** makes up the difference with Earth's 365 days and accounts for leap years: 105 span of darkness that mark the turn of a new year. The first cycle of the year correlates with November on Earth. There is a cold and a warm season in Galavan, six cycles each. The cycles are named as follows:

Wane, Wither, Nadir, Serene, Falcate, Kernel – Cold season, November through April.

Bloom, Apogee, Garner, Scorch, Fallow, Yearning – Warm season, May through October.

Hallow's End – End of Year festivities in perpetual darkness, used to perform maintenance on all the contraptions that keep the skyveil from collapsing.

Appendix B: Galavan's Economy & Currency

Galavan's current economy is a hodgepodge of free enterprise, collectivist policies and protectionism against Earth products.

Magical stasis and transportation make it trivial to acquire human goods and capital. Unfortunately, rampant abuse of these methods would also expose the wicked to the world, as well as encourage witches to abandon the coven in favor of going rogue on Earth. This is why the Departments of Wealth, Travel and Transportation, and Scouting and Supply work together to control imports into Galavan and *discourage* witches who'd go astray.

Products from Earth are limited in nature and distributed only to sanctioned outlets. Prices fluctuate but are incentivized to remain low. This stops non-exotic contraband from becoming profitable, and low-level government-appointed jobs able to support a comfortable living. There is a pervasive under-economy of contraband regardless, which goes mostly unpunished as long as it hews to small-scale commodities and baubles.

For Galavan-produced merchandise, licenses aren't required to buy or sell as long as the goods are not magical in nature. Magical artifacts aren't tightly controlled but can only be manufactured and / or sold by licensed vendors. Obtaining a license is relatively easy and question-free, and the level of scrutiny is proportional to the scale of the operation. This market is largely driven by merit-based capitalism, without even regulation to prevent collusion and price-fixing. The Council simply intervenes on a case-by-case basis. Corruption is common, but not rampant.

All these factors have resulted in two separate economies nearly independent from one another: the high market, with high-end Galavan-made products and spark't food for the wealthy, and the low "bottomfeeder" market, dealing with all the basic items witches might use for sustenance and comfort in modern times. Witches are unruly by nature and a pleasant standard of living is a high priority for the Puritan coven in order to maintain stability.

There is no official conversion rate between Galavan's currency and USD, as all sanctioned travel to Earth will be provided with the appropriate funds for the region. The underground contraband economy will charge whatever they can get away with for currency exchange, and always in one direction: no witch is reckless enough to sell Galavan currency in exchange for human coin. For an approximate value, Meredith can buy a box of Honey Nut Cheerios for 5P and 9 at the day market.

P stands for Piggy Coin (ŧ), the standard unit of currency. There are 1, 2, 5 and 10ŧ coins, all square. A 2ŧ coin is a "pared". A 5ŧ coin is a "footer". A 10ŧ coin is a "set". In modern times, note versions of these amounts have replaced a good half of the coins in circulation, though witches are stubborn and averse to change and so they still keep to coins as much as they can.

Twenty clippings, or clips, make 1₺. Clip coins are half-moon-shaped and come in three varieties: 1, 5, and 10 clips. Two boog-shims make a clip, though boog-shims are rarely used in current times due to inflation.

All piggy coins are iron, clips are aluminum, both coated in an ultra-thin layer of silver. The value of the metal is irrelevant; their value resides in the anti-tampering sigils and the tiny trace of spark imbued in each.

A peep note is worth 100₺. A knob note is worth 200₺. A stem is worth 10 peep notes, or 1,000₺.

The nomenclature is a holdover from the bartering of olden days, when witches would trade among themselves using the currency most valuable to the wicked. . . .

Appendix C: Concept Compendium

Alchemy – The discipline of creating mixtures of agents with magical or outlandish properties, often by processing and manipulating plants grown through infused **Botany**. Reagents and concoctions are often terribly volatile.

Apostate – A witch who actively preaches against the **Puritan Doctrine** or who's been proven to renege it.

Artificing – The discipline of crafting **Trinkets**. The surfaces of the trinket are inscribed with interconnected wordpaths, rows of **Source language** glyphs that recite **Incantations** when **Spark** flows through them. Extremely complex contraptions can be devised in this way.

Attunement (magic) – A witch's capability to link the flow of power from herself to a source of energy and / or the target of her **Incantation**.

Botany (infused) – The discipline of channeling wordless **Infusion** into plants as they grow for greatly enhanced properties. Extremely time-consuming and endurance-demanding. Colloquially referred to as "Chanted growth."

Bottomjosh – Laughingstock.

Breeder – A female **Serf** whose womb is used to spawn new witches.

Brood – A witch's lineage. Two broods are combined through genetic manipulation and brought to term through in-vitro fertilization in a **Breeder**'s womb.

Brood-sisters – Spawns of the same **Brood** combination that share a **Breeder**'s womb.

Broodspawn – A witch brought about, or *hatched*, by way of breeder womb. All witches currently residing in Galavan are broodspawn.

Chanted growth – See **Botany** (infused).

Chud – Slang for money.

Corenbound – Cardinal point in **Galavan** equivalent to Earth's North.

Council (The) – The ruling body of Galavan, led by the Head of the Coven. Councilors are willful by nature and voting sessions habitually devolve into shouting matches. Members are not elected in an official capacity but rather hand-picked by the Council itself— the reason often being popular support. Currently comprised of twenty-five members, six for each of Galavan's settlements plus the Head of the Coven.

Coven (The) – A loose term referring to all witches in the **The Masquerade**, the concept of **Wick't** cooperation in general, the **Council**, or simply a gathering of witches.

Culling conflict – Picking your battles.

Dayturn – Midnight

Department of Mercy – A sub-branch of the **Judicar**s in charge of monitoring any and all infractions concerning the treatment of humans and **Apostate**s.

Department of Progeny – The Puritan department in control of wick't reproduction. The secretive officials in charge of this department have more control over Galvani affairs than most Councilors.

Department of Harvest – The Puritan department in control of spark extraction, storage and distribution. Although it's a separate entity from the Department of Progeny, the departments overlap substantially, especially at the decision-making level.

Dermaturgy – The discipline of layering, carving and scarring wordpaths into flesh for non-verbal spellcasting.

The Desolation – the **Puritans**' solution to centuries of strife and depravity among witches: all witches are born barren through in-vitro fertilization of genetically concocted **Broods**. Human hosts are designated for the task—often, but not necessarily, Earthborn witches.

Distalways – Cardinal point in **Galavan** equivalent to Earth's West.

Draw a line – Understand, figure out.

Dud – (1) A female youth without **Spark**. (2) A defective **Brood** spawn without **Magical Talent**. (3) A human female **Serf**.

Fel (alchemy agent) – A volatile or otherwise noxious active reagent in **Alchemy** .

Fellingwise – Cardinal point in **Galavan** equivalent to Earth's East.

Flipside (The) – The bottom of **Galavan**'s landmass. Formerly used as a waste dump, currently used as a form of lethal punishment for criminals. It's breathable but barren and desolate, so victims can survive for a long while before dying.

Fuffled – Annoyed, chafed, bothered.

Fury / Furies / The furies – A fury is a prominent witch in **Galavan** history, be it through fame or infamy. It will often refer to the founding furies: Caterina Galvan, Head of the Coven; Helena Tremmel, the Hag, The Marrow Banshee; Shrewd Valen, Architect of Realms; Tarka the Gorgon, Supreme Magister. More modern furies include Sabrena the Mad Crone, Mergat, Chen Yaniwa (temporarily) and Agnes Vanuuren, among others.

Galavan – The realm witches call home after their exile from Earth. It resides in **The Hollow**.

Golem – An artificial biomechanical servant of wide-ranging potential intelligence.

Golemancy – The discipline of crafting and maintaining **Golem**s, in truth a highly specialized branch of **Artificing**. Temporarily a forbidden art after the Golem Revolts, but a severely shackled form of the discipline has resurfaced in modern times.

Gourdmonger – Pumpkin peddler, a pejorative way to refer to a merchant of questionable quality goods.

Gracious ravens – Expression of dismay, roughly equivalent to "goodness gracious!"

Hold to mind – Take to heart, remember well.

The Hollow – The pocket of empty space housing the realm of **Galavan**, tethered three-fold to Earth's gravity well.

Hollowhead – Dunce, airhead.

Humanists – Incumbent and losing faction of **Galavan**'s civil war. The Humanists weren't so much a doctrine as they were the status quo: a long-degenerated society of anything-goes customs where both wick't malevolence and human convivence were commonplace. Both escalating outrage at the depraved chaos and a desire to break free from the **Hunger** that drove it gave rise to the **Puritan Doctrine**.

Hunger – A witch's addiction to **Spark**. Some witches find it more urgent than others. Its effect was greatly reduced, but not negated, by **The Desolation**.

Incantation – Casting a spell through **Infusion** of spoken **Source language**.

Infusion (magic) – The act of imbuing words with magical power so that the Universe will "listen" to the spell. It feels somewhat similar to forcing a belch into words.

Inquisitor – **Judicar** officer: Detective, minister and judge rolled into one.

Joys and cheers to X – Glad to hear X.

Judicars –The law-enforcing branch of the **Puritan Doctrine**.

They operate the **Department of Mercy**.

Juditor – Ground-level enforcer of the **Judicars**.

Magical Talent – An amalgamation of a witch's potential for **Infusion**, the extent of her **Attunement** and her available **Spark** load. It manifests in a perfume-like aura that's not smelled, but sensed the same way someone might sense a stalker creeping up behind them.

The Masquerade – A term to encompass all the hidden wick't tendrils of **Galavan**'s witches on Earth and all the measures taken to keep them hidden from the general public. Agents of the Scouting and Supply Department are closely scrutinized to ensure long term exposure doesn't compromise their contempt for humanity.

Mezzocraft – The discipline of crafting replacement or enhancement body parts and organs. Arbitrary enhancements are generally frowned upon by **Puritan Doctrine**, but replacement limbs are commonplace. Extensive anatomical knowledge and surgical precision are required.

Mol (alchemy agent) – A mollifying or otherwise neutering active reagent in **Alchemy** .

Moppet – Slang for money.

Mumjob – the act of removing a **Serf**'s tongue. Communication between serfs is kept to the absolute bare minimum since the human rebellions. This practice predates the rebellions.

Near glean – Suspect.

Nexus – Plural: nexūs. Due to Earth's rotation and the shape of **Galavan**'s tethers to the planet, travel between the two worlds can only happen to certain places at certain times. To prevent a complicated times and places schedule, the availability was simplified and codified into the **Nodework** to meridian bands over one span intervals. Two separate meridian bands are available during each span every day.

Nodework – Short for node network. A vital set of artifacts in **Galavan**, as they facilitate its viability as a habitable space. It's comprised of a hundred and twenty-four nodes, and their functionality is many-fold: they configure the **Nexus** to Earth, project the **Skyveil**, enable communications by bouncing signals similarly to Earth's satellites, provide surveillance, and more.

Parse earnest – Take seriously, believe wholeheartedly.

Paw the gourd patch – Egregiously waste time.

Pecked at my heckles – Nipped at my heels.

Puritans – Faction opposing the **Humanists** during **Galavan**'s civil war. A reactive, authoritarian Doctrine focused on elevating witches above human rabble and curbing debauchery by any means necessary. Currently the oligarchy ruling Galavan.

Puritan Doctrine – (1) See **Puritans**. (2) The core tenets of the Puritan faction, an extensive collection of mandates and criteria dictating both law and proper conduct.

The Riven Circle – A society of merciful witches operating in the shadows to liberate as many **Serf**s as possible, which isn't very many. Their long-term goal is to bring about a more compassionate cohabitation with humans without returning to the corruption of **Humanist** rule.

Shrewd (for an object) – Of the dankest quality.

Shroudwise (to someone) – Unbeknownst to someone, behind someone's back.

Soot and ash – Expression of dismay.

Tarkisward – Cardinal point in **Galavan** equivalent to Earth's South.

Thank the Stones / furies / ravens / Crones – Expressions of relief, roughly equivalent to "thank goodness."

Thogwash – Nonsense.

Toughchop – A tough chunk of dried meat, like beef jerky.

Trinket (magic) – An artifact imbued of magical power.

Twaddlebag – Nonsense of the most foolish nature.

Serf – human slave labor.

Skyveil – Semblance of Earth's sky in **Galavan**. A dome-shaped membrane upon which the **Nodework** projects day and night cycles. The sun doesn't provide heat and doesn't travel, it fades instead from one position to the next with the turn of every **span**. The moon goes through thirty increments, one for each night in a moon cycle, from full to new and back to full. The stars remain static and do not mimic Earth's constellations, they're purely aesthetic.

Source language – A conceptual language that, under proper conditions, resonates with the properties of reality. It requires very precise diction. It can be written phonetically to facilitate **Incantation**, or in glyphs to store magical instructions in **Trinket**s.

Spark – the main fuel of wick't power. Highly addictive for some witches, but not all. Only minor cantrips are possible without it. It naturally occurs in some humans at a young age, until their **Sparkwane** upon maturity. The cause of occurrence isn't fully determined but it loosely correlates with both genetics and locations on Earth.

Sparkwane – the fading of **Spark** from a human youth. It happens over a year, approximately, during puberty.

Stemhoard – Moneybags.

Stunt – (1) A male youth without **Spark**. (2) A human male **Serf**.

Wary's Worth – Expression for parting. "Stay safe."

Wealth-latch – Gold digger.

Whislegab – Blab, incriminate.

Wick't – Pertaining to witches.